"I have to believe that David is innocent," Liz said.

"And therefore, these murders are the work of some avenging ghost . . ." Roger said.

"David wasn't here when Audra was killed," Liz reminded him. "He was on a cruise ship somewhere in the middle of the Atlantic, with *me*."

"That's a pretty solid alibi."

"So whoever killed these three people—"

"You don't believe the three deaths could be unrelated?" Roger interrupted.

Liz shook her head emphatically. "No. That's just impossible to believe. The same killer murdered Audra, Jamison, and Rita—and for similar reasons, I believe. And whether human or something else, something we can't explain, there is some connection to this house." She paused and looked over at him. "To Dominique."

"What do you intend to do now, Liz?" Roger asked.

"I'm not sure. I need to speak with David before I do anything. But then . . . I don't know what I'm going to do, but I'm certainly not just going to sit around here and wait for the next knife to swing through the air. Because I'm pretty sure the next target will be me . . ."

Books by William Patterson

SLICE

THE INN

DARK HOMECOMING

Published by Kensington Publishing Corp.

DARK HOMECOMING

WILLIAM PATTERSON

PINNACLE BOOKS
Kensington Publishing Corp.
www.kensingtonbooks.com

PINNACLE BOOKS are published by

Kensington Publishing Corp.
119 West 40th Street
New York, NY 10018

All Kensington titles, imprints, and distributed lines are available at special quantity discounts for bulk purchases for sales promotions, premiums, fund-raising, educational, or institutional use. Special book excerpts or customized printings can also be created to fit specific needs. For details, write or phone the office of the Kensington sales manager: Kensington Publishing Corp., 119 West 40th Street, New York, NY 10018, attn: Sales Department; phone 1-800-221-2647.

PINNACLE BOOKS and the Pinnacle logo are Reg. U.S. Pat. & TM Off.

ISBN-13: 978-0-7860-3659-2
ISBN-10: 0-7860-3659-1

First printing: February 2016

10 9 8 7 6 5 4 3 2 1

Printed in the United States of America

First electronic edition: February 2016

ISBN-13: 978-0-7860-3660-8
ISBN-10: 0-7860-3660-5

1

Mrs. Hoffman had a face like a hockey mask. Hard, white, and plastic. She'd had so much cosmetic surgery that her eyes looked feline and her mouth had trouble making "O" sounds. Her cheeks were unnaturally round and shiny and her eyebrows never moved. Liz felt as if she were meeting a wax statue.

Only the eyeballs were animated. "Welcome to Huntington House," Mrs. Hoffman said, looking Liz up and down like a Disney automaton.

Liz glanced away from the middle-aged housekeeper, murmuring a soft, polite, "Thank you." She let her eyes take in the place she now called home, the fabled Huntington House. The floor was marble and the ceilings were very high, dripping with sparkling crystal chandeliers. A fireplace nearly the size of a garage stood at the far end of the room, and on the walls hung gilt-framed portraits of somber-looking forebears. Liz hoped that her own children, if she had any, would not inherit such dour genes from their father.

"Mr. Huntington wrote and told us all about you,"

said Mrs. Hoffman. "We were all so very eager to meet his new bride."

Liz turned her gaze to the assembly of chambermaids, housemen, cooks, and chauffeurs who had lined against the far wall of the drawing room for her inspection. For some reason they reminded her of the living deck of cards that Alice met in Wonderland. They all seemed flat and faceless, just a collection of spindly arms and legs. Liz offered a smile in their direction. She detected none coming from them in return.

"And where *is* Mr. Huntington?" Mrs. Hoffman inquired.

"He's at the stables," Liz replied. "When the car dropped us off out front, he told me to head up to the house while he went down to see his horses."

"Of course," Mrs. Hoffman said, showing slightly more teeth than before, which Liz assumed was the best she could manage for a smile. "How Mr. Huntington loves his horses. He always visits them first thing after a long trip away from home. He and his late wife rode every morning and every evening. Have you brought your jodhpurs?"

"I . . . I don't ride," Liz told her.

Mrs. Hoffman gave her a look that suggested that if she could have raised her eyebrows, they would have reached her hairline. "You don't *ride*?" the housekeeper asked.

"No. David has promised to teach me."

Mrs. Hoffman said nothing. She just stood there staring at her.

"I'd like to freshen up," Liz said after several moments of uncomfortable silence. "Perhaps one of you would show me to my room."

"Oh, but of course," Mrs. Hoffman said. "You must be exhausted from your long trip." She clapped her hands. "Jamison!"

A tall, reedy boy with freckles and wispy strawberry blond hair, dressed in a cream-colored shirt and matching trousers, stepped forward.

"Take Mrs. Huntington's bags to her room," the housekeeper instructed.

Jamison nodded and lifted the two small pieces of luggage that Liz had carried into the house. Mrs. Hoffman gestured to Liz to follow her up the stairs.

"I've prepared your suite, but since I wasn't sure of your favorite flowers, I filled it with daisies," the housekeeper told her as they began their climb, a few steps behind Jamison. "I trust they will be satisfactory."

"Well, of course," Liz said. "How very kind of you."

"Daisies were Mrs. Huntington's favorite."

Liz thought she should remind the housekeeper that she was Mrs. Huntington now, but thought better of the idea. She was sure it was just an old habit. Mrs. Hoffman had served David's late wife for many years. Liz was certain she didn't mean any disrespect.

As she climbed the stairs, she still couldn't fully believe she was here. Had it been just a month ago she'd met David? A month and a handful of days. He'd been sitting out there in the audience in the theater of the cruise ship, and their eyes had met across the footlights. In her sequined dancer's costume, Liz had spotted him looking at her. At least, it seemed as if he was. As she'd tapped and shuffled her way through the carefully choreographed routine, Liz had kept glancing out at the tables, and sure enough, the man at the front table, seated alone, never took his eyes off her. Surely it was her imagination, Liz had told herself. But when David had introduced himself to her after the show, she'd realized her instincts had been right.

Two weeks later, at the end of the cruise, after several romantic dinners and long swims in crystalline blue waters, the captain of the ship had married them. Liz's family, when she called with the news, was stunned. Her mother was still angry she'd been denied the chance to give Liz a big traditional wedding. But Liz didn't want that. She just wanted David.

Their cruise-ship idyll had been followed by an even more idyllic honeymoon, hopping from Rio to Cancún to Miami Beach in David's private jet. Liz had never imagined what being in love would feel like. She had thought she'd been in love before, but what she'd felt for that weasel Peter Mather, her college boyfriend, didn't come close to what she felt for David. Certainly nothing had prepared her for a man like David Huntington growing up in her working-class neighborhood in Trenton, New Jersey. David was thirteen years older than she was, thirty-five to her twenty-two. It was true, as her mother kept telling her, that there were still many things she didn't know about her new husband. But from the moment Liz had felt his gaze on her from the audience, it had seemed that she had known David all her life.

She looked up as she reached the landing of the staircase. There, in front of her, gazing down the stairs, was an enormous portrait in a magnificent gilt frame of a beautiful, dark-haired woman dressed all in white.

The portrait was so large, so majestic, that for the slightest of moments it took Liz's breath away.

Beside her, Mrs. Hoffman was smiling that strange,

limited, plastic smile of hers. "Yes," she said, looking up at the woman in white. "She was beautiful, wasn't she?"

"That's Mrs. Huntington?" Liz asked, aware that she'd just called her predecessor by the name she now rightly bore.

"Indeed. She was born Dominique DuBois. Even the name is lyrically beautiful, don't you think?"

"Yes," Liz said in a small voice, forcibly moving her eyes away from the portrait.

"Come along, dear," Mrs. Hoffman said, gently nudging her to resume walking. "Your room is right down the hall."

Liz noticed the glance Jamison gave to the housekeeper.

At the end of the hall, they turned in to a large, airy room looking out over the gardens. The windows were open and a soft spring breeze was tickling the sheer white curtains. The walls were painted a soft cream color and the wooden floor was polished to a high gloss. Comfortable chairs surrounded a sleek modern coffee table and a gigantic flat-screen television. A daybed was strewn with colorful pillows. Tall black vases filled with crisp white daisies stood on every table.

"How very lovely," Liz said.

"The bathroom is off here," Mrs. Hoffman said, opening a door at one end of the room and revealing the sparkling white tiles within. "And over here," she continued, walking now across the room, her low-heeled black shoes making a hard tapping sound on the wooden floor, "is the bedroom."

Liz followed her inside. A large bed on a white platform, draped in white satin from an enormous canopy, sat in the center of the room. Enormous windows allowed in a flood of light. And as in the outer room, black vases filled with daisies were everywhere.

"I'll let you get settled and freshened up," Mrs. Hoffman said. "Welcome once again to Huntington House."

"Thank you so much," Liz said, standing in the middle of the room, feeling a little out of place in such grandeur.

"Jamison," the housekeeper called over to the young man. "Just place Mrs. Huntington's bag there and then go back downstairs and bring up any other luggage that Mr. Huntington has brought. And don't dawdle! I am sure they are both exhausted."

With that, Liz was left alone in her room.

It was like a dream.

She gazed around at all the magnificence. This was *her* room. It boggled the imagination. It had all happened so fast—and such impetuousness wasn't like Liz. Everyone who knew her had been stunned. Her mother was furious that she'd never get to host a reception for her at the local VFW hall. Liz's best friend, Nicki, another dancer on the cruise ship, had questioned her sanity for marrying a man she'd known for just two weeks. But when Nicki had learned how rich David was—that he was the scion of the wealthy Huntington family of New York and Palm Beach, Florida— she'd changed her tune. "What a life he can give you, girlfriend," Nicki had said, all wide eyes and excitement.

But it hadn't been David's wealth that had impressed Liz. For the first week she'd had no clue that he had any money. He was a widower, he told her. He was taking a cruise by himself to heal. At first Liz worried that she was a rebound lover, that David was fixating on her only because he was heartbroken over the loss of his wife. But he'd assured her that was not the case, that he loved Liz for herself, and that she was, in fact, very different from Dominique—precisely the reason he loved her, he said.

Liz stood at the window looking down at the gardens, the well-tended topiary and sparkling fountains. Very different from Dominique. Having now seen how beautiful, how glamorous, David's late wife was, Liz wasn't sure that was much of a compliment.

She stole a glimpse of herself in the mirror. She was pretty, but her hair was a light, indistinct brown compared to the luxurious ebony tresses cascading over Dominique's shoulders in her portrait. Liz had a trim, lean, dancer's body, with shapely legs, but her small breasts and hips could hardly match the voluptuous curves of David's first wife. How could a wren compare to a raven?

"But he told me I was beautiful," Liz whispered to herself, her eyes still on her reflection. "He told me I was exactly what he wanted in a relationship."

David never spoke much about Dominique. He would say only that they had been happy once. Her death had been sudden and tragic—a boating accident, a terrible, unexpected event. Dominique had drowned. No one was to blame. A sudden storm had come up, and Dominique, out on the yacht on her own, without a captain, had been unable to steer the boat to safety. But whenever Liz asked for more details, her husband would grow silent. He told her he preferred not to talk about the past. He wanted to concentrate on the future. *Their* future.

Looking around the room, Liz imagined that their future would be quite bright. This house was big. Liz wasn't used to having servants. It would all take some adjustment. She wasn't sure she could ever get used to ordering people around.

But there was one request she'd make of the staff: the removal of the portrait of Dominique from the stairway landing.

Liz wouldn't ask right away. It might sound crass. But really, how could they start their marriage walking past the towering presence of David's dead wife every day?

Suddenly the room was suffused with the most glorious fragrance. Liz couldn't determine what it was at first, but then it struck her. Gardenias. That's what it was. Liz inhaled deeply. There must be gardenias growing in the garden below. How wonderful to wake up every morning smelling gardenias! She thought she'd enjoy living at Huntington House very much.

Liz looked over as Jamison and another young man, in an identical cream-colored uniform, entered the room carrying the luggage Liz and David had brought back from their honeymoon. Mrs. Hoffman followed, observing their actions with a keen eye. She looked up and spotted Liz.

"I'm sorry if we disturbed you, Mrs. Huntington," the housekeeper said.

"Not at all. I was just admiring the beautiful gardens."

Mrs. Hoffman's hard mask shifted ever so slightly—her approximation of a smile. "Yes, they are magnificent, aren't they?" She took a few steps toward Liz. "Do you have a green thumb?"

"I'm afraid not," Liz admitted. "I can barely keep a houseplant alive."

"I see." Mrs. Hoffman's face returned to its former hardness. "Well, we have a very talented groundskeeper. He keeps the gardens full of color all year long."

"Well, the gardenias smell so lovely," Liz said. "I can hardly wait to see them. I was just standing here and caught a whiff and it was just unbelievably beautiful."

Mrs. Hoffman looked at her. "Oh, it wouldn't have been gardenias that you smelled, ma'am."

"No? But I was sure—"

"At one time, we did indeed have many beautiful gardenia shrubs lining the house. But you see, Mr. Huntington had them all pulled out by their roots."

"Why would he do that?"

Mrs. Hoffman offered her a tight smile. "Well, it was just that . . . gardenia was Mrs. Huntington's signature scent. She always wore it. And I suppose the fragrance of the shrubs reminded Mr. Huntington of his wife, and so, in his grief, he had them all torn out."

Liz just looked at her, completely at a loss for what to say.

"Are you finished with the bags?" Mrs. Hoffman was asking, moving away from Liz to speak to Jamison.

"Just one more downstairs," the young man replied. "I'll go get it."

"Well, be quick about it. We need to stop disturbing Mrs. Huntington. I'm sure she wants to rest after her flight."

Jamison hurried out of the room with his companion.

The housekeeper turned to look back at Liz, who was still in the doorway, still unable to speak.

"I saw Mr. Huntington in the yard and he said to tell you he'd be up momentarily."

"Thank you," Liz managed to say.

"Good day, Mrs. Huntington," Mrs. Hoffman said, giving Liz a quick nod and then striding out the door, her heels clicking against the wood as she departed.

It must have been something else that I smelled.

Liz turned and looked back out the window.

The fragrance was gone.

Gardenia was Mrs. Huntington's signature scent. I suppose the fragrance of the shrubs reminded Mr. Huntington of his wife, and so, in his grief, he had them all torn out.

Liz wished David would get here quickly. She realized that these few minutes in the house had been the only time so far in their sixteen-day marriage that they'd been out of each other's sight. She certainly didn't want to become too dependent on her husband. But all of a sudden Liz was feeling very much alone, and very, very much out of place. And she knew the moment that David came bounding through the door all those feelings would evaporate.

She heard a sound and turned in anticipation.

"David?"

But it was just Jamison, with the last of the bags.

"I'm sorry, ma'am," he said. "Only me." Liz noticed he had a very thick Southern accent, probably from Georgia or South Carolina.

"Thank you, Jamison. Did you see my husband downstairs?"

"Yes, ma'am," the servant told her. "He's speaking with Mrs. Hoffman."

"Okay, thanks."

Liz turned to start unpacking when she realized that Jamison was still standing there. She looked back at him. What was he waiting for? Ridiculously, she thought he might be waiting for a tip—like the bellboys who carried luggage up the staterooms on the cruise ship. But one didn't tip one's own staff.

"Is there something else, Jamison?" Liz asked.

"Ma'am . . ." The young man's voice was tremulous. "I feel I need to . . ."

Liz realized he couldn't get the words out.

"What's the matter?" she asked him, reaching out and placing a hand on his shoulder. "Is everything all right?"

Still he struggled to speak.

"Go ahead," Liz told him. "You can speak freely to me."

"I need to warn you!" Jamison finally blurted out. "I couldn't sleep if I didn't!"

"What is it, Jamison?"

"She won't tell you," he said, "but I gotta."

"Who's she? Mrs. Hoffman?"

Jamison didn't reply, just went on with a rush of words that seemed to surge up from his gut and tumble out of his mouth. "A girl was killed! And it was because she came in this room!"

"What are you talking about? What girl? Killed—how?"

Jamison seemed near tears. "She was a pretty girl, like you, Mrs. Huntington. Young and pretty! And she killed her!"

"Who killed her?"

"Mrs. Huntington!"

Liz didn't understand what he was trying to say.

"Dominique killed her!" Jamison cried, and Liz saw the utter terror that filled the young man's eyes.

"But Dominique is dead," Liz said, her own voice sounding miles away to her ears.

"Yes, she is," Jamison acknowledged. "But she's still here. And she'll kill you, too, Mrs. Huntington, just like she killed that poor girl!"

2

"Welcome home, Mr. Huntington," the young housemaid said.

The master of the house paused on his way up the stairs. He looked around at the young woman standing off to the side, her cream-colored maid's uniform crisp and pressed.

"Well, hello, Rita," Mr. Huntington replied, and then he smiled.

Rita melted. That smile of his had a way of erasing all the pain and the anger. David was so handsome. So tall and broad-shouldered. And that smile of his . . . with his bright white teeth and full lips and dimples in his cheeks . . . Rita wanted to cry.

"I'm glad you've come back," she managed to say, her throat tight with emotion.

Mr. Huntington took a step closer to her. "Are you, Rita? Are you truly?"

She nodded, dropping her eyes to the floor. She couldn't meet his gaze.

"I'm glad to hear that," he told her. "I hope we can be good friends."

"Of course," Rita told him.

David lifted her chin with his hand so that she had to look at him.

"You were very special to me at a very difficult time, Rita," he told her. "I hope you realize how special you were, and how I'll always treasure our times together."

She nodded.

"But you do understand that now things will have to be different," David said.

"Of course," Rita answered.

"My wife . . . she's, well, she's not used to all the fuss we make around here. You know, with the dinner parties and the horse shows and the servants in and out of her room. She didn't grow up with a staff of people in her house. So she'll need friends here, friends who can help her get used to the way we live." He paused. "I hope you'll be a friend to her, Rita."

"Of course," she told him.

"Thank you, Rita." He smiled again and moved away from here.

But she was lying.

She wasn't going to be a friend to his wife.

Rita hated the new Mrs. Huntington. Just as she'd hated the old Mrs. Huntington.

She watched David climb the stairs. Pulling her eyes away from him, Rita headed back toward the kitchen. Mrs. Hoffman was probably lurking around as usual, ready to reprimand her. Mrs. Hoffman didn't like the staff fraternizing with Mr. Huntington.

If she only knew.

Rita figured that the domineering head housekeeper

probably suspected that she'd had an affair with David. Very little ever got past Mrs. Hoffman.

He loves me still, Rita thought. *He couldn't say it, but I could see it in his eyes*.

Once again she felt his rough hands on her breasts, his hot lips on her neck . . .

Lost in her memories, Rita wandered into the kitchen. The place was a vast cavern of shiny chrome and marble, with three ovens and five sinks and a refrigerator large enough to store rations for an army. Rita didn't notice the tall black woman standing at the marble countertop and staring at her from across the room.

"I saw you talking to him again."

Rita looked up. The tall woman spoke in a heavy Haitian accent, and the sound of her lyrical voice startled Rita out of her reverie.

"So what?" Rita snapped. "I just welcomed him home."

The Haitian woman folded her arms across her chest. "You can't fool Variola. I know what went on between you two."

Rita smiled. "Oh, that's right. I forgot that you're a witch."

The Haitian woman shook her head. "I can see things. And that way is not safe for you, Margarita Cansino."

"I appreciate the warning, Variola," Rita told her, gathering the dishes to set the table for dinner. "But I think I can take care of myself."

"Audra thought that, too."

Rita just laughed. "What does Audra have to do with any of this?'

"She was one of his favorites as well."

Rita spun at her, nearly dropping the dishes from her hands. "That's a lie! That's ridiculous gossip spread by people who don't know what they're talking about! David barely knew who Audra was!"

Variola just shrugged. She returned to what she had been doing when Rita came into the room, chopping green peppers. "Just heed my advice," she told Rita again. "I don't like to see trouble in this house."

The young housemaid made no further reply. No one was going to tell her what to do. Not Variola. Not Mrs. Hoffman. And certainly not that silly little wife David had just brought home.

Rita carried the dishes out to the dining room.

Friends! David wanted her to be friends with his wife! Rita laughed.

She'd show the new Mrs. Huntington just how good a friend she could be.

3

Liz was staring out the window into the garden, watching the way the fronds of the palm trees that lined the estate swayed gently in the breeze, when she heard the door close behind her. She spun around.

"David!" she cried, as if she hadn't seen her husband for weeks instead of a matter of minutes.

"Darling," he said, flashing her that smile of his, the one that had first ensnared her while he'd sat out in the audience, watching her dance. "How do you like the house?"

"It's more than I could possibly have imagined," Liz replied, rushing to him, putting her arms around him and resting her head on his chest.

David stroked her hair. "Did Mrs. Hoffman show you around at all?"

"No, she just brought me here." Liz looked up at him. She tried to hide the unease she was feeling, but David seemed to spot something in her eyes. Her husband's smile disappeared.

"Is it satisfactory?" he asked. "If not, we can always take a different room . . ."

Jamison's words were still resounding in her mind. She was unsure how much she should say to David right away. So she just asked, "Is there anything that should disqualify this room?"

"This is the most beautiful room in the house. I mean, look at the view of the gardens! It's got the largest closets and the largest sitting area, and of course the bathroom is pretty luxurious."

"Yes," Liz agreed. "Two sunken tubs." She pressed further. "But—there's nothing here that disturbs you?"

"Do you mean the fact that it was my first wife's room?"

Liz nodded, watching his eyes.

"It's your room now, Liz," he said, embracing her. "*Our* room."

Liz remembered something that David had said to her while they were still on the cruise ship. He didn't do well with people who complained. It was the part about being a boss that bothered him the most—putting up with people who constantly bitched and moaned. She knew she'd eventually have to tell David about what Jamison had just told her, but she couldn't do it yet, not at this moment. He had been so anxious for Liz to see the house—and to love it—that she couldn't start blathering right off the bat about what some servant boy had told her.

She tightened her arms around her husband. "So long as I'm with you," she said, "I'm satisfied."

David leaned down toward her. They kissed. Her husband's kiss still had the power to make Liz feel dizzy.

Gently he broke their embrace. "Well, you must see the rest of the house. It's quite the place, really. Built in the 1920s, during Prohibition. There are still all sorts of sliding panels all over the house where my great-grandfather hid his liquor."

"Sounds as if there's a lot of history here."

"There sure is. And a lot of staff. Did you meet them?"

Liz laughed, trying to appear merrier than she felt. "Mrs. Hoffman had them all lined up at attention waiting for me when I came in," she told him. "It was as if I were Queen Elizabeth reviewing the troops."

The smile bloomed on David's face again. "In this house, you *are* a queen."

"Oh, David, I'm not used to all of this. I mean, the idea that some maid is going to come in and make my bed every day . . ."

"It will free you up to do other things," David told her.

"Like what, David?" Liz frowned. "I mean, all I know how to do is dance . . ."

This was one of the things that had worried Liz. Would she be happy being a stay-at-home wife? She was giving up her dream of being a dancer by marrying David. She hadn't even given her career a chance to take off: her gig on the cruise ship had been her first job out of college. Liz had jumped at the opportunity to see the world, but also knew the experience would look good on her résumé. She'd expected that when she finished the cruise she'd be auditioning in New York, or, failing that, in Orlando for a gig at Disney World. She was young. She had plenty of time to get to the top. Liz's dream, ever since she was a kid, was to sing and dance in a Broadway musical.

Now she was a Palm Beach society lady. At twenty-two! Would she be happy?

She was sure she'd be happy as David's wife—she loved him more than she ever thought it was possible for a woman to love a man—but would she get bored when he was off on business trips or overseeing his various projects? David's family ran a vast number of businesses, mostly in the financial sector, all over the globe. David's father was president of Huntington Enterprises, and more and more he was handing David control, grooming him for eventually taking over the business from him. Liz wasn't quite sure what David actually did, even though he'd tried explaining it to her; she'd never understood numbers and money very well. All she knew was that his work would take David away from home for chunks of time, sometimes for up to three weeks at a time.

And when he was gone, was she going to be bored wandering around this big, glamorous, sparkling clean house?

David seemed to be reading her mind. "You know, babe, I've been giving this some thought. There's no reason you need to give up dancing just because you're my wife."

"You want me to audition for a show?"

"No. I want you to audition other people."

Liz didn't follow.

David smiled. "Why not open your own dancing school? Believe me, some of the snooty Palm Beach ladies would love to send their children to be instructed by a gen-u-wine high-stepper with a college degree."

"I'm not sure how impressed they'll be by the College of New Jersey."

"It's a great school."

"Yes, it is, but—I mean, *me*, teach dance to kids?"

"And some of those ladies might be interested in an adult class as well."

Liz didn't know what to say. It hadn't been so long ago that *she* was the student in a dance class. She didn't think she had enough experience yet to teach . . .

"I . . . I don't know," she said.

"Well, think about it, sweetheart. We could get you a studio in town."

He moved into the bathroom, turning on the faucet at the sink and lathering up his hands with soap. He continued talking with Liz as he did so, telling her about his horses and what the stable hands had reported and what horse shows were coming up . . .

But, in fact, Liz wasn't listening. She had gone back to ruminating over what Jamison had told her.

A girl was killed! And it was because she came in this room!

And Dominique had killed her.

She's still here. And she'll kill you, too!

That was absolute craziness.

The boy must be mentally ill. That was the only explanation Liz could think of. Or deliberately trying to scare her for some reason. Why would he say such a thing? That a dead woman—her husband's dead first wife—would kill her?

Liz was glad she hadn't blurted out what had the boy had told her the moment David walked into the room. She would have looked hysterical. But she couldn't stay quiet much longer. If this Jamison kid was unbalanced, or deliberately trying to cause trouble for a reason, Liz had an obligation to let David know.

He was coming out of the bathroom now, drying his hands.

"David," Liz said, trying to appear nonchalant, "there *was* one thing about this room I wanted to mention . . ."

"What's that?" David asked.

"Well, it's ridiculous, I'm sure, but . . ."

David's face had grown serious. "Tell me, Liz."

"It's just that one of the boys who brought up our bags seemed a little . . . unusual. Do you know him? His name is Jamison?"

"I might, sweetheart. Probably by face, I would. I don't remember all the staff's names." He smiled, a little uncomfortably. "Mrs. Hoffman and Dominique always handled the hiring and supervision of staff. And if I did know his name once, I no doubt have forgotten it now." He looked out the window in a sort of wistful gaze. "I was away from this house an awfully long time, you know."

Liz did know. Soon after his wife's death, David had left Palm Beach. That was a little over a year ago now. He had thrown himself into his work, traveling the world on behalf of the family business. And then he'd taken the cruise . . . where he'd met Liz. He hadn't been back to Huntington House in all that time.

"How was this boy unusual?" David asked. "Did he say something inappropriate to you?"

Liz hesitated. "He told me that a girl had been killed in this room," she said. "In Dominique's room."

David's face blanched. "The little son of a—"

"You mean it's true?" Liz cried.

"No!" David hurried to her, taking her in his arms. "Not here. Not in this room. But yes, a girl was killed on the estate several months ago. It was while I was away. Mrs. Hoffman phoned me and told me about it and I spoke with the police."

"Who was she? Who killed her?"

"She was a housemaid here. I barely knew her. Dominique had hired her. Her name was Audra."

"But who—why—how—?"

"Sweetheart, I wish I could tell you. It was a totally random act. Probably the killer was somebody she knew, the police speculated. She had broken a few hearts, apparently. Somebody followed her onto the estate one day and—"

David stopped talking. He moved his eyes away from Liz.

"Go on, David," she said. "How was the girl killed?"

"She was stabbed to death."

"Oh, God!"

David pulled her closer to him. "I'm sorry you had to learn this your first day here. It had nothing to do with anyone here at Huntington House."

"Jamison said it was in this room."

"He's wrong about that."

"And he said . . ." Liz stopped. She couldn't finish the sentence.

"What else did he say?"

But Liz just couldn't bring herself to tell her husband that Jamison had said the ghost of his dead wife had killed the girl.

Yet, in some strange way, David seemed to know what Jamison had said. "Some of the boys who worked here," he said, struggling for words, "they became almost . . . I don't know . . . obsessed with my late wife."

"What do you mean, obsessed?"

"They tried to get her to pay attention to them. They imagined all sorts of things about her . . . this boy must have been one of them. One of those who thought everything that happened in this house was because of Dominique." He slammed his fist down onto a desk. "Even after she's gone, everything has to be about Dominique!"

Liz was stunned by the ferocity of David's response.

"The boy is fired." David's lips were tight with anger.

"Oh, David, no . . ."

"He had no right to repeat such gossip to you. Mrs. Hoffman told me that all sorts of rumors sprung up after the girl's death. There were stories that said a drug lord had killed her. Apparently Audra had a drug habit. Police thought maybe the killer was an old boyfriend she'd dumped. But none of the stories involved Dominique!"

Liz let out a long breath. "David, let's just forget that he said anything. So long as the girl wasn't killed in this room . . ."

"Darling, she wasn't even killed in the house! It was somewhere on the estate, out on the grounds." David walked over to stand in front of the window. "Mrs. Hoffman found her body."

"Well, I'm still weirded out by it, but at least it didn't happen in this room."

David looked around at her. "That's why that boy's ass is out the door. How dare he spread such unfounded gossip?"

"You're sure that's all it is? Gossip?"

"Liz, I've told you! All sorts of stories started swirling about the poor girl's death. Each one crazier than the last."

Maybe that was so, but Liz couldn't get David's words out of her head: that the boys here at Huntington House had been obsessed with Dominique. It was easy to see why. She was beautiful. Far more beautiful than Liz . . .

But she wouldn't dwell on it. The sooner Liz pushed the entire episode out of her mind, the better. But she wasn't sure that Jamison should be sacked.

"Look, David," she said, "I hate to think that on my first day here, I get somebody fired. It might turn the rest of the staff against me."

"Liz, that boy cannot be permitted to go around spreading ridiculous stories, and especially not to you on your first day here. That's insubordinate. That's unacceptable."

She supposed it was. "Do what you think best, David," she said.

He took her in his arms again. "I want you to be happy here," he said, his lips brushing against her ear. "I don't want anything to upset you."

Liz thought about the portrait of Dominique on the landing of the stairs. She wanted to ask David to take it down. If he didn't want anything to upset her, then he'd do it. But she decided not to say anything quite yet. Even with her husband's arms around her, Liz wasn't feeling very secure. If she pushed too much, became too demanding, he'd leave her. That was Liz's secret fear—a fear that had always lived inside her, ever since she was a little girl and her father had walked out on the family all because of her.

4

Liz was eight years old when her father left and never came back. And forever after, she blamed herself.

"Daddy," the little girl had asked, "where are you going?"

He stood there in front of her wearing his overcoat and holding a suitcase. The television was blaring some rerun of *Friends* in their messy little house in Trenton, New Jersey, and Liz's three-year-old sister, Deanne, was screaming at her five-year-old brother, George, to give her back her Pop-Tart, and the family dog had just pissed on the carpet. Liz's mother was nowhere to be found.

"I'm going away," her father replied. "I can't take any more of this."

He turned and walked out the front door. He never came back.

Standing there alone in her living room, a Cheerios box overturned on the couch, the little o's filling up the valley between the cushions, Liz blamed herself for her father leaving them. Her mother had asked her to watch the children and clean up the living room because she had a headache, and she'd told her she'd better be quick about it, because Daddy was getting fed up. Liz, however, had not done what her mother had asked. Instead, she'd sat there watching television, becoming lost in the make-believe world of Monica and Rachel and Ross. She hadn't told Deanne and George to keep their voices down. She'd just let them rant and rave. She hadn't cleaned up the Cheerios or the dog piss. And so Daddy had left.

From that moment on, Liz grew up believing that if she didn't always make things right, everyone else would leave her, too.

Certainly that had been the case with her first boyfriend. Peter Mather had been a freckle-faced redhead whom Liz had started dating during her last year in high school. They both went on to the College of New Jersey, where Liz had studied music and dance, and they stayed together all through their freshman and sophomore years. Liz had even allowed herself to imagine marrying Peter. He was studying engineering, so he was certain to get a good job, which was a good thing, since she'd be off auditioning for shows and trying to make a career for herself as a dancer. She would tell Peter that when she made it big—dancing on Broadway in some big successful musical hit—she'd support him and pay him back for all the years supporting her.

But at a party during their junior year, Liz had walked into a room to find Peter going at it with some girl with long blond hair and big breasts. Lots of tears had followed, but at the end of her grief, Liz had decided to forgive Peter. Men will be men, after all, and, after all, he'd been drunk. She was devastated, then, after telling Peter that she forgave him, he looked at her and said he was leaving her. "I'm bored in this relationship," he explained. For the last two years, Peter told her, Liz had been boring him more and more. He'd only stayed with her because all his friends had girlfriends and he didn't want to be the odd man out.

Liz just wasn't good enough, Peter explained—or pretty enough, or smart enough. At least, that was what Liz had heard. Maybe those hadn't been the exact words he used, but those were what Liz heard. Once again, she hadn't taken care of things—she had let things go, she hadn't taken care of someone else's needs, she had been boring and inattentive—and someone she loved had left her. Soon Peter was dating the big-boobed blond girl, who Liz imagined was never boring and always very attentive.

After that, Liz moved back home, commuting her last two years of college. It was a good thing, too, as Mom was drinking more. Deanne and George tended to avoid and ignore Mom's problem, but Liz did her best to intervene. If they didn't take care of Mom, Liz argued, they'd lose her. Liz tried so hard to make things right for Mom. She took care of her mother through every one of her drinking binges, cleaning up the messes that she made, calling everyone Mom had offended and apologizing for her. When Mom finally got sober, after a long and agonizing ordeal, she said she owed her life to Liz. For once, Liz had done what she was supposed to do, and she had the results to show for it: she hadn't lost her mother.

But her mother became determined that she'd never lose Liz either. "I still need you, honey," Mom had said when Liz had announced she was taking the job on the round-the-world cruise ship soon after her graduation from college. The idea of Liz being so far away for so long unnerved Mom—and it unnerved Liz, too, who worried Mom would backslide and start drinking. An email from Deanne, which Liz received somewhere off the coast of Iceland, confirmed Liz's worst fears. Mom had indeed hit the sauce again. She'd wrecked the car. Liz blamed herself for going away, for not sticking around to keep Mom in line. See what happened when she didn't do what she was supposed to do? Her guilt threatened to ruin the rest of the voyage for her.

"But baby," Liz's best friend, Nicki, counseled her, sitting on the upper deck under a full white moon as the ship sliced through the cold waters of the North Atlantic, "you can't blame yourself. You can't go on living your life for your mother. You have your own life to live! This cruise was a golden opportunity for you to see the world and to do what you love most—dance! You can't go on being your mother's keeper."

When Liz met David a short time later, she saw the wisdom of Nicki's words. If she hadn't taken the job on the ship, she never would have met David.

And to her relief, Mom's relapse didn't last. With the help of her friends in AA, Mom had once again committed to sobriety, and Liz was proud of her. Still, she wondered, deep down, if she had been the cause of Mom falling off the wagon, and if without her around, the same thing might happen all over again.

But she had hesitated only a moment when David had asked her to marry him and move with him to Florida. Nicki's words came back to her. *You can't go on living your life for your mother.* An amazing man had just asked Liz to marry him. He was kind and decent and extraordinarily wealthy. She said yes gladly.

Take that, Peter Mather!

Mom hadn't been happy when she learned that Liz had eloped. She was furious, in fact. But what upset her more was that Liz was moving permanently so far away from her. At least before, her mother had consoled herself that the cruise ship gig would eventually end. Now Liz was taking up residence more than a thousand miles away. Liz had tried assuring her mother that if she ever needed her, she would come to her. David could afford to fly her anywhere at any time. But Mom was still brooding about it. There was an edge to her voice every time Liz called her. Liz constantly worried her mother would start drinking again.

Liz had rocked the boat, quite literally, by going off on the cruise, and Mom had suffered. Now she had married and moved away—leaving Mom on her own to fend for herself. Sure, she had Deanne and George, but George was a pothead and Deanne was still in school.

Once again, Nicki's words: *You can't go on living your life for your mother.*

But Mom was only as fragile as she was because Dad had left her, and Dad had only left because Liz and her siblings had been too much to handle.

That was the guilt that festered in Liz's heart of hearts.

And that was why she didn't want to rock the boat with David. That was why she was so timid with him, so reticent about asking him hard questions or requesting he take down his first wife's portrait right away.

She wasn't going to make a big deal about comments made by an unhinged young man. If Jamison needed to be fired, that was David's decision. But Liz wasn't going to speak of it again. If she did—if she proved to be too much trouble, if she didn't do what she was supposed to do—she believed subconsciously that David would leave her, just as Daddy did all those years ago.

5

That night, at Mickey's Bar, a very dejected young man asked for a beer. The bartender complied, filling up the glass at the tap and sliding it across the bar toward the young man. He took a sip, getting foam on his upper lip.

"Why so glum, Jamison?" a female voice asked from behind him.

Jamison turned around. "Oh, hello, Rita," he said.

The pretty maid from Huntington House sidled onto the next stool. "You look like you just got run over by a truck," she said, signaling to the bartender to pour her a beer as well.

"I might as well have," Jamison replied. "I was fired."

"No way!"

"Mr. Huntington fired me. Told me to get out and not come back."

Rita sipped her beer, daintily wiping her lips with her napkin. "That doesn't sound like Mr. Huntington. He's usually so nice."

"Well, he wasn't very nice tonight."

"But whatever did he fire you for? What reason did he give?" She smiled, batting her lashes lightly at him. "I think you're a very hard worker, Jamison."

The young man scowled. "He fired me because I told the truth."

Rita lifted an elegantly manicured eyebrow in his direction. "The truth?"

Jamison nodded. "I told the new Mrs. Huntington about Audra."

Rita was silent for a moment, seeming unable to absorb what Jamison had just said. Then a small smile tickled the ends of her mouth. "You . . . did . . . not!"

"I did. I just couldn't see that poor unsuspecting girl brought into that room and not being told about what had happened there." Suddenly Jamison banged his fist on the bar, nearly upsetting his glass of beer. "I was raised to be a good Christian, Rita, and you just don't withhold that kind of information from someone! That's not being very charitable, to say the least. If anything had happened to Mrs. Huntington, and I hadn't said anything, then I'd be partly to blame." He looked intently over at her. "We all have to watch out for each other. That's Christ's teaching, right there."

"Well, I admire your convictions," Rita said, "but telling the boss's new wife something like that before he has the chance to tell her himself was really asking for trouble, Jamison. You have to see that."

"He *wasn't* going to tell her," the young man insisted. "That's just it. That's why I had to speak up."

"How do you know he wasn't going to tell her?"

Jamison's eyes were big like saucers, full of indignation. "Mrs. Hoffman told me before they arrived that

Mr. Huntington would never say a word to his wife about Audra, or about anything bad that had happened in the house since the first Mrs. Huntington died." He slumped back on his stool, chin on his chest. "I just felt she had a right to know."

"Maybe so, but it wasn't your place . . ."

His eyes darted back up to her. "I ask myself every day: What would Jesus do? And I believe Jesus would have told her."

"Yeah, but Jesus doesn't work for Mr. Huntington."

Jamison took another sip of his beer. "I don't care. I did what I did and I'm glad. He can stuff his stupid job up his stupid ass."

"That kind of talk is hardly Christlike," Rita gently scolded, unable to suppress a smile.

"Pardon my language," Jamison said, slumping back on his stool again.

"But are you sure Audra's body was found in that room?" Rita leaned in toward him. "I've heard so many crazy stories since her death. I heard she was found outside on the grounds and it was some old boyfriend of hers who surprised her and slashed her—"

"She died in that room! I know! I saw her! I helped Mrs. Hoffman move the body!"

Rita was even more dumbfounded upon hearing this news than she had been before. "You—did—*what*?"

"I've kept it a secret all this time, but what the heck, I no longer work there." Jamison chugged down a long gulp of beer. "I was working late, when all of a sudden Mrs. Hoffman came running in to find me, all out of breath. She begged me to help her. She was really freaking out!"

"I can't imagine that plastic mannequin ever getting that worked up," Rita said.

"Well, she was this night. She told me to follow her upstairs, to Mrs. Huntington's room—the *late* Mrs. Huntington—and there, right in the middle of the floor, I saw Audra's body in a pool of bright red blood."

"Oh my God, Jamison. What did you do?"

"Mrs. Hoffman was terrified. I thought she was going to start screaming. I asked her who had done this." Jamison shuddered. "I'll never forget what she said."

"What? Tell me!"

"She just said, 'Her.'"

"Her?"

"Yes. *Her*. She was looking around the room, as if she was scared to death."

"But what did she mean by *her*?"

"She meant Mrs. Huntington." Jamison looked directly into Rita's eyes. "The late Mrs. Huntington."

"Dominique Huntington."

The young man nodded.

"Oh, come on, Jamison," Rita said. "You don't believe in ghosts, so you? A good Christian boy like you?"

"I believe in the devil. And I remember the things Mrs. Huntington used to do . . . the things she and Variola used to talk about . . . those secret meetings and the chanting . . ."

"Oh, but they were just fooling around," Rita said. "Variola always talks about that black magic stuff from the islands. I've never taken her seriously."

"You should. Because that night, I saw the work of

the devil." Jamison finished his beer, then looked hard at Rita. "Bloody footsteps . . . leading away from Audra's body, then disappearing at the wall."

Rita frowned. "Are you saying . . . Dominique's ghost slashed Audra to death, then walked away through the wall?"

"The evidence was right there." He smirked. "Ghosts can walk through walls. It's one of the perks of being dead, I guess."

"This is crazy."

"I'm telling you the God's honest truth. But Mrs. Hoffman—she said it would never do to find the body in that room. It would cause a panic. It would be too much of a scandal for poor Mr. Huntington."

"So you moved the body?"

Jamison nodded. "I'm not proud of the fact. But I did. I was so scared. And I didn't want to lose my job." He frowned, then gestured toward the bartender for a refill of his glass. "Lot of good my cooperation did. I'm still out on my ass."

"You carried the body down the stairs?"

He nodded. "We wrapped it in a shower curtain and I carried poor Audra down to the backyard, where I placed her on the grass. Only then did Mrs. Hoffman call the police."

Rita had seen enough *CSI*s and *Law & Order*s to know that forensics would have spotted something not quite right. "Why didn't the police notice there wasn't much blood under her on the grass? They would have suspected she'd been moved . . ."

Jamison smiled tightly. "It was pouring rain. By the time Mrs. Hoffman called and by the time the cops got to the estate, poor Audra was soaking wet, lying in five inches of mud."

Rita just shuddered.

"I'm going to the police and telling them everything I know," Jamison said, taking a sip of his second beer. "Mr. Huntington made a big mistake firing me."

"I gather Mrs. Hoffman didn't know he did so?" Rita asked. "I imagine she wouldn't be happy knowing you were let loose carrying this particular secret of hers."

Jamison nodded. "That's right. She had gone to bed. At first, I wanted to wake her, and tell her I was being fired. I figured she'd want to keep me, so I wouldn't tell what I knew. I even thought of telling Mr. Huntington—telling him that I had moved Audra's body out to the grounds, and that I hadn't been lying when I'd told his new wife that the poor girl had died in her room. I figured I could threaten him with dredging up the scandal and making things worse." He took another gulp of beer. "But then I thought: Why do I want to work in a place like this? A place possessed by the devil?" He narrowed his eyes at Rita. "He's still there, you know. The devil. He operates freely at Huntington House."

"I don't believe in the devil," Rita said.

"Well, you should. And so should that poor girl Mr. Huntington just married." He drank down the last of his beer, and seemed a bit drunk all of a sudden. "I'm going to the police in the morning and tell them everything. It's the least I can do for that poor girl."

"How will telling the police help the new Mrs. Huntington?"

"It might get her out of that room. Maybe even the house."

Rita smiled. "You think it would drive the poor girl away? You think she might leave Mr. Huntington?"

"Well, if she knows the crime that was committed there, and covered up . . ."

Rita looked over at him. "Mrs. Hoffman might be charged with lying to police, with tampering with evidence in a murder investigation."

"So be it. She's the devil's handmaiden, after all. You remember how close she was to the first Mrs. Huntington."

"Yeah, she was a freakishly possessive of her. Like some sort of kinky girl-crush."

Jamison was nodding. "If Dominique and Variola were casting spells, I'm sure Mrs. Hoffman was part of it."

Rita smiled. "You silly boy. Believing in such things as spells and ghosts." Her smile disappeared. "But clearly something happened in that house. Something is being covered up. You should definitely go to the police. If you don't, they might charge you with the same things they might charge Mrs. Hoffman with. After all, you moved the body."

"But if I confess, they will probably not press charges." He got up off his stool, standing shakily beside the bar. "And if not, if they arrest me, then so be it. I did wrong. I'll take my punishment."

"Are you all right to drive home?" Rita asked as Jamison turned to leave.

"I can handle two beers," he replied.

She lifted hers in salute. "Thanks for telling me all this stuff."

He looked back at her. "You should know. Everyone should know. That way you can get out of that devil's house."

Rita just smiled.

She had no intention of leaving Huntington House.

At least, not without David.

6

Driving across town, making his way over the Royal Palm Bridge in his beat-up little Toyota Corolla, Jamison realized he was drunker than he'd thought. Just two beers, and his head was spinning. What was wrong with him? He gripped the steering wheel tightly in his hands and concentrated on the road. A light mist of rain speckled his windshield.

He was feeling pleased with himself for his decision to go to the police. It was the right thing to do. These past several months had been wearing on his conscience. He had covered up a crime, he had lied to police, he had assisted in preventing justice for a young woman's horrible death. Such actions could not be allowed to stand.

Ever since he'd been a boy, growing up in rural Georgia, Jamison had tried to do the right thing. His father had been the pastor of Marin Hills Baptist Church, and for many years Jamison had proudly worn his WWJD bracelet on his wrist: *What would Jesus do?* But while taking classes at the local community college—Jamison had intended on becoming a dental hygienist—he'd lost that bracelet, and, no surprise, he'd lost his way as well. He'd started smoking and drinking, and getting too familiar with fast girls. He ended up dropping out of school. His father was deeply disappointed in him, and told him he could no longer depend on him to pay his way. Jamison had to move out of his parents' house. He didn't know where to go, except he knew he needed to get out of town, far away from his father's disapproving eye. He'd lived in various little towns between there and here, finally lucking out by landing the job at Huntington House.

The first Mrs. Huntington had spotted him bagging groceries at the local Publix. She'd struck up a conversation with him. Jamison had been taken with how beautiful she was. Before long, Dominique Huntington had offered him a job, at a very good wage, as a houseboy on the Huntington estate. Jamison had felt like God was giving him a second chance, and as His messenger, he had sent the most beautiful angel He could find.

But now Jamison knew it had been Satan who had sent Dominique into that Publix that day. It had to have been Satan, since now Dominique's ghost walked the earth—killing people.

Still, at the time, Jamison had been glad for the job. It was more money than he had ever made before. It allowed him to leave the boardinghouses and shelters he'd been staying in ever since he left home and move into his own place, a little apartment above a convenience store that smelled constantly of kielbasa and popcorn.

He pulled into the parking space behind the apartment. His head was still spinning, and he craved a cigarette. What had he done? He was very angry with himself. He'd drowned his sorrows over being fired in beer—and not just one but two! What was he thinking?

Jamison knew it was a slippery slope from a couple of beers to a bottle of Jack. He had been doing so well, too. He'd gotten his life back together when he'd been hired at Huntington House. Who cared if he was a houseboy instead of a dental hygienist? It was an honest living. He'd made good money with the Huntingtons. His father had welcomed him home, telling him he was proud of him.

And then Audra had to be found facedown in a pool of blood.

It was Satan's doing, getting me that job, Jamison thought.

He got out of the car and locked the door. The night was damp and muggy, with a mist in the air. Jamison climbed the back stairs to his apartment and let himself inside. He flicked on the overhead light. "Home sweet home," he said to himself.

It wasn't much, but it was his. The couch, which had come with the apartment, was cobwebbed with a light blue mildew. The kitchen table had a broken leg. The linoleum on the kitchen floor was peeling. And always those smells rising up from the store below. But it was *his*—the first place Jamison could ever call his own.

There were three rooms in the apartment: the living room, the kitchen, and Jamison's bedroom, none of them much larger than six by eight feet.

And yet, even this he wouldn't be able to afford much

longer, now that he was out of a job. He hoped Dad would allow him to move back home.

"He will," Jamison said to himself, as he flopped down on the couch, rubbing his temples, trying to get his head to stop spinning. "Once he hears how I did the right thing and went to the police, he'll let me come home."

But he'd also learn that Jamison had lied at first. He'd also discover that Jamison had been living for the past year in a house with the devil.

And some devilry can rub off.

Jamison regretted the fact that he had run to a bar for consolation the moment he learned he'd been fired. Why hadn't he run to a church and prayed? No, he'd gone right back to his old ways and made his way to a bar. He'd had two beers and craved a cigarette. He'd even had impure thoughts sitting next to Rita as she'd tried flirting with him.

"Begone, Satan!" Jamison suddenly bellowed, his hands over his ears.

In that moment, the overhead light went out and Jamison was left in darkness.

He looked around. The little green light on his television was also out. The hum of the refrigerator had stopped.

We've lost power, Jamison thought to himself, standing and looking out the window, bumping his shin against the coffee table as he did so. He let out a little cry of pain. It got so dark in this place at night.

Jamison peered down to the street below. The convenience store underneath him was closed, but he could see the red glow of its neon sign. And through the haze, he could make out that the streetlight some yards away was still burning.

Could it just be his apartment that lost power?

Jamison figured a fuse had blown. He wasn't even sure where the fuse box was. Without a flashlight, he stumbled through his living room, whacking his shin again and suppressing the urge to curse. He remembered the little metal door on the wall in the hallway near the bathroom. That must be the fuse box. He felt his way along the wall, turning at the hallway and running his fingers across the plaster until he felt the metal door. He used his phone for a little bit of light, but still he had to strain to see the fuses. He had no idea what was what.

"Well," Jamison said, "here goes."

He switched each one in turn back and forth. But the power didn't come back on.

Suddenly he felt as if he might faint. That beer was still messing with his head. A year ago, Jamison could have drunk most of his friends under the table. Now he couldn't even handle a couple of beers!

He needed to lie down. He'd deal with the power outage in the morning. He'd call the landlord right before he went down to the police station.

All he wanted to do right now was sleep.

He yanked off his pants and left them in a clump on the floor. He lay in his shirt, underwear, and socks on the bed, staring up into the darkness. He wished the room would stop spinning.

He heard something from the other room. It sounded like a footstep in the kitchen. For some reason Jamison became frightened. He listened again. He heard nothing. It must have been the wind or the rain against the house.

He was feeling jittery. His heart was beating fast. He needed to relax. After everything that had happened today, he needed very badly to chill out. But he was having a difficult time doing so.

Of course, there was one way he could chill out fast.

One way he could forget all his distress about being fired and his anxiety about going to the police and telling what he knew and his fear of his father's disapproval. One way he could block all that out of his mind.

He could smoke a joint.

Jamison had been so good this past year. He'd barely had a sip of alcohol (until tonight) and he'd not had one whiff of pot. But suddenly he wanted to get high so bad. It would stop his head from spinning. It would relax him, settle his mind, allow him to sleep.

He reached over to the bedside table and slid open a drawer. Far in the back, behind his Bible, buried among his dozens of wax-smudged earplugs, he'd stored something in the event of an emergency. Jamison withdrew a small remnant of a joint and held it in front of his face, close enough so he could make it out in the dark.

It was more than a year old. But he figured it might still do the trick.

From the drawer he took a lighter and ignited the little flame. Bringing the joint to his lips, Jamison inhaled.

"Forgive me, Jesus," he said as he let out the smoke.

It was stale, but it was still potent enough.

He smoked the joint until it was just a brown crisp smoldering between his fingers. Resting his head back against the pillow, he allowed the wave of good feeling to wash over him.

But then he heard the footstep in the kitchen again.

He pushed the sound out of his mind and closed his eyes. He just wanted to sleep. In the morning, he'd feel better, and he'd go down to the police and get all of this devilry off his chest. He wasn't sure how the police were going to stop the ghost of Dominique Huntington from killing again, but they could at least arrest that plastic-faced Mrs. Hoffman.

Another footstep, then two.

Jamison opened his eyes. The pot was maybe making him a little paranoid. But it seemed that someone was in his apartment and walking around in the dark.

That's crazy, Jamison told himself. *I locked the door behind me when I came in tonight.*

Didn't I?

Of course he did. He shook off the paranoia and closed his eyes.

He was fading off to sleep, but some small voice inside his head forced its way through the marijuana haze and got him to wonder.

Did I lock the door?

It doesn't matter. Ghosts can walk through walls.

Jamison opened his eyes again. The room was pitch-dark. He listened. A soft sound nearby. Maybe it was the light rain hitting against the window.

Or maybe, Jamison thought, it was someone breathing.

He fumbled his hand through the dark to the bedside table and found his phone. Grabbing ahold of it, he hit the switch, casting a soft amber glow through the room. Jamison looked around and saw nothing.

What would Jesus do?

Jesus would go to sleep, Jamison thought.

In that instant, the glow of his phone picked up the steel of the blade that was swooping down toward him, which then slit Jamison's throat so deeply it nicked bone.

7

"Oh, no, David, no!" Liz cried.

"I'm sorry, darling, but it's true," her husband replied.

"Why now? We just got here!"

Patiently, David took her hands and explained that the family business had a lot of interests around the world, and right now, there was trouble in their Amsterdam office. His father was putting all his trust in him that he'd be able to resolve that trouble. "It will only be for six days," he told her. "Not even a full week."

"But David—"

"I can't let Dad down," he went on. "I need to prove to him that I'm capable of taking over the business from him one day soon." He smiled kindly, seeing the stricken look on Liz's face. "And when that day comes, darling, I'll be able to delegate others to go off on these trips, and I'll get to stay home with you."

Liz wasn't very consoled by that. "David, it's just that I—well, I don't know these people, and I'm not sure of my way around—"

She stopped herself. She heard the sound of her voice. Whiny and scared and needy. The same voice she'd used the night her father walked out on them.

I'm going away, her father had said. *I can't take any more of this.*

She stopped whining.

"Sweetheart," David was saying, "believe me, if I didn't feel it was urgent, I wouldn't go."

"It's okay, David," Liz forced herself to say. "I understand."

"Do you?"

"Yes. I'm disappointed that you won't be here for me to get to know Huntington House, but I do understand. It's very important that you show your father that you can handle situations like these."

"That's my girl," David said, cupping her chin in his palm.

Liz didn't like it when he called her a girl. It felt patronizing. But for the moment she let it slide. Better to have him patronizing her than considering leaving her.

Liz was fully aware that she had some serious codependency issues to work through. Nicki was always informing her of the fact. "Sweetheart," Nicki would say, "you better work through that codependency stuff or you'll never have a satisfying relationship." One time, somewhere between Gibraltar and Corsica, Nicki had been particularly adamant, giving Liz a long list of relationship dos and don'ts.

Liz had laughed. They had been drinking wine on the quarterdeck. "If you're such an expert on relationships, how come you're not in one?"

"Because I'm in the middle of a cruise, baby," Nicki replied, "and I'm just having fun. But someday, when we're back on dry land, I intend on settling down. And I'm going to do it right. None of this letting the man set the terms."

But Liz knew that was exactly what she had done with David. She had allowed him to make all the decisions about when they got married, where they would live, what their household would look like. It had been hard to say no to the promise of Huntington House, of course. Liz couldn't deny being intrigued by the idea of all that land, all those rooms, all those servants. Growing up as she had, with a mother always struggling to pay the bills, Liz had been a bit dazzled by David's descriptions of his estate.

He was packing now. Liz watched him with a sinking heart.

"Oh, but David, I don't know any of the details of running this house. Like preparing grocery lists and menus and coordinating the staff . . . I don't know any of that yet."

"That's what Mrs. Hoffman is for, sweetheart. You don't have to trouble your mind with any of those details. You just relax and explore the estate. Have one of the chauffeurs drive you around town. Look for a property for your dance studio. You're going to need something to do with your time, baby."

Liz wasn't all that keen on David calling her "baby" either. She wasn't a baby. She was a grown woman—his wife. But it was just his way of showing affection.

David snapped his suitcase shut. "And I'll be back in just six days, sweetheart. Not even a full week."

He kissed her. Liz gave him a smile. This wasn't what she expected married life to be exactly, but she figured she'd have to get used to it.

8

Variola had seen many things in her day. Back in Haiti, before it had been devastated by the earthquake, she had watched as her mother had changed stones into flowers and healed little children of influenza with just a sprinkle of her special powders. When she was just seven years old, Variola had seen a dead man get up and walk. So nothing surprised Variola.

She was in the kitchen, preparing breakfast for the new Mrs. Huntington. The late Mrs. Huntington had been very particular about her meals. They had to be vegetarian and wheat-free and always topped with fresh raspberries. The late Mrs. Huntington had had other requests of Variola as well, and most of them had had nothing to do with her culinary skills.

"I've brought you to this house for a reason," Dominique had said to her on Variola's first day there. "You understand that reason, do you not?"

Variola had thought she understood. Later, she wasn't so sure.

She'd asked Mrs. Hoffman if the new mistress of the

house would have any special dietary requests like the former mistress. Mrs. Hoffman had replied that she suspected the new Mrs. Huntington would be satisfied with a Happy Meal from McDonald's. How Variola had laughed at that, with her deep, from-the-lungs laugh that echoed through the house like the gong of a giant bell. She didn't care for Mrs. Hoffman all that much, but still, what she had said had made Variola laugh.

She was a tall, strikingly beautiful woman with glossy chocolate skin, a pile of black hair, and great, dark, saucer eyes. In Haiti, she had broken many a man's heart; many men had wanted her, many had tried to possess her. But no one owned Variola but Variola. Indeed, the only time her own heart had ever been broken was when the earthquake had come and devastated her cherished homeland. Her family scattered, her fortunes depleted, Variola had been forced to leave Haiti and come here, to this house.

She had quickly made it her own. Mrs. Hoffman didn't like that, especially now that the first Mrs. Huntington was gone. But even Hoffman knew that Variola answered to no one.

She never had.

There was little that escaped Variola's notice in this house. She heard the whispers of the servants. She saw the comings and goings of the Huntingtons themselves. Her eyes were always alert, her ears always attuned.

Like now. She heard Mr. Huntington come down the front stairs and the soft pitter of footsteps that hurried from the parlor to meet him.

Like a cat, Variola moved soundlessly to the doorway of the kitchen, and from there, hid herself in the small alcove that led to the pantry where, through a space in the doorway, she had a clear view of the front staircase.

Mr. Huntington was carrying a suitcase. So he was leaving again, Variola thought. So soon after bringing his new bride home . . .

The master of the house looked preoccupied. He checked his wristwatch. He didn't notice the woman who had come to the foot of the stairs to meet him.

But Variola had seen the woman approach—and wait like a spider in the shadows, ready to entrap her prey.

"David," Variola heard Rita whisper.

Mr. Huntington lifted his face and saw the maid in front of him. "Oh, hello, Rita . . ."

"You're leaving?"

"Yes, I have to get on a plane. I don't really have any time to talk . . ."

Rita reached up and gently gripped Mr. Huntington's lapels. "David . . . I have to see you. I know I said I'd accept the fact that things were different now . . ."

"You *must* accept it, Rita," he told her coldly, stiffening, trying to break the hold she had on him.

"It's not possible, David. I thought about you all night. Remembering . . . those times . . ." She pulled close to him, pressing herself against his chest.

"Rita, stop this."

"Don't you remember them, too, David?" She was purring, moving her lips softly against his neck. Even from where Variola stood, she could get a whiff of Rita's perfume, so sweet, so toxic. Gardenia. It was the first Mrs. Huntington's scent.

The man was struggling in her grip, recoiling from her—but he did not thrust her away.

"Oh, David, you said it yourself to many nights, in that room in the servants' quarters . . . you said that you had never known such passion as you found with me."

"Rita, it was different then. Very different circumstances. I'm married now."

"You were married then."

"Please, Rita, my wife . . ."

"She never needs to know," Rita purred, and her lips kissed Mr. Huntington's neck. Variola smiled at the girl's boldness.

Mr. Huntington seemed ensnared. He stood there, no longer recoiling, seemingly under the spell of Rita and the fragrance of gardenia.

The housemaid moved in for the kill. She pressed her lips against her lover's. Variola let out the smallest sound of laughter. What a show the girl was putting on!

They kissed standing there at the foot of the stairs. A deep, hard, hungry kiss. Anyone could have seen them.

But as it was, only Variola witnessed the event, safe in her hiding space in the pantry.

"Oh, David, David . . ." Rita moaned.

"No, you mustn't," David muttered. "I mustn't . . ."

"We *must*!" Rita replied. "We can't resist! I love you, David!" And she tried to kiss him again.

But finally he pushed her away. "If you keep this up," Mr. Huntington said, "I'll have to let you go. I don't want to fire you, Rita, but this behavior is unacceptable."

"You kissed me," she seethed. "You still want me."

"You are very attractive, Rita. But this can never happen again." He pushed his way past her toward the front door. "There's a car waiting for me outside. Remember what I told you, Rita. I need you to be a friend to my wife. If you care about me as you say, then you will do that for me. You will be a friend to Mrs. Huntington."

Rita said nothing, just turned her face away from him.

Mr. Huntington hurried out the front door. In moments, Variola heard a car driving off down the driveway.

She stepped out from her hiding place into full view. Rita looked up and realized she had witnessed the entire episode.

"I don't care if you saw it all," Rita spit, before Variola had a chance to say a word. "Go ahead and judge me."

"Oh, I don't judge," Variola replied, in that spicy-sweet island patois. "I only observe."

Rita set her chin in defiance. "I will get him, you know. I will get him back."

"He used you, sweet girl. When he was bereft and hurt and lonely. You should hate him, not love him."

"He didn't use me. He loves me. You weren't there when we would make love. You didn't see how he was when we were together."

Variola just smiled in reply. Silly child. Didn't she know Variola saw all?

"Excuse me," Rita said, attempting to step around Variola. "I have to work to do."

"That's apparent," Variola said, a smile tickling her lips. "You have a great deal of work to do, but you'll only get it done if Variola helps you."

Rita glared at her. "What do you mean?"

"Mr. Huntington is a stubborn man."

Rita said nothing.

"I warned you to stay away from him. Your way will only lead to heartbreak—or worse."

"Why would you care about that?"

"I have my reasons."

Variola considered herself a kind woman; she had been brought up by a mother who had seemed an angel on earth, using her special potions and enchantments to heal the sick and make gardens grow. Variola was fond of Rita; she didn't want to think of her heartbroken over a man who didn't love her or respect her.

But that was not why she offered to help the girl. Variola had a sense that she was going to need allies in this house now that Mr. Huntington had brought home a new bride. What if she was like the last one? What if she formed the same sort of bond Dominique had with Mrs. Hoffman? There would come a point, Variola was sure, that she would have to go head-to-head with Hoffman. And if that happened, she needed friends, supporters, followers—*acolytes*, she thought. *Disciples*. As she had once had in Haiti, back before the earthquake. Rita Cansino might be her first disciple, *if* she felt indebted to Variola.

"If you really want to get him back," the chef said to Rita, "then you will need more than your soft lips and a squirt of Dominique's gardenia perfume. To stay safe, you need Variola."

Rita huffed. "I don't need any of your island mumbo jumbo, if that's what you mean," she said, sneering, and continuing down the hallway.

"Woe to those who do not believe," Variola shouted after her.

But Rita wasn't hearing anything else. She turned and disappeared into the parlor.

She's as stubborn as he is, Variola thought.

And a fool.

She thinks her little kisses and soft words will get him.

Variola laughed.

She'll be back. She'll come back begging to Variola.

They all did, eventually. Except for Hoffman.

But Hoffman could be dealt with.

9

Without David in the house, Liz felt adrift, unsure of herself and unsteady on her feet. She hated feeling this way, hated how she suddenly felt like a timid and insecure little mouse after so many years as a strong, independent woman.

She had blossomed after Peter dumped her. She'd been fine on her own, really committing to her studies of music and dance. That was when her dreams started taking shape. She wanted to perform onstage, to hear the applause. Someday she wanted to choreograph a great show—one of the classics, perhaps, or something new and modern. She had been a little nervous accepting the job on the cruise ship—she'd never been away from home for that long or that far before—but she'd taken it, and she'd performed well. The cruise director was very sorry that Liz left the gig early to get married. "You're a good dancer, Liz," she had told her. "You have a great style and a great rhythm. You'll direct your own shows someday, if you don't give up your dreams."

But that's what Liz had done. She had given up her

dreams. David's idea of a local dancing school hardly matched choreographing a show at Lincoln Center.

Still, she loved him. She'd find a way to dance, but for now, she was going to make her first ambition her marriage.

If only she didn't feel so anxious.

It was just that she was so out of her element in this great big imposing mansion. On the second day that David was away, Liz dressed early and went downstairs with a cheerful grin on her face, trying to learn the routine of the house. She asked Mrs. Hoffman to show her around and explain how things were run. But the icy housekeeper only smiled at her. "Don't worry about such things," she said. "I have everything under control." As mistress of the house, she insisted, Liz should enjoy a life of leisure. "Why don't you take a stroll through the gardens and enjoy all the beautiful flowers?"

So that was what Liz did, feeling as if she'd just been banished from her own house.

The gardens were extraordinary, however. Huge tropical blossoms looking like alien life-forms towered over her as she walked down the path. Calla lilies and birds of paradise were clustered against spiky yuccas, and exotic rosebushes grew along a trellis. But when Liz took a corner she stopped short. There, along the path in front of her, were the remnants of a row of bushes yanked out by their roots. A few scattered roots remained; the soil was still disturbed and unleveled.

The gardenias.

These were the gardenias.

The fragrance Liz had thought she'd smelled on her first day in this house.

The fragrance that Dominique had always worn.

The bushes David had ordered torn out by their roots since the smell of them reminded him of his heartbreak.

Liz suddenly felt overcome, as if she should run away from this place forever. She turned, prepared to bolt somewhere—anywhere—

—and there was Mrs. Hoffman standing behind her, staring at her with those terrible eyes, her plastic face shining in the afternoon sun.

"You seem warm," the housekeeper said, her lips moving in that way that passed for a smile. "Might I suggest you take a dip in the pool?"

"The pool . . ."

"Yes. And afterward you can just lounge in one of the chairs. We have a mister system—cool mist sprinkling down that keeps you from ever getting too warm. It's rather like a tropical paradise, Mrs. Huntington used to say. Such beautiful flowers and greenery surround the pool. It will be as if you're on vacation in the Caribbean."

"I feel as if I should be . . . helping . . . doing something . . . instead of just lounging around."

"There's nothing to be done, ma'am. Perhaps you'd like to take one of the cars instead, and drive into town, do some shopping . . ."

Liz blushed. "I don't have a driver's license. I let it expire when I was on the ship. I'll need to renew it."

"Oh, I see. Well, then, we could have one of the chauffeurs take you . . ."

The idea of going out and exploring Palm Beach without David made Liz uneasy. "I'm not feeling very peppy today, I'm afraid," she said. "I guess maybe sitting by the pool and reading a book sounds like the best idea for now."

"You'll love the pool. I'll have Rita set out a pitcher of iced tea. You go on upstairs now and change into your swimsuit."

Liz gave her a half-smile. Maybe Mrs. Hoffman wasn't so bad. Maybe Liz's nerves and everything that had happened since she got here had made her too uneasy around her. Maybe she really *was* trying to be kind to Liz.

Back in her room, Liz slipped into her bathing suit. It was a light blue one-piece, cut high in the hips. Liz looked at herself in the full-length mirror. She could see the tautness of her leg muscles had softened. On the ship, dancing every day, she had been lean and tight. But she hadn't been keeping up with her gym routine since she'd married David. How could she have? They'd been jetting from place to place on their honeymoon, eating far too many cakes and pastries and drinking more cocktails than they could count. Liz was going to have to join a gym somewhere, and soon. And she really, *really* needed to start dancing again. Maybe David's idea of opening a dance studio wasn't so bad, after all.

But even if her legs were less toned than they were a few months ago, they were still pretty damn shapely, Liz told herself, admiring them in the mirror. What satisfied her far less than her legs, however, were her breasts. She'd always been rather flat-chested, and when she was younger she used to feel terribly self-conscious about the fact. The boys in high school used to tease her; one day, when she'd innocently remarked that her mother had taken some sweaters out of a hope chest, the boys had latched onto the phrase and started shouting, "Liz is hoping for a chest!" Liz had laughed, putting on a good face, but inside she was mortified.

So when Peter Mather had left her for a woman who was far more stacked than she was, all of Liz's insecurities had flooded to the surface. How she used to cringe when she would see the two of them walking around the campus together, Peter's new girlfriend seeming to go out of her way to flash her big tits in everybody's face. Liz knew that was probably only her own perception, but she couldn't help but look at the two of them and feel completely inadequate.

The memory of all that humiliation, however, receded into the past the moment she stepped out poolside. Mrs. Hoffman was right. The pool was magnificent. And it was hers. She had married a man who loved her, who thought she was beautiful, who had given her all this.

Set as if into the side of a cliff, the pool meandered around rocks and little manmade islands, perfect to stretch out on under the Florida sun. Palm trees provided plenty of shade if one wanted it, and at the deep end of the pool a waterfall cascaded from above. The fragrance here wasn't gardenia—Liz was glad about that—but tropical flowers. Soft, tinkling music was piped in from somewhere. On the other end from the waterfall a cushioned lounge chair waited for her, and beside it sat a glass table bearing a pitcher of iced tea and some glasses.

Rita, one of the chambermaids, stood apart, watching Liz take in the surroundings.

"I hadn't been out here yet," Liz said, more to herself than Rita. "It's . . . lovely."

"Is there anything else you'll be wanting, ma'am?" Rita asked.

Liz thought she detected a coldness in the young woman's voice. "No, thank you," she replied. "Thank you for bringing out the iced tea."

Rita nodded and quietly slipped through a side door into the house.

Liz took a seat on the lounge. The sound of the music and the waterfall was almost hypnotic. She thought she could fall asleep out here. But first she determined she would take a swim. If she was serious about getting back into exercise, she could start right now.

She rose, walked to the edge of the pool, and tested the water with her toe. Perfect temperature. Not too hot, not too cold. She stepped gingerly down the ladder into the pool. The water enveloped her body like a warm silk blanket.

Liz began to swim. It felt wonderful to be moving her muscles again, making her legs and arms and shoulders work. She swam three laps, then stopped, looking up into the waterfall, her eyes caught by the kaleidoscope of color. How peaceful it was here.

"Excuse me, Mrs. Huntington."

A voice cut through Liz's reverie. She turned to look. It was Mrs. Martinez, one of the kitchen workers whom Liz had met briefly.

"Yes, hello, Mrs. Martinez."

"I've brought you some fruit salad. Variola made it special for you."

"Oh, isn't that sweet, thank you," Liz said, hopping out of the pool.

As she did so, she caught a glimpse of herself in the

large glass windows that lined the pool area. What a sight. Her hair was wet and stringy, plastered down over her shoulders. She wore no makeup, of course, and this ill-fitting bathing suit announced her loss of muscle tone and lack of curves more than she'd anticipated.

Liz looked away from her image. Mrs. Martinez, a short, plump, middle-aged lady, was standing in front of her, holding a bowl of chopped mango and watermelon and what looked like basil and feta cheese.

"Variola hopes you will enjoy," Mrs. Martinez said, handing the bowl to Liz.

"I'm sure I will. Please tell her thank you for me."

After Mrs. Martinez left, Liz ate the fruit and allowed herself to relax, perhaps for the first time since she had come to this house. The waterfall was so soothing. She placed the empty bowl on the side table and lay back on the lounge. She closed her eyes. The sweet aroma of plumeria flowers filled her nostrils. Within moments Liz was asleep.

She awoke with a start. How long had she been asleep? The sun seemed slightly different in the sky. But the waterfall and the music were the same.

Liz turned her head. On the table next to her, the empty bowl of fruit was gone. In its place stood a photograph in a frame.

Liz looked closer.

It was a picture of the pool. But stretched out in a lounge chair, in the exact spot where Liz now sat, was Dominique. She was wearing a bikini.

She might have been a *Playboy* model, Liz thought, with her large breasts and tiny waist and full, curvy legs. Her long, dark, lustrous hair framed her exquisitely beautiful face.

And standing behind her, beaming into the camera, was David.

Liz sat up, horrified.

Immediately she spotted Mrs. Hoffman walking toward her.

"Ah, you're awake," the housekeeper said. "I came out earlier and you were asleep. I trust you're enjoying the pool."

"This . . . picture . . ." Liz managed to say.

"Oh, yes. I thought you might like to see it. It was taken just after the pool was put in. As you can see, only a few stones had been set at that point. And if you'll look, the waterfall hadn't yet been installed."

"I . . . see . . ."

Liz looked away from the photograph. Why did she feel certain that Mrs. Hoffman had placed it there not to show her the changes in the pool, but to intimidate her with Dominique's beauty? To point out that Liz could never hope to measure up—quite literally?

At that moment she felt more eyes on her. Instinctively Liz turned, and there, standing on the other side of the glass separating the pool area from the rest of the house, she saw half a dozen staff members arranged in a row. Rita. Mrs. Martinez. And several men. All watching her.

This was their idea of a joke! They had all been waiting to see what Liz's reaction to the picture of Dominique would be. Liz's face burned with embarrassment. She could imagine their schemes. Let's show her that she's a miserable substitute for Dominique! They were laughing at her, just like the boys in school had once laughed at her.

"I think I'll go upstairs now," Liz said, standing. "I . . . I have a headache."

"Oh, I'm so sorry to hear that, ma'am," Mrs. Hoffman said. "I had hoped the pool would relax you. Is there anything I can get you?"

"No," she managed to reply, as she pushed past the housekeeper, self-conscious of all the eyes on her. Liz felt naked in this terrible, ugly swimsuit. She wished she had a blanket to wrap around herself. She hurried upstairs. In the privacy of her room—it had been Dominique's room, too, she knew—she sobbed on the bed.

She needed David to come home. She needed his arms around her.

But in that moment, thinking of how happy David had looked in that photograph with his beautiful wife, Liz felt she would never trust his arms again.

10

Variola made her way down into the wine cellar where she kept some of her more exotic spices. She was looking for something specific. A very special recipe was called for.

She had seen what Mrs. Hoffman had done to the new Mrs. Huntington. A cruel trick.

So that is how it will be, Variola thought. No alliances there. Mrs. Hoffman does not intend to accept the new wife.

And where would that leave Variola?

Mrs. Hoffman was a cruel woman. Variola had never liked the old plastic-faced harridan, even if she'd had to work with her, and make her peace with her, these past few years. But from the day she had first met the housekeeper Variola had seen deep into her soul, and discerned only darkness there. A cold, bitter darkness.

Variola opened a small wooden box she kept on a low shelf, beneath the burgundies. She withdrew a dried flower. She was about to place it to her nose and test its fragrance when she heard a step behind her. Variola spun her head around like an owl, eyes blazing.

"I'm sorry to disturb you," came a soft voice.

"Mrs. Martinez, what are you doing down here?"

"She frightens me," the older woman said.

"Ah, you have no need to be frightened of Mrs. Hoffman. What she did was needlessly cruel, but Variola can take care of her."

Mrs. Martinez frowned. "Mrs. Hoffman troubles me, but it is not she who I fear."

"Then who?"

"Mrs. Huntington."

Variola laughed. "Are you becoming like all the rest of them now? Afraid of a ghost that walks these halls?"

"No, not the first Mrs. Huntington," Mrs. Martinez replied. "This one! The new one."

Variola laughed again, a sound that echoed through the cold, damp wine cellar. "And why should that little sparrow frighten you? She could barely frighten a mouse!"

"You know why she frightens me."

Variola's dark eyes hardened as they bore down on Mrs. Martinez. "No. I do not know why she frightens you."

"Because of what might happen." The older woman paused. "Happen again."

"You disappoint me. You have no faith in Variola."

"Oh, but I do, but—"

Variola smiled. "No buts. Tell me, Mrs. Martinez. If it happened again, whose side would you rather be on? Mine or Mrs. Hoffman's?"

The older woman wasn't sure how to answer. "I believe you have a kinder heart, but she . . . she will stop at nothing."

"When the time comes, you will be on my side," Variola told her.

"I'm still frightened."

Variola waved her away. "Go upstairs, Mrs. Martinez. Speak no more of this. None."

All of them fools, Variola thought, sniffing the dried flower and determining it to be perfect. Why couldn't they all trust Variola to make sure everything worked out?

11

"I'm so glad you called, David," Liz said into the phone. "It's been so wonderful talking to you . . . I miss you so much . . ."

"I miss you, too, darling, and I'm sorry this call has to be so short." David's voice sounded so far away. "But we have a revolt of investors on our hands. I've got to rush from meeting to meeting, soothing ruffled feathers and making promises . . ."

"I understand, David. But when will you be home?"

"It might be another week."

"Another week!"

"Liz, I can't help it. I'm sorry."

"But you said just six days . . . it's been five already . . . another week?"

"Really, darling, there's nothing I can do."

She pulled back, careful not to sound too needy. "All right," she said. "I'll just count the days, David."

"That's good, sweetheart, so will I. In the meantime, keep enjoying the pool . . ."

"David," Liz said, cutting in before he could say goodbye.

"What is it?"

"I had a crazy thought . . . I don't know . . . maybe . . . maybe I ought to consider some breast implants . . ."

There was silence on the other end of the line. Liz worried the call had been dropped.

"David?"

"I hope you're joking, Liz."

"Well, I—"

"I can't believe you'd say that! Don't even think about such a thing! Jesus Christ, what did you have to say that for? Now, I'm late. I've got to go."

"David, I didn't mean to anger you. It was just a silly thought."

"A very silly thought. Goodbye, Liz."

He hung up the phone.

Liz stood there holding her phone. A soft knock came at the door of her room.

She opened it to see Rita holding a tray.

"You wished your dinner sent up to your room, Mrs. Huntington?"

Liz nodded. "Thank you. You can put in on the desk there."

Rita did as she was instructed. Liz couldn't help but notice how attractive the maid was, how full her breasts and hips were.

"Is there anything else?"

"No, thank you."

Rita nodded and left the room.

Liz sat down at her desk. As she picked at her pasta primavera flavored with Caribbean spices, she logged on to her computer and was thrilled to find Nicki—her darling Nicki—online.

"So, how's it going?" her friend messaged her.

"Wonderful," Liz messaged back without delay.

"Liar."

"Why would you say that?"

"Because I know you. You always say things are wonderful when they're not. If they were really wonderful, you would have said something like 'amazing' or 'awesome.' "

Liz admitted Nicki was right. They clicked onto Skype so they could see each other. How wonderful— or rather, how awesome—it was to see Nicki's face. Her shiny black eyes, her easy smile, the way she tossed her thick brown hair back when she laughed.

"I'm finally heading back home," Nicki announced. "I'm leaving the ship and the world tour early."

"Whatever for?" Liz asked. "I thought you were having a great time."

"I thought you were, too, then you up and got married."

Liz smiled weakly. "Has the same thing happened to you, too, Nicki?"

Her friend laughed, tossing her hair. "No way, sugarbabe. I'm immune to Cupid's arrow, remember? No, I just got a better gig in Atlantic City, and the cruise ship is being kind enough to let me out of my contract, just like they let you."

"What's the gig?"

"Harrah's, baby! The biggest resort in town! I'm starting at the top! One of the lead dancers in a new nightly revue—*and* I get to help choreograph and design the whole thing!"

"That's . . . that's amazing, Nicki."

Liz was envious. She listened as Nicki rambled on about the details of her new job. She asked a few questions and Nicki responded with undisguised glee. How exciting it was, Liz thought, to be going to Atlantic City, to be able to design and choreograph a new show. That was something Liz had always wanted to do herself, something she had looked forward to doing someday in her career.

Then she'd up and gotten married.

Immediately Liz rejected her envy of Nicki. Her friend didn't have what she had—a terrific husband who loved her very much. The very fact he'd gotten so angry at her for suggesting cosmetic surgery meant that David loved Liz exactly the way she was. She had to believe that. She thought about how much she loved David in return—how the sight of him still caused her heart to leap a little, how the touch of his lips on her neck still thrilled her beyond anything she'd ever experienced. She wouldn't trade David for all the shows in Atlantic City, even if she got to choreograph them all! She had to remember that. She had to!

But it was difficult, given how alone and disliked she felt in this big house.

"So, tell me," Nicki said. "What's wrong?"

"Nothing's wrong," Liz said.

"As I said before, you're a liar."

"Really, Nicki. Nothing's wrong. David is the most amazing husband. I adore him. It's just that . . ." Her words trailed off.

"Just that what?"

"Well, he had to go away on business."

"How long has he been gone?"

"Almost a week."

"Poor baby, but I guess the honeymoon is over."

"That's just it," Liz said, finishing the last of her

wine. "We had such a marvelous honeymoon and now . . . well, now I'm afraid this is what my life is going to be like. Stuck here in this big house alone for much of the time while he travels on business."

"Is it such a terrible place to be stuck in?"

"Oh, it's a gorgeous house. And the gardens are equally as beautiful. I don't want for anything. There are maids and houseboys to wait on my every need, and a magnificent chef . . ."

Liz's mind passed quickly over the faces of all the people who worked in the house. She remembered the eyes of those staring at her out at the pool. Maybe she'd been mistaken. Maybe they hadn't been laughing at her. Maybe they had just been told to be there in case Liz had requested anything. They were her servants, after all, who were supposed to be at her beck and call. But Liz couldn't get used to that fact. A woman like her didn't have servants.

"I'll bet you'll get pretty good at bossing them all around," Nicki said.

"I hardly think so. I just kind of keep to myself. The whole time David's been gone, I've eaten in my room."

"Sweetie—you can't be a hermit! It's your own house!"

"Yes, but until David gets back, I don't feel at home here."

"Look, Liz, you married a very successful man. You knew right from the start that he was going to be away from home a great deal. You've got to find your own rhythm. You've got to learn to do your own thing."

Liz nodded. "David suggested I open a dance studio."

"Brilliant idea! You'd be terrific!"

"I don't know. I'll think about it."

Nicki drew closer to her camera, so that her face nearly filled Liz's computer screen. It made Liz miss her friend a great deal.

"So, the sixty-four-thousand-dollar question."

"What's that?"

"Have you talked to your mother since you got back from your honeymoon?"

Liz sighed. "I've tried. I've called several times. But she's either been asleep or out. At least, that's what Deanne tells me. I think she might be fibbing, however."

"You think your mother is avoiding talking to you?"

"I'm beginning to think so. She's still upset that I got married without her there. And David and I never got the chance to see her when we got back from our honeymoon. We had to get down here. We'd planned on going up to see Mom in a week or so, but now, with David being called away, I don't know if those plans will change."

"Fly her down to see you. I'm sure David can afford a private jet to get her."

Liz couldn't help but laugh. "Mom, here? Oh, no. I don't think so."

"I'm sure your siblings would come with her."

"Even worse! George would be out smoking weed on the back patio and Deanne would be sprawled out on the couch watching the Home Shopping Network all day!"

Nicki smiled. "They're your people, Liz."

Liz smiled herself. Yes, they were. And suddenly she missed them, too. A wave of guilt surged through her.

I abandoned them. I walked out on them, just as Daddy did.

"Okay, and now for the second sixty-four-thousand-dollar question," Nicki said.

"What else could there be?" Liz asked.

"Any mementos of the dead wife lying around?"

The question stopped Liz cold. If thoughts of her family disturbed her, the mention of Dominique chilled her to the bone.

"Only like everywhere I look," Liz responded.

"No way!"

"There's a huge portrait of her in the stairwell that I have to pass every time I go up or down. That's part of the reason I've been staying in my room." Liz paused. "She was very beautiful."

"Tell David to take that thing down!"

Liz shook her head. "I can't. Not yet anyway. Eventually, when he gets back."

"Um, hello, when did the body snatchers make off with my tough friend Liz? Cuz I don't recognize this milquetoast." Nicki shook a finger at her. "It's your house now, sweetheart. Not hers."

Liz laughed lightly. "I just don't feel that way yet. Her fragrance—gardenias—is everywhere. Sometimes I think the servants still spray it everywhere so they can remember her." She paused. "They were apparently very devoted to her."

"I can't believe that David left that portrait hanging! I'd confront him if I were you, Liz."

"I will," she said, though she knew she didn't sound convincing. "When he gets back I'll ask him to move it somewhere else."

"Really, Liz, honey, you're going to have to stand up for yourself."

"I know . . ."

"I'm not sure you do. You're hiding out in your room!"

"You're right, and so I should get going," Liz said, deciding to end the conversation. It was becoming increasingly uncomfortable. "I'll go downstairs and try to be social. Most of the help will be going home soon for the night anyway, and I should say goodbye before they go."

"No live-ins?"

"Just Mrs. Hoffman and the chef, Variola. Everybody else goes home. We have a couple of shifts here at Huntington House, seven to three and three to eight. By eight-thirty the entire place is dark and quiet—unless there's a party. David tells me in those circumstances, everybody gets overtime."

"All right, baby, you go downstairs and be social. Don't forget—you're the mistress of the house now." She blew her a kiss. "Keep in touch, okay? Once I'm off the ship, you can call me anytime."

"I will. And congratulations on the new job. Really."

"Love you, Liz."

"Love you, too."

They signed off.

Liz stood and took a deep breath.

She really *should* go downstairs. Make small talk with the staff. Learn something about them. Like their names, to start. She only knew Rita and Variola by their first names. She had no idea what Mrs. Hoffman's first name was, or Mrs. Martinez's for that matter. Any others' names, if she'd been told them, she had now completely forgotten.

I'm terrible, Liz thought to herself. *I should go down there right now and project confidence and cordiality and everything will get better.*

But she didn't want to. All she wanted to do was crawl into her bed—that big, canopied haven—and go to sleep.

Liz became aware of the ticking of the clock on her mantel. It was a soft, reassuring sound, background noise throughout the day. She glanced over at the clock and saw that it was nearly seven-thirty. The sun was beginning to set, filling the room with crimson light.

But there was a sound competing with the ticking clock, Liz realized. How long had that sound been there? A knocking sort of sound, a banging of some kind. Soft and muffled. Sometimes it seemed to fade away, but when Liz listened closely, it was still there. *Tap, tap, tap* . . . She drew closer to the mantel. No, it wasn't coming from the clock. It seemed to come from another part of the room . . .

Liz tried to follow the sound, but suddenly she lost it. She listened, but all she heard once again was the ticking of the clock. She dismissed the sound as the rattle of a pipe.

Looking back over at her desk, Liz spotted her dinner plates. Was she going to place the tray with its dirty dishes outside her door, in the hallway, as if she were staying in some hotel?

No, she told herself. *Take them downstairs yourself. Be friendly. Make them like you.*

As much as they seemed to have liked her.

They *did* like Dominique, Liz believed.

Mrs. Hoffman sure seemed to. She lost no opportunity in bringing up the name of the late Mrs. Huntington. How witty Dominique was. How charming. How eloquent. How talented. How beautiful.

The young men of the house, like that impertinent Jamison, had been obsessed with Dominique. What was it that David had said? *Some of the boys who worked here became almost obsessed with my late wife. They tried to get her to pay attention to them. They imagined all sorts of things about her . . .*

"They had thought she was the most beautiful creature to ever walk the earth," Liz said out loud, looking at her pale reflection in the mirror.

That was why Jamison tried to frighten me on my first day here. I was daring to replace his beloved Dominique!

All Liz's insecurities came bubbling back to the surface.

She'd have to face everyone eventually. She knew that. But not tonight. Her fears and anxieties were just too raw at the moment. No way was she going downstairs to try to win them over tonight. Maybe tomorrow. But not tonight. Liz placed her tray outside her door in the hall, then turned off her light and went to sleep.

12

What Sergeant Joe Foley thought of as he looked over at the scene in front of him was the candied apples his granddad used to buy him at the county fair. An apple on a stick would be dipped into red sugar glaze, which would then harden over the apple, encasing it in a dark red shiny shield.

That's what the dead body on the bed in front of him reminded Joe of. The head and upper torso were encased in a hard dark red translucent shell—probably hardened blood. The body had been lying here all that time, Joe guessed. From the looks of it, the young man's throat had been slit and he'd bled out.

The landlady of the apartment building was still shaking as she gave her statement to Joe's partner, Sergeant Aggie McFarland.

"I took a delivery for him this morning," the chunky, middle-aged woman said, clutching the apron she wore around her waist. She was the proprietor of the convenience store downstairs. "It was marked 'perishable.' It looked like it came from his parents up in Georgia. His mother's always sending him fruitcakes and pastries.

Well, I kept knocking on his door, but he didn't answer, even though his car was in his parking spot. It's been there all week. I thought maybe he was getting a ride to work, that the car had died on him, like it's done before. I really wasn't suspicious at all until he didn't open the door, even after I told him that I had this box for him. Finally I figured he must have been away, gone off with some friends. I figured I'd just let myself in and put the box in his refrigerator. But then, when I went inside, I saw . . ." The woman's voice trailed off in horror.

"Go ahead, Mrs. Marino," Sergeant McFarland encouraged her.

"I saw through the open door to his room that he was in bed. And I just peeked in, didn't want to disturb him, and then I saw all the blood!"

"This was when?"

"Just an hour or so ago. I screamed and called down to my son, who was in the store below. He came running up, took one look, and then called the police."

Joe Foley turned away from the corpse on the bed and walked over to the trembling woman, who wouldn't glance into the bedroom, having already been traumatized enough. "You say his name was Jamison Wilkes," Joe said. "Can you tell us any more about him?"

"He was a good boy, though I think he'd had some hard times of it during the past few years," said Mrs. Marino. "I had a feeling he was struggling."

"Did he work for you?"

"Oh, no," the woman replied. "He worked over at Huntington House. He was very proud of his job over there, how he had to wear nice pants and a nice cream-colored shirt every day."

Aggie was taking all of this information down in her investigator's notebook. Joe took a moment to glance over at the dead young man again. So he worked at Huntington House.

Not so long ago, Joe had been up to that sprawling estate. He'd been investigating the death of the young woman who'd been found on the lawn. Her name was Audra McKenzie. She was a pretty girl. Just twenty-two. She'd been stabbed repeatedly in the chest and neck. She'd bled out, too, like this Jamison Wilkes, though most of Audra's blood was gone by the time they'd gotten to her, seeped into the earth. She'd been lying in the grass for hours in a torrential rain.

And now a second employee of Huntington House had been murdered.

Two dead employees. Not to mention the mysterious death a little over a year ago of Mrs. Dominique Huntington. A tragic accident on her boat. No foul play involved according to the verdict of the investigating team. Joe had only recently joined the force at that point; he'd played no role in that investigation. But the case had always struck him as odd. Mrs. Huntington takes the yacht out on her own—without its usual captain—and runs into a storm. She drowns. Joe had started thinking about the death of Dominique Huntington again when Audra McKenzie was found dead on the estate, and now he thought about it again.

Could there be a connection between these three deaths?

Joe took a few steps closer to the dead man encased in that glaze of dried blood. A retaliation killing? Revenge for something? Whoever slit this kid's throat was known to him. The door was locked from the outside. And Jamison's key was still on his ring. So whoever killed him had a key to his apartment. And only a friend would have a key.

It appeared Joe would need to drive out to Huntington House again.

Joe noticed something on the floor beside the bed. He stooped down, looking at it closely.

It was the tiny charred remnant of a marijuana cigarette, if he wasn't mistaken.

And he wasn't likely to be mistaken. Joe knew very well what a joint looked like. He'd smoked more than a few in his day. When he was a teenager, growing up outside Greensboro, North Carolina, he had been a bit of a rebel, driving around a beat-up old Camaro with a Confederate flag on its license plate, smoking pot and swilling Jack Daniel's. But he'd never been a bad kid, really. Drove too fast, partied too much, but never broke any real laws. He knew he wanted to be a cop since the age of ten, when he got hooked watching *America's Most Wanted* on television. More than anything else, even more than smoking weed with Maribeth Sinclair in the back of his Camaro, Joe had wanted to catch killers.

No doubt that was because no one had ever caught the killer who'd ended Joe's mother's life that terrible day in August when Joe was eight.

But Joe didn't like to think about that much. Instead, he concentrated on the dead body in front of him. Solving the murders of other people had to suffice, since neither Joe nor anyone else had ever been able to solve the murder of his mother.

He went over the details of Jamison's death in his mind.

The kid may have been high when he was killed. Or he had smoked the joint before falling asleep, then his friend had slipped inside the apartment and slit his throat.

Or perhaps the friend had been in bed beside him.

The coroner and the forensics team were arriving. "Hey, boys," Joe said, "snap some pictures of this roach on the floor, then see what you can find on it. Also, I'll want to know if the kid was smoking pot shortly before he died."

Aggie drew close to him, speaking softly. "Are you thinking what I'm thinking about Huntington House?"

"I am indeed," Joe told her. "Shall we take a ride out there together?"

"Let's," she said.

They exited the apartment to the sound of snapping cameras.

13

"Mrs. Huntington?"

Liz opened her eyes. Glancing around the room, she saw that it was late. The drapes were still pulled, but enough bright sunlight was making its way into the room that she could tell it was getting close to noon. And now someone was softly rapping at her door.

"Mrs. Huntington?"

It was Mrs. Hoffman. Liz pushed aside the white satin covers of her bed, swung her legs over the side, and placed her bare feet on the floor.

"Just a moment," she called. "I overslept."

"I'm sorry to bother you," the housekeeper replied through the door. "I just wondered if you wanted some breakfast sent up to your room."

"No, that's all right," Liz told her, getting up, finding herself a little dizzy and steadying herself against one of the posters of the bed. "I'll come down."

"Very well," said Mrs. Hoffman.

Liz tried to wake up. She had slept so soundly. She felt as if she had gone far, far away during the night . . .

She had been back home in her dreams, in her mother's house, and her father was standing outside on the sidewalk, refusing to come in, despite Liz pleading with him to do so. Then her dream had shifted, becoming vague and unclear, except that it was David standing there, beckoning to her, but she couldn't reach him . . .

She hopped into the shower in the bathroom adjoining her bedroom, hoping the hot water would bring her fully awake. For such a deep long sleep, Liz didn't feel rested. She felt as if she must have tossed and turned all night. She always felt that way when she had dreams about her father. As the water cascaded over her face, she wondered where her father was now. He had sent Mom child-support payments for about a year, then vanished, presumably finding another life for himself, possibly with other daughters—better behaved daughters, more obliging, more obedient, who didn't make him want to run away.

Or maybe, Liz thought as she toweled herself dry, *Daddy's dead.*

But she didn't think so. She imagined him still out there, walking his beautiful, obedient daughter down the aisle in a magnificent church wedding. He would lift her veil and tell her how much he loved her and how proud of her he was.

Liz got dressed, combed her hair, and ran a lipstick lightly over her lips. It was time she went downstairs and faced this life she had found for herself.

Mrs. Hoffman was waiting in the dining room. She smiled at Liz's entrance, though her cheeks and eyes barely moved as usual.

"I trust you slept well then," the housekeeper said.

"Yes, thank you," Liz replied, taking her seat.

"Rita," Mrs. Hoffman called to a maid. "Will you bring Mrs. Huntington her breakfast?"

Liz watched as the young woman carried a tray into the room. Just as she had seemed that day at the pool, Rita was pretty—very pretty, in fact. Dark hair and dark eyes.

Just like Dominique.

"Here you go," Rita said, placing the plate of what looked like scrambled eggs, rice, and tomatoes in front of Liz. "Variola said she made it special for you. Ham and egg jambalaya. A Cajun dish."

"Smells delicious," Liz said. "Thank Variola for me. She needn't have gone to any trouble. I could just have had some toast."

"But you haven't joined us for breakfast since you've been here," Rita replied. "Variola has been waiting to make you something special, and we've all been waiting to get to know you."

Liz looked over at the young woman's face. The other day she had seemed distant, but now her eyes were kind. She offered Liz a sincere smile. Liz was touched.

"Thank you," she said. "I'm very grateful to everyone here for all they've done since I arrived, and everything you all did to prepare for my arrival. I'm sorry if I've been staying mostly in my room. It's just—"

"I understand, ma'am," Rita said. "It's a big house. It's a lot to get used to. If there's anything I can do to help you get adjusted, please let me know."

Liz smiled. "You're very kind," she said.

"Isn't she, though?" Mrs. Hoffman asked, moving over to stand beside Liz. A look from those frozen eyes sent Rita scurrying back into the kitchen. The housekeeper dropped her gaze down to Liz. "I'd watch out for that one," she said once Rita was gone.

Liz had begun eating her jambalaya. It tasted as good as it smelled. "But she seemed so sweet . . . so sincere . . ."

"It's just that she can get overly familiar," Mrs. Hoffman said. "I know Mrs. Huntington was always just a little wary of her. Excuse me. I meant the *first* Mrs. Huntington."

"Well, I'll keep your words in mind," Liz said. "But I prefer to make my own judgments of people."

"Of course. And I'm sure you'll find everyone here to be most accommodating of you. In time, I'm sure they will all learn to love you as they loved her."

"You mean Dominique?"

"Yes," Mrs. Hoffman replied, still standing over Liz, watching her like a hawk as she ate. "How devastated the entire staff was when she died. But their grief was nothing to match the master's . . ."

"I'm sure it was a shock for all of you."

"A terrible day. A beautiful, sunny morning, much like this one. When suddenly there came the chimes of the doorbell . . . and there stood an officer from the Coast Guard, come to give us the terrible news that Mrs. Huntington had drowned."

"A tragedy," Liz said quietly, wishing the old hag would move away from her.

"Now," Mrs. Hoffman said, changing the subject, "I need to know any wishes you have about the household. Do you usually sleep late? If so, I will adjust the time that Variola prepares breakfast . . ."

"No, I usually—"

"And then I need to know any likes and dislikes you have." She moved away from the table, toward the doorway, before turning around to face Liz again. "We wouldn't want to prepare you dishes that you have no taste for. The vegetarian jambalaya, for instance, was Mrs. Huntington's favorite. But for all we know, you might have very different tastes."

Her cold, unmoving eyes locked onto Liz's.

Suddenly Liz lost her taste for the jambalaya. She placed her fork down onto her plate.

"Actually, I'm usually awake at the crack of dawn," Liz said, "and I like most anything. I'm not very picky—"

Her words were suddenly cut off by the deep chime of the doorbell. Liz saw the look that entered Mrs. Hoffman's eyes. Her facial muscles didn't move, of course, but the sudden shine to her eyes seemed to indicate that, for her, the chime of the doorbell would always summon memories of the terrible day Dominique died.

"Excuse me," Mrs. Hoffman said, and strode out of the dining room to answer the door.

Liz pushed the jambalaya away from her. Why did the fact that it was Dominique's favorite make her lose her taste for it? She didn't know, nor did she care to ponder the reason. She just poured herself a cup of coffee from the silver pot set on the table and drank it black. It tasted so good going down.

From the foyer she could hear Mrs. Hoffman talking with someone. She couldn't make out their words. But then, all at once, the housekeeper was back in the doorway.

"I'm sorry, Mrs. Huntington, but you should probably come in and be a part of this conversation."

"Who are you talking with?" Liz asked.

"The police."

"Oh my God," Liz said, rising quickly from her chair. "Has something happened to David?"

"No, not Mr. Huntington. Please come with me, won't you?"

Liz followed Mrs. Hoffman out into the parlor, where two police officers, a man and a woman, were standing. The man was tall, red-haired, and scruffily handsome; the woman was almost as tall, with piercing blue eyes that locked onto Liz as soon as she approached them from across the room.

"This is Mrs. Huntington," Mrs. Hoffman said, introducing Liz to the officers.

"I'm Sergeant Foley," the male officer said, "and this is Sergeant McFarland." He indicated the female officer, who nodded in Liz's direction.

"Congratulations on your recent marriage," Sergeant McFarland said, though she didn't smile as she spoke. "Welcome to Palm Beach."

"Thank you," Liz replied. "What can I do for you officers?"

"We want to ask you a few questions about an employee of yours," Sergeant Foley told her.

"Oh, I'm afraid I don't know much about any of them yet. Mrs. Hoffman would know more—"

"His name was Jamison Wilkes," Sergeant McFarland interrupted her.

Liz didn't miss the use the use of the past tense. *His name* was *Jamison Wilkes*. Liz couldn't speak.

"Mrs. Hoffman just informed us that Mr. Wilkes had recently been fired from your employ," Sergeant Foley went on.

"And at your directive," his partner added.

"*My* directive?" Liz looked over at Mrs. Hoffman in surprise. The housekeeper's face remained immobile. She just looked at Liz with those feline eyes of hers. "No, I didn't fire him . . . my husband did."

"Mr. Huntington said he was acting on your wishes," Mrs. Hoffman explained. "That's what I told these officers."

"No," Liz protested. "It was David's decision. I just—"

She turned and looked at the police officers.

"What's happened to Jamison?" Liz asked.

"He was murdered," Sergeant McFarland informed her.

"Oh, dear God."

"We wondered if there was anything you could tell us that might help us find the person or persons who did this."

Liz could barely speak. "I don't know anything . . . I spoke to him only once . . ." She felt as if she might faint. "How was he killed?"

"His throat was slit, possibly while he was sleeping. He was found in his bed."

"Oh, dear God," Liz moaned again.

"Could you tell us why he was fired from his job in this house?" Sergeant Foley asked.

"It had nothing to do with anything that's happened," Liz insisted. She suddenly felt her body trembling. She was sure everyone noticed.

"Why don't you let us be the judge of that, Mrs. Huntington?" Sergeant McFarland suggested.

Liz glanced over at Mrs. Hoffman. She stood there so implacably, so undisturbed by it all. She was just staring over at Liz.

"Mrs. Huntington," Sergeant Foley said, his voice becoming compassionate, "I know this must be a shock to you, and so soon after you arrived here. But we need you to answer our question. Why was Mr. Wilkes fired from his job in this house?"

In her mind, Liz saw the young man once more. He was standing there in front of her in his cream-colored uniform, in her room—in Dominique's room—looking at her with such plaintive eyes, warning her about this house.

I need to warn you! She won't tell you, but I gotta!

She was a pretty girl, like you, Mrs. Huntington. And she killed her!

"But Dominique is dead," Liz had said.

Yes, she is. But she's still here. And she'll kill you, too, Mrs. Huntington, just like she killed that poor girl!

"Mrs. Huntington?"

Liz looked up from her reverie. It was Sergeant Mc-Farland.

How could she tell them that story? She couldn't! She remembered David's distress. She knew how much Jamison's death would upset him . . .

"My husband is the one who fired him," Liz said again. "It was his decision. I wasn't there. You'll need to speak to David about this."

"We plan to, but we understand from Mrs. Hoffman that he's away," said Sergeant McFarland.

"Yes," Liz replied. "On business."

"So, until we get in touch with him," the sergeant went on, "we were hoping you might tell us whatever you know. Why would your husband tell Mrs. Hoffman that he was firing Mr. Wilkes on your directive?"

"I have no idea," Liz whispered.

"Had he done something offensive?"

Liz looked over at Mrs. Hoffman again. What did the housekeeper know? How much did David tell her?

"He came into my room . . ." Liz began, her voice failing her.

"Into your room?" McFarland asked.

Liz nodded. "He said . . . well, he told me about a girl who had been killed here on the estate . . ."

As she spoke the words, the enormity of the situation became obvious to Liz. Another murder! There had to be a connection! She was suddenly terrified, both for herself and for David.

"I assume he meant Audra McKenzie?" Foley asked.

"Yes," Liz replied, her voice shaking. "I believe that was her name. That happened before I came here, however." She added that last remark instinctively, almost as if she felt she needed to protect herself in some way.

"Interesting," McFarland said, looking over at her partner. "He speaks of Audra's death and a few hours later he's murdered."

"It happened that same night?" Liz asked.

"That's what forensics is telling us," Sergeant Foley replied.

His partner had another question for Liz. "Did Jamison say anything else to you?" Sergeant McFarland wanted to know.

Once again the dead young man's words echoed in

Liz's mind. Should she tell them? Should she tell them that he'd insisted Audra had died not on the grounds but in her room—and that she had been slain by the undead hand of Dominique?

Liz felt the gaze of Mrs. Hoffman upon her. When she glanced over, sure enough, the housekeeper's cold cat eyes were burning into her, her face a frozen plastic mask, devoid of all emotion.

"No," Liz managed to say. "All he said was that Audra had been killed here."

"And for that he was fired?" Foley asked.

Liz gathered her wits together. "Yes. My husband felt it was impertinent to tell me something like that on his own." She took a deep breath. "It rather upset me, you see, on my first night here."

"That's understandable," Sergeant Foley said. He seemed satisfied with her response. He looked over at Sergeant McFarland, who nodded.

"Could there be a connection?" Liz asked. She was terrified; she almost didn't want to know the answer. "Between what happened to Audra and what happened to Jamison?"

"That's what we'd like to know," Foley said. "Wasn't he the same boy who was with you, Mrs. Hoffman, when we came that day after you called and notified us of the girl's death?"

"Yes, he was," the housekeeper acknowledged.

"But it was you who found the body in the grass, was it not?"

Mrs. Hoffman nodded. "Yes, it was I who found the poor girl's body. I asked Jamison to stay with me until you arrived. I was rather upset, as you can imagine."

"Of course," Foley replied.

"I think the episode deeply disturbed Jamison." Mrs. Hoffman's face betrayed no worry or concern. "He was very devout, you see, a very religious young man." Her lips tightened. "It was difficult for him to come to face-to-face with the work of the devil."

"The devil?" Sergeant McFarland asked.

"Surely whoever could kill like that was influenced by the devil."

Foley was writing this all down. "Did Mr. Wilkes have any connections to Audra's friends?" he asked. "Anyone who might have wanted to kill him, for whatever reason? Could they have blamed him in some way for Audra's death?"

"I wouldn't know," Mrs. Hoffman said, almost dismissively. "I have very little knowledge of the private lives of the employees here, or what they do or whom they see in their off hours."

"Well, we'll be checking it all out," Sergeant McFarland said. "Before we go, is there anything else you can tell us about Jamison?"

"Until the episode the other night, he had a spotless record working for us," Mrs. Hoffman declared.

"I wish I could tell you more," Liz said. "This is all just so horrible. I feel so badly for him . . ." She found herself crying all of a sudden, which embarrassed her. "He may have been inappropriate, but he was just trying to . . . in his own way . . . protect me . . ."

"Protect you from what?" asked Sergeant Foley.

Liz wiped her eyes. "From not knowing, I guess. He felt it wasn't fair that no one told me about what happened here before I arrived. And he was right. David should have told me."

"Mr. Huntington simply didn't want to upset you," Mrs. Hoffman said.

Liz nodded. "I know. But Jamison's statement to me wasn't malicious." She looked over at the police officers. "I didn't want you to have that impression."

Sergeant Foley smiled at her. "Thank you, Mrs. Huntington."

"Thank you both," his partner added. "That's all we need for now. But we may be back in touch."

"Of course," Liz said. "You'll be calling David?"

"Yes," Foley assured her. "Mrs. Hoffman gave us his card."

Liz escorted them to the door. Sergeant McFarland strode out to their waiting cruiser, but Sergeant Foley looked back at her and gave her a small smile.

"I regret that your arrival here should be so unpleasant," he told her.

Liz just smiled sadly. What a kind man Sergeant Foley seemed. His strawberry blond hair was cut short, and he sported some day-old ginger scruff on his cheeks and chin, not heavy enough to disguise a pretty deep dimple in his chin. His eyes were pale blue and very reassuring. Liz was glad he was on the case.

She closed the door and looked back at Mrs. Hoffman.

"You're new in your role as mistress of this house," the housekeeper said. "I understand that. But I believe Mr. Huntington would want me to point something out."

"What's that?"

"Never reveal more than what is necessary about what goes on here, not even the slightest, most innocuous detail. And never, *ever* show weakness to outsiders."

"Was I being weak when I cried? Is that what you mean?"

"Mrs. Huntington always smiled, no matter what the situation. She always faced outsiders with a smile and a steeled back."

"I see," said Liz.

"Just a helpful comment," Mrs. Hoffman said. "If I were you, I'd put all this unpleasantness aside and move on. It has nothing to do with our lives in this house."

Liz said nothing. She just watched as the housekeeper hustled off, to do whatever it was she did to run this glittering mansion.

A glittering, bloated, oversized monstrosity that Liz suddenly thought she could never learn to call home.

14

Standing off in the shadows behind the grand curving staircase was Rita. She had heard the entire conversation with the two police officers.

Jamison—dead!

Murdered!

The housemaid stepped out of the shadows and resumed her task of dusting the tables. But her mind was reeling.

She couldn't shake the image of that sweet boy, his throat slit. The blood must have been everywhere.

Rita felt as if she might get sick.

She slipped out of the parlor and into the hall bathroom, the one reserved for guests. Mrs. Hoffman would have a fit if she ever caught Rita in here for anything other than cleaning. But Rita needed to steady herself, and if her breakfast of coffee and toasted blueberry muffin was going to make a reappearance, she wanted to be near a toilet.

Jamison! Dead!

She looked into her eyes in the mirror. He must have been killed soon after they had spoken to each other at

Mickey's Bar. Jamison had told Rita some really disturbing things as they sat there drinking their beer.

He had admitted to tampering with evidence, helping Mrs. Hoffman move Audra's corpse from Mrs. Huntington's room to the grass outside. He had been planning to go to the police and reveal all he knew.

But someone had stopped him from ever squealing.

The door to the bathroom suddenly rattled. Someone tried to turn the knob, but found it locked. Rita tensed.

A rapping. "Who's in there?" a voice called through the door.

Mrs. Hoffman's voice.

Rita quickly began wiping the sink with her dust rag with one hand while unlocking the door with her other. "I'm just doing some cleaning," she replied, opening the door behind her.

Mrs. Hoffman stood there, filling the door frame with her imposing presence, her frozen face as white as the ceramic of the bathroom. Only the eyes showed any life. They were blazing.

"Why was this door locked?" the head housekeeper asked icily.

"*Was* it locked? Oh, I must have accidentally hit the lock when I came in here."

"I asked you to dust the parlor. What were you doing in here?"

"I told you. I was cleaning. I noticed there was some residue in the sink. Perhaps Mrs. Huntington used this bathroom . . ."

"There was no residue in this sink," Mrs. Hoffman seethed. "I've told you, Rita, time and time again, that the servants may use the bathrooms at the back of the house, off the kitchen. Not any of those in the front of the house. You must know your place in this house!"

"Really, Mrs. Hoffman, I wasn't using—"

"Just get out and get back to work," the older woman said, and Rita quickly complied.

She hustled back into the parlor. The nausea had passed. Now it was anger that surged up from Rita's gut.

That wicked old witch, Rita thought. *If anyone had reason to kill Jamison, it was her.*

After all, Jamison knew the secret she was keeping from police—that, under her direction, Audra's body had been moved.

As Rita halfheartedly dusted off the mantel, her mind was far, far away from her task.

Not only did she suspect Mrs. Hoffman of killing Jamison, but she suddenly believed the old harridan had killed Audra as well.

Rita had never bought into Jamison's talk of ghosts and devils. It had been Mrs. Hoffman who had stabbed Audra to death. It had to have been! No ex-boyfriend of Audra's, who cops thought the most likely suspect, would have been inside the house. No, it must have been Mrs. Hoffman who'd wielded the knife, ending the poor girl's life, and then she had roped Jamison into helping her move the evidence of her crime. When Jamison had been fired, she'd had no choice but to kill him as well.

Rita's heart suddenly began to pound in her chest. A fear overtook her. Did Mrs. Hoffman know that Jamison had spilled the beans to her before he died? Did she know that Rita knew the truth—that the truth hadn't died with Jamison?

It wasn't likely. The police officer said it looked as if

Jamison had been killed in his sleep. That was more likely. Mrs. Hoffman wouldn't have wanted to tangle with him awake. Jamison wasn't a big guy, but he was bigger and stronger than old Mrs. Hoffman. How much easier to just slit his throat while he slept.

So there had been no chance for Jamison to reveal that he'd told Rita the truth about the night of Audra's death. Mrs. Hoffman had no idea that her secret still lived on.

"A penny for your thoughts, Rita, my dear."

The voice startled her, and she spun around. Variola stood there across the parlor, smiling at her and gazing at her with those mysterious black eyes.

Could Variola read minds?

"Oh, I doubt they're worth even that much," Rita said, trying to smile.

"With you, your thoughts are always rich," the house chef observed. "Whenever I see you so far away in thought, I think to myself, 'There is a master schemer at work.' "

Rita shook her head, trying to mask her thoughts, just in case Variola could see inside her head. It was a crazy idea, but still, Rita worried about it. "I was just thinking about my mother and what to buy her for her birthday."

"Ah, but Variola thinks you were contemplating someone much farther away than that." She smiled at Rita again. "Someone who right now, I believe, is in Amsterdam."

Rita didn't know David's exact itinerary, but she knew Amsterdam was one of the frequent stops on his business trips. She smiled back at Variola. Better that the chef believe she was thinking about David than thinking about Mrs. Hoffman being guilty of murder. Rita didn't trust Variola; the chef had her own agenda, and she'd use information for her own purposes.

"You can believe whatever you want," she said.

Variola laughed—that magical, tinkly, musical sound—and headed out into the kitchen. Rita let out a breath in relief.

Perhaps, on second thought, she *could* trust Variola. After all, Variola had spotted Rita and David together and she'd never said a word. If Variola *had* told Mrs. Hoffman about the affair with David, the old witch would have definitely fired her—she was very insistent that the staff not fraternize with the Huntingtons. She didn't even want them sharing the same bathrooms! So Rita was pretty sure that Variola had kept her secret about David.

Maybe she should take her up on her offer for some potion or some island herb to magically win back David's love. But Rita hadn't yet given up on accomplishing that task all on her own.

It was thinking about David that made everything suddenly so clear to her.

I know why Mrs. Hoffman killed Audra, she realized.

Rita's previous conversation with Variola came back to her. She'd implied that David had had an affair with Audra . . . Rita had dismissed the idea. But what if it was true?

What if, when she'd discovered Audra's misbehavior, Mrs. Hoffman had killed her? Maybe it was an impulsive move—a rash act of anger on the housekeeper's part. How she hated when any staff did not know their place in this house! Audra had dared to impose herself on Mr. Huntington and Mrs. Hoffman had had enough!

But there had to be more to it than that.

That was when Rita remembered the obsessive devotion Mrs. Hoffman carried for her late mistress, even now.

Mrs. Hoffman had worshiped Dominique. Some of the staff even whispered it was sort of an unrequited lesbian crush that the older woman had on the younger. Mrs. Hoffman would follow Dominique around slavishly, attendant on her every need, watching her with eyes filled with adoration as she dropped her robe and dove naked into the swimming pool. After Dominique's death that day on the boat, Mrs. Hoffman had been devastated. She had insisted that everything be kept as her late mistress had left it, and that Dominique's enormous portrait remain hanging in the stairwell, as if she were still watching over the house. And how angry she had been when Mr. Huntington had dug up the gardenia bushes, not wanting to be reminded of his late wife.

So Mrs. Hoffman had killed Audra because she had dared defile the sacred memory of Dominique by sleeping with Dominique's husband.

If that was so, then what fate did Mrs. Hoffman have in mind for the new Mrs. Huntington, who was now doing the same thing?

As Rita began setting the setting the dining table with plates and silverware for lunch, she was hearing Jamison's words in her head.

If anything had happened to Mrs. Huntington, and I hadn't said anything, then I'd be partly to blame.

Jamison had been worried Audra's fate might befall little Liz.

We all have to watch out for each other. That's Christ's teaching, right there.

Rita was torn. If Liz was found stabbed to death, she'd have a pretty good idea who did it. But she'd also have David, free and clear.

Maybe she was overreacting. Maybe Jamison was killed by a burglar, or someone totally unconnected to Huntington House. Maybe he was unstable, and all that talk about moving Audra's body had just been in his mind. The police had never questioned anything about Mrs. Hoffman's story, after all. They had seemed to be convinced the killer was an ex-boyfriend of Audra's.

For now, Rita would say nothing. But she would keep her eyes open. Wide open. Especially when Mrs. Hoffman came lurking around.

15

"Darling!" David's voice crackled over the phone. "Sorry I haven't called in a while. Have you gotten my emails?"

"Just one," Liz said, her heart pounding in her chest as she heard David's voice.

It had been nearly two days since the police had been there, giving her the news of Jamison's death. How desperately Liz had tried to reach David after that. She couldn't call him, because he'd said his international mobile phone was out of service; he'd have to call her. But he had not done so. Except for one short email, telling her that he'd call soon, there had been no communication from David. Liz had been so worried that something had happened to him. "Oh, David," she gushed. "I'm so glad to finally speak with you. Did you hear from the police?"

"Yes, and I told them that we knew nothing about that kid's death. Darling, don't freak about this, okay?"

"But now there have been two murders here . . ."

"No! Not there! Jamison died at his own apartment.

His death had nothing to do with Huntington House. There is no connection, darling. None! The police can see absolutely nothing that links the two cases. You must understand that it's just a horrible coincidence and not let it freak you out."

"That's what I keep trying to tell myself, David, but—"

"It's the truth, Liz." He seemed impatient with her. "Darling, I really need you to be strong about this. I'm in a bit of a crisis over here. Two of our Dutch subsidiaries are near a melting point. And I'm dealing with a hostile takeover at our German company, and I just really need you to be strong and not get hysterical."

"I'm not hysterical," she said plainly.

"If the police come around again, just tell them that you've told them all you know, and ask them to leave you alone."

"But I didn't tell them all I knew."

"Of course you did!"

"No, David, I didn't tell them that the reason Jamison was fired was because he told me that Audra had been killed in my room."

David sighed. "Well, I told them."

"You did?"

"Well, I told them he was fired because he was telling you lies on your first day at Huntington House to frighten you. Things about Audra. I told the police officer who called me that the kid was impertinent and out of line. He agreed, and that was that."

Liz hesitated. "David, are you certain there's no connection to—"

"There is no connection between Jamison's death and Audra's," he interrupted. "None!"

"That wasn't what I was going to ask," Liz said, in a very small voice.

"Then what?"

She hesitated again, then finally asked David what was burning through her mind. "Is there no connection between both of these deaths . . . and Dominique's?"

There was utter silence on the other end of the phone.

"David?" Liz asked.

"What can you possibly be thinking?" her husband finally responded.

"I never told you everything Jamison said that night." She summoned the courage to say what she had been hiding. "He said that . . . he said that Dominique killed Audra."

"Dominique! She's *dead*, Liz!"

"I think Jamison meant . . . her ghost . . ."

"This is crazy talk," David snarled, "and I don't have time for crazy talk."

"I know it is. But he said it, David. I was too . . . horrified . . . nervous . . . dismissive of it to tell you before."

"So you think Dominique's ghost walks Huntington House, killing Audra and then floating over to Jamison's apartment to kill him too?"

"No . . . but I . . ."

"But what?" David snapped.

"Forget I ever brought it up," Liz said.

"Good idea." David was angry with her. "I have got to go, Liz. Please stop all this nonsense and I will be home as soon as I can."

"Just a few more days, right, David?"

"It might be a few days longer now. This hostile take-over isn't going to be easy to manage."

"But David . . ."

"Liz, don't you realize how important this is? How this is my big chance to prove to my father I know how to run the business?"

"Yes, I'm sorry. I know your work is important." She could feel the sarcasm creeping into her voice. Even if she had wanted to hold it back, she couldn't. "Much more important than my little problems here at the house. Like dealing with murder investigations."

"Liz, please . . ."

"It's *fine*, David."

They hung up quickly after that, barely saying good-bye.

David might be angry, but now Liz was angry, too. How dare he be so cavalier about all this? She took a deep breath, strode over to the window, and looked out.

A storm was fast approaching, rolling up the coast. The clouds were deep brown, tinged with gold. The air was thick with moisture.

Liz smelled gardenias. The fragrance was unmistakable.

Dominique's fragrance.

But the gardenia plants had all been ripped out.

Liz headed out of her room. She would go mad if she stayed in there any longer. She gripped the bannister and started down the stairs.

Dominique's portrait stared at her from the landing.

It was enormous. Monstrous. Those big black eyes. That lustrous hair. Those big heaving breasts under that flowing white dress.

It was intolerable.

And it was coming down.

Liz found Mrs. Hoffman in the study, seated at a desk, going over a ledger.

"Might I have a word with you?" Liz asked.

The housekeeper looked up at her. "Of course."

"In the garage are some of the framed photographs I brought with me, stacked against the far wall."

Mrs. Hoffman gave her that rigid expression that passed for a smile. "Yes, I've seen them."

"I'd like them brought into the house. I took them, and I'd like them hung in the house."

"There's very little photography on the walls, as you've no doubt noticed," Mrs. Hoffman said. "The Huntingtons have always preferred original paintings."

"Well, there will be photography now," Liz told her. "This is my house now. I'd like the photos brought in from the garage and I will direct where they will be hung."

Mrs. Hoffman regarded her uneasily. "Very well. I'll have our caretaker, Thad, bring them in at once."

"The largest of them—the shot of the volcano in Iceland—I'd like hung in the landing of the staircase."

Mrs. Hoffman's hard plastic face looked as if it might crack. "But that's where the portrait of Mrs. Huntington hangs."

Liz drew in close to her. She could feel the anger trembling along every fiber of her body like an electrical current. "I'm Mrs. Huntington now," she said, very carefully, articulating each word.

"Of course you are." Mrs. Hoffman closed the ledger and stood. "I might point out, however, that the portrait of the first Mrs. Huntington is nearly six feet tall and more than four feet wide. Replacing it with the photograph in question, which is, what, maybe three by two—?"

"Yes, that's the size of it."

"Well, the landing is an awfully large space, and the photograph—which is quite lovely, I'm sure—will look rather small and out of place there."

"That's where I want it." Liz surprised herself with the calmness of her voice.

"Very well." Mrs. Hoffman regarded her impassively. "And where shall I have the portrait of Mrs. Huntington hung?"

"It's going into the garage."

Mrs. Hoffman visibly tensed.

"It's time we had an understanding, Mrs. Hoffman," Liz said. "I mean no disrespect to David's first wife. But she's passed away. She's not here anymore. I am. And I simply don't find it appropriate that her portrait remains hanging in this house."

"I see," said Mrs. Hoffman. "I assume you've discussed this all with Mr. Huntington."

"He told me I was in charge of the house."

The two women held eye contact for several seconds.

"Very well, then, Mrs. Huntington," the housekeeper said at last. "I'll get Thad to work on this request of yours immediately."

"Thank you," Liz said.

She watched as Mrs. Hoffman walked out of the room. She felt suddenly as if she might collapse, but she also felt good. Powerful.

Nicki would have been proud of her.

She stood there in the study, listening to the first rumble of thunder in the distance.

And then she smelled it again.

Gardenias.

Overwhelming. Overpowering the room.

16

"You've never spoken so much about your mother before," Aggie said as she stood from the table where she'd been sitting with Joe to walk across the room and close the window. Rain was beginning to patter against the glass. Thunder rumbled on the horizon.

Joe shrugged. "Yeah, normally I don't like to remember. I guess these recent killings have brought all that back up for me again."

Aggie returned to her seat. They were going through photographs on Joe's laptop of various boyfriends and acquaintances of Audra McKenzie, trying to see if any of them might have some connection to Jamison Wilkes. But conversation had drifted to Joe's mother.

"It must be so hard to live with that," Aggie said, giving Joe a compassionate smile. "I don't know how I'd do it."

"Thanks, Agg." Aggie was a good friend and partner. People sometimes asked him why he and Aggie weren't an item. Quick, easy answer: partners should never be romantically involved. Second quick, even easier answer: Aggie was already happily married, and she and her husband had two kids. But even if neither of the above were true, Joe thought they still wouldn't have been involved. And it had nothing to do with Aggie.

It had everything to do with him.

Joe had had plenty of girlfriends in high school, back when he would race his car around town and smoke several joints a day. Even when he was at the Police Academy and started acting more responsibly, he'd dated a couple of girls, and at least one of them had thought they were getting serious. Joe had had to break it to her that it wasn't so. He just couldn't get serious with anyone. Sometimes Joe thought he had a chip missing—the chip that controlled commitment, or even the desire for commitment. He didn't want it.

And, as he'd just told Aggie, he was pretty sure that all went back to his mother.

"You were only eight years old," his partner said, looking at him, her eyes shining. "What a thing for a little boy to see."

"Thing is," he told her, "it was like I had a sixth sense. Dad told me to go in and wake Mom. It was strange that she wasn't up before us. She always was. And so even as I walked over to her tent and pulled down the zipper, I knew she was going to be dead. Somehow, I just knew it. And she was—covered in—"

Aggie reached over and placed her hand over his. "It's okay. You've told me what you found. No need to relive it again, Joe."

But it was too late. In his mind, he saw once more the inside of his mother's tent.

They had been out camping. They went every summer, the three of them, Mom, Dad, Joe. Mom cooked the fish her two guys caught in a nearby brook over an open fire. How Joe had loved to go camping with his parents.

But when he'd pulled down the zipper of Mom's tent, all he'd seen was bright red blood.

He'd first thought a bear got her. Mom was always talking about bears, worrying the animals would get them. But a bear would have simply torn her tent apart. No bear could unzip the tent, slip inside, then step back out and zip it closed again.

Only one kind of monster could do that.

"But I think the worst part," Joe said, "was that the first person the police suspected was my father. Being a cop now, I know that's pretty standard. But back then, I was so angry at them for thinking Dad could have done such a thing."

DNA evidence had ruled Dad out as a suspect. And his utter despair and near-catatonic grief was the punctuation point on that theory if anyone still needed convincing. When Dad died a couple years later of lung cancer—he'd never smoked a cigarette in his life—Joe secretly believed what had really killed him was a broken heart.

After that, Joe was raised by his grandparents in Greensboro. No wonder Joe had acted out after his parents' death, smoked too much pot. No wonder he had become hooked on cop shows on television, fascinated by tales of cold cases finally solved so many years later.

Because his mother's case was as cold as it got. No suspects were ever identified.

Every once in a while, Joe dug out his mother's file, poring over it for clues the original detectives might have missed. The cops up in North Carolina had been very good to send it to him, welcoming his help. But there was nothing. The DNA that was found linked to no one in any database. It was too inconclusive to give them much to work with, except to rule out who the killer was not. Mom and Dad had no enemies. They weren't controversial people. Dad was a construction worker. Mom volunteered at the United Church of Christ. The murder, the cops had concluded, had been utterly, horribly random.

"Well," Joe said, "I guess it's back to looking at photos."

But Aggie wasn't quite ready to let the subject drop. "I worry about you sometimes, Joe. I wish you would spend more time with Terry and me and the kids. Or join a group or something. Sign up for Match.com. Go to church. Anything. Find an activity other than police work."

"Oh, I'm fine, Agg," he assured her. "I'm on season three of *Breaking Bad* now. Walter White, Jesse Pinkman, and a bowl of popcorn are plenty sufficient for me after a hard day of tracking down killers." He laughed.

"Joe Foley, you're not even thirty-five yet. You're handsome and smart. None of us are meant to be alone."

"How do you know that? Maybe some of us are."

"I do not believe that. I refuse to believe that."

He shrugged. "It's a free country. You can believe what you want." He clicked to the next photo. "Hey, is this the girl?"

Aggie looked down at the photo staring up at her

from Joe's laptop. Dark eyes, dark hair. Very pretty. "Yep, that's her. Rita Cansino."

"The one the bartender at Mickey's remembered seeing with Jamison the night he died?"

Aggie nodded. "Yes. He overheard them talking about Huntington House. And yes, Rita was working there when Audra was killed. We interviewed her."

Joe scribbled her name down on a pad. "Well, looks like we'll be interviewing her again."

17

Liz stood at the bottom of the stairs supervising the removal of Dominique's portrait from the landing. Thad, the estate's caretaker, a big, blond, lumbering man who stood over six feet tall, was setting the aluminum ladder against the wall. He seemed uncomfortable with the task. Perhaps, Liz wondered, he'd been one of the men in the house who'd been "obsessed" with the late Mrs. Huntington.

"Is there a problem?" Liz asked.

"No, ma'am," Thad answered.

He paused before taking the first step up the ladder and pulled on a pair of cloth gloves. Mrs. Hoffman, who stood beside him, watching with those intense eyes of hers, had instructed Thad not to damage the portrait. It was "priceless," she insisted.

Liz stared up at Dominique's dark eyes.

Your time is over, she thought, holding the gaze of the portrait.

Gardenias.

She smelled gardenias.

Outside the storm had settled directly over the house.

The day had turned deep purple. Wind lashed the eastern exposure, rattling windows in their frames. Rain pounded the roof. Violent cracks of thunder were followed by explosive bursts of lightning.

Liz watched as Thad took the first step up the ladder.

Get it down. Get that woman's face out of my life.

Mrs. Hoffman watched, her hands clenched in fists at her sides.

Thad took a second step up the ladder.

The wind found some tiny space at the window and began to howl through the house. For a moment Liz turned to look, worried that the glass might shatter in over all of them.

Thad took a third step. He was now at a point where he could grasp the lower frame of the portrait.

That's it. Grab her. Take her away!

"Be very careful now," Mrs. Hoffman said.

"I hung this portrait of her, didn't I?" Thad asked, his voice thick. "I will take it down just as carefully as I placed it here."

Liz studied the man on the ladder. Strong, broad, his face a canyon of crags. He must have been late forties, or maybe early fifties. His skin was burnt leather. He'd been with the Huntingtons since he was a teenager, he'd told Liz when they met. He was utterly devoted to the family, he said, a fact which David had confirmed.

Liz watched as Thad's hands gripped the frame.

When Mrs. Hoffman had given him the instructions to remove the portrait from the stairway, Thad had seemed horrified. His face had fallen. His mouth twisted. Had he loved Dominique so much he couldn't bear the idea of removing her portrait?

Liz looked up at the dark eyes of the woman in the portrait. Dominque really had been that beautiful, that charismatic. Even after death, she still held men in her power. More than ever, Liz wanted her portrait gone.

"Steady now," Mrs. Hoffman said as Thad took hold of the bottom of the frame, ready to lift it off the wall.

Get it down! Liz thought.

Gardenias suddenly overwhelmed her.

Just as Thad attempted to lift the portrait, the loudest thunderclap yet reverberated through the house. The caretaker jumped, startled, and tottered backward on the ladder. Liz watched the action unfold as if in slow motion. Thad swayed back and forth for what couldn't have been more than a second, but to Liz it seemed like many minutes. There was no way Thad could keep his balance on that ladder. The scream was already out of Liz's mouth as the caretaker fell backward, as if he were a great oak cut down by a lumberjack's ax. Thad hit the bannister of the staircase with his shoulder, then tumbled over and over all the way down the stairs, until his massive body lay sprawled in a heap at Liz's feet.

"Oh my God, are you all right?" Liz shouted, dropping to the fallen man's side.

Thad groaned.

Mrs. Hoffman came hurrying down the stairs.

"I'm all right," Thad said, sitting up, rubbing his shoulder.

"Are you certain?" Liz asked. "Try to walk. Shall we call a doctor? Does your shoulder hurt?"

The caretaker attempted to get up, but collapsed in pain. "My shoulder's fine, but not my ankle," he groaned. "I think I broke it."

Mrs. Hoffman shot Liz an intense glance.

"We never should have tried to take it down," Thad moaned, a big, burly man reduced to quivering on the marble floor. "I knew it wasn't wise. I knew she wouldn't let it happen!"

Liz swung her eyes up the stairs. The portrait of Dominique was slightly askew, but still it hung. Still those black eyes stared down at her.

"I'll have one of the drivers take you over to the ER," Mrs. Hoffman told Thad. "Don't try to walk."

She hurried off. Thad was staring up at Liz.

"Should never have tried to take it down," he said hoarsely again.

"I'm sorry," Liz told him. "We'll take care of everything, any costs, any time off."

Thad just nodded.

Thunder crashed again.

Other servants were gathering around now, asking if Thad was okay. Thad repeated his belief that they should never have tried to take the portrait down, and the others nodded their heads.

"You can't all believe in ghosts," Liz said.

But their eyes told her otherwise.

Liz moved off toward the parlor, where Mrs. Hoffman was talking with one of the drivers and pointing over in Thad's direction.

They're blaming me, she thought.

They're blaming me because I tried to take down their mistress's portrait.

Liz turned and hurried out into the foyer. She had to get out. Maybe she'd take a drive—whether she had a valid driver's license or not. She needed to get out of this house!

But what she saw at the front door both startled and gladdened her. The door was being opened by Rita, and in from the wind and the rain stumbled—

David!

How was that possible? David was in Amsterdam . . .

But it *was* him! The same dark hair, dark eyes, square jaw—his face partially hidden behind the upturned collar of a raincoat. And Rita was greeting him, "Hello, Mr. Huntington."

"David!" Liz cried, running toward the door.

But as he turned to look at her, it became clear that the man at the door was not her husband. He looked a great deal like him, but he was not David.

"This must be Liz," the man was saying. "And bless her heart, she thinks I'm David."

Liz stopped short, confused and embarrassed.

The man approached her, dripping water all over the tiled floor of the foyer. "I'm so sorry to have gotten your hopes up, my dear," he said. "But I'm Roger Huntington. David's brother." He smiled, the same dazzling, dimpled smile that David possessed. "And your brother-in-law."

"Roger," Liz said weakly.

David had told her that he had a brother . . . but he'd said he lived far away. He wasn't involved in the family business. A bohemian sort, David had said, implying they weren't close. There had been plans for Liz to meet his parents as soon as possible, but David had never mentioned anything about meeting his brother.

"Rita, sweetheart, will you take this drenched coat for me?" Roger asked, doffing his sodden outerwear. "I'd like to be able to greet my new sister-in-law appropriately."

"Of course," Rita said, helping Roger out of his raincoat.

When he was free of it, he approached Liz again. "How wonderful to meet you," he gushed, extending his arms. "May I?"

Liz didn't know what to say or do, so she simply nodded.

Roger threw his big arms around her and pressed her into his chest. He smelled musky—sweaty and vaguely sweet. He was harder, more muscled than David.

"David isn't here," Liz managed to say when Roger let her go.

"I'm aware of that. I spoke with my father last night and he told me he'd needed David to go to Europe on business. That damn company of theirs." Roger smiled down at her, and his chocolate brown eyes, so much like David's, seemed kind. "I'm not a big fan of the corporate sort of life that the other men in my family lead. So when I heard you were here all alone in this mausoleum, I thought I ought to come by and say hello."

"Oh, that's nice of you, but I'm fine—"

Roger made a face. "How can you possibly be fine here?" He leaned in closer, dropping his voice to a whisper. "With that old harridan Mrs. Hoffman haunting the place like a ghoul?"

Liz struggled to keep from betraying her own thoughts about the housekeeper.

"Rita," Roger called over his shoulder, "will you have some extremely hot coffee brought in to us in the study? I want to take the chill off and get to know my new sister-in-law. And would you tell Mrs. Hoffman there's no need to fuss over my being here?"

"She's tending to Thad at the moment, arranging to have him driven to the ER," Rita informed him.

"What's happened to Thad?" Roger asked.

Rita looked over at Liz to provide the explanation.

"Oh," Liz said, supremely uncomfortable. "He fell on the stairs. He may have broken his ankle." She felt as if she might cry.

"Well, a big old buck like Thad will rebound just fine," Roger said. "Give him my best."

Rita nodded, then headed out of the foyer.

When they were alone, Roger turned his eyes back to Liz. "I shouldn't be so presumptuous to whisk you away from your duties and call for coffee like I'm the master of the place. Forgive me. Maybe you had plans for the day . . ."

"No, no," Liz said. "It's fine, really."

"Are you sure?" Roger smiled again. "You're okay with having some coffee with me in the study and talking a bit? Getting to know one another?"

She returned the smile. "Of course."

"Because I wouldn't want to impose on your plans. I can come back another time when it's more convenient. After all, you're the mistress of Huntington House. You make the rules."

Liz sighed wearily, trying not to fret over the irony in Roger's words. "Let's go into the study. Did you tell David you were stopping by?"

"He's maddeningly difficult to get ahold of on his business trips."

Liz certainly knew that to be true. They took seats on sofas opposite each other. Liz tried to steady her shaking hands by folding them in her lap. Roger noticed.

"Are you all right, Liz?" he asked.

"Oh, I guess seeing Thad topple down the stairs just upset me," she replied, withholding the unspoken fear that was gnawing away at her: that it was *Dominique* who had pushed him.

But that was absurd. It was the crack of thunder that startled him.

I smelled gardenias, Liz reminded herself.

"I take it he's okay, though?" Roger was asking. "You said maybe his ankle . . ."

"I hope it's just a sprain. You see, he was doing a job I'd asked him to do . . ."

"On the staircase?"

Liz held Roger's gaze. "Yes. I had asked him to take down the portrait that's hanging there."

"Dominique's portrait," Roger said softly.

Liz nodded.

At that moment Rita entered, carrying a tray with a pot of steaming coffee, two mugs, and some cream and sugar. She placed the tray on a table between Liz and Roger. "Will there be anything else?" Rita asked.

"Would you like something to eat, Roger?" Liz inquired.

"No, thank you, just some hot coffee to take off the chill from that storm outside."

Rita left them alone.

They each poured themselves a cup of coffee, both of them taking it black. Roger looked up at Liz over the brim of his mug.

"I would hope Thad's accident won't deter you from getting that damn thing off the wall."

Liz was struck by his words.

"I can't believe my brother left it hanging there

when he brought his new wife home to live here." He set his mug down on the table, shaking his head. "Really. How insensitive."

"I'm sure he would have taken it down if he'd been able to stay."

Roger looked over at her, narrowing his eyes almost as if he were entering a conspiracy with her. "I suspect David would have taken it down soon after Dominique died. But you know who insisted they leave it hanging up there, don't you?"

"I could probably guess."

"If you were to guess Mrs. Hoffman, you'd be right."

Liz wanted to speak freely, wanted to say exactly what she was thinking about this house and its chief housekeeper. Roger seemed so natural, so kind, so trustworthy—but still she had to be careful. She'd just met him, and she couldn't say anything that might get back to Mrs. Hoffman and make things worse for her.

"Well," Liz said, choosing her words, "I understand Dominique and Mrs. Hoffman were very close friends. I'm sure it's been hard for her to accept that she's gone."

"But she's going to have to! I mean, Dominique took the big gulp more than a year ago."

"Roger," Liz said, taken aback by her brother-in-law's callous words.

"I'm sorry if I sound disrespectful of the dead. But Dominique and I . . . weren't always the best of friends."

"Oh?"

He smiled. "Ancient history." Roger reached over and reclaimed his mug for another long sip of hot brew. "I won't bore you with all the details. We've moved past all that. There's a new mistress of Huntington House, and I think I'm going to like her much better than the last."

How much he looked liked David. It was almost uncanny—the way he moved his mouth, the little lift of his eyebrows, the dimples, the voice.

"David implied that you lived far away," Liz said.

"Far away? If two miles down the road is far away, I guess so." Roger laughed. "Our father divided the original family property in two when he and Mom decided to make Manhattan their base. David got the north part of the estate, I got the south."

"I see. He never mentioned that."

"Too busy closing some big corporate deal, I expect. David's always working."

Liz lifted an eyebrow in agreement.

"That was why I was so glad he took that cruise," Roger went on. "He really needed it after Dominique's death. I knew it would do him a world of good. And it did—he came home with you!"

Liz smiled. "I hope I can live up to your expectations of me."

"You already have." He returned her smile, kindly and sincerely. "You have no airs about you. That's a refreshing change in this house."

"So Dominique put on airs?"

"That's an understatement. She considered herself the queen of Palm Beach society."

"That will hardly be me."

"Have you met Dad and Mom?"

Liz shook her head. "Not yet. David's planning on having them visit . . . or maybe we'll go up to New York when he gets back."

"David's a carbon copy of Dad. All work and no play."

Liz smirked. "Well, I've seen David play a bit . . ."

Roger laughed. "Well, I hope you have!"

"He was so much fun on the ship and on our honeymoon. We partied late into the night in Rio—he was so much fun, singing songs and dancing—"

"David? Singing and dancing?"

"Yes!" The memories of her honeymoon lifted Liz's spirits. "We went scuba-diving and rock climbing and he was always surprising me with bottles of champagne . . ."

Roger was grinning. "You're good for him, apparently."

"I hope so." Her high spirits deflated. "But as soon as we got here, he had to rush off to work. I hope . . . I hope he doesn't have to stay away much longer."

"David is always trying to please Dad." Roger put his hands behind his head and leaned back into the cushions of the couch. "Me, I gave up trying to do that a long time ago."

"You didn't follow into the family business."

He shuddered. "Stocks and bonds and money markets and hedge funds . . . oh man, can you imagine anything more boring?"

"So what is it that you do?"

"I'm an artist."

"Wonderful! What kind?"

"I paint. People sometimes, but usually abstract."

"How interesting, and how very different from David."

"Right now I'm experimenting with color. I find the color inside my subjects and bring it out. Like, for instance, you've got a lot of blue."

"Blue? And here I thought my coloring was a rather mousy brown."

"Oh, no, you've got a beautiful, iridescent blue inside you, with traces of violet around the edges." Roger laughed. "Maybe you'll let me paint your portrait. Replace the one that's in the stairway."

"Well, I'll have to talk to David about that."

"I have a gallery in town. I have a show coming up soon—not my work, but of a very exciting new artist from New York. I hope you'll come."

"I'd enjoy that."

Liz liked Roger. After being so upset a few moments ago, she was suddenly feeling happy and light. For the first time since she'd come to this place, she was actually enjoying a conversation with someone. For the first time, she'd met someone she thought she might be able to call a friend.

A light tapping on the open door of the study drew her attention.

It was Mrs. Hoffman, looking at Roger with those beady eyes.

"Excuse me, Mrs. Huntington," she said, moving her gaze over to Liz, "but I just wanted to let you know that Clarence has driven Thad to the ER. Shall I have another of the servants attempt to remove the portrait?"

"No," Liz replied. "Let's just leave it for now."

"Good afternoon, Mrs. Hoffman," Roger said, standing.

"Good afternoon, Mr. Huntington."

"We were just talking, my sister-in-law and I, about something to put up there in the stairwell instead. Don't you think that I ought to paint the new Mrs. Huntington and give her the place of honor she so deserves?"

"Only if you paint her as realistically as you painted the first Mrs. Huntington," the housekeeper replied. "I would think your current, more abstract style wouldn't suit the house, or Mrs. Huntington, for that matter."

Liz looked over at Roger. "You painted . . . the portrait that hangs there now?"

He smiled rather sheepishly. "Yes, I plead guilty."

"Mrs. Huntington sat for him for several weeks," Mrs. Hoffman told her, seeming to bask in the memory. "I think he captured her likeness brilliantly."

"She . . . sat for you?" Liz asked.

"That's when Dominique still liked me," Roger replied.

"Why didn't you mention that you had painted it earlier?" Liz asked.

He shrugged. "It was clear you wanted it down. And I agree with you. It *should* come down." He shot his eyes over at Mrs. Hoffman. "I think it's horrible of David to leave that portrait hanging when his new bride walked into the house."

"It's such a lovely piece," Mrs. Hoffman said. "I believe it's your masterpiece. Why would anyone want to remove it?" She smiled. "Mr. Huntington, will you be staying for lunch?"

"No, thank you. I've got to get over to the gallery and get ready for my show."

"Very well then," said Mrs. Hoffman. "Good day, Mr. Huntington." She turned to Liz. "If you need me, I'll be in the parlor."

Liz nodded. The housekeeper turned and left them alone.

"It's a wonder she can speak at all," Roger said

under his breath. "She's had that face pulled and stretched and pumped so full of Botox it's a wonder it doesn't crack and fall off."

Liz suppressed a smile. "You're a breath of fresh air, Roger. You really are."

"I'm sorry I didn't tell you about painting the portrait. I didn't want you to feel guilty about wanting it down."

"It is very good. Technically that is. I can see you're very talented."

He smiled, then gulped down the last of his coffee. "I do need to get to the gallery," Roger told her. "I just wanted to stop by and introduce myself." Liz stood and followed him as he moved over to the doors. "Let's have dinner soon," Roger said as they headed into the corridor. "If David can't—or won't—come, then let's you and I go out on our own."

"All right," Liz said. "It's a date."

They walked into the foyer and toward the front door.

"Don't let this house get you too down," Roger was telling her. "It can be mighty depressing. David rarely socializes. Force him to get out and do things."

Liz nodded. "Roger," she said. "Before you go . . ."

He lifted his eyebrows in anticipation of her request.

"Why did you and Dominique have a falling-out? You said you were friends once . . . when you painted her portrait . . . but then something happened." She stopped talking, thinking better of herself. "You don't have to tell me. It's none of my business."

"It's fine, Liz. Nothing really happened between us. I think I just . . . I just became aware of the pretension

Dominique lived with. The airs she put on. I got tired of it all. And Dominique resented that I could see through her."

"Sometimes . . ." Liz paused. "Sometimes I think I can still feel her here."

"What do you mean?"

As soon as the statement was out of her mouth, she regretted it. But she couldn't take it back now. "I don't know. Her fragrance . . ."

"Gardenias."

"Yes. I smell it . . . so often . . ."

"No wonder. She used to douse herself with the stuff so much it's probably rubbed off on the furniture and the drapes." Roger laughed. "Dominique was anything but subtle."

"I guess I'm just worried about not living up to her. You said she was the queen of Palm Beach society. If that's what people here are expecting of me, that's not what they're going to get. They're going to be very disappointed."

"They'll like you just the way you are." Roger gently cupped her cheek in his hand. "Obviously David liked you well enough. He married you."

"He hardly ever speaks of her. Hardly ever says her name. Says he doesn't like talking about the past. On our honeymoon, I didn't think much of it. He was so focused on me, I never gave his first wife a thought." Liz shivered. "But since coming here . . ." Her voice faded away.

"Go on. Since coming here what?"

"I worry that David sees that I'm nothing like Dominique and he's disappointed. He was very angry at me on the phone."

"What about?"

"One of our former employees was murdered."

Roger reacted. "A former employee? You mean—in addition to Audra?"

Liz nodded. "A young man. Not here on the grounds. He was found dead in his apartment in town. The police came by asking questions about him and I was upset about it. David was not very understanding when I spoke to him on the phone."

Roger became angry. "My brother can be a total boor sometimes. Of course you were upset! Did the police think there was a connection with Audra's death?"

Liz shrugged. "I don't know. They were just asking questions."

"No wonder you were upset," he said, and without warning he pulled Liz into him, wrapping his arms around her again. "You poor kid."

She thought for a moment she might cry in his arms. How good it felt to be held . . .

But she stiffened. It wasn't right. She gently withdrew herself from Roger's embrace.

"I'm sure David was just busy when we spoke on the phone," Liz said. "Things aren't going well with the business."

"No excuse for him to be hard to you."

"He wants me to be strong." She smiled ironically. "I imagine Dominique was strong."

Roger glared at her. "Believe me, Liz, David does *not* want you to be like Dominique."

She held his gaze for a moment. At last Roger reached over and gave her a kiss on the cheek.

"I will see you very soon," he promised. "In the meantime, I want you to relax and stop worrying. In a day or two, I'll come by and pick you up and we'll go on a tour of the town. Would you like that?"

"Very much," Liz said.

"And if David's not back, you'll come to my gallery show as my guest."

"Deal," she told him.

Liz watched Roger go with grateful eyes. At last—someone here who had been kind to her. Genuine and thoughtful.

Even more than her own husband had been.

18

Variola was spreading out dough with a rolling pin on the counter, her hands dusted with flour. She planned on serving a rum-flavored coconut cream pie for dessert this evening. The delicacy had been one of Mrs. Huntington's favorites. Variola wondered if the new lady of the house would like it as much. She seemed to have much simpler tastes . . .

She had hardly seen the new mistress. She rarely took her meals in the dining room. But Variola had heard all about the incident on the stairwell. The attempt to remove the portrait of Dominique.

So she does have some spirit inside her, Variola thought about Liz.

Variola had nothing against the young woman. But she had no use for her either. It was clear she was not going to be another Dominique. So that rendered her irrelevant in Variola's eyes. She wouldn't want to have to hurt the poor girl. But she might have to take advantage of her, for everybody's good.

Because Variola could feel something happening. When she woke up in the mornings, she could feel a tugging at her mind, as if someone was trying to siphon off her power. She had a pretty good idea who could be doing such a thing.

A showdown was coming. Variola had known it would come for a long time now. She had made a special offering this morning to Papa Ghede at the little altar she kept in her room. She'd burned some rosemary and dried nasturtium and muttered a prayer over the smoke. She needed to stay strong.

I should never have come here, she thought to herself as she rolled the dough. *But what choice did I have? The island was devastated. I had lost everyone. And Mrs. Huntington had made such promises . . .*

She thought again of the first day she stepped foot on this estate. Dominique had greeted her, her face covered in bandages.

"I am tired of this," Dominique had told her.

"Tired of what, madam?"

She'd indicated the bandages. "Surgeries and facials and fillers. I want to be young, Variola. Young and beautiful. You can make me that way."

When she'd first come to this house, Variola had had no idea how much vanity and cruelty and selfishness and greed she would find there. But she'd had no choice but to come. Before the earthquake that had leveled her beloved Haiti, Variola had presided over a thriving community, all devoted to the fine arts of the island and following the tenets of Papa Ghede. Variola knew that silly Americans, so conditioned by television and movies, would have called her community a "coven." But to Variola they had simply been family.

When the earthquake came, she'd lost that family— if not to the earthquake itself, than to the death, disease, and financial ruin that followed. Yet by then her fame had spread far and wide. Her reputation as a great sorceress had reached many parts of the globe, including one particular mansion in Palm Beach, Florida. Her spells and enchantments, her potions and her powders, had brought about some amazing transformations and they had become the stuff of legend. She'd restored a woman's hair after it was burned off in a fire. She'd corrected a boy's lazy eye. She'd melted the pounds off a dangerously obese man. So, yes, she could make someone look younger. A simple job, in fact.

And so Variola had accepted the offer from Dominique Huntington to come live with her and teach her the arcane arts. She would be well compensated for her efforts, of course.

Once again she heard her mother's voice in her head. *Papa Ghede grants us certain powers, Variola, but we mustn't waste time on frivolous purposes. That is not why we are here. The powers we have should never be used for reasons of selfishness or revenge. Papa Ghede does not tolerate evil. Remember that.*

Variola sighed as she fitted the dough into the pie plate. In Haiti, they all knew that Papa Ghede was the spirit of the first man who'd ever died, who waited at the crossroads to escort souls into the afterlife. When a child fell sick, the whole village would pray to Papa Ghede. He was a good spirit, and fair, but he was also strict, and he had the ability to read minds. Papa Ghede knew everything that went on in the worlds of the living and the dead.

So he would have seen clearly that Variola's work for Mrs. Huntington had been the very definition of frivolous. Mama would have shaken her head and sniffed that Variola was wasting her talents. But at least Variola's work had not been evil.

Not in the beginning, anyway.

She didn't need to look up from her task to realize that eyes were staring at her.

"And what orders do you bring me this afternoon, Mrs. Hoffman?" Variola asked, arranging the dough in the pie plate with her fingers.

"No orders," the housekeeper told her.

Still Variola didn't look up at her.

"I just wanted to let you know that Roger was here."

That brought Variola's big black eyes up. "Really, now. He came to see her?"

Mrs. Hoffman nodded. "I asked him if he would stay for a meal, but he declined."

"Does Mr. Huntington know that his brother paid a visit to his wife?"

"I doubt it very much."

Variola returned to her work. "Will he come around again?"

"That I don't know. But I suppose it's possible." She paused. "Perhaps likely. They seemed to get on quite well, the two of them."

"Of course they did."

Mrs. Hoffman sniffed. "He has a way with women."

Variola laughed. "But not with you, eh, Mrs. Hoffman?"

The housekeeper didn't seem amused. "The other news is . . . the portrait remains."

Variola's lips stretched into a smile. "Did you ever expect it not?"

"She may try again."

"Oh, I'm sure she will try a great many things. She is the mistress here, whether you like it or not, my dear Mrs. Hoffman."

"This house will only ever have one mistress," the housekeeper said, her eyes moving behind her hard, plastic face as if she were wearing a mask.

Variola chuckled lightly as she returned to work. Mrs. Hoffman, having said all she intended to say, turned and left the room.

Variola placed the piecrust in the oven. Yes, she could feel the tug—as if someone were yanking at her mind and her soul, trying to rip them right out of her. She resisted.

I'm stronger than anyone in this house, Variola thought.

Still, just the same, she would burn more rosemary and nasturtium for Papa Ghede this evening.

19

Rita came through the front door of her parents' house and removed her wet, dripping raincoat. It was still pouring out there though the thunder and lightning had at last stopped. Her mother asked her if she was hungry, and Rita replied that she had eaten at Huntington House. She was tired, she told her mother, and she was going to bed early.

But in the privacy of her room, sleep was the furthest thing from Rita's mind.

She had just come from talking with the police. Detective Foley had asked her to come down to the station. He wanted to keep their conversation private, he said, just between him and Detective McFarland and herself. They didn't want anyone else at Huntington House to know they'd spoken with her. Was Rita okay with that?

She told them yes.

They wanted to know about Jamison. Was it true she had seen him at the bar the night he was killed? Yes, Rita, admitted, it was true. And yes, she knew he'd been fired.

But that was all she told them.

When they asked Rita if she knew *why* Jamison had been fired, she had lied and said no. She hadn't told the detectives anything that Jamison had told her about Audra. She had thought long and hard about whether she should say anything about her suspicions that Mrs. Hoffman had killed both of them. She had thought it might be good revenge against the cruel old house-keeper, and give her a freer hand at the house if Mrs. Hoffman was removed. But telling the police what she knew, Rita had decided, might hurt David and his business and his reputation, and Rita would never hurt David.

On her phone she tapped in David's mobile number. She knew it would be the middle of the night in Amsterdam or wherever he was at the moment. But she also knew that David always answered his phone, no matter what time it rang. Whatever call came in on this line was important. Only a select few had David's private mobile number; Rita suspected he hadn't even given it to his new little wife. He'd never given it to Dominique; why would he give it to this one? This number was only for David's closest business colleagues—and his father, of course, who was also his boss. But Rita had the number. David had given it to her back in those terrible days before Dominique died, when he was so upset, so unhappy. How vulnerable he had been the day he gave her this special number. How much like a little lost boy. How cruel Dominque had been to him. She was always trying to make him jealous, to make him feel inadequate. And so David had reached out to Rita and gave her his private number. It was then that Rita had known he truly loved her.

She'd used the number only once, the day Domi-nique died, and Rita was desperate to know if David was okay. Now, she figured, it was time to use it again.

David answered on the second ring.

"Why are you calling me?" he snapped.

"I wouldn't be calling you if I didn't think you wanted to hear what I had to tell you, David."

Rita could hear the anger simmering in his voice. "What is it?" he asked.

"Your brother."

"My brother?"

"He came by the house today to see your wife."

There was silence on the other end of the phone. The silence was so complete that Rita thought for a minute the call had been dropped.

But then she heard David let out a breath.

"What's the problem with my brother coming by to welcome his sister-in-law to her new home?" he asked her. "It's a perfectly natural, kind, family gesture. Why would you think I needed to know such a trivial little thing?"

"Because I remember what happened—"

"Listen to me, Rita," David seethed, cutting her off. "You remember nothing. Do you understand? You re-member nothing because nothing happened. Not be-tween us, not between me and anyone else. *Do you understand?*"

It was Rita's turn to fall silent. Finally she replied, "Yes, David."

He hung up on her.

Rita boiled. How dare he just discard her this way? How dare he try to deny everything they'd been through—everything she had witnessed?

She had protected him! She had thought of him first and no one else in those terrible days after Dominique died. How would he like it if she went back to Detective Foley and told him everything she knew? Everything!

Sitting there, staring out the window as the moon rapidly revealed itself from behind the dissipating clouds, Rita vowed one of two things.

She'd get David back, and everything would be just as it was.

Or else she'd make sure that no one—no one!—ever had David again.

Including his mousy little bride.

20

At Huntington House, Liz was looking out at the moon as well.

Thin ribbons of clouds were drifting away as the moon rose in all its white shiny glory, reclaiming the sky from the wind and the rain. The moon made Liz happy as she watched it, as if the end of the storm symbolized the end of all her unhappiness since she'd come to this place.

But it wasn't the moon that made her feel better. Not really. It was Roger.

At last Liz felt as if she had a friend here. Someone who understood her and, critically, who understood David. Roger had said things that reassured her, most importantly: *David does* not *want you to be like Dominique*. Roger had reminded Liz that David had married her because he had liked her, loved her, for exactly who and what she was.

But even more: Roger promised her an escape from the dreariness of this house.

Liz had found Roger's gallery on Facebook and sent him a message, telling him how much she'd like to attend his opening. He'd quickly replied that he'd love to pick her up tomorrow—if she was free—and show her around town. Since Liz didn't have a driver's license yet, he was glad to be her chauffeur. Although Liz had her pick of drivers at Huntington House, she much preferred the idea of being shuttled around town by Roger. She'd told him that yes, she was free, and yes, she'd love to go out with him tomorrow.

Liz pulled away from the window. For the first time since coming to this house, she was going to sleep honestly looking forward to the next day.

But as she crossed the room to her bed, she was distracted by a sound.

The same sound she had heard before—heard a number of times over the last couple of weeks, in fact.

The low, muffled banging—from behind the wall—or perhaps it was above her.

Liz could never quite be sure where the sound was coming from. But there it was again.

She stopped the clock on the mantel and pressed her ear against the wall. There was *definitely* a sound.

The soft rapping of a hammer?

Or . . . a series of footsteps?

Then, as always, the sound ceased as suddenly as it began.

But this time, with the end of the sound, came the sudden overwhelming fragrance of gardenia.

21

Mrs. Martinez wasn't pleased by the conversation she overheard in the kitchen when she reported to work the next morning. Rita was standing in the middle of the room, speaking in hushed tones to Variola. But Mrs. Martinez could hear all too clearly what the maid was saying.

"You said you could help me," Rita implored.

"Of course Variola can help you." The chef smiled. "The question is, what is it that you truly want? The man you claim to love, or happiness and well-being?"

"I'd say they're one and the same."

Variola rolled her eyes. "Oh, such a foolish child. Very well. Variola will help you nonetheless."

"Why have you offered to help me?"

Variola shrugged. "I thought maybe we could be better friends."

"And you need friends," Rita said. "To help you against Mrs. Hoffman."

"Now, girl, you are just concocting scenarios."

"I've watched you. I've watched you both for a long

time. There is a rivalry there. She was once your pupil. I saw the two of you, in the garden, picking flowers, boiling them on the stove, chanting words over the steam that rose from the pot."

Variola nodded. "She was interested at one time in the magic and the remedies of the islands. I taught her. She and the first Mrs. Huntington were both my pupils."

"And Mrs. Hoffman has learned maybe a bit too well?" Rita asked.

Variola leveled her black eyes at her. "She has concluded her lessons. I no longer teach her."

"But you can teach me," Rita said.

The chef was nodding. "If you want to learn."

"I do."

"Let me tell you something, Margarita Cansino," Variola said. "Papa Ghede is a compassionate deity. But he can take back as much as he gives if your aims are impure. And your desire to lure a man away from his marriage . . . that is impure. That is selfish. That is evil."

Rita laughed. "But you've offered to help me, to teach me the ways to do just that."

"What I will teach you," Variola said, "is how to go after what you think you want and how to understand that what you get is what you deserve."

"Whatever," Rita said, seeming to become bored with all the talk. "Just help me get him."

"You'll only get him if it's meant to be," Variola cautioned her.

Rita folded her arms across her chest, impatient. "It

is meant to be. He'll realize that soon enough. He just needs a little . . . *shove* in that direction."

"If he truly loves you, why is he so resistant?"

Rita stiffened. "He's under a spell."

From her hiding place, eavesdropping on the conversation, Mrs. Martinez winced.

"Is he now?" Variola asked. "Who placed this spell on him?"

Rita frowned. "When I came to work here," she said, "shortly before the first Mrs. Huntington died, I heard the whispers about witchcraft being practiced in this house. Even after seeing you and Mrs. Hoffman brewing up your potions, I didn't believe the stories. But Jamison did." She paused. "When he was killed, I realized the stories had been true."

"So you believe I have bewitched Mr. Huntington."

"Either you, or Mrs. Hoffman."

In the shadows, Mrs. Martinez tensed. Did the child not realize how dangerous her words were becoming?

"Why would either of us do such a thing?" Variola asked.

"Because there is a war between you two. You want control over this house. Over the Huntingtons. Over their money and their estate."

Variola smiled. "My, you have us pegged as real go-getters. So, help me to understand. You come to me looking for talismans or potions to break this spell? You offer yourself as my ally if I will undo the spell I have placed on your lover? Is that it?"

"That about sums it up."

Variola turned from her in disgust. "I have placed no

spell on Mr. Huntington. He operates of his own free will."

"Then Mrs. Hoffman has done so," Rita said. "It is Mrs. Hoffman who cast the spell." She took a step closer to Variola. "And I will help you destroy her. I know you want her gone. I can help you make that happen, in exchange for what you can give me."

"How can you help make such a thing happen?"

"I know things about Mrs. Hoffman. Things that could remove her from this house for good."

Variola smirked. "You think Variola doesn't know such things as well? You think Variola does not know things about everyone in this house, including yourself, that would destroy them? You promise me things that I do not need."

"But you're intrigued, nonetheless," Rita said. "You want to know what I know."

Variola's smile disappeared. "You come back this afternoon. I will give you what you want. But remember, Rita. I am giving this to you on two conditions. One, that whatever it is that you go after, you shall get it only if it is *supposed* to come to you, only if it is *right*."

"Oh, it's right, believe me," Rita said. "Nothing has ever been more right."

"And two," Variola went on, "that you are, as you proclaim, on my side."

"I understand."

No more words were exchanged between the two women. Mrs. Martinez waited until Rita had left the kitchen. Then she stepped out of the shadows.

"After hearing all that, I'm more afraid than ever," she said in a tiny voice. "Is she right? Is there some sort of contest brewing between you and Mrs. Hoffman? What is this talk of sides? Will we be asked to choose?"

Variola didn't even bother looking over at her. She opened the refrigerator, took out some apples and pears, and placed them on the chopping board beside her. "You have got to stop being so afraid, Maria," she said over her shoulder. "Fear gets in the way."

"I have children," Mrs. Martinez said. "And grandchildren."

She thought of little Marisol and Luis. How sweet and innocent. These sorts of things could ricochet. Mrs. Martinez knew that. Variola had taught her that. If the powers in this house were ever turned against her, no one in her family would be safe.

"Your family will be fine," Variola assured her. "There was no trouble before, was there?"

"But there might have been. You told me yourself. We were all in danger . . ."

Variola looked up at her, black eyes flashing. "But nothing happened, did it? We were fine! And we will be fine now, too."

Mrs. Martinez clasped her hands together to keep them from trembling. "You are going through with it? You will use the girl's silly fantasy about Mr. Huntington for your own purposes."

"She will learn."

Mrs. Martinez was about to reply when they both heard a step. They fell silent, busying themselves in the kitchen.

In an instant, Mrs. Hoffman presented herself at the kitchen door.

"She will eat lunch in the dining room today," the head housekeeper announced.

"Oh, really now?" Variola asked. "She gifts us with her presence more these days."

"She is coming out of her shell, it seems."

Variola smiled slyly. "Will Mr. Roger be coming for dinner?"

"No." Hoffman's face turned dark. "Why would you ask such a thing?"

"I just thought, since they had gotten on so well yesterday . . ."

"I have not heard from Roger."

"I'll make a little extra just in case."

Mrs. Hoffman stiffened. "There's no need to do so."

Variola looked up at her. "You don't trust Variola's instincts? Even still, after all this time, you don't think I can know these things, that I can't sniff them out?"

"It would seem to me that you should hope Roger stayed far away from here. He is trouble for all of us. You know that all too well. You remember what happened before." She shuddered. "If Mr. Huntington knew that his brother was coming around again . . ."

"Maybe he does know."

"Why do you say that?"

Variola laughed. "Instinct, Mrs. Hoffman. Why will you not trust me?"

Mrs. Hoffman pursed her lips tightly. "All I know is, she has called for lunch in the dining room."

"I appreciate the information," Variola said.

Mrs. Hoffman turned on her heel and strode out of the room.

Once the housekeeper's footsteps had faded off down the hall, Mrs. Martinez returned to Variola's side. "I cannot help it," she said, her face pale and drawn. "I am frightened."

This time Variola made no reply.

22

Liz tapped lightly on the open door of the servants' sitting room in the back of the kitchen, just behind the back stairs. This was where they came to take their breaks, to eat their lunches. The caretaker, Thad, his bandaged foot in a slipper, sat at the table, eating a sandwich he'd brought from home. His long legs were stretched out in front of him.

"I can't believe you came into work, Thad," Liz said, entering the room. "I told Mrs. Hoffman you could stay home until the cast came off. You'll receive all your pay . . ."

"No, ma'am, I can still get around," Thad said, his craggy face creasing into a small smile. "It was just a bad sprain. I just walk a little more slowly than usual. The doc said I'll be fine in a day or two. But I appreciate your thoughtfulness." He looked up at her. "Really, I do."

Liz sat down beside him. Thad's sandwich was tuna fish on white bread, and a baggie filled with Oreos was waiting for his dessert. For some reason this big, burly man's simple little lunch made Liz feel even worse for him, and all the more guilty. "I'm so sorry for what happened to your foot, Thad," she told him. "I feel responsible."

"Oh, no, ma'am, it's not your fault."

"I know the lightning startled you, but if I hadn't asked you to—"

"It wasn't the lightning either," Thad said plainly.

"What do you mean?"

"It was *her*."

Liz felt her blood run cold.

"Dominique," Thad said. "She didn't want her portrait taken down."

"Oh, Thad," Liz said, but her admonition was weak.

He took a bite of his tuna fish, chewed a while, swallowed, and then continued. "She's never left this house, you know. Ever since she was washed off that boat, her spirit has been stuck here. I shouldn't say such things perhaps. But while I was stretched out in the emergency room, waiting for the doctor to come in and bandage up my foot, I knew I had to speak plainly about this. After all, that poor kid got killed."

"You mean . . . Audra?"

"Well, I was thinking of Jamison, but Audra, too."

"Surely you can't be saying . . ."

"But I am, ma'am. Dominique killed both of them."

Liz stiffened. "That's ludicrous, Thad."

"You're a kind lady, Mrs. Huntington. That's the truth. You coming in here and checking on me like this. That proves you have a good heart and soul. She would never have done such a thing."

"You mean, you didn't like Dominique? I thought . . ."

"You thought what, ma'am?"

"I thought you *did* like her, given how resistant you were to taking down her portrait."

"That wasn't because I liked her, ma'am. Not at all. It was because I didn't want to touch her."

Liz wanted to hear more. "So she wasn't friendly to you?"

Thad grinned. "Oh, she tried to be. She tried to be *real* friendly with all the men in the house. She thought every man would fall in love with her. But I was immune to her charms."

"How so?"

Thad wiped his mouth with a paper napkin, having finished his sandwich. "I'm gay, ma'am."

"Oh, I see." Liz tried to hide the surprise on her face.

"It's okay, ma'am, no one thinks I'm gay at first. I don't fit the stereotype. And that took Dominique by surprise, too. But you see, because of that fact, I could discern the truth about her. I could see right through her phony charms." Thad laughed. "She didn't quite get the same sort of response from me that she got from other men."

Liz was unable to suppress a small smile.

Thad opened the baggie with the Oreos. "Would you like one, ma'am?"

"No, thank you, Thad."

He popped an Oreo into his mouth. "Well, maybe I shouldn't be saying all this," he said, his mouth full, "but the first Mrs. Huntington was a terrible flirt. She was very vain."

"Was she?"

"She and Mrs. Hoffman were always going off to have more plastic surgery. Faces stretched, lips plumped, breasts filled out."

"She had . . . breast implants?"

"They seemed to get bigger every year."

"And what did Dav—Mr. Huntington say?"

"Oh, he didn't like it. He didn't like it one bit."

Liz was getting far more than she had expected when she'd come in, out of courtesy, to check on Thad. Suddenly she had some brand-new insights into her predecessor's character—and to David's relationship with her.

"I may be talking out of turn," Thad said. "But that little fall down the stairs seems to have woken me up." He gazed at her intently. "I love this place. I love this family. Your husband's mother and father hired me when I was just a kid, and I owe them everything. I can't keep quiet when I realize there's danger lurking around. There are forces at work in this house, and I can't be silent about them. Not anymore."

"Well, Thad, I must say that . . ." Liz hesitated, not sure if she was being truthful in what she was about to say. "I don't believe in ghosts."

"You will." He finished his last Oreo. "Dominique was a bad woman in life, and she's an even worse one in death. She's not giving up her control of this house just because you're here."

"If she's that powerful," Liz asked, "aren't you afraid of her? Aren't you afraid that, if what you say is true, her spirit will take revenge on you next?"

Thad shook his head. "Not afraid. Not anymore. After that tumble I took, I knew I needed some protection." He reached inside his open shirt collar and withdrew a pendant on a chain. It was a small green stone. It looked like jade. "Variola gave it to me. Protects against the undead. She promised it was so."

"Variola gave this to you because you told her what you believed?"

"Sure did." He grinned. "Had to pay her fifty bucks, but it was worth it."

Liz smiled sadly. The poor man had been taken for a ride, she thought. "Well, if it makes you feel better to wear it," she said.

Thad replaced the pendant under his shirt. "It does. And you need to get one, too, Mrs. Huntington. I was planning on telling you so. Everyone here should wear one. I expect Variola won't charge you or Mr. Huntington like she charged me."

Liz stood. "Thanks. I think I'll pop in and have a word with Variola."

"Good idea." He smiled up at her. "You're a fine lady, Mrs. Huntington. I'm glad you're here. Your good, strong energy will help to drive away any of the bad forces."

"Thank you, Thad. I hope so."

Liz headed out into the hall. It seemed it was time she had a conversation with their enterprising chef.

23

"What do you have for me?" Rita whispered to Variola, who took hold of her wrist and motioned for her to step into the pantry.

Variola motioned for her to be quiet.

"You told me to come back! You told me you'd have something for me!"

"You speak too openly, girl," the chef cautioned her. "There are ears everywhere in this house."

Rita sneered. "Everyone talks, everyone hears. Everyone knows you're a witch. Give me a pendant like you gave Thad. He believes it will keep him from any more accidents like falling down the stairs."

Variola smiled indulgently. "Poor, sweet, simple Thad. Of course he believes that."

"You're saying his pendant has no power?"

"If he imbues it with power, then it has."

Rita frowned. "I don't want something like that then. You told me you could help me. I want something that really *works*."

Variola's black eyes danced. "Oh, for you, dear Rita, I have something special."

She opened a cabinet and withdrew a small wooden rectangular box about six inches long and four inches wide. A tiny gold padlock secured the lid of the box.

"And here is the key," Variola said, producing a small gold key from her apron pocket.

"What's in the box? And why do you keep it locked?"

Variola handed it over to Rita, who accepted it with a little apprehension. Then she held up the key for her to take.

"Go ahead," the chef said. "Open it and see for yourself."

Rita took the key. Her hands were trembling.

"Why do you fear Variola?" the woman with the dancing dark eyes asked her. "You came to Variola for help. Why do you fear that help is not what I am giving you?"

"Because I don't know yet what kind of payment you'll be asking for."

"Your friendship is all," Variola insisted.

"You want me on your side when the time comes," Rita said.

Variola nodded.

"What will happen?" Rita asked. "When—"

Variola laughed, a small tinkle. "You'll learn all in good time. We all will. Now go ahead, dear Rita. Open the box."

Rita gingerly fit the key into the lock and turned. The padlock sprung open.

"Lift the lid," Variola instructed.

Rita obeyed. And there, lying in the box as if it were a tiny coffin, was a wooden doll about five inches long. The doll was painted beige, with crude red dots to indicate eyes, nose and mouth, and loosely wrapped in fabric of some kind. Rita recognized what it was.

"That's one of David's neckties," she said softly.

"He has so many. He won't miss one."

Rita fingered the silk of the tie. It was a pattern of blue, white, and green stripes. She had seen him wearing it several times. She had once unknotted it at his throat, then slid it out from under his collar before unbuttoning his shirt.

"Is this what's commonly referred to as a vodou doll?" she asked Variola.

The other woman shrugged. "You can call it what you want. But so long as you possess it, you can make your wishes come true. But your wishes must be pure, Rita. This is not some black magic granted us by the devil. Do you understand? Whatever you ask for, it comes to you only if it's *meant* to come to you."

"If it's meant to come to me," Rita asked, "why do I need a vodou doll?"

"Even fate sometimes needs a little *shove*, as you described it."

A woman's voice suddenly interrupted them.

"What's all this talk about fate?"

Rita turned her head quickly. Standing in the kitchen, glaring at them, was David's wife. Little Liz.

24

Liz noticed that Rita quickly closed the lid of the box that Variola had just given to her. The maid seemed mortified to be caught in the pantry, though Liz couldn't imagine why. Variola, on the other hand, just smiled sweetly when she noticed Liz standing there.

"I've just given Rita some island medicine to cure her menstrual cramps," the chef explained. "She doesn't have much faith in my medicines, but I told it was sometimes better to take action instead of just leaving things up to fate."

"I'm sorry," Liz said. "I didn't mean to pry."

"It is all right," Variola replied, coming out of the pantry, Rita following. "You are the mistress of this house. We can have no secrets from you."

"I'll . . . I'll be getting back to work now," Rita said. She smiled awkwardly at Liz. Liz returned her smile.

Once she was gone, Variola asked, "And what may I do for you, ma'am? I trust your meals have all been satisfactory. I'm happy to accommodate any dietary requests you have."

"Every meal has been superb, Variola. Truly. You've spoiled me."

"That is my job, ma'am."

"Well, I'm deeply grateful." Liz paused. "But that's not what I've come to talk to you about."

"Oh, no? Then tell me what it is, ma'am."

Liz sighed. "I know I've been a bit of a recluse since I came here. It's not because I didn't want to get to know all of you. It's because I haven't had an easy adjustment to moving here, what with Mr. Huntington leaving so soon after we arrived, and then the disturbing news about Jamison, and also learning about the young woman who was killed here a while back."

Variola gave her a sympathetic face. "Oh, I am sure that has made the transition terribly difficult for you, ma'am. What can I do to help you?"

"Well, maybe you can start by helping me understand the culture of the house."

Variola lifted her elegantly shaped eyebrows. "The culture of the house, ma'am?"

"I must admit . . . there are all sorts of stories swirling around."

"What sorts of stories, pray tell?"

"Ghosts. Witchcraft."

Variola laughed, and Liz thought it sounded like the ringing of chimes. "You've probably heard some of them call me a witch. Is that why you're here?"

"I just spoke with Thad. He told me about his pendant . . ."

"Oh, yes. It's a sacred tradition where I come from. In the islands, there is the belief that one can imbue certain talismans with power. If you believe it strongly enough, it will do what you wish it to do. It's really all about the power of suggestion."

"That doesn't sound like witchcraft to me."

Variola shook her head. "My mother taught me the religion of vodou. Some call that witchcraft. But in fact it is a faith, a system of beliefs. It is a blend of African tribal religions and Roman Catholicism. The power of vodou is real, but it is not what the movies would have it to be, all black magic and zombies. It is, rather, the herbs and roots and flowers of the islands." She laughed, that sound of chimes again. "What seems like witchcraft to some is increasingly recognized by health care givers all over the country as sound, proven medicine. Have you never taken echinacea when you've had a cold, Mrs. Huntington? St. John's Wort when you're feeling down? Goldenseal for indigestion? They're all in my bag of tricks, but they are also sold in the heath food store downtown."

"I pass no judgment on your beliefs. I just want to understand what goes on in this house."

Variola gave her another sympathetic smile. "What is it that troubles you, ma'am? You can speak freely with Variola. I do not betray confidences."

For some reason, Liz suddenly felt as if she could trust this woman. "All right. It started on my very first day here. Jamison told me that Dominique's ghost still walks this house. Thad is convinced of the same."

"I have heard those tales, too."

"You gave Thad a pendant for protection against her."

"His pendant protects him from whatever dangers he believes he faces because he gives it the power to do so. Not me."

"But why does he believe that Dominique haunts this place? Why did Jamison believe it as well?"

Variola sighed. "She was a very . . . formidable figure. Perhaps they have a hard time believing she is really gone."

"Formidable? In what way?"

"Well, she was very beautiful."

Liz nodded. "I can see that from the portrait."

"She was also charismatic and vain and demanding and not always very pleasant, though she could be exceeding charming when she chose to be."

Liz swallowed hard. "My husband loved her . . . seemed to love her very much."

"Is that what he has said?"

Liz realized David had never actually said such a thing, at least not in so many words. "It's been obvious to me. He took a cruise around the world to get over the grief of her death. Whenever her name comes up, he is stricken . . . I can see the pain on his face."

"Well, he was her husband," Variola replied. "I'm sure her death was hard on him."

Liz hesitated. "Do you . . . do you believe her spirit is still here?"

Variola smiled kindly. "You are asking me if I believe in ghosts?"

"I suppose so, yes."

"I do believe that the dead can come back. I have seen many things that cannot be explained by science alone."

"So you believe Dominique's ghost—"

Variola shook her head. "Her ghost does not walk here. Variola could see if it did."

"Are you certain of that?"

Variola evaded giving her a direct answer. "I take it, then, that you *do* believe in ghosts, Mrs. Huntington?"

Liz smiled weakly. "I didn't before I came here . . ."

"But now you do? Because of the babbling of frightened men?"

Liz leaned in closer to Variola. "I've smelled gardenias."

"Ah. Her fragrance."

Liz nodded.

"You are aware that Rita wears the fragrance, too?" Variola asked.

"No, I hadn't noticed . . ."

Variola grinned. "She frequently does. And I wouldn't be surprised if Mrs. Hoffman still sprayed the fragrance to remind her . . ."

"Mrs. Hoffman! That would make sense . . ."

Variola folded her arms across her chest and gave Liz a knowing look. "Tell me why that would make sense, Mrs. Huntington."

Liz held the chef's gaze. "Because . . . they appear to have been very close."

"Very," Variola confirmed. "As thick as thieves sometimes." She took a step closer to Liz and lowered her voice, as if she were about to reveal a secret. "They brought me to this house. Dominique and Mrs. Hoffman. They were interested in learning the fine arts of the islands. They were like little girls eager to find hidden treasure." Variola's face darkened. "But they weren't interested in art or culture or faith or religion. They were interested only in how my heritage could benefit them. They were greedy. Selfish."

Liz was surprised to hear the chef speaking so plainly. "Do I take it that you don't like Mrs. Hoffman?"

"I work fine with her," Variola assured her. "You needn't worry about that."

"I'm not sure she likes me," Liz offered.

Variola arched an eyebrow. "Mrs. Hoffman has only ever liked herself and Dominique."

Liz decided to trust the chef some more. "Many times since I've come here, she's made me feel as if . . . as if I don't measure up."

Suddenly Variola leapt at her and grabbed her hands, gripping them tightly in her own. "Don't you listen to Mrs. Hoffman when she starts talking like that! You hear me? You are a good woman. Variola can see that now. Can see that clearly." Her dark eyes reflected Liz's own. "Your husband married you because he loved you. You must know that. Variola can see that, too, as clear as I can see the nose on your face."

Liz felt as if she might cry. "Oh, thank you, Variola, you have no idea how much it means to me to hear that."

Variola let her hands go and smiled craftily at her. "I think we will be good friends, Mrs. Huntington. I think we can help each other."

"I hope so," Liz replied.

"You come to Variola," the dark-eyed woman told her, "if you ever feel lost in this house. Variola will make it right for you." She lowered her voice again. "And pay no attention to the honeyed words of Mrs. Hoffman. Beware her. She is not your friend. The time will come when we will stand up to her. Variola will make sure you are safe in this house."

"Safe from what?"

"From everything you fear," Variola told her.

Liz appreciated the support, though she realized it probably hadn't been wise to get herself involved in what was apparently a domestic rivalry between these two women. Still, what Variola had just told her made her extremely happy.

Your husband married you because he loved you. Variola can see that, too.

In that moment, Liz's cell phone jangled. She grabbed at it, suddenly convinced it was David, telling her that he was coming home. But it was a number she didn't recognize . . .

"I think you should answer that," Variola told her.

Liz did so. It was Roger, asking if he could take her to dinner tonight.

"Oh, I don't know," Liz said.

Overhearing the conversation, Variola smiled at her. "Invite Mr. Roger here to the house for dinner," she said. "Tell him I'll make him his favorite curry goat."

Liz relayed the offer, and Roger accepted.

After Liz had hung up the phone, Variola said, "You might let Mrs. Hoffman know we will have a guest tonight."

Liz said she would do so.

Yet neither she nor Variola were aware of the eavesdropper who was standing just outside the kitchen door in the shadows, listening to every word of their conversation.

25

In the servants' washroom, the door locked securely behind her, Rita wrapped the necktie tightly around the little wooden doll.

A part of her thought what she was doing was utterly and ridiculously mad. She had never believed in such things before. She had told Jamison he was crazy to talk about ghosts and devils. But then Jamison had been killed for such talk . . .

Rita thought back to the day she first came into this house. She'd answered an ad she'd found online, looking for a chambermaid. Mrs. Hoffman had interviewed her, looking her up and down with those creepy eyes—the only part of her face that ever moved. Rita had felt as if the older woman was peeling off her clothes with her eyes—her clothes, her skin, seeing right into her soul. Rita had shivered. At the end of the brief interview, she was given the job.

Rita had been thrilled, because she'd really needed the job. She was saving to move out of her parents' house and go back to school. She'd started beauty school a year earlier, but had had to drop out when her father lost his job and could no longer help her pay tuition. How Rita ached to live on her own, to have her own life.

But the life she observed at Huntington House had made her want a very special sort of existence—one that no job as a cosmetician would ever give her.

Very quickly Rita had spotted the way Mr. Huntington looked at her. When he was around his wife, he seemed very much in love—completely devoted to Dominique, in fact—but when she wasn't around, David's eyes wandered. Rita saw how he looked at her, and she learned how to hold his gaze for that tenth of a second longer than was acceptable. Finally, one day, in the solarium, as David sat reading and Rita watered plants, she'd deliberately brushed past him, stumbled just a bit, and nearly fell into his lap. He'd responded by kissing her. Dominique was away for the day, on another plastic surgery adventure, and they'd had the rest of the afternoon to themselves. Rita had never known such lovemaking. She had decided then and there she would not only be David's mistress, but she would someday be his wife as well.

Oh, yes—she wanted everything that Dominique had. She wanted everything that vain, imperious woman lorded over her. Rita wanted her clothes and her cars and her spending allowances. But she wanted her husband, most of all. And Rita would love David in a way that Dominique had apparently been unable to do.

Rita could see that something had been missing from the Huntingtons' marriage. When they were together, David had refused to ever let Rita speak his wife's name—almost as if he could not speak it himself. At first, Rita had thought he was simply guilt-ridden about the affair; as time went on, however, she discerned something else was going on. David never spoke Dominique's name around her because he *hated* her—he was desperately unhappy being married to her. Yet for some reason he could never bring himself to admit that to Rita, always changing the subject when she tried to bring it up.

So when word came that Dominique had been washed overboard on their yacht, and no amount of plastic in her body had kept her from drowning, Rita hadn't felt in the least bit regretful. The woman had never been kind to her. She'd snapped her fingers and expected Rita to come running. She'd kept David on a short leash—while at the same time, flirting outrageously with every male member of the staff. How the bellboys and chauffeurs had been dazzled by her. Rita wouldn't have been surprised if Dominique had been carrying on affairs with all of them. She was simply a horrible woman, and Rita was glad she was dead.

Finally David was free! But he had left the house in such a miserable state—after tearing up the gardenia plants in the garden because he wanted no memory of Dominique in the house. But if hated her so much, why had he been made so distraught by her death? He hadn't loved her. All that attention he gave her in public was just a show. It couldn't have been real—not with the way that David brought such passion to his relationship with Rita. Rita believed deep down in her bones that David was glad that Dominique was dead. But for whatever reason, he'd left Huntington House for all those months after her death—and when he came back, he brought that little drip of a new wife with him.

It made no sense to Rita.

That was, it made no sense until after Jamison was killed. It was the only answer. All the talk she'd heard ever since coming to this house—all the talk of witchcraft and black magic—must be true. It was the only thing that could explain David's attachment to Dominique. He was under some kind of spell. When Dominique wasn't around, David could break somewhat free of it, and find some moments of true happiness with Rita. And when Dominique died, he had been shattered—almost like an alcoholic who suddenly gives up alcohol cold turkey.

But who had put David under the spell? It might have been Variola, on Dominique's order. Variola had never possessed any particular love for Dominique, so no doubt she was being paid to cast her spells. And Rita suspected Variola wanted to continue that profitable enterprise by keeping her hold over David. That's what had caused him to act so uncharacteristically and so impulsively and marry some cheap little dancer he'd met on a cruise ship. Rita didn't think little Liz knew that her husband was under a spell, or that he'd married her only because Variola had directed him to do so. She suspected that Variola would make her schemes and her demands known to the new mistress of the house in time. Then she would go back to controlling the house once again and enjoying whatever forms of payment she received.

And if it wasn't Variola who cast the spell, then it must have been Mrs. Hoffman, but had she truly learned enough of Variola's black magic to keep David under such control?

Rita looked down at the vodou doll in her hands. She didn't trust Variola, but she believed the chef when she said that she wanted Rita as her ally. She suspected the two women, Variola and Mrs. Hoffman, were in a struggle for control of Huntington House. Whoever controlled David, of course, won. And what better way to control David than to reignite his affair with Rita? Quite possibly, Variola was using Rita as a weapon in her fight against Mrs. Hoffman. But her reasons didn't matter. Rita had the doll. She was going to use it.

And soon she would have David back in her arms.

"You're missing me, aren't you, David?" Rita said, looking down at the little doll.

Its painted red eyes stared up at her.

Rita tightened the silk necktie even more. If the doll were human, it would be struggling to breathe.

"You need to come home, David," Rita said. "You are filled with thoughts of me, aren't you? Remembering the way I kissed you. The way we made love to each other. You are filled with thoughts of my face. You are overcome by my scent. You want me. You need me. You must have me."

She loosened the tie, then tightened it again.

"You are coming home, David. You are getting on an airplane and coming home to me. It is *me* you yearn for. Me. Say my name. *Rita*. David and Rita."

She lifted the doll from its little coffin and cradled it at her breast.

"You are coming home because the spell is broken, and you no longer love that silly little twit you married. You are coming home to tell Liz that your marriage was all a mistake and you want a divorce."

She kissed the doll's little painted mouth.

"You want a divorce and you want to marry me."

She replaced the doll in its box.

"Once the spell is broken," Rita whispered, "you will see that you truly love me. This is not an enchantment to make you love me, David. You already love me deep in your heart. It is merely a spell to free you so you can embrace your own true feelings."

She tightened the necktie once more, choking the little doll.

"Come home, David," Rita purred. "Come home."

26

The day was bright and sunny, without even the slightest shred of humidity. Liz strolled across the green manicured lawn of the Flagler Museum, exulting in being out of the house for the first extended period since she'd arrived. How beautiful Palm Beach was! How marvelously lush and green and balmy. And how marvelous was her tour guide: her husband's handsome, charming brother, Roger. Liz felt as if she were a bird, freed at last from its cage—and she was enormously grateful to her liberator.

"This beautiful mansion," Roger was telling her, "was given by Henry Flagler, one of the founders of Standard Oil, to his wife as a wedding present."

Liz gazed upon the tall white columns that fronted the mansion. "Was she happy here? His wife?"

Roger shrugged. "That much I don't know. But who wouldn't be happy in a place like this?"

Liz looked again at the mansion glittering in the sunlight, the tall palm trees swaying gently around it, the bright red bougainvillea popping out everywhere.

"Oh, I don't know," she said. "One can be unhappy even in the most beautiful of places."

Roger smiled kindly at her. "I know what you're thinking. You're thinking of another young wife given a mansion to live in when she married a rich man. A wife named Liz."

She smirked. "How'd you guess?"

"Liz, you will be happy in Huntington House. I promise you. Once David comes home, everything will be different."

How kind his eyes were. Roger looked so much like David, but the kindness . . . that was different. Had Liz ever seen kindness in David's eyes? She thought she had, when they'd first met on the ship. But maybe all she'd seen then was grief—his terrible sadness over losing Dominique—and she'd mistaken that vulnerability for compassion. Because the David she'd been speaking with on the phone—indeed, the David her husband had become the moment they arrived at Huntington House—had shown not a smattering of kindness or compassion. All he'd demonstrated to Liz was impatience and annoyance.

Roger had come for dinner the previous night. How they'd laughed. For the first time since she'd come to that house, Liz had laughed out loud and easily. Roger told her tales of his boyhood—when he was constantly showing up to elegant, snooty parties thrown by his parents dressed in T-shirts and flip-flops. David, of course, had obediently worn the requisite suit and tie, but Roger—the bohemian, the artist—was always dropping canapés on the dresses of society ladies and winking at their daughters.

Then he started in on the stories of setting up his art gallery, and how he outraged Palm Beach society with his irreverent exhibitions of art from the inner cities. Once he hosted a performance artist who got naked on-stage and covered herself in chocolate and invited patrons to lick it off her. The police had closed down the show after complaints that it was obscene. Roger had fought the closing in the courts and won. "I'm always upsetting apple carts," he told Liz, and she had spied the way Mrs. Hoffman had pursed her lips when she overheard the remark. Mrs. Hoffman, Liz realized, didn't like Roger. That made Liz like him all the more.

He'd insisted that Liz finally get a tour of her new city, and he told her he'd be back to pick her up in the morning. He arrived bright and early, and Liz was ready for him. They'd sped all over town in Roger's black Porsche Carrera, the top removed, the wind in her hair. Liz had loved everything she'd seen. The white, sandy beaches and the crashing blue surf. The tall silver buildings glistening in the sun. The trendy shops along the palm-shaded downtown streets. The fabulous Mar-A-Lago, once the home of Marjorie Merriweather Post. And finally the Beaux-Arts architecture and exquisite furnishings of the Flagler Museum.

"Come here," Roger said suddenly, grabbing Liz's hand and tugging her away from the mansion. "Over here—look at this! One of my favorite things in all of Palm Beach."

Not far away stood an enormous, strange, and beautiful tree covered in white flowers. It looked like something out of a children's book, with its peculiar, twisting branches stretching into the sky. Behind it glittered the towers of the city. Liz was entranced.

"It's called a kapok tree," Roger told her. "It's one of the biggest specimens around."

Still holding her hand, he pulled her close to the tree, where they stood within the enclosure of one of its gargantuan roots, dwarfed against its trunk.

"This is magnificent," Liz said. "I've never seen anything like it."

Roger was looking into her eyes. "And I've never seen anything like you," he said. "Just getting you out of that house—wow, I can see the way your eyes suddenly sparkle!"

Liz blushed, glancing away.

From there it was on to the luscious Pan's Garden, where exotic flowers grew in clusters and bright orange butterflies danced around a statue of the god Pan playing a lute.

"It's so beautiful here," Liz gushed. "Everywhere we've been today—everything has been so beautiful." She laughed. "So much more color and style and fragrance than my hometown of Trenton, New Jersey."

"I'm sure there's beauty there, too," Roger said, as they strolled down a path lined with bright orange birds of paradise. "Especially if you come from there."

"Okay, mister, you can turn off the charm," Liz said, laughing some more. "I like you. You've won me over!"

"I'm glad, Liz, because I like you, too." He smiled over at her, and once again he looked so much like David. "I'm glad we're part of the same family now."

Liz nodded. She tried to say something, but the words didn't come. She wasn't sure just what to say.

"Ah," Roger was saying. "And here we come to my favorite part of the gardens."

They turned down a quiet path overhung in places with bougainvillea, bright red against the sharp blue sky. Roger gently placed his hand on Liz's shoulder.

That was when she caught the fragrance.

Gardenias.

She saw the flowers then, growing on bushes along the sides of the path, delicate white blossoms amid the deep, emerald green leaves. The scent was almost overpowering.

Liz stopped walking.

"What's the matter?" Roger asked her.

She looked at him. She couldn't bring herself to say what she was thinking, but finally she saw understanding flicker across his face.

"The gardenias," he said. "Oh, I'm sorry, Liz . . . I didn't think . . ."

"It's all right," she said. "It just brought me back to the house, that's all. Made me think about that place after forgetting about it all day."

"Look," Roger said, "let's take another path . . ."

"No, that's crazy. I can't run away from a scent! Gardenias are beautiful and they smell so wonderful . . . almost otherworldly in their sweet fragrance. Let's keep going, Roger."

"That's the girl."

"Really," Liz said as they resumed their walk. "I'm over all that silly nonsense. I had a good talk with Variola yesterday."

"Oh, really? The chef?"

"Yes. She's a very kind woman. I think we'll be friends."

Roger smiled at her. "Well, I'm delighted. I guess I

never thought Variola was the type to be . . . all that welcoming."

"She was very happy to include you for dinner last night," Liz pointed out.

"You're right. She was." He smiled again. "What did the two of you talk about?"

"I confided in her some of my silly ideas. Did you know some of the servants talk about ghosts and witches?"

Roger nodded. "Oh, they always have. Dominique encouraged such talk. And so does Variola, I must admit. But you couldn't really have been thinking that there was something supernatural going on at the house?"

"Oh, I let myself get freaked out about silly things. Like the fragrance of gardenias and the occasional sound of footsteps when no one was around. They sounded like they were coming from inside the walls."

"Sounds like something out of *Jane Eyre*."

"And then Dominque's portrait . . . the way the thunder had clapped just as Thad tried to take it down and then the way he had fallen, almost as if she hadn't wanted him to do it." Liz laughed. "A hyperactive imagination, I guess I could say I had."

"No wonder your imagination got the better of you, Liz. The two deaths of Audra and Jamison would have unnerved anyone who'd just showed up to live in a new place."

Liz was nodding. "But it wasn't only that. Variola told me some other things that helped me, too."

"Like what?"

"Like that Dominique wasn't always such a wonderful person, and that I was just as good as she was, and I shouldn't ever compare myself to her."

Roger smiled. He stopped walking and took both of Liz's hands in hers. "Didn't I tell you the same thing?"

"Yes. Yes, you did, Roger."

"I told you that David wouldn't want you to be like Dominique, that he would want you to be just the way you are."

"Do you really believe that? He's seemed so impatient with me on the phone whenever I've spoken to him."

Roger lifted Liz's left hand to his lips and kissed it. "Sweet Liz. My brother can be a boor sometimes."

"Until he comes back," Liz said, "I'm just so confused. I worry sometimes . . ."

"What do you worry about?"

"That I married him too quickly. It was impulsive. We barely knew each other. My mother was not happy at all. And I gave up so much . . ."

"Like what?" Roger asked, genuinely interested.

"My career. I was really hoping that once the cruise was over, I could start auditioning for musical productions. I wanted to be a choreographer. It was a dream I've had most of my life."

"You don't have to give up your dreams just because you're married."

"You're right. But David was so . . . oh, I don't know, so *eager* that I come here, and live here, and be part of Palm Beach society as the mistress of Huntington House." She said the words rather pompously for comic effect.

"Once he gets back, you need to talk to him about all that."

"That's just it. Without David here . . . I'm not sure

what our life is going to be like together. I just can't picture it."

Roger let go of her hands. "David's always been a klutz when it comes to knowing how to treat a woman. He was a fool to leave you so soon after you arrived here. If there's anything David needs to learn it's that sometimes—no, not sometimes, *most* of the time— business must come second to relationships."

"I hope he does learn that," Liz said.

Roger touched her cheek. "I hope he does, too."

There was a second when they held each other's eyes. And then, from out of nowhere, a sudden black cloud appeared in the sky over them, raining down a mist on their cheeks. They had only time to look up and spot the unexpected storm before the downpour came. In seconds they were both soaking wet.

Liz shrieked. Roger whipped off his blue blazer and held it over their heads.

"Let's make a run for the car," he shouted. "Welcome to Florida! You never know when a rainstorm might blow in!"

They ran down the path that had been turned into a river. Despite being drenched, Liz didn't mind the rain. It was warm and felt surprisingly refreshing. Liz and Roger laughed as they hopscotched through the puddles, and when Roger slipped and felt into a bed of calla lilies, they couldn't contain their hysterics. They tumbled into Roger's Porsche wet and muddy but laughing so hard tears were coming down their cheeks.

"My gallery's nearby," Roger said as he started up the car.

The rain was coming so fast and furious the Porsche's

windshield wipers could barely keep up with it. Liz's hair was dripping down in front of her eyes, and her clothes were so drenched that every move she made brought forth a sloshing sound. That only made her giggle harder. Roger called them "a couple of creatures from the black lagoon."

They pulled up in front of the gallery. They hopped out of the car and made a mad dash for the entrance. As they tumbled through the front door, a young man at a desk looked up in surprise at them. "Karl," Roger called. "Bring us some towels from the back room."

The young man hurried off to comply with his employer's order. Within moments he had returned, and Liz was drying her hair with a fluffy white terrycloth towel.

"Come on inside," Roger was saying to her. "Karl, do we have coffee brewing?"

"Yes, sir," the young man replied.

It was only at that point, as Liz made her way following Roger across the room, that she really got a look at the art that was hanging on the gallery's walls. And what she saw nearly stopped her in her tracks.

The paintings were strange, to say the least. One was of an armless woman with a mouth open as if in a scream, standing against a bloodred background. Another was an enormous eye, filling the entire canvas. Others were of dark figures marching across bleak, gray terrain, dressed in black hoods so the viewer couldn't see their faces. Still other painting displayed hands growing out of the earth as if they were ferns.

Roger noticed Liz looking. "Not my work," he said, as if sensing her unease. "I'm showing an artist from

New York. She's very good, but rather disturbing some-times."

"I'd agree with the disturbing part."

"Karl and I just hung her show. She's all the rage in the art world. Her name's Naomi Collins. Her show has its official opening next week, and she's coming down from New York to be here for it. I hope you'll come."

A painting of a decapitated head on a platter caused Liz to look away.

"Here we are," Roger said. "Some hot coffee."

They sat in a small lounge off the main gallery. Liz cupped the hot mug in her hands and drank. At the same time, she kicked off her wet shoes to let them dry.

"I enjoyed our time today," Roger said, looking over at her.

Liz smiled. "As did I. I needed to get out of that house. Thank you, Roger."

"You know, Liz," Roger said, "when I'm with you, I . . ."

His words trailed off. Liz looked at him, waiting for him to continue.

But Roger said nothing more. He blushed suddenly, looking away. And then he was saved by his assistant popping his head through the door of the lounge.

"Mr. Huntington, you have a visitor."

"Who is it, Karl?"

"Mrs. Delacorte."

"Oh!" Roger stood quickly, setting down his coffee. "Bring her back, of course." As Karl hurried away, Roger turned to Liz. "Mrs. Delacorte is one of the gal-lery's biggest patrons. One of the richest women in Palm Beach."

"Oh, I see," Liz said, standing herself now. "Should I make myself scarce?"

"Not at all. She'll want to meet David's new wife."

Liz suddenly felt mortified. She was still drenched, her hair a mess. She was about to ask Roger to let her run to the ladies' room and try to freshen herself up, but before she had a chance Karl had returned with a tall, plump lady. She had iron-gray hair and wore a long strand of knotted pearls hanging over her ample bosom. Whether Liz liked it or not, she was about to have her first interaction with Palm Beach society.

"Roger, darling!" Mrs. Delacorte trilled, air-kissing either side of his face, fat fingers crusted with rings gripping his shoulders like talons.

"Mrs. Delacorte, how nice to see you," he said.

Liz saw the woman's large blue eyes latch on to her.

"Allow me to introduce my sister-in-law, Liz," Roger said, gesturing for Liz to join him in greeting the woman.

Liz extended her hand. "I'm pleased to meet you. Please excuse us . . . we just got caught in the rainstorm . . ."

Mrs. Delacorte took her hand but quickly moved her eyes back to Roger. "This is David's wife?" she asked him.

"Yes. They've only been married a short time."

Mrs. Delacorte looked back at Liz, but continued addressing Roger. "But where is your brother? Word around town is that he brought her to the house and then took off again."

"That's right," Liz said, refusing to stay silent and let Roger answer for her. "It was unavoidable. Business. He's in Amsterdam at the moment, but I expect him back very soon."

Mrs. Delacorte deigned to address her directly. "And where do you come from, dear?"

"New Jersey," Liz replied.

Mrs. Delacorte lifted an eyebrow. Liz felt for certain she could see the little house on the working-class street in Trenton where she had grown up.

"Mrs. Delacorte," Roger said, cutting in, possibly aware of Liz's discomfort, "did I understand your message correctly that you wished to buy one of the Naomi Collins pieces before the opening party?"

"You most certainly did," the large woman told him, turning her gaze away from Liz. "I'm not going to get into any kind of bidding war with Amanda Merriwell."

Liz assumed that was another of Palm Beach's great ladies.

"Well, normally I prefer to wait until—"

Liz noticed how Roger's voice cut off the moment Mrs. Delacorte raised her other eyebrow.

"But of course, for you, I'll make an exception," Roger said. "Which image do you want?"

"Which is the most expensive?"

He hesitated. "The armless woman, I believe. It's thirty-five thousand dollars."

Liz almost fell over when she heard the price.

"Then that's the one," Mrs. Delacorte said, taking a seat and pouring herself a cup of coffee. "Will you get all the paperwork completed so I can have it with me at the opening? Just in case Amanda Merriwell gets any ideas."

"Absolutely," Roger said. He looked over at Liz. "I'm just going to head to my office and get some forms . . ."

"Of course," she told him, taking her seat again, this time beside Mrs. Delacorte.

"Pretty grisly stuff, don't you think?" the lady was saying.

"You mean the paintings?"

"I don't mean the wallpaper," Mrs. Delacorte said, taking a sip of coffee, "though that could use some sprucing up, too."

"I understand Naomi Collins is highly regarded in her field," Liz said, playing as diplomatic as she could.

"Yes, she certainly is, and that's why I must own a piece of hers." Mrs. Delacorte smiled. Her thin lips were outlined in a lipstick that looked almost orange. "I can't imagine where I'll hang it, but I want it. You know all the other ladies in town will want one, too."

"Then Ms. Collins's show here will be quite the success," Liz said.

"Any show here is a success. Any artist Roger takes under his wing becomes rich and famous. He's *brilliant* at spotting talent." She smiled. "And of course, he does pretty well himself. It's about a fifty-fifty cut between artist and gallery, you know."

"I wasn't aware of the percentage," Liz replied.

Mrs. Delacorte stared off, not looking at Liz. "It's funny, you know, how successful Roger has become. He was always the wanderer, the ne'er-do-well in the family. Practically the black sheep." Her blue eyes found Liz again. "Your David, on the other hand, was always the achiever. He was always putting Roger to shame. His parents despaired of Roger, always pointing to the shining example of David."

Liz didn't know quite what to say. She just looked

out into the hallway, hoping Roger would come back soon.

"And then, all of a sudden, Roger's fortunes changed. He settled down, purchased this gallery, and the rest is history. Now every emerging artist begs to be shown at the Roger Huntington Gallery. Roger can make or break a career. He's in all the art journals. It's been quite amazing, the success and respect this little art gallery has brought him."

"Well, I'm pleased to hear that."

"Are you?" That eyebrow shot up again. "I'm surprised that David's wife would be wishing Roger well." She sniffed. "I'm surprised David's new wife would be here in Roger's gallery at all."

"Why is that? He's my brother-in-law."

"Maybe you're too new to the family to know that the two brothers haven't always seen eye to eye."

Liz stiffened. "I'm not sure I should be discussing family matters."

Mrs. Delacorte smiled. "You say David is returning soon? We must have a party, welcoming you to Palm Beach. It's been ages since I've seen David. Not since that terrible business with the family yacht . . ." She seemed to appraise Liz. "How interesting that you're not like Dominique in the least bit."

Liz's defenses flared up. No, she thought. *I'm not as polished or as sophisticated as Dominque. I won't fit in with your snooty society parties the way she did.* But before Liz had a chance to respond, Roger had returned, paperwork in hand, and placed it on the table beside Mrs. Delacorte to sign. Karl was with him, standing beside his boss with a ready pen.

"Liz, it's going to take me a while with Mrs. Delacorte," Roger whispered, taking Liz aside.

"That's all right. I should be getting back to the house anyway."

"If you can wait half an hour, I can drive you . . ."

"No, I'm just going to call a cab," Liz said, taking out her cell phone.

"Oh, no, please let me drive you . . ."

She smiled. "There's no need. You've done so much for me today already. Thank you for everything, Roger."

"Are you sure?"

"Positively. Go back to Mrs. Delacorte." She smiled. "I can see she's a handful."

He returned the smile. "You'll come to the opening?"

She sighed. "All right. I'll be here."

Roger beamed. He kissed her on the forehead.

Liz headed out of the gallery, avoiding any further glances at the bizarre artwork on the walls. How she'd get through an entire opening party, walking around all night looking at that stuff, she wasn't sure. But she owed it to Roger.

She also wanted to show Palm Beach that there was harmony in the Huntington family.

If there had ever been bad blood between the two brothers, that was in the past. Liz would insist on that when David came home.

She needed Roger in her life.

Without him, she didn't think she'd last long at Huntington House.

27

The next morning, Liz awoke with a terrible cold. Her head throbbed, her nose was stuffed, and her throat felt as if someone had taken a knife to it. She blamed it on being caught in the rain and getting soaked to the bone the day before. Picking up the phone beside her bed, she rang the kitchen, asking Variola to send her up a pot of hot tea.

A short while later came a soft rapping at her door.

"Come in," Liz rasped.

But instead of Variola or one of the maids, Liz saw it was Thad carrying in the tray of tea. "I'm sorry, ma'am," he said, "but no one else was around . . ."

"Oh, thank you, Thad," Liz said. "My throat is killing me."

Thad looked terribly worried about her. He set the tray beside the bed and poured her some tea. Steam rose from the cup like an Indian smoke signal. Liz accepted the tea gratefully and took a tiny sip.

"What do you think ails you, ma'am?" Thad asked.

"I guess I caught a cold yesterday," Liz replied. "I got caught in a rainstorm."

"Awfully quick for a cold to set in, if that's the case," Thad grumbled. "Drink your tea, ma'am. I hope it makes you feel better."

Something seemed to be troubling Thad; Liz wasn't sure what it was. She gave him a smile as he left the room. She supposed it *was* a rather a fast onset if her cold indeed grew out of her rainstorm adventure yesterday, but no matter how she'd caught it, she was really suffering today. She sipped her tea again. It soothed her throat a little bit. She lay back against her pillows, closing her eyes, hoping the pounding in her head subsided.

She must have fallen asleep, for suddenly she opened her eyes. The light in the room was different, and the cold hard face of Mrs. Hoffman was looming over her.

"I'm terribly sorry to have to wake you, Mrs. Huntington," the housekeeper was saying. "But Detective Foley is downstairs, wishing to see you."

Liz tried to shake off the sleep and gather her wits. "Detective . . . Foley?"

"Yes, ma'am. I told him you weren't feeling well, but he asked that I inquire if you could just spare him ten minutes."

"Yes," Liz managed to say. Her throat was still sore, but her headache was gone. "I'll put on a robe and come downstairs."

"Very well," Mrs. Hoffman said, striding out of the room.

Liz stood, feeling a bit dizzy. Steadying herself against one of the posters of the canopy bed, she slipped into a large flannel robe. Despite the sun streaming in through the windows and the warm temperature of the room, Liz felt cold, and she took some comfort inside the flannel. She glanced at herself in the mirror and shuddered. She had no strength to make herself look more presentable to Detective Foley, but neither did she want to send him away. Perhaps he had more information about the deaths of Audra and Jamison. And if so, Liz wanted to hear what he had discovered.

Heading down the stairs, she passed the portrait of Dominique that dominated the landing, those great dark eyes staring down at her. Liz looked away, shivering under her robe.

Waiting for her at the bottom of the stairs was Variola, holding a steaming mug on a tray.

"More tea for me?" Liz asked.

Variola shook her head. "Not tea, ma'am. This is better. Variola's concoction for what ails you."

Liz caught a whiff of the strong brew. A mix of coffee and spices, she thought. But also something else. Something bitter.

"Drink it, ma'am," Variola told her. "It will make you better."

Liz smiled. "More island witchcraft, I presume."

"Indeed, ma'am. Brewed up by Variola in her cauldron."

Liz lifted the mug by its handle and took a sip. It tasted like nothing she'd ever tasted before. Not coffee. Not even very spicy. But also not unpleasant. Thick, rich.

"Thank you, Variola," Liz said.

"There is a man waiting for you in the parlor," the chef told her.

Liz nodded. "Yes, I know. Detective Foley."

"Drink, ma'am. It will make you strong."

Liz clutched the mug with both hands as she entered the parlor. The police detective was seated on the divan, looking idly around the room. He stood when Liz entered.

"Detective Foley," she said.

"I'm sorry to rouse you when you're not feeling well," he told her.

"It's just a cold. How can I help you? Have you discovered anything new?"

She took a seat on the opposite divan. Foley sat back down.

"Nothing really new, Mrs. Huntington, I'm sorry to report. But I've been going over the reports with a fine-tooth comb. I wonder if I could ask you about a couple of other things."

Liz took another sip of Variola's elixir. "By all means. Go ahead."

"Do the names Jeanette Kelly or Tonesha Lewis mean anything to you?"

"No. Who are they?"

"Friends of Audra McKenzie." Foley paused for the slightest moment. "Friends who went missing in the weeks after her murder."

"Do you think there's a connection?"

"I have no idea." Again that slight pause. "But I've learned to trust my hunches."

"Did either of them have any connection to Huntington House?"

Foley shook his head. "I interviewed Mrs. Hoffman before you came down. She didn't recognize the names either. She said neither had ever worked here or, to her knowledge, ever been to Huntington House, though she couldn't say if either had ever visited Audra at any point while she was employed here."

Liz clutched the mug in her hands, seeming to draw strength from it, just as Variola had promised. "They might still be alive."

"They might be. But their families have had no contact from them in months."

"That's terrible."

"I only made the connection when I was going over our investigations of Audra's murder. I saw that we had interviewed Tonesha, who had spoken with Audra earlier on the night she was killed. The name sounded a bell for me, and sure enough, I had received a notice of a missing person with the same name from neighboring Broward County."

"It seems too obvious to just be coincidental."

"Perhaps."

"But Detective Foley, you see, I've only been here a short time, as I've told you. I didn't know Audra. You're going to have to speak to my husband when he gets back—"

"I understand that, Mrs. Huntington. But it's the very fact of your newness here that makes me want to speak with you."

"I don't understand."

"Since arriving here, has anything seemed—oh, I don't know, curious? Strange? Has anyone seemed as if they might be keeping secrets from you?"

Liz was flabbergasted. How could she respond? Yes, indeed, all of that was true. But could she admit it all to a police officer? What would David think?

"Why . . . why do you ask?" was all Liz could manage to say.

"What do you know of your husband's first wife's death?"

"It was an accident. It had nothing to do with—"

"What do you know about the accident?"

"Just that it was on the yacht, and that she drowned . . ."

"Who was with her on the yacht?"

"I don't know . . . I believe she was alone."

"Are you sure? Was your husband with her when the accident occurred?"

"No! I mean, I'm only going by what I've been told."

"What *have* they told you about the accident?"

"Very little, actually." Liz thought better of his question. "Who do you mean by 'they'?"

"Any of them here. Mrs. Hoffman. Your husband."

Liz stiffened, her hands tightening around the mug. "I don't think I should talk to you anymore until David has returned."

"If that's what you wish," said Detective Foley.

Liz felt a strange sort of panic growing in her stomach. "Surely, you can't think that Dominique's accident was in any way connected to the killings of Audra and Jamison?"

"My job is to ask questions, Mrs. Huntington."

"But it was an accident! Mrs. Hoffman said that the

doorbell rang and there was a Coast Guard officer at the door, telling her there'd been an accident."

"And where was your husband at the time?"

"I . . . I don't know."

"He's never spoken about where he was when he learned of his wife's death?"

Liz felt foolish. "No. He hasn't." She began to tremble. "He doesn't like to speak of it. And I've never pressed him."

Foley looked skeptical. "He's never told you about the inquest that followed her death, or about his testimony?"

Liz shook her head. "As I said, Detective, I don't think I should talk to you anymore until David is home."

"All right." He stood. "Well, I hope you're feeling better soon, Mrs. Huntington."

Liz stood as well. "Actually," she said, "I'm feeling much better."

It was true. Her sore throat was gone. Her nose was no longer stuffed. She felt fine.

She looked down at Variola's potion in her hands. What was in it?

Liz walked Detective Foley to the front door. "You understand that I'm only trying to get to the bottom of these cases," he said to her. "I'm not accusing or suspecting anyone at this point."

"I understand," she said. "You're only doing your job."

He smiled at her.

Once he was gone, Liz turned. Mrs. Hoffman was standing across the foyer, staring at her, rock still. Liz stared right back. Neither woman said a word, and neither moved from their places for several moments. Their eyes burned holes into each other. Then Liz made her way across the room, climbing silently up the stairs, still clutching Variola's mug in her hands.

28

"She's trying to kill her," Thad said.

Mrs. Hoffman turned around to glare at him.

"Who's trying to kill whom?" the housekeeper asked him in a cold, bored monotone.

"Dominique. Trying to kill that poor girl."

Mrs. Hoffman gave him that expression that passed for a smile on her plastic face. "Dominique is dead."

"That don't matter. She's still here, and you know it."

"You've been spending too much time with Variola, talking about spirits."

She tried to walk past him, but Thad grabbed her arm, stopping her.

"How dare you!" Mrs. Hoffman hissed. "Let me go."

"I know too much—I've seen too much—for you to just dismiss me. And I'm not going to let anything happen to that poor girl. Enough is enough."

"Let me go," Mrs. Hoffman said again, in a low and furious voice.

Thad complied. "You'll see. I'm going to drive Dominique's spirit from this house. I'm going to find a way. I'm not going to let her kill again!"

29

The sun was setting, a big wet canvas of red and gold, as Joe Foley drove Aggie McFarland home to her husband and kids. Palm trees were silhouetted against the sky and long blue shadows were filling up the streets.

"I'm not sure where you're going with this line of investigation," Aggie was saying to him as she flipped through the reports on her lap.

Foley stopped at a red light. "You don't think two of Audra's friends going missing not long after her murder is suspicious?"

"Sure it is, but what does it make us suspect? That they were killed by the same person, only we haven't found their bodies yet?"

"Possibly."

"But they didn't even live in Palm Beach at the time of their disappearances. Look, Joe, all three girls lived rather fast lives. They were all involved in drugs to some degree."

"So maybe there's no connection." The light changed and he started to drive again. "But maybe there is. You know me and my hunches."

Sometimes Joe just knew things were true. Like that horrible day he knew his mother was dead in her tent, and not just sleeping late.

"I agree we need to look into both cases," said Aggie, "but I just caution you against making any quick assumptions."

"Caution well taken," he said.

"But what I really don't get," Aggie continued, "is this inquiry into the drowning death of the first Mrs. Huntington. There was an inquest at the time. Her death was ruled an accident."

"Without any body ever being found."

"When someone falls off a yacht that far out to sea in shark-infested waters, it's rare that a body ever is."

"True." Foley turned to look at her. "But read the captain's statement."

Aggie flipped through some pages, then found what she was looking for.

"Do you see what I mean?" Foley asked.

His partner just looked at him.

"This isn't going to go over well with the chief," she finally said.

Foley pulled into Aggie's driveway. The front porch light came on. A couple of kids appeared at the door.

"I can deal with the chief," Foley said.

Aggie tossed the reports at him. "Thanks for making our lives even more difficult," she said, getting out of the car.

"See you in the morning," Foley said.

Aggie just made a face. Foley watched her as she went inside, kissing the kids on the tops of their heads. He could smell pot roast cooking from the open front door.

He placed the reports on the empty seat beside him. He'd go home, pop a Lean Cuisine into the microwave, and look the reports over again to see what he could figure out.

He would crack this oyster. He vowed on his mother's grave that he would do it.

30

"This is quite possibly the most delicious dessert I have ever tasted," Roger enthused, spooning another helping of Variola's pudding into his mouth.

"I agree," Liz said. "What is in it? Mango, for sure. Cinnamon . . . what else?"

"Who knows? Whatever it is, it's magnificent!"

They were sitting out by the pool, the sun on their faces, the sound of the gushing waterfall in their ears. Liz was feeling perfectly content and happy, something a week ago she could never have dreamed she'd be feeling in this house.

"She did tell me it was packed with herbs to keep that cold from coming back," Liz told Roger. "She said it was the healthiest dessert ever made!"

"If only everything healthy tasted this good," Roger replied, laughing. "Usually healthy crap tastes like cardboard and dead leaves."

Liz laughed, licking her spoon. Variola's pudding had the consistency of yogurt but none of the bitterness. She'd slivered almonds on the top and sprinkled it with cinnamon. "Eat this," the chef had told her, "and you will stay strong and healthy."

"What do you say we take a walk?" Liz suddenly asked, standing. "I've yet to really explore the grounds here, except for a couple of pass-throughs. It's such a beautiful day. Let's see what kind of backyard I've married into!"

Roger smiled. "David certainly pays enough for its upkeep. We might as well enjoy it."

They wandered off along a path that wound through the gardens. Enormous red hibiscus grew on either side, accented by tall spiky yellow flowers that Liz couldn't name.

"I expect it does cost a great deal to keep these gardens maintained," she mused. "I have no idea about the finances, or what it takes to run Huntington House. David's never shared any of that with me, and I've never thought to ask."

"Money is a boring topic."

"Yes, but I should know, shouldn't I? If I'm going to be expected to plan parties and things like that . . ."

"I'm sure you'll learn everything you need to know."

She paused to admire a garden of orchids. "So beautiful," Liz said. "Sometimes, I still can't believe how my life has changed . . ."

"Is it really so different from before?"

Liz laughed. "Only like the difference between night and day. Roger, I grew up very middle class. The only landscaping we had to do to our yard was mow it twice a month."

"Well, you have gardeners now to take care of that."

"That's what I'm talking about. I married David so

quickly . . . and now I find myself in a world that seems so beautiful and yet . . . so intimidating."

They stopped walking, and Roger took her hands in his. "There's no need to feel intimidated. You are going to be fine here."

"Because of you, I've started to believe that," Liz replied. "Thank you."

The held each other's eyes for several seconds. Liz finally looked away.

"Have you heard from David?" Roger asked as they resumed their walk.

Liz shook her head. "No. I've tried calling, emailing . . . nothing."

"When he gets wrapped up in business . . ."

"Don't make excuses for him. I've decided that if we are going to make this work, he and I are going to need to have a very honest conversation when he gets back."

"That's probably smart."

"He can't just go off like this anymore with only the occasional contact. Maybe his first wife allowed it. Maybe it didn't bother her. But I'm not okay with it."

"Oh, I think it bothered Dominique as well. She just . . . found other distractions."

"What do you mean, other distractions?"

"Well, she became so . . . involved in her causes, you know."

"What causes?"

He shrugged. "Various clubs."

Liz sighed. "I don't see myself ever being a Palm Beach club lady."

"No. I don't see you that way either."

"Anyway, David and I are going to have to come to some terms. I'm trying to remember the warm, caring David I knew when we met on the ship, and the man who was so sweet, so considerate, all during our honeymoon. It was really such a magical time. He was so kind, so interested in everything I thought and felt . . . I have to believe that David is still there."

Roger gave her a small smile. "There are many sides to David."

Liz was about to reply when she caught sight of something up ahead on the path. "Are those statues?" she asked.

"Yes. A sculpture garden. David bought most of the pieces from my gallery. Well, Dominique bought them, but it was David's money."

Liz was walking faster. "Is that an angel up front?"

"Yes," Roger was saying, and he sounded a little embarrassed or uncomfortable. "It's a sort of angel, I guess."

He hung back, walking more slowly as Liz hurried toward the sculpture garden. What struck her first about the angel was that its wings were black, despite the rest of the piece appearing to be white marble. But as she got closer she let out a little gasp as she discerned the sculpture's head.

It wasn't like any angel she had ever seen before.

It had the head of a cow.

"What the heck?" Liz asked, standing in front of it, looking up into the cow's flared nostrils.

Roger still stood a few feet away, almost as if he didn't want to come any closer. "I knew you were going to find it bizarre. I saw how you reacted to Naomi Collins's pieces at the gallery. You're going to think the only art I feature is strange and twisted."

Liz laughed. "Everyone's got to have an angle, right?"

She made her way into the sculpture garden alone.

"And I guess 'strange and twisted' does describe these things," she said, getting a look at the other pieces standing on pedestals.

Some of the sculptures seemed innocuous enough to Liz's eyes: a plain copper triangle; a six-pointed star made out of metal; a white marble obelisk that looked like a miniature Washington Monument. But others were just as weird as the cow angel. A porcelain little girl with three eyes, hands raised to the sky. A dog with two heads. A hand reaching up from a box.

"Dominique picked these out?" Liz asked. "And David actually paid for them?"

Roger didn't answer right away.

Liz had approached the porcelain little girl, inspecting her three eyes up close. No pupils had been etched into the porcelain. The eyes looked blank.

"Do these have some sort of meaning?" Liz asked Roger. "I mean, is there some sort of symbolism I just don't get?"

Again Roger didn't answer. Liz looked up. She didn't see him.

"It's okay," she said. "I'm not judging you or your gallery. I've never understood art, especially abstract art. I guess I'm just a Thomas Kinkade sort of girl. Norman Rockwell. I like art that is easy to understand."

Still no reply.

"Roger?"

Liz turned, wondering where he had gone. As she

did so, she noticed movement between two of the sculptures a few feet away from her.

"Roger?" she called.

Had he just run between the obelisk and the two-headed dog?

Someone had. There was someone standing there.

"Roger?"

Liz approached.

"Roger, why don't you answer me?"

Suddenly, the person hiding behind the sculpture leapt out at her, maybe a foot and a half away from her.

And it wasn't Roger.

It was a woman. She had long, cascading gray hair and was wearing a white robe. And her face—it was the most hideous thing Liz had ever seen. Twisted, broken, burned. It was almost as if there was no face at all surrounded by all that hair—just a pulpy purple mass with two black holes for eyes.

Liz screamed.

"Liz!"

In her terror she could hear Roger's voice behind her. She turned and ran—and not knowing where she was running, suddenly collided with him. His arms wrapped around her.

"Liz, what is it?"

"That—woman!"

"I know these sculptures are weird, Liz, but you don't have to be scared of them."

"No! That woman! Over there!"

She pulled her face off Roger's chest and looked behind her.

"Where?" Roger was asking. "What woman?"

She was gone.

"She must have run away," Liz said, casting her eyes through the sculpture garden. There was no movement anywhere, only the occasional flutter of chirping birds in the trees.

"She frightened you terribly," Roger observed.

"Her face! Oh, Roger, her face! It was all . . . deformed!"

He looked at her oddly. "Are you certain you saw a woman, Liz?"

"Yes, of course I am. She was right in front of me. I saw her clearly, as plain as I'm seeing you right now."

"Because . . . I was approaching you at the moment you screamed. Your back was to me. And I saw no one."

"You had to have seen her. She was right there." Liz pointed to the spot beside the two-headed dog. "Right there! She jumped out at me."

"I believe you. I just didn't see her."

Liz looked from the spot up into Roger's eyes. "How could someone like that get on the property?"

"Well, that's just it. No one can get onto the estate. You've seen the gate out front. And the wall that surrounds the estate is pretty damn high."

"She must have climbed over. She looked mad, Roger. Not just deformed, but insane. Her eyes—it was if she had no eyes at all!"

He took her hands in his. "You do know you're sounding a little hysterical, don't you?"

"But I saw her!"

"I believe you."

"We need to tell Thad. Get somebody out here looking for her."

"Yes, of course." He sighed. "But Liz, you do realize you're sounding rather like . . . well, like the way you did when you were talking about witchcraft and ghosts."

Liz broke free of his hands. "You think I imagined it. You don't believe me at all."

"I believe that you believe you saw something. That you're convinced of it."

"She was standing right there!"

"I'm just saying . . ."

Liz let out a long breath. "Do you think I . . . do you think it's possible that I . . . imagined what I saw?"

"I don't know, but it's possible. You've been pretty on edge these last few weeks, living here in this house. And these sculptures . . . they can get anyone's imagination racing."

Liz covered her face in her hands. "It was so real. *She* was so real!"

"And maybe she was. We'll have Thad make a thorough search of the grounds. Point is, I just don't want you getting yourself all upset and anxious again."

"Right," Liz said, more to herself than to Roger. She lowered her hands. "I don't want to feel that way again. It was horrible, terrible. You brought me out of all that." She looked over at Roger. He smiled at her.

"Liz, you're an extraordinary woman," he said, drawing close to her. "I really hate seeing you in distress."

She managed to smile. "Now that you're here, I feel better."

He touched her chin with his thumb and forefinger.

And—before either seemed aware of what was happening—he kissed her.

For a second, Liz felt as if she were floating on air. Her head tingled. Every muscle in her body seemed electrified.

And then she pulled away.

"I—I am so sorry," Roger said.

"It's all right," Liz said, not looking at him.

"No, it's not. I—I shouldn't have done that! I didn't intend to—it just—it just happened!"

"I know," Liz said, finding the strength to look at him again. "It just happened to both of us. It was the intensity of the moment—and our connection these last few days."

"I'm sorry, Liz."

"It's all right." She tried to smile. "It was nice."

"That it was," Roger said.

"But it can never happen again," Liz added.

"Of course not," he agreed.

"Let's go inside. Have Thad check the property. If he doesn't find anyone, then I guess I imagined it. But I'm telling you, Roger, there could very well be some homeless woman out there who climbed over the fence . . ."

Even as she said the words, Liz glanced up at the wall that surrounded the estate. The nearly eight-foot-tall, solid stone wall . . .

". . . or got through the front gate somehow . . ."

"Of course," Roger said. "Let's go in and make the report."

Liz stopped. "Will you do it for me? I hate to ask but . . . well, Thad is already a rather superstitious sort . . .

he'll get talking about ghosts and I'll just get all worked up again."

Roger nodded. "Of course. I completely understand. I'll speak to Thad."

"Thank you."

They headed back inside. Overhead, in the trees, a green, black-hooded parakeet began to squawk, setting off a handful of others, until the entire property echoed in angry cries.

31

Rita felt the thing move from across the room.

She had left the vodou doll in her purse, which was strapped tightly closed and hung on a hook in the servants' lounge. But as soon as Rita walked into the room, she felt it move, as if she were holding it in her own hands.

She rushed over to her purse and opened it, looking down inside.

Sure enough, the doll was moving, writhing, its little arms reaching up toward her.

"David," Rita breathed, and she felt her heart leap.

The doll continued to rock back and forth.

"He's coming home!" Rita whispered to herself. "He's coming home!"

32

"Did you speak to Thad?" Liz asked Roger as he came in from outside.

She was standing anxiously at the window, looking out into the lush greenery, trying to convince herself that she'd hallucinated the whole thing. But what was worse? That some strange woman was prowling the grounds, or that she, Liz, was still so unstable as to imagine such a horrible thing?

"Yes," Roger assured her. "He said that he and some of the others would look over the whole estate."

"Then I'm just going to put it out of my mind for now," Liz said.

"That sounds like a good idea."

He stepped toward her. Liz felt a twinge of nervousness, remembering their kiss, and feared her hands might have been a little sweaty when Roger took them in his, a gesture that had always reassured Liz, up until now.

"I don't want to leave until I know you're okay," he said to her. "And that *we're* okay."

"I'm fine," Liz said, trying to sound convincing. "And so are we."

She looked into his eyes. His beautiful, kind, compassionate eyes.

"Good," Roger said. "You know you can call me whenever you need—"

"Well," came another voice, booming through the room and interrupting them, "she won't need to do that anymore."

They both turned.

David was standing in the doorway to the parlor, glaring at them. Immediately Liz and Roger let go of each other's hands.

"David!" Liz exclaimed.

He said nothing, just kept looking at them.

Liz rushed to him. "You're home! Why didn't you let me know?"

"I thought I would surprise you," he replied. "Apparently I have."

"Welcome home, brother," Roger said.

David didn't respond. He didn't even look at Roger. He kept his eyes on Liz.

"How long have you been here?" Liz asked, taking David's hands, aware that she was trembling.

"About half an hour. I went down to see my horses. Always the first thing I do when I come home." His eyes were burning accusation at her. "Then I hoped to find my wife waiting for me . . . happy to see what I had brought her."

"Brought me what, David?"

He gestured with his head back into the parlor. Liz peered past him and let out a little gasp.

The parlor was filled with flowers—roses mostly, white and red, accented with the occasional yellow daisy.

"I sent them on ahead, to arrive a few minutes before I did," David explained.

Liz wandered into the parlor, overwhelmed by the rich, sweet, musky fragrance of the roses. "Oh, David, how beautiful . . . why didn't Mrs. Hoffman come and get me?"

"Apparently she didn't know where you were," David said. "She said you were out on the estate somewhere."

"I was showing her the sculpture garden," Roger explained, coming up behind David. Liz saw the look that passed between the brothers.

For a moment, Liz considered telling David what she'd seen—or what she'd thought she saw—out there in the sculpture garden. But she knew she shouldn't. Not yet. Maybe not ever, if Thad's search of the property turned up empty.

"David," Liz said, taking her husband's hands again, "if I had known you were coming, I would have been here waiting to greet you at the front door!"

"You're all she's been talking about ever since you've been gone," Roger added.

David said nothing, just kept looking at Liz.

"The roses . . ." Liz lifted one to her nose and inhaled the scent. "David, they're so beautiful. Thank you."

"I'm going to leave you two alone," Roger said, smiling broadly. "Remember, you're still newlyweds. Three's a crowd, I think."

"David," Liz said, anxious to extinguish any suspicion that might be brewing in David's mind, "Roger's been very kind to me. He showed me around town, kept me company. He knew how lonely I was for you."

"Well, then," David said, finally addressing his brother, "I guess I owe you a great deal of thanks."

"No thanks necessary. It was my pleasure." Again Liz saw the look that shot between the two brothers, weighted with so much unspoken. "All I ask in return is that you both will be my guests at my upcoming gallery show. Liz has the details."

"We will make sure to be there," David told him, but his voice was cold, not warm.

"Excellent." Roger smiled again. "Now—the two of you need to spend some time reuniting. Please don't bother showing me out. I know the way."

"Yes, you do," David said, turning away from him.

"Thank you, Roger," Liz called after him. "For everything."

He gave them a little wave and then disappeared into the foyer. Not until she heard the front door open and close did Liz speak again.

"David, I'm so happy you're home."

"Are you?" He turned cold eyes to hers.

"Of course I am. Surely you're not thinking—"

"Surely I'm not." His expression softened. "Darling, my brother isn't to be trusted. He's always been a rebel in our family. A troublemaker."

"He was the perfect gentleman with me," Liz said, her eyes flickering away as she recalled their kiss.

"I'd prefer you not see him alone from now on," David said.

Liz felt a little electrical jolt of anger. She spoke carefully but firmly. "Look, David, I'm not a child. I'm your wife. An equal partner in this thing we call our marriage. You left me alone for weeks in a strange house and a strange town. He showed me some friendship, offered some companionship. I can't be told whom I can see and whom I cannot."

"Liz, I'm just telling you—he's a troublemaker—"

"I don't know what happened with Dominique." Liz surprised herself by how strong and confident she sounded. "I know she didn't like Roger, and he didn't like her. But now that you're back, David, it's time we got one thing straight." She paused. "I am not Dominique."

He looked at her as if she were mad. "I am well aware of that, Liz."

She allowed her voice to soften, but just a little. "I am very happy you're home, David, and a part of me just wants to run over there and jump up into your arms and go upstairs with you and make love all the rest of the day. But not until I have a chance to say what's been on my mind these last couple of weeks."

"Okay, go ahead."

"You were a real jerk to leave me so soon after we got here. You were an even worse jerk to get angry with me on the phone for being upset about being questioned in a murder investigation. And you were pretty jerky, too, in not telling me everything about what had happened in this house, and the stories about your dead wife."

"What stories?"

"That she practiced witchcraft and that her ghost still walks these halls."

David shook his head. "These damn servants . . ."

"Yes, maybe they are all a pack of superstitious gossipmongers, but that's precisely the reason you should have prepared me before you left."

He sat down on the couch quickly, as if he might suddenly have felt faint, nearly upsetting a spray of red roses on the table beside him. "I'm sorry, Liz," he said. "Truly I am."

"There's so much that I had to learn on my own," she said, standing over him. "For one, that Dominique was a vain, unpleasant woman who nobody but Mrs. Hoffman seems to have liked. I spent my first several days here convinced that everyone was judging me for not being as pretty or as a good or as accomplished as she was."

David just sighed and covered his face with his hands.

"You never told me about her death," Liz went on. "I had to hear from Detective Foley that there had been an inquest . . . and that you had to testify."

"Liz," David said from behind his hands. "Please stop."

"I'm sorry if this is painful, David. I really am. But we can't go on with so much unspoken between us. We're still practically strangers, you and I. If we're going to make a go of this marriage, we have got to start speaking honestly with each other. We have to be here for each other. We can't retreat. We can't hold back. We can't run away."

Her husband looked up at her. He looked as if he might cry.

"Oh, David," Liz said, suddenly overcome with sympathy for him. She sat down beside him, taking his hands in hers. "Don't be afraid to talk to me. I love you."

"I shouldn't have left you," he said weakly. "I've been so . . . caught up in proving myself to my father . . . that I put that ahead of what was best for you. And for us."

"Was that the only reason you went away, David?"

He looked off across the room. "I suppose . . . coming back here was harder than I thought."

"Did you love her that much, David? Or was it that you didn't love her at all?"

"I . . . Oh, Liz, please don't make me talk about it. Not yet. Not so soon after I've come home." He took her in his arms. "Please. Let's do what you suggested. Let's go upstairs and make love. There's time for talking later. For now, please, darling, let's be the newlyweds we are."

She held his gaze for several seconds before replying. "All right, David. But on one condition."

"What's that?"

"Tonight that portrait of Dominique in the stairwell comes down."

He hesitated only a second. "Of course, darling. It should have come down long ago."

What made them turn at the moment, Liz didn't know. There was no sound. No sense that anyone was in the room. But turn they did, both at the same time, to face the doorway into the foyer.

There stood Mrs. Hoffman, her plastic, expressionless face watching them.

"Mrs. Hoffman," David said, standing up. Liz thought he seemed afraid.

"Mr. Huntington," the housekeeper said. "Welcome home."

"Thank you." He looked down at Liz and grabbed her hand. "My wife and I don't want to be disturbed for a while. Will you have a couple of the boys bring my luggage up to my suite? It's still in the car outside."

"Of course," said Mrs. Hoffman.

David tugged at Liz's hand to follow him as he moved across the room. She complied.

"And afterward," David went on, just as they were passing Mrs. Hoffman in the doorway, "have them take down the portrait in the stairwell."

"Very well," Mrs. Hoffman said, not missing a beat, her eyes not making contact with Liz's. "And where shall we store it?"

"You can burn it for all I care," David said.

Liz saw the flicker of outrage in the housekeeper's eyes, but it lasted just a second. Then Mrs. Hoffman turned and headed down the hallway.

Liz and David started up the stairs.

"You know what I think, darling?" David asked as they passed Dominique's portrait, Liz looking at her predecessor's big dark eyes for the last time. "I think we should throw a dinner party."

"A dinner party?"

"Yes," he said. "It's time everyone sees that you are my wife now."

"Who would we invite?"

"All the Palm Beach ladies who are so eager to get a look at you."

Liz smiled. "I met Mrs. Delacorte at Roger's gallery."

"Oh, definitely Mrs. Delacorte, but all of them. Mrs. Clayton. Mrs. Merriwell." He smiled at her. "We'll even invite Roger and my parents."

Liz felt a moment of apprehension. "Whatever you think, David."

"I think it's a grand idea." They had reached the top of the stairs. "It's time everyone saw just how happy we are."

He kissed her, hard, hurting her lips. Liz felt how

strong her husband was, how powerful his arms were wrapped around her. He could snap her in two, she realized, like a twig.

Then he led her down the hall and into their bedroom, locking the door behind them. They made love, three times in a row, for the next six hours straight.

33

"Mr. Huntington, if I could just have a few minutes of your time . . ."

Detective Joe Foley saw the look Roger Huntington exchanged with his assistant when he came through the front door of his gallery. The young man—he'd said his name was Karl—shrunk back against the glare of his employer. Roger seemed extremely perturbed that Karl had allowed the detective to wait here for him. The assistant sat there with a remorseful look.

"Detective," Roger said, turning his attention to Foley, "I'm preparing for an opening here in a few days . . . I'm incredibly busy."

"I promise it will only take a few minutes," Foley replied.

"I don't have a few minutes."

"It would really help me in the investigation I'm doing."

"Oh, all right," Roger said, sighing and giving in. "Karl, hold all my calls. I'll take the detective into the lounge."

"Yes, sir," Karl said. Foley figured the kid was going to get a lecture for not finding a way to get rid of the nosy policeman. But Foley knew the power of flashing that badge of his. It made most people very cooperative.

Most people. Not everyone. Foley's badge didn't seem to have any effect on Roger Huntington, who made it very clear he resented this intrusion into his day. Once they were settled in the lounge, the door closed against any eavesdroppers, Roger gestured for Foley to sit down.

"Would you like some coffee?" Roger asked. "Tea?"

"No, thank you. I promised you this would be quick."

"All right then. How can I help you?"

"I'd like to ask you a couple of questions about your sister-in-law."

"Liz? What's Liz done to draw your interest?"

"No, not that sister-in-law. Your *late* sister-in-law." He paused for just a second. "Dominique."

"Dominique?"

"Yes. According to the inquest notes, you saw her on the day of the accident."

"Why are you asking about Dominique? I thought you were investigating the deaths of Audra and Jamison."

"Oh, I am."

Roger laughed derisively. "Are you suggesting there's a connection between two barbarous murders and Dominique's accidental drowning on her yacht?"

"Oh, I'm not suggesting anything. Just asking questions. Is it true you saw Dominique shortly before she went out that day?"

Roger shifted uncomfortably in his chair. "Yes. I told everything I knew at the inquest. If you've read it, you have all the information. Ask your chief. It was Chief Davis, working for the D.A.'s office, who conducted the inquest."

"Oh, yes, I remember that well. The chief did it as a special favor for the D.A."

"Yes, so all the information I have is already down in that report."

Foley scratched his chin as he stared at Roger. "It's just that there are a few inconsistencies in the report. I've been reading it over."

"What kind of inconsistencies?" Roger acted as if he didn't believe him.

"Well, the report of Captain Hogarth, for example. The man your brother and his wife regularly employed to captain the yacht."

Roger sniffed. "Hogarth? He's a drunk. Chief Davis noted that. He discredited Hogarth's testimony."

"Yes, I know, but it's just peculiar. Hogarth at first testified he didn't take the yacht out that day. But later he backtracked and said, yes, he *was* at the helm, taking Mrs. Huntington out on the water . . ."

"I'm well aware of the change in his testimony. He was clearly angling to try and pull some kind of shakedown of my brother. It was an attempt to get money. Extortion. The guy should be locked up. Ask Chief Davis. He discredited Hogarth's second testimony."

"But I'm confused. What kind of shakedown of your brother could Hogarth engineer by changing his testimony?"

Roger shrugged. "I have no idea. Ask the chief. Ask my brother."

"The official inquest determination was that Mrs. Huntington took the yacht out on her own that day, that she was alone on board when the accident occurred. So that means she was fully capable of steering the yacht on her own?"

"There wasn't much Dominique wasn't capable of doing," Roger said.

"So I take that as a yes? She could captain the yacht on her own?"

"Yes."

"And you saw her that day, just about an hour before she went out?"

"Yes."

"And she told you she was going out on her own? That she was not asking Hogarth to take her out?"

Roger hesitated. "I gave my statement to the inquest."

"If you don't mind, Mr. Huntington, I'm asking you to give it to me again."

"Yes!" Roger snapped. "She said she was going out alone."

Foley nodded. "That's all. Thank you for your time."

Roger stood. Foley started to do the same, then sat back down. He loved pulling this little trick.

"Oh, wait," he said. "There was one more thing."

"What's that?"

"Are you aware of the actual statements Hogarth made in his second, discredited testimony?"

Roger glared down at him, a version of the same angry look he had given his assistant earlier. "All I know is that he said he *did* take Dominique out that day."

"Why would he say such a thing, do you think? It left him open for possible accusations of negligent homicide, that he steered the yacht out into stormy seas and then couldn't manage it, resulting in Mrs. Huntington's death?"

"I have no idea. He's a drunk and a crook. You'll have to ask him if you want to know."

"I intend to."

Roger stared down at him. "Does Chief Davis know you're reopening the inquiry into Dominique's death?"

"Oh, I'm not reopening it. Just asking questions."

"Well, are you through with me now?"

Foley finally stood so he could look Roger straight in the eye. "I will be, once I tell you what Hogarth actually said in his second testimony, since you say you don't know the details."

Roger said nothing, just continued to meet Foley's gaze.

"He said that he *thought* he was taking Mrs. Huntington out alone, but once they were out at sea, he realized a man was on board. He heard voices. Angry voices. A great deal of shouting. He looked down and he saw a man on deck—a man he identified as your brother. But he didn't see Dominique anywhere. All at once, Hogarth reported, a storm came on—he'd never seen waves so high—and he had to concentrate on keeping the yacht steady. So he never had a chance to speak to your brother. The storm only got worse, and eventually Captain Hogarth lost control—the yacht was capsized. He grabbed a life jacket and made it back to shore safely. But as far as he knew at the time, both Mr. and Mrs. Huntington had been lost with the ship."

"Well, that's absurd, isn't it?" Roger asked. "Because David was very much alive back at Huntington

House when the Coast Guard reported finding the capsized yacht."

"They never found its lifeboat."

"They never found half the things that were on the
yacht, including Dominique's body. Are you trying to
imply that David threw his wife overboard, then made
it home in a furious storm in a lifeboat?"

"I'm not implying anything. I'm just asking questions."

Roger laughed. "Hogarth's story is ridiculous! Now
that I know the details, it was clear he was trying to get
some money out of David. Everyone back at Huntington
House could, and probably did, attest for his where-
abouts that day. I'm sure that's why Chief Davis dis-
counted Hogarth's second testimony. In my opinion, he
should have arrested him for attempted extortion." He
sneered. "Really, Foley. You should have spoken to
your chief before coming to talk to me. He'd be able to
answer you better than I can."

"I plan to speak to the chief." Foley smiled. "Well,
thank you for your time, Mr. Huntington. Good luck with
your upcoming opening. Quite an eccentric collection
of art, if I might say so. I got a peek on my way through."

"Naomi Collins is a very hot artist at the moment,"
Roger said, opening the door and striding back out into
the gallery. "At least she is considered so among those
with an appreciation and understanding of art."

"I'm just a country boy, so what do I know?" He followed Roger out of the lounge. "I imagine your brother
and his wife will be here."

"I've invited them," Roger said, not turning around.
"Now, if you'll excuse me, Detective, I really am very
busy . . ."

"Of course," Foley said. "I can show myself out."

Roger disappeared down a hallway without another word.

Foley gazed at one of the paintings on the wall. A girl with no arms staring at him with enormous purple eyes.

Yes, indeed, eccentric. Who'd ever buy such a thing? Where would you possibly hang it? Over your couch? In your dining room?

Foley shuddered.

34

Rita couldn't quite believe what she was seeing when she arrived at Huntington House for work the next morning.

Carrying freshly laundered sheets upstairs, she paused on the landing. The portrait of Dominique was gone!

In its place was merely its outline, a large dusty rectangle. The blue wallpaper that had been behind the portrait was a more vivid color than the sun-bleached paper around it.

So it had finally come down . . .

Rita heard a voice from the top of the stairs.

David's voice. Talking on his cell phone.

She hurried up to the second floor. She spotted David in his study. His back was to her, and he was giving instructions in Dutch to some overseas business colleague. She slipped into the room without him noticing, closing the door behind her.

Setting the sheets in her arms down on a chair, she moved quietly across the room to her intended target.

As soon as David ended his call, Rita's arms snaked around him.

"Jesus Christ!" David shouted, shaking her off and looking back at her.

"What's the matter, David?" Rita purred. "Aren't you happy to see me?"

He glared at her, saying nothing.

Rita smiled. "Don't you realize why you had such a sudden and overpowering desire to come home?"

"Rita," he seethed, "I told you to leave me alone . . ."

"I left you alone all day yesterday, even though I was *dying* to see you."

"Look, Rita . . ."

"Really, David. Haven't you stopped to wonder? Why did you feel so compelled to come home, David? It was *me*. Admit it. You were thinking of me."

Rita knew it must be true. The doll that Variola had given her . . . it had enabled her to break the spell on David and allow him to once again feel his love for her. While she refused to win him back through hocus-pocus, all the doll really did was liberate David so he could admit the truth . . . *that he loved her*.

But his face appeared far from loving.

"Get this through your head, you stupid, stupid girl," he snarled. "I *didn't* think of you. I *never* thought of you! The only time you came into my mind was when you so inappropriately called me on my private phone to tell me about my brother."

"David, I know you love me . . ."

"Look, Rita, I tried to be kind to you. I tried to be careful of your feelings. But you just won't get it!" His face was beet red. "I *don't* love you! I *never* loved you! I *used* you, Rita! I was an unhappily married man and I *used* you! Get that through your head!"

It was as if David had physically struck her. Rita took a few steps back, staggered.

"I came home because I was concerned about my *wife*," David told her. "My wife—to whom I intend to remain married. My wife, whom I love very much."

"No . . . it was me . . . me who brought you home . . ."

David pushed past her. "One more scene like this, Rita," he told her, "and you are fired."

He pulled open the door and stormed out into the corridor.

Rita didn't know what to do, what to say, what to think.

That doll Variola gave her . . . it was worthless!

Variola was a fraud!

But so was David.

He lied to me all that time, Rita thought. *He let me think he loved me when he was just using me.*

His words echoed in her ears.

I never loved you! I used you, Rita! I was an unhappily married man and I used you!

In that instant, all of Rita's affection for the man mutated. Soured, corroded.

Changed into hate.

Now she didn't want his love.

Now all she wanted was revenge.

Rita picked up the sheets she had set down on the chair. When the moment was right, she decided, she would tell that dear, sweet little wife of his all about her husband's affair.

David had asked her to be Liz's friend. And good friends told each other things they needed to know, didn't they?

Then she'd go back to Detective Foley. She'd reveal everything she knew. She'd tell him what Jamison had revealed to her the night he was killed—that Audra had been killed right in this very house, and that Mrs. Hoffman, quite possibly with David's knowledge, had had the body moved out to the grounds.

Wouldn't Detective Foley love to know that? Wouldn't little Liz love hearing it, too?

Oh, the scandal Rita would bring to Huntington House.

A scandal that might even ruin David financially, if it appeared he covered up a murder in his house.

Maybe he'd even go to jail . . .

Rita walked out into the corridor carrying the sheets in her arms and wearing a smile that stretched across the entire width of her pretty face.

"What's got you in such a cheery mood?" Mrs. Hoffman asked her when she saw her.

"It's such a beautiful day," Rita responded, "why shouldn't I be smiling?"

And she went on smiling for the rest of the day.

35

Liz held tight to David's arm as they made their way into Roger's crowded gallery. The Naomi Collins opening gala appeared to be a great success: the room was packed with people, so full that Liz could barely see the art on the walls—which, having seen it before, she really didn't mind. David seemed to know everyone there. From the moment they arrived he was stopped, greeted, embraced, and enthused over. "David, how good it is to see you!" "David, I'm so delighted you've come!" "David, you look marvelous!" A mass of floating faces—men, women, mostly old, all obviously wealthy—overwhelmed Liz. Usually David introduced her—"This is my wife, Liz"—whereupon the eyes of Palm Beach society briefly studied her before offering a tepid "How nice to meet you" or "I've heard so much about you." Liz wondered what they had heard, and from whom. Their names she tried to commit to memory but they all quickly blurred together. She and David did not pause to talk with anyone; they just kept pushing through the crowd, Liz clutching on to her husband as if for dear life. Where they were going, Liz wasn't sure. She just let David lead the way.

A harpist was playing at the back of the gallery; the soft music lilted through the dull roar of milling conversations. Given how hot the evening was, most everyone, Liz and David included, was dressed in beige or tan linen; temperatures were still in the nineties. But the occasional red dress stood out from among the crowd. Everywhere Liz went, eyes seemed to follow her: *there she is, David's wife, how different she is from Dominique.* Liz tried not to meet their gazes, keeping her eyes on the back of David's head as they pushed through the mob.

He was, thankfully, once again the man she had married, the man she had fallen in love with. How good, how considerate, he had been to her this past week. There had been very few business calls, and plenty of time together, lounging at the pool, taking walks on the beach, sharing candlelit dinners, just the two of them. And he had made love to her with such skill, such tenderness, that Liz thought she would never again know such bliss. "We're still newlyweds," he'd reminded her, quoting his brother. That they were.

A couple of times, lying in his arms after sex, Liz had carefully ventured into areas she knew David was not comfortable speaking about. But he hadn't pushed her away.

"I wish you had told me more about Dominique, and about the unhappiness here at Huntington House," she'd said softly one night.

"I'm sorry. I should have. I'm sorry I let the servants fill your head with their stories . . ."

"Did Dominique really practice witchcraft?"

"Oh, she and Variola were always brewing something up . . . island mumbo jumbo . . . but I suppose it was really nothing more than herbs and flower remedies."

"Sometimes," Liz said, almost dreamily, "I smell gardenias. I know that was Dominique's scent. I smell it sometimes . . . even when no one's around."

"Liz, you're too smart to believe such things."

"But I've been frightened, David." She hesitated. "I thought I saw something the other day."

He looked over at her sharply. "What did you think you saw?"

"A horrible woman . . . a terrible face. Dressed in an old robe, prowling around the sculpture garden."

He had sighed. "We've had some problem with vagabonds getting onto the estate. There's an area where the wall is fairly easy to scale. I'll have Thad keep an eye out."

Liz supposed that could have been the case. She remained convinced that she *had* seen someone that day. She'd never questioned Thad to find out what, if anything, he had discovered after Roger told him about the trespassing woman. She hadn't wanted to hear more talk of witches and ghosts. Surely Thad, with all his superstitions, would claim it was Dominique, back from the dead.

"It's just all been very strange, David," Liz said. "The fragrances . . . the sound of footsteps coming from a place I can't pinpoint . . . from behind the walls . . ."

He took her gently by the shoulders. "It's my fault, darling. I should have told you more before I left, instead of letting your imagination run wild."

"So tell me now," Liz had said. "Tell me about Dominique."

David had leaned back against the pillows. "I was very much in love with her once," he said. "But then . . ."

Liz had waited, wondering what he might say.

"The love didn't last," David finished. He went quiet. That was all he was willing to say.

"Why didn't it last, David?" Liz asked.

"I don't want to talk about the past." David had sat up at that point, pulling Liz close to him. "I now have a wife whom I love very much. Can't we just focus on the future?"

She had murmured her consent and let the conversation end there. It wouldn't do to harass him. He would just clam up again.

But another night, after another round of tender lovemaking, Liz had tried once more to discover her husband's secrets.

"Why didn't your brother like Dominique?" she'd asked.

David had lifted one eye up to her. "He didn't tell you on one of your outings?"

"He just said that Dominique wasn't always the nicest person." She began tracing David's face with her forefinger. "Yet clearly he'd been fond of her at one point—after all, he painted the portrait of her that was hanging in the stairwell."

"Oh, yes," David said, closing his eyes. "He painted the portrait. That he did."

"I can tell that Mrs. Hoffman doesn't care for Roger. Given how close she was to Dominique, I can't help but wonder why . . ."

"You'll have to ask her then. What went on between

Dominique and Mrs. Hoffman, I never much delved into. It seemed every time they came home from a trip into town they had more plastic in their cheeks and their lips had turned into suction cups."

Liz smiled. "She's quite the sight, isn't she, Mrs. Hoffman? Does she actually think all that work has made her look younger?"

"She was encouraged in it by Dominique. It all started the day Dominique turned thirty. She was desperately scared of getting old. That was when she hired Variola, and began taking all her potions and treatments." He laughed lightly. "That's what their witchcraft, if you can call it that, was all about. Keeping Dominique young."

"Thirty isn't old," Liz said.

"I hope you still think so when you get there," David said, opening his eyes and looking up at her. "There's too much focus around here on looking young. Such a premium placed on youth. Don't listen when Mrs. Hoffman starts in on how you look, or someone else looks."

"She can be very hard," Liz acknowledged, remembering the day by the pool when she'd placed Dominique's photo beside her.

"Hoffman's a strange old bird, but she knows this house better than anyone. She's been here since my parents ran the place. Just let her do her thing, darling, keeping the house running, while you carry on with your own life. Don't let her get you down."

"I just don't understand why she doesn't like Roger . . ."

"I told you, Liz. My brother is a troublemaker."

"Is that why you said he lived far away?"

"I said we lived in different worlds. You took me literally."

"Well, all I know is, he was very kind and sweet to me."

"Yes, so he could get under my skin, and make me feel guilty for leaving you, which I do." David pulled her close and kissed her. It made Liz think of the kiss Roger had given her—and made her feel all the more troubled by it now.

"All my life," David went on, "Roger has been jealous of me. He always felt I was Dad's favorite. If I was, it's because I didn't get in trouble. I applied myself. I went to school and joined the family business. I made Dad proud. Roger hung out with musicians and artists and got himself arrested for marijuana possession any number of times."

"When was this?"

"Back when he was a kid."

"David, I'm not going to judge anybody for smoking pot, especially when they were kids . . ."

"But he's still underhanded, darling. I'm sure of it. Where does he get his money? Dad's given him nothing except his house, and Roger still manages to live like a king. Fancy cars, elegant parties . . ."

"His gallery has become very successful," Liz said.

"You mean to tell me he makes that much money selling weird art?" He shook his head. "How he's ever managed to hoodwink people like Mrs. Delacorte and Mrs. Merriwell, I have no idea. These ladies are pillars of society. My mother's friends. And they're buying junk from my brother."

"He's a good salesman," Liz said. "Nothing wrong in that. And maybe he's right. Maybe we just don't get 'art.'"

She was suddenly yanked out of the memory by the sudden burst of applause from the crowd all around her. She looked around Roger's gallery. Everyone was turning to look at something.

David stopped walking. "Shit," he grumbled. "I was hoping to get to some private corner before they started all this."

"May I have your attention, ladies and gentlemen?" The voice was Roger's. He had hopped up onto a chair to get the crowd to stop talking. "I'd like to introduce our artist."

Catching Liz's eye, he gave her a little smile before going on with his announcement.

"Tonight I am thrilled to have Naomi Collins with us, a brilliant new force in the art world, someone who challenges our notions of beauty and power and faith."

The crowd parted to reveal a tall woman with short black hair, a shiny helmet with bangs cut straight across her forehead that made her look like that old silent movie star—what was her name? Louise Brooks, Liz thought. Naomi Collins was wearing a bright red dress, and she'd joined Roger up on a chair, offering a small, bashful wave to the assemblage. Liz clapped her hands along with everyone else. She noticed that David did not.

Roger was going on about what Collins meant to the art world—how she was pushing boundaries and changing definitions—but Liz tuned him out as she looked around at the crowd. They all looked so chic and fashionable and very, very rich. Watching Roger intently was Mrs. Delacorte, and Liz noticed several other well-dressed ladies of a certain age hanging on his every word. Occasionally one of them would glance over at

Liz. She saw the disapproval in their eyes. *Really,* they seemed to be thinking, *that little mouse has married a Huntington?*

"Will you look at that?" David whispered to her. "Nearly every painting has a red dot next to it."

"What do the red dots mean?"

"They've been sold. And look at the prices. Ten, fifteen, thirty thousand dollars! Jesus, my brother's made a fortune tonight."

Roger had finished speaking. Naomi Collins was thanking the crowd for coming. Then there was another round of applause and everyone went back to milling about and sipping wine. David took Liz's elbow and guided her over to a corner, whispering to her that they'd made an appearance and now they could leave. But just at that moment he was approached by a tall older man with a short clipped white beard and deep-set green eyes who started talking about stocks and bonds, and Liz knew they wouldn't be leaving quite yet. David sighed and introduced the man to her as Paul Delacorte. "Paul's on our board of directors," David explained.

"Oh," Liz said, shaking the man's hand. "I believe I've already met your wife."

"Delighted to meet you, Liz," Mr. Delacorte said as his creepy green eyes looked her over. His wife had been condescending to her, but Delacorte was an old lech as he appraised Liz up and down. She even saw the tip of his tongue slither out from between his lips for a second, like a snake.

She was about to slink off and grab a glass of wine when she felt a hand on her shoulder. She turned around. It was Roger.

"Thank you for coming," he said to her.

"What a successful event," she said. "Congratulations, Roger."

He smiled. "This is the first time my brother has ever been to my gallery. That's your doing, Liz, and I'm grateful."

"You're coming to our dinner party next week, aren't you?"

"Actually, I'm afraid I . . ." His voice wavered. "Unfortunately, I have a conflict. A previous engagement. But thank you for inviting me."

"It's David, isn't it? You think David doesn't want you there."

"No, Liz, I'm telling you the truth. I have to be somewhere else."

She frowned. "I'm sorry, but I don't believe you. Look, David came tonight. I want the two of you to be friends."

"Perhaps you and I being friends is the best we can hope for."

She felt a twinge of missing him. How much fun they'd had. How much of a savior Roger had been when Liz had been feeling her lowest.

"I told David I wanted you at the party. He didn't object. Besides, your parents are flying down from New York."

Roger smirked. "That's hardly an enticement to get me there, Liz."

"I could use the moral support meeting them myself."

"I'd love to support you, Liz, but I simply have a conflict I can't break."

Liz looked at him. "It's not David, is it? It's me."

She saw the confirmation in his eyes. She remembered their kiss. Did Roger have feelings for her that he worried might complicate things?

"We're friends, Liz," Roger said, smiling kindly at her. "Let's be happy about that."

At that moment, David stepped up, slipping his arm around Liz's waist.

"Well, Roger," he said, "quite the show you put on."

"I'm pleased you came, David."

"And just as I feared, I'm cornered about business wherever I go." He nodded in Paul Delacorte's direction. "You'll understand if we duck out."

"That's why I decided not to go the corporate route all those years ago," Roger replied. "Seems you're never off the clock."

"Given the money you raked in here tonight, I'd say you made a wise choice," David said. "Sorry you can't make our dinner party."

Liz looked up at him. So David already knew that Roger wouldn't be coming.

"I'm still hopeful you can change your appointment and come," Liz said. "I'll see to it that we leave a place open for you. Show up even at the last minute if you'd like."

She saw the frown that slipped across David's face at her words.

"You are too kind, sister-in-law. But that would throw off Mrs. Hoffman's seating plans, I'm sure."

Liz snorted. "If Mrs. Hoffman thinks she's organizing my dinner party, she's got another thing coming."

"Come on, Liz," David said, nudging her forward. "It's time we went home."

"Thank you both again for coming," Roger said.

"Congratulations again on such a successful show," Liz told him.

He smiled. Liz and David made their way through the crowd. When Liz turned around just before they left the gallery, she saw Roger still standing where they'd left him across the room, still looking after her.

36

Variola had known this moment would come, sooner or later. They were alone in the house. No one could hear them. From across the marble floor of the parlor, Mrs. Hoffman stared at her. Variola stared right back. They were like two cats, glaring at each other in that fraught moment before each pounced.

"You are getting lax," Mrs. Hoffman said at last.

Variola laughed. "Me? You accuse *me* of being lax?"

"We can't have what happened the other day happen again."

"That was *your* failing, not mine."

Mrs. Hoffman's eyes radiated anger, even if the muscles of her face did not move. "You have responsibilities, and you have not been vigilant."

"I have done my best to keep doors from opening. I conduct the ritual of enclosure every morning. But it is not I who oversees the locks on the doors."

"She is getting stronger."

Variola nodded. "Yes, she is."

"That unnerves you."

"I have done what I can. But at a certain point, you will have to accept that she is not coming back."

"I will *never* accept that," Hoffman hissed, her anger threatening to explode out of her plastic face. At that very moment, a vase on a shelf fell and shattered to the floor. Neither woman paid any attention to it.

"I don't care if you ever accept it. But you will have to accept the fact that responsibilities are shifting in this house, even as we speak." She smiled. "Your allegiances may have to change."

"Never."

Variola laughed—that rich, deep, musical sound. "You've been afraid of me ever since I came here."

"If I was once, I no longer am."

"You have learned your lessons well. I will give you that."

A tight smile suggested itself on Hoffman's face.

"All but one. Papa Ghede does not bestow power to his followers for use in cruelty or revenge. If that is your motivation, then there will be a price to pay."

"I do not follow Papa Ghede," Hoffman said. "I am not some vodou priestess from the islands."

Variola frowned at the insult, and a second vase went flying from the shelf, hurtling across the room before smashing into smithereens on the floor. Once again, neither woman reacted.

"You brought me here to form a community," Variola said bitterly. "I was to teach you . . ."

"You were brought here to teach us, yes, but the coven was ours."

Variola made a face in disgust. "Coven," she spit. "That was your word. Not mine."

"She was our leader," Hoffman said. "And she will be again."

Variola laughed in derision. "You poor deluded creature."

Mrs. Hoffman folded her arms across her chest. "You think I'd ever swear allegiance to you? That I'd ever recognize you as leader of our coven?"

"I believe there will be others who will do so. Others who are not as foolish or as deluded as you are to think she can ever be brought back."

"I'm not threatened by your alliances with chambermaids."

Variola smiled. "But Mrs. Hoffman. I've decided to embrace the new mistress of the house. She has expressed an interest in the fine arts of the islands."

It was Mrs. Hoffman's turn to laugh. "I am even less threatened by *her*."

"You have repudiated all I taught you!" Variola shouted, angry all of a sudden. Every single glass object in the parlor—every vase, every figurine, every ashtray—suddenly went flying around the room. Mrs. Hoffman had to duck to avoid being hit, though she did so with only the slightest alarm. "You have corrupted my faith! Papa Ghede will not stand for it!"

"You agreed, Variola," Hoffman seethed. "You promised to bring her back! You were paid very well to bring her back!"

"I kept my promise," Variola said, her voice a low growl.

"At what cost?" Mrs. Hoffman demanded, her eyes suddenly filled with emotion. It looked as if the plastic mask might crack.

"The cost you insisted on," Variola told her softly. "What we have today is all because of you."

"But I have been taking steps to correct it, to make things better," the housekeeper said, even as she waved a hand around her. The shattered glass nearest to her reassembled as if in reverse motion and returned to the shelves. "I have been doing what I could to bring her back even as you have sat idle."

"I have done all I can to bring her back," Variola said, waving her own hand now. The remaining shattered glass was quickly and efficiently restored.

"There must be more that you can do," Mrs. Hoffman said. "Or I will have to continue doing things my way."

"Your ways don't work," Variola told her. "There must be no pain . . ."

"Then step up and do what you were asked to do," Hoffman replied. "What you promised to do that terrible day of the accident."

Variola was silent. The two women resumed staring at each other without speaking any words. Memories of the year past thrummed between them.

This time it was Variola who broke the silence. "And what about Mr. Huntington? He is a wild card, you know. Will he do as you say?"

"He has no choice, does he?" Hoffman replied.

Variola sighed.

Mrs. Hoffman turned, walking stiffly out of the parlor and up the stairs. Variola sighed once more, turning herself and returning to the kitchen, chanting a prayer to Papa Ghede under her breath.

37

"Mom, don't hang up the phone," Liz said.

She'd been trying to reach her mother for weeks, but Mom would never return Liz's calls or emails. Every time Liz called, she always ended up getting Mom's voice mail. Apparently, when she saw it was Liz calling, Mom wouldn't pick up the phone. Finally, this morning, Liz had had enough: she blocked her number when she called, so her mother wouldn't know it was her. And, sure enough, Mom picked up on the first ring.

"Why would I hang up on you?" she asked Liz.

"Because you clearly have been avoiding me."

"You're paranoid, Liz."

"You never even called to congratulate me after the wedding!"

"Congratulate you? After you ran off and got married to some guy I'd never even met?"

"Mom, we've been over this. We were on the ship—it was spontaneous—romantic—"

She heard her mother sniff. "Spontaneous! Romantic! More like impulsive and foolhardy. Liz, you barely know this man you've made your husband."

"I know him very well," she replied, even if, down deep, she still worried sometimes that she didn't know David all that well. Despite how wonderful things had been between them lately, Liz hadn't forgotten how he'd abandoned her and left her here to deal with all that unpleasantness on her own. She'd forgiven him, and she felt pretty certain he regretted his behavior—but Mom's words just raised her doubts all over again, although she'd never give her mother the satisfaction of knowing that.

"Besides," Mom was saying, "you denied me the chance to plan a wedding for you. You denied your sister and brother the chance to be a part of your big day."

"That's what I'm calling for, Mom. I want you and Deanne and George to come visit. We're having a dinner party next week—it's a big deal, David's pulling out all the stops. His parents are coming, too."

Her mother harrumphed. "We can't afford to fly down to Florida for a dinner party."

"Mom, David's going to fly you down. It's time you met him. He wants so much to meet you."

There was silence on the other end of the phone.

"Mom?" Liz asked. "Are you there?"

"I'm here."

"He's got his assistant working on the tickets now. I was thinking, the day after the party, we could maybe drive down to Miami—or would you rather go to Orlando, maybe take in Disney World? You know how much Deanne and I always wanted to go there as kids."

"Right, and I could never afford to take you."

"Well, now we can go!"

"Sorry, Liz, but we have a prior engagement next week."

"What?"

"You can't just call us up after ignoring us for weeks and tell us your rich husband wants to jet us around and take us places. Sorry, Liz. We're not at your beck and call. Maybe your houseful of servants, but not us."

"Mom, you're being unreasonable. Put Deanne on the phone . . ."

"She's out. And I have to be somewhere, too. Thanks for the invite, Liz, but I'm afraid it came a little too late."

Mom hung up the phone.

Liz was steaming mad. She was about to call her sister—Deanne would be very happy to come, she was sure—but then she took a deep breath. She knew how sensitive her mother was. She'd raised them on her own, struggling to overcome her own problems. Maybe Liz had touched a nerve calling her this way. She could feel her anger subsiding as she remembered how Mom had fought so hard to get sober, and how abandoned and alone she'd felt when Liz took the job on the cruise line. Liz was still hurt by David's abandonment of her—but hadn't she abandoned her mother in the same way?

The old tape loop of guilt started playing in her head again. Down deep, Liz believed that everything that went wrong in her life was ultimately her fault.

She knew who could shake her out of that sort of thinking. She hit Nicki's name in her contacts on her phone.

"Hey, this is Nicki," her voice mail announced. "I'm back on dry land, so leave your message and I will get back to you."

"Hey," Liz said after the beep. "Are you in Atlantic City? Have you started the new job? Hope things are going well. Call me when you get this. I just want to vent a little bit about my mother." She drew out the two syllables in the word *mother*. "Oh, and David is back home and everything is great and happy and wonderful again. Call me. Love you."

Great and happy and wonderful. Liz stood there at the window, her phone in her hand, looking out over the topiary. In the distance she could spy a bit of the sculpture garden—the wings of that hideous cow-angel. Great and happy and wonderful.

That was really how things were—weren't they?

Standing there, she caught a whiff of gardenia. She told herself she must be imagining it.

38

"How does such a handsome, obviously success-ful man as yourself end up sitting at a bar like this one, all alone on a Saturday night?"

The blond woman sitting next to him with the tattoo of a star on her neck lifted her martini glass in a sort of toast.

Roger clinked his glass with hers. "Well, truth is, I was invited to a gala dinner party tonight, but I had to decline."

"Because you'd rather sit here, drowning yourself in gin?" She winked at him. "I've been counting. That's your third."

"Fourth," Roger corrected her. "I had one at my gallery, before I came over here."

"You hold your liquor well." She looked him over. "Gallery? What kind of gallery?"

"An art gallery. Uptown."

The woman snickered. "I don't really understand art."

"That's all right," Roger said, taking a sip of his mar-tini. "I don't really either."

The bar was a dive, wedged between a check-cashing

business and a boarded-up building with signs posted declaring it had been condemned by the city. The bar smelled of beer and urine, and the lights were low. The countertop was sticky.

"You come here often?" the woman asked.

Roger sighed. "My first time. I needed to go somewhere where no one knew me. Where I could, as you say, drown myself in gin."

"Well, my name is Lana, and now, someone knows ya."

They clinked glasses again.

"So," Lana said, "what's her name?"

"Excuse me?" Roger asked.

"Her name. The woman you're drowning yourself over. The woman you'd rather be with tonight, instead of here, in this dive."

Roger looked down at his glass. "You're a smart girl," he said.

"Not really. Just wise to the ways of men." She took a drink. "You haven't told me your name."

"Roger," he said quietly.

He looked over at her. She was pretty enough. Blond, blue-eyed. The star tattoo on her neck suggested she was a bit of a free spirit. She wasn't all that young, but she wasn't old either, despite the lines around her eyes and her mouth. She was a smoker, Roger suspected. But there was a vitality to her that intrigued him.

Lana smiled. "How about if we finish our drinks and go take a swim? My apartment isn't far from here, and we have a nice pool."

"I don't have a bathing suit with me."

She winked. "You won't need one."

He downed the last of his gin.

39

Liz stood in the foyer, greeting the guests as they arrived. They had invited eight couples, and all but one had accepted, seemingly eager to get an up-close look at David's new wife. The Delacortes were there, of course. Mrs. Delacorte air-kissed Liz as if they were old pals, though she never made eye contact with her. Mr. Delacorte winked at her, which made Liz distinctly uneasy. He was introduced as "Dr. Delacorte," but what kind of doctor he was, Liz had no idea. The Merriwells were incredibly snooty, calling Liz "Lisa" three times before she corrected them. The Claytons were a little better; when Liz told Mrs. Clayton that she was from New Jersey, the older woman had replied that she was, too. For a moment Liz had thought she'd found a friend—until the overly made-up lady (her pancake and rouge had to be half an inch thick) leaned in and said, "But my parents insisted I go to school in Connecticut and Massachusetts. Miss Porter's, then Smith." Her eyes twinkled. "Where did *you* go to school, Liz?"

"Trenton High," she replied. "And then the College of New Jersey."

Mrs. Clayton retreated to her dinner plate and didn't speak to Liz again.

Most everyone was in their fifties or sixties; only two couples seemed to be in their thirties, and only one had a wife anywhere near Liz's age, though she was a textbook example of a gold digger. "You did good, honey," she said, leaning into Liz, her bracelets jangling. "We gals from the wrong side of the tracks have to be pretty damn shrewd if we want to catch a big fish." And then she giggled, jangling away on her wealthy husband's arm.

So that's what they think of me, Liz thought, steaming. *That I'm some floozy from "the wrong side of the tracks" who married David for his money.*

They all had some connection to David's business. The older couples had been friends with his parents for years. All of them came expecting the elder Huntingtons to be there. Indeed, Liz had expected the same thing. But a few hours before the party David had told her that his mother and father had declined.

"They can't get away from New York," he'd said. "Too much going on."

"Talk about canceling at the last minute."

David had looked away.

"David," Liz had said, a realization dawning on her. "You knew about this! How long?"

"I'm sorry, darling. I forgot to tell you . . ."

"You forgot? David, that's not something you forget. Here I was, all anxious about meeting your parents, and you don't let me know they're not coming . . ."

"I'm sorry, Liz. Dad mentioned it yesterday when we were on the phone talking about business matters. It slipped my mind."

"Why aren't they coming?"

He still hadn't looked at her. "I told you. There's too much going on for them. To fly down to Florida would just be too much . . ."

"They've known about this for some time!"

"Dad was very apologetic."

Liz had glared at him. "They don't want to meet me. Isn't that it? They don't approve."

"Liz, stop imagining things. Stop playing the victim."

"Playing the victim? Listen, David—"

"Can we not argue, darling? Let's just have a wonderful dinner party without them. All right?"

So Liz had refrained from saying any more. But all through the event she couldn't shake the idea that David's parents had canceled because they didn't want to give their friends the impression that they approved of their son's marriage to this girl from the wrong side of the tracks.

At the table, the silver and china sparkled under the light of the chandelier. Mrs. Hoffman had had the maids polishing and shining all day. Liz sat with Mr.— or rather Dr.—Delacorte on her right and some man whose name she'd forgotten on her left. Mrs. Merriwell sat opposite her. The conversation mostly went over Liz's head. The men talked business with David; the women talked about people they all knew but whose names meant nothing to Liz. She mostly stayed quiet, picking at her salad, not in the least bit hungry.

"And do you have a career, Liz?" Mrs. Merriwell asked at last, startling her into life.

"I'm a dancer," Liz replied. Eyelids flickered around

the table as people tried to get a look at each other, as if to say: *A dancer?*

David chimed in helpfully. "She's thinking of opening her own dance academy here in town."

Liz saw Mrs. Clayton sneak a peek at Mrs. Delacorte as she forked a slice of tomato from her salad into her mouth.

"I haven't decided definitely on that yet," Liz said. "But possibly."

"Are your parents still living?" Mrs. Merriwell asked.

Here it comes, Liz thought. *They're trying to find out what sort of family I come from.*

"I don't know if my father is still alive," she said honestly. "He walked out on us years ago."

A chorus of *ohh*s sounded from around the table.

Liz considered adding, just to slake their curiosity, that her father had been a traveling salesman before he took off, and that her mother was currently working in a Laundromat. But she figured she'd given them enough information to chew on for the moment.

"If you'll excuse me," she said, standing, "I'll see about the soup."

She felt eyes on her as she walked out of the room into the kitchen.

Waiting for her was Rita.

"Is everything all right, ma'am?"

"Yes," she lied. "I just thought I'd let Variola know that we're . . . we're ready for the soup."

Rita surprised her by taking her hands in hers. "They're horrible people, aren't they?" Rita asked. "They think they're better than you. Better than all of us."

Liz didn't know how to respond. "Rita, they're Mr. Huntington's friends . . ."

A small smile spread across the maid's face. "I'm sure he knows how phony they all are, and why he subjects you to them, I don't understand. Well, stay strong. Don't let them make you feel bad about yourself."

Liz was speechless.

"I'll let Variola know about the soup, and we'll bring it out right away." Rita squeezed Liz's hands, then let them go. "Everything is going to be all right, Mrs. Huntington. You can trust me." Her smile broadened. "I'm your friend."

Liz still didn't know what to say. She watched Rita hurry off. Taking a deep breath, she returned to the table.

"It is hard getting and keeping good help these days," Mrs. Merriwell was saying as Liz sat back down. "You can never be sure if they're legal, first of all, and second of all, you can never be quite sure whom you can trust. I'm always afraid they're going to steal the silver."

Mrs. Delacorte was nodding. "It's terribly unfair that we can't feel safe in our own homes."

Dr. Delacorte smiled at his wife, then leaned in toward Liz. "Do *you* feel safe in your own home, my dear?" he whispered.

Liz thought it a very odd question, given everything she'd been through. "Now that David is back home," she replied, "I feel very safe and very happy."

"Oh, that's good," Delacorte said, looking at her with his sunken green eyes in such a way that Liz felt very uncomfortable. "I like it when pretty girls like you are happy."

Liz was eager to change the subject. "So what do you do at Huntington Enterprises, Dr. Delacorte?" she asked.

"Oh, I don't work for Huntington. I'm just on the board of directors. And a stockholder, so I have a stake in any advice I give David." He chuckled. A piece of lettuce was stuck between his teeth. "The rest of the time, I'm an anesthesiologist."

"An anesthesiologist," Liz repeated.

"Yes. I put people to sleep."

Liz thought this entire dinner party was putting her to sleep.

Suddenly she felt a hand on her knee. Delacorte was grinning up at her. Even as his wife was speaking, sharing her rich-people's problems, he was slipping his hand under the table to make a pass at his host's wife.

Liz moved her leg sharply, knocking his hand away.

Horrible people, indeed.

40

A couple of maids were carrying the soup—a hot Caribbean blend of fruits and spices—out to the table when Rita noticed a girl she'd never seen before.

The girl was coming through the back door into the kitchen. She was pretty, but Rita noticed she was a little bit older than the other maids, with blond hair and a tad too much makeup. Mrs. Hoffman would definitely not approve if she got a look at her. Since she wasn't wearing a maid's uniform, Rita assumed she's been hired as extra kitchen help. Variola often requested assistants for big dinner parties like this one.

But the girl never joined the chef at the stove. After she came through the door, she turned abruptly and headed straight up the back stairs. How very odd, Rita thought. This unknown girl just walked in here like she owned the place, and now she was heading upstairs as if she knew exactly where she was going. Who the heck was she?

Rita decided to find out.

Stealing through the kitchen, sidestepping sous chefs

and Variola herself, who was busy chopping red and green peppers, Rita made her way to the back stairs.

She caught a glimpse of the girl turning down the upstairs hallway.

Who was she? Where was she going?

Suddenly Rita thought she knew.

Hurrying up the steps, she reached the top just in time to see the girl enter the last room on the left. Rita knew what that room was. It was an unused servant's bedroom. Occasionally, when the servants were asked to stay overnight for special events, they would use these small, plainly furnished rooms. And that last room on the left had a special significance for Rita. She'd stayed overnight in that room dozens of times, when the first Mrs. Huntington was alive. That was where David would meet her. How quiet Rita had been when she'd slipped inside that room, waiting for the arms of the man she loved to wrap around her. How quietly David would arrive, after everyone was asleep, after Mrs. Hoffman assumed Rita had left for the evening. How quietly they'd make love. Rita would start to fall asleep, her head on David's chest, listening to his heartbeat, when he'd nudge her gently and tell her it was time to leave.

All the while his wife slumbered, unaware, in another part of the house.

And now another woman waited in that room. Rita noticed how quietly, how carefully, the strange girl had closed the door to the room. Just as she had once done, when she'd wait there for David.

She could already imagine how the night would go. After their guests would leave, David would tell Liz that he was too wired to sleep; Dr. Delacorte or Mr.

Merriwell or Mr. Whoever, he'd say, had gotten him all worked up about business. He was so worried about plunging stock prices or excessive overhead or some bullshit that he needed to make some business calls. That's what he'd tell his wife. In Europe, he'd point out, they were just getting up. He wanted to call and talk to his associates before they began their day. David would tell Liz that she should go on up to bed on her own, and that he'd be up in a while. He'd go into his study and do a little work. It was the only way, he would tell her, that he'd ever be able to fall asleep.

He'd do work all right. He'd sneak into the last room on the left and fuck the brains out of that blonde. Then he'd send her away as he used to do with Rita and creep back to his wife.

Oh, no. Not anymore.

Rita had wondered just how she was going to have her revenge on David. Just how she'd tell Liz the truth about her beloved, deceitful husband.

Fate had just given her a wonderful opportunity. How luck she had been to see that floozy slip in the back door.

David's fun was over.

Rita would see to that.

41

"Are you certain, Rita?"

Liz looked into the maid's deep brown eyes. She had come back into the kitchen to see about coffee—that horrible dinner was nearly over but Liz had nonetheless needed another break from their pretentious conversation, so she'd ducked once more into the kitchen—and while there, she had been approached by Rita, who'd taken her aside and whispered something very strange to her.

"I'm absolutely certain, ma'am," Rita told her.

"Are you sure she's not a temporary employee?"

"Very certain, ma'am. I asked Variola if she had hired anyone for this event, and she said she had not. It was only the regular staff on tonight."

Liz tried to make sense of it. "So you're telling me you saw a woman you didn't recognize come in through the back door, go up the back stairs, and go into one of the servant bedrooms."

"Exactly, ma'am. And she hasn't come out either. I've been watching."

They were standing near the back stairs. Liz glanced up. It was dark at the top of the stairs.

"Well, why are you telling me? You should let Mrs. Hoffman know. She's in charge . . ."

"I thought you would want to know, ma'am." A thin smile bloomed on her lips. "After all, you're mistress of the house. You should know what goes on under your own roof."

Liz looked at her strangely. "What are you saying, Rita?"

"Just that I think you should find out who that woman is."

"I . . . I should get David to go . . ."

Rita gently took her hands again, her dark eyes imploring. "If you send Mr. Huntington up there, I guarantee you that he'll report back that there was no girl there."

Liz held her gaze. "How can you guarantee that, Rita?"

"Trust me, Mrs. Huntington."

For some peculiar reason, Liz did.

"I'll go with you, ma'am. Let's go up and find out who that woman is, why she's trespassing in this house."

"But . . . the guests . . . they expect me back at the table . . ."

Rita smirked. "Those snobs can wait."

Liz looked up the stairs again. Could the woman who was up there be the same she'd seen that day on the estate? But Rita had said nothing about any deformities. Still, David had said they'd had problems in the past with "vagabonds" getting onto the property. Could this be another one?

But for some reason, Liz didn't think so. Rita said the woman had seemed to come into this house with a purpose. And she was implying that she knew what that purpose was.

"I should get Thad . . ." Liz said in a small voice.

"You need to see for yourself, ma'am," Rita said. Her voice, though still a whisper, was becoming urgent. "You need to know what's going on under your own roof!"

Liz looked at her. She could see the fierceness in Rita's eyes.

What was she trying to tell her?

Without another word, Liz began climbing the stairs.

42

As they headed down the hallway to the last door on the left, Rita could barely hide her jubilation. How wonderful this was going to be! Liz would discover that David was cheating on her. If her nervous behavior these last few weeks was any indication, Liz wouldn't be able to contain her anger, and she'd confront David right in front of all those horrible Delacortes and Merriwells—oh, what a scene she'd made! The dinner party would be ruined! David would be humiliated! Rita couldn't wait.

"The door will no doubt be locked from the inside," she whispered to Liz as they grew close. "But I've brought a pin we can use to pop the lock."

Liz turned to look at her. "Why do you say, 'no doubt'?"

"Because that's what the instructions always were," Rita replied.

"What are you talking about?"

"I suggest you ask the woman who is waiting in that room."

Liz looked as if she could strangle Rita. But the maid just smiled, as if to say, *Don't blame the messenger.*

They reached the door. Liz took hold of the knob. As Rita had predicted, it was locked.

"Who's in there?" Liz called, rapping on the door.

There was no answer.

Rita handed her the pin. "We're coming in," Liz announced, sliding the pin into the hole of the knob and moving it around until she heard the pop of the lock.

The door swung open. The room was dark. Liz switched on a light.

They looked around.

A plain twin bed. One small wooden dresser.

No woman.

Rita pushed in ahead of Liz. "This can't be!" she shouted. "I saw her come in here."

Liz stood staring into the room, silent.

"I swear to you, ma'am! I saw someone come in here!" She looked under the bed. Nothing there but dust. "And I've been watching! No one came out!"

She flung herself at the closet, yanking the door open. But nothing in there but a couple of empty wire hangers dangling from the rod.

"Well," Liz said. "I'm not sure what this was all about, Rita, but tomorrow I'd like some answers from you."

"Mrs. Huntington," Rita insisted, "I don't have any answers! I saw a woman come in here! I swear to you!"

"The answers I'll be looking for, Rita, concern the insinuations you've been making. You clearly know something about this room and I am going to ask you to tell me what that is."

Rita stood silently staring at her.

"But not tonight," Liz went on. "Tonight I need to get back to my husband and my guests. I'd suggest that if you truly think there is an intruder in the house, you let Thad know. He can do a thorough search of the place."

Rita said nothing as Liz walked away.

She looked around the room again.

How was it possible? She was certain she saw a woman come in here.

And the door was locked—from the inside!

How was that possible?

Shaking her head, her heart pounding in her ears, Rita returned down the stairs into the kitchen. Mrs. Hoffman was waiting for her.

"Mrs. Huntington just came down these stairs and she did not look happy," the housekeeper said, her eyes practically vibrating in her unmoving face. "What has been going on?"

Variola came into view over Mrs. Hoffman's shoulder. "I saw them go upstairs together."

Rita's eyes moved back and forth between the two of them.

"Did you upset Mrs. Huntington in some way?" Mrs. Hoffman wanted to know.

"It wasn't I who upset her," Rita said softly.

Mrs. Hoffman looked over at Variola. "Will you be needing Rita any more tonight?"

"No," the chef said, returning to the stove. "I'm through with her."

"As am I," Mrs. Hoffman echoed. "You may go home, Rita."

Rita stood her ground. "I'm scheduled to work until midnight. For cleanup."

"I think we are well staffed for that," Mrs. Hoffman said. "Please get your things and go home, Rita."

"Very well," she said bitterly.

She knew Mrs. Hoffman intended to fire her. After all, she'd been wanting to do so for some time, and now she'd found her opportunity. Rita fully expected that when she came in tomorrow morning, Mrs. Hoffman would hand her a pink slip. But that was okay. She was prepared for it. Besides, Rita intended that her departure from this house would be memorable. She wouldn't leave before she told sweet little Liz everything she knew.

Rita intended to go out with a bang.

43

The last of the guests were heading out the front door. Dr. Delacorte winked at her as he stumbled out, having imbibed one Beefeater martini too many. Liz looked away, disgusted.

"And so, that's done," David said, smiling at her as he closed the front door. "You handled yourself marvelously, Liz."

"That's bull, and you know it, David. I was like a deer caught in the headlights." She shuddered. "They are not very pleasant people."

"No, I suppose they're not. But you don't give yourself enough credit, darling. You held your own against them."

He took her arm and they headed into the parlor. Maids and busboys were busy tidying up the house, carrying empty glasses and plates out to the kitchen. Liz noticed that Rita was not among them.

"David," she said. "I'd like to talk to you about one of the servants."

He lifted an eyebrow in her direction. "Which one?"

"Rita."

Liz noticed a subtle yet definite change of expression cross David's face. He dropped her arm and sat down on the couch. "What about her?" he asked.

"In the middle of the party tonight, she asked me to go upstairs with her."

"Upstairs where?"

"To the servants' rooms."

Liz noticed a definite flush cross David's cheeks.

"She said she saw a woman come in through the back door and go up the back stairs."

David appeared genuinely perplexed at that. "And where did she say this woman went after she went up the stairs?"

"To the last room on the left."

David stood. He was enraged. "Rita is unstable. I've always thought so . . ."

"She wanted me to go in there so I could find out, in her words, what was going on under my roof."

David shot her a look. "Did you go in the room?"

"Yes." She paused for just a second. "But no one was there. The door was locked, from the inside, but no one was there."

"Of course no one was there," David said. "I'm telling you, Rita is unstable."

"She's seemed a little strange at times, but never unstable. I've never had a problem with her."

"Well, I have."

Liz stared at him. "How so, David? What kind of problems?"

"I've found her to be insubordinate at times."

"You talk as if you're a military commander and the servants your soldiers."

"I just mean—"

"Never mind, David. Just tell me. Do you have any idea what Rita might have been talking about? Whether or not there really was an intruder in the house, what could she have meant when she said I should know about what's going on under my roof?"

"I have no idea. You shouldn't take anything Rita says seriously. I'm telling you. She's an unstable girl."

Liz sighed. "Well, the idea of intruders does worry me. After all, I still feel certain I saw that woman on the grounds."

"Then by all means, let's have Thad search the place."

"He's gone home for the night."

"Then *I'll* search, if it makes you feel better."

Liz sighed again. "No, it doesn't matter. I suppose you're right that I'm being silly." She tried to smile and take his hand. "Let's just go to bed. Tonight really wore me out. Those people are quite the crew. I could use your arms around me."

But David ignored her outstretched hand as he stood up from the couch. "No, no, no, I'm going to search around the house. Now you have me worried. If something's going on under our roof, I should find out what it is."

Liz frowned. "I thought you just said we shouldn't take anything Rita says seriously."

David kissed her quickly on the forehead. "You go on to bed, darling. I'll be up in a while. I'll look around the place just to make sure. I'm too revved up to sleep right away, anyway. Paul Delacorte filled my ear all night with talk about the company's stocks."

Liz wanted to add, *while his hand was on my knee*, but she refrained.

"All right, David," she said. "But don't be long, okay?"

"I'll see you shortly, darling." He kissed her forehead again.

Liz watched as he hurried out into the corridor.

She switched off the lights in the parlor. She could hear the last of the dishes being put away in the kitchen and the pantry. The dining table was completely cleared off and polished. There was no evidence of a dinner party ever having taken place. David's foot soldiers were an efficient army. They'd all be going home now, Liz knew, except Mrs. Hoffman and Variola, who would retire to their rooms in the back of the house before getting up tomorrow and starting all over again. Liz wondered if she would ever feel like this was her home, and not some hotel she'd wandered into by mistake. Tonight had been difficult all the way around. The interaction with the Delacortes and the Merriwells had been bad enough, but that strange episode with Rita had left Liz with all sorts of questions, questions she couldn't even quite formulate in her mind. It all left her with a rumbling feeling of unease and distrust. She thought the only thing that might console her would be David's arms around her as she fell asleep, but now he was out wandering around the house. She hoped he wouldn't be long.

She started up the stairs.

44

"Have all the servants gone home?" David asked, striding into the kitchen.

Variola looked up from the last of her tasks for the night, wrapping the remnants of her dessert pudding and placing them in the refrigerator. Across the room, Mrs. Hoffman, standing stiffly like a sentinel, also looked over at their employer.

"Yes," Mrs. Hoffman answered. "The last of them just left."

"All right," David said. "I need to speak with you both."

"Has your wife gone upstairs?" Variola asked, approaching.

David nodded. "She can't hear us."

"She is a smart lady," Variola said. "Smarter than one thinks, upon first meeting her."

"Liz is indeed very smart," David agreed. "That's why I must know what's going on here."

"Going on?" Mrs. Hoffman asked, in that plastic, robotic way of hers. "What do you mean, sir?"

"I mean," David said, his sharp, intense eyes moving between the two women, "I want to be assured that what happened before will not happen again. If the two of you are still playing your silly games . . ."

"Sir," Mrs. Hoffman said, "I can assure you that we are fully in control of this house."

"That's not the assurance I was looking for, Mrs. Hoffman. Your little games are over, are they not?"

"Our little games, as you call them, saved this house, and *you*." Mrs. Hoffman's voice was quiet and severe.

David looked over at Variola. He seemed to think he couldn't reason with Mrs. Hoffman, so he turned elsewhere. "Are they over, Variola? Tell me the truth."

The chef smiled. "If you want them to be over, sir, then they are." She sensed Mrs. Hoffman stiffening beside her.

"Not only do I want them over," David replied, "but I will *make sure* they are over."

"You need not worry, sir," Variola told him.

He grimaced. "What does Rita know?"

"Rita?" Mrs. Hoffman practically spit her name. "The little twit. She knows nothing. You need not worry about her."

"Are you certain about that?"

"Yes," Variola assured him. "She knows nothing more than rumors and gossip, like everyone else."

"Well," David said, "she brought my wife to a room upstairs tonight, claiming to have seen some unfamiliar woman come in through the back door and enter that room."

Variola felt the anger rise from her gut, and looked sharply over at Mrs. Hoffman. "I don't like the idea of strange people coming and going through my kitchen. Do you know anything about a woman coming in here tonight?"

"Of course I don't," she said, but Variola didn't believe her. She had threatened to continue doing things her way, and that was apparently the case. Variola steamed.

"I won't have what went on here before starting up again," David said.

Variola watched as Mrs. Hoffman's back arched and her chin lifted in defiance. She took several steps toward David.

"You think you have any authority here," the housekeeper said, her voice burning with anger and resentment. "You think you can tell me what to do."

Variola saw the life drain from David's eyes. She had seen this once before, in the aftermath of the accident, when his wife's body lay here, on the kitchen counter, dripping with seaweed, cold and blue. Mrs. Hoffman had spoken to him in the same way then as she spoke to him now, and Variola realized that all of her lessons of the fine arts of the islands had created a monster. She pulled back now, slightly afraid, and fear was not an emotion Variola was familiar with, or comfortable with.

Mrs. Hoffman stood in front of David with those hard, cold eyes of hers. "Rita is a lunatic," she said. "And we all know why that is."

He looked away. "My fault."

"Yes, your fault," Mrs. Hoffman agreed.

"I'll take care of her," he said, in a small voice.

"The only reason Rita thinks she can get away with

whatever she wants to do is because you have given her delusions of her own power."

David ran a hand through his hair. His anger from earlier had been replaced by anguish. His eyes were locked on to Mrs. Hoffman's. He was a little boy, frightened of the schoolmarm. "I'm sorry, Mrs. Hoffman. Believe me, I am. I take full responsibility. I was weak . . ."

"Yes, weak! That's what you were. Weak and cruel. And you hurt her. Hurt her terribly."

Variola realized she wasn't talking about Rita.

"How she loved you," Mrs. Hoffman said, drawing closer to David, her voice dropping into a hushed, angry whisper. "Do you remember when her body lay here, dripping and cold? That was your fault, too!"

David was crying.

"How devoted she was to you. It was only because of her pain and her sense of betrayal that we started what you so condescendingly call our 'little games.' "

Variola was astounded at how quickly he had been overcome by Hoffman. He hadn't even put up a fight. She felt pity for the man, tinged with contempt.

"She would still be here, with us," Hoffman was saying, "the mistress of this house—"

"But Liz is the mistress of the house," David said quietly, unconvincingly.

"That's not so! There will always be only one mistress here, and you know it!"

David shuddered. He had come into this room so full of authority. Now he was small and shriveled.

"You remember her as she was, don't you, David?" Mrs. Hoffman was saying, drawing even closer to him, speaking almost directly in his ear. "How beautiful she was . . ."

"So . . . beautiful . . ." David murmured.

"We were so happy together."

"So . . . happy . . ."

"And how you loved her."

"How I loved her," David repeated.

"Until Rita came along."

All at once, David's eyes clouded over with bitterness.

"And now," Mrs. Hoffman hissed, "another woman sleeps in her place."

David's face twisted in anger.

Mrs. Hoffman pulled back, her voice becoming subordinate again. "Forgive me, sir, if I have been out of line in speaking so plainly," she said. "But I think you know everything I say is true."

"True," he repeated, almost incoherently.

Mrs. Hoffman smiled.

"I . . . I need to go outside . . ." David was mumbling, trembling hands running through his hair. "I need to walk . . . think . . ."

"Of course you do, sir," Mrs. Hoffman said. "The night air will do you a tremendous amount of good."

He said nothing more, just stumbled out the back door.

Variola looked over at Mrs. Hoffman. "That was audacious," she said.

The housekeeper sniffed in derision. "I can't stand it when he starts trying to act like he's in charge around here."

"But he's right," Variola told her. "This can't go on."

"It goes on until we are done. Until we are successful."

"We have tried. It is not possible. When will you accept that?"

"How *dare* you give up?"

Variola frowned. "I have enough blood on my hands."

"You took an oath."

"To someone who is no longer here."

Mrs. Hoffman bristled. "How *dare* you give up on her?" she repeated, more forcefully.

Variola folded her arms over her chest. "He is right. The games, as he calls them, must end. Too much blood has been shed." She narrowed her eyes at Hoffman. "Who was the woman who came into the house tonight? How did she get here? What has happened to her?"

Mrs. Hoffman ignored her questions. "If and when our games are to end, *I* will give that command. *You* will not tell me."

"I took no oath to you."

"I speak with her authority."

"Ah, but you haven't been listening to me, have you, Hoffman? The rules are changing. She doesn't have authority anymore." Variola smiled. "I do."

"Don't you *dare* to presume supremacy here."

"It is *you* who should not dare." Variola lifted her chin as high as Mrs. Hoffman's. "Remember who I am. Why you brought me into your games. Do you really want to go head-to-head with me? Are you really that confident of your abilities, Hoffman?"

The other woman backed off, but just a little bit. "I'm confident of hers, and she won't stand for insubordination."

That only made Variola burst out laughing. The sound of chimes echoed through the room. When she caught her breath, Variola started to reply, to say something in response to Mrs. Hoffman's threat, but then she decided against it. Her laughter was all the response that was necessary. So she laughed again, and kept laughing as she climbed the stairs to her room. Mrs. Hoffman stood staring after her, her fists clenched at her sides.

45

Rita paid the bartender for her beer. "Thanks," she said. "I should be getting home."

"They ever find out who killed that kid?" the bartender asked as Rita slid off her stool.

"Which one?"

"The boy you were here with a while back."

"Nope." She felt a little woozy from the beer. She shouldn't have had two. She should have just had a glass of wine. "But I expect they will soon."

Tomorrow morning, after she had told sweet little Liz all about the affair she'd had with David, Rita planned to go down to the police station and reveal everything that Jamison had told her to Detective Foley. Then she would sit back and watch the show.

She couldn't wait.

Rita stepped outside of Mickey's Bar into the cool night air. The sky was a dome of stars, little pinpoints of light in a vault of endless midnight blue. A light breeze rustled the fronds of the palm trees overhead. The beer sat uneasily in Rita's stomach, making her a little nauseous. Once again she wished she'd just had a glass of white wine.

She was parked out in back of Mickey's, near the Dumpster. When she'd gotten here, the lot had been packed; it was the only spot she could find. She walked through the parking lot, her feet crunching the gravel, her head starting to pound. She was feeling low as well as sickly. What was she about to do? Did she really want to do it?

She loved David, after all. Did she really want to destroy his life?

But how vicious he'd been to her. How cruel. His words still sounded in her ears.

I don't love you! I never loved you! I used you, Rita! I was an unhappily married man and I used you! Get that through your head!

She covered her ears with her hands, as if to block out the memory.

But maybe she could still win him back . . . maybe . . .

No, she told herself. *It's over.*

All that was left for her was revenge.

But did she really want that? Was she really as bitter as all that?

She reached her car. She opened her purse, searching for the fob to unlock the door.

Behind her, she heard the crunch of gravel.

She turned, not in any way alarmed, just indifferently curious, and what she saw was a figure in the darkness, moving quickly toward her.

Rita never had time to be afraid.

She barely had time for pain.

The sound of the blade through the air was immediately followed by a cold, burning sensation against her belly, and in the last seconds of consciousness, she caught a glimpse of red blood and amber beer exploding onto the side of her car.

The blade came swinging at her throat, and everything went dark for Rita.

She had never even screamed.

46

Liz woke with a start. Glowing green through the darkness, the clock read 3:15.

All at once, she felt cold and realized David wasn't in the bed beside her. She'd fallen asleep waiting for him to come upstairs, but apparently that had never happened. Liz sat up and switched on the light.

She gasped. David was sitting in a chair across the room, wrapped in a bathrobe, just staring straight ahead at her.

"David?" Liz asked. "Are you all right?"

"No," he replied in a soft voice.

"What's the matter?" she asked.

"I have to leave in the morning."

"What do you mean?" Liz swung her legs out of bed and placed her feet against the floor. "David, you can't be serious!"

He stared over at her with dead eyes. His voice was monotone. "Delacorte sent me an email he just received. A Dutch company is going to launch a takeover bid of our entire European holdings."

"You just got back from Europe," Liz said feebly.

His expression didn't change. "I thought I'd put the problems to rest. Apparently I didn't."

"How long will you be gone?"

"I'm not sure."

David didn't smile, didn't apologize, didn't show any sign of any emotion. If he was upset that he had to leave, he didn't express it. If he was glad, he didn't express that either.

"Are you telling me the whole story?" Liz asked. "Is there something else wrong?"

"Nothing else is wrong." He continued staring at her, which made Liz supremely uncomfortable. "But I have to save the company. Or else my father will blame me."

"Oh, David," she said in a low voice, lying back down and pulling her legs up to her chest.

He continued to sit there.

"At least come back to bed for a couple of hours?" Liz asked.

"I wouldn't be able to sleep. A car is picking me up at five o'clock. I'll be meeting Dad's private jet at the airport at six." He stood. "I should get ready."

Liz heard him walk across the room and step into the bathroom. The door closed behind him. The water in the sink went on. The shower stayed off, however. It had appeared to Liz that David, wrapped in that bathrobe, had already showered. His hair seemed wet and he was barefoot.

Why was he so unapologetic? Why did he seem so utterly resigned to going? After everything Liz had said to him last time, she would have thought he'd at least express some regret about having to leave for Europe again. What the hell was going on with him?

She sat up when he came out of the bathroom and started to get dressed.

"David, please tell me if something else is going on."

"I've just got to go," he said, knotting his tie.

Liz got out of bed. "Did something happen? Please tell me."

He moved those blank eyes over to her again. "What happened was a Dutch company initiated proceedings to take over our holdings."

"Fine," Liz said. "I guess this is what our marriage will be. You taking off unexpectedly and going away for who knows how long."

"I'm sorry, Liz."

Finally an apology. She looked over at him.

But he kept his eyes averted. He slipped on his jacket and grabbed a small suitcase.

"I'll call you," he said, brushing his lips against her hair.

She said nothing. She just stood facing away from him, her arms wrapped around herself, listening as he opened the door and walked out. She listened to his footsteps down the hall until they faded away.

47

"The body's over here, Detective," the cop called to Foley, who was just getting out of his car in front of Mickey's Bar, a cup of coffee in his hands.

"What a way to start our day, huh?" Foley asked Aggie, who was getting out of the passenger side of the car. "How many murders are we supposed to juggle at once?"

"I'm beginning to feel like Benson and Stabler," she quipped.

They crunched across the gravel parking lot. Out in back of the bar, near a Dumpster, an area had been cordoned off with yellow police tape. Half a dozen officers in blue uniforms were milling about. One of them was motioning to Foley.

"The victim's a Latina female, sliced up pretty good at the throat and the stomach," the cop, a tall black man, was saying. "The guy who came to get the trash this morning found her. Looks like she was killed sometime last night."

"And nobody found her until this morning?" Aggie asked.

The cop shrugged. "Parked way back here, I guess nobody noticed."

"That her car?" Foley asked, nodding at the silver Toyota Corolla with blood splattered along its driver's side door.

"Appears to be. She's got a key fob in her hand."

Foley bent down at looked at the dead woman on the ground. She was lying on her side. Her pretty face was pressed down into the gravel. Her eyes were still open.

Her eyes . . .

"Joe," Aggie said, bending down next to him. "I know her . . ."

"Yeah," Foley said. "Yeah, we both do. We interviewed her. About the murder of Jamison Wilkes."

"Right. She said she knew nothing about it."

"Excuse me, detectives."

It was the cop who'd been speaking with them. Joe and Aggie stood.

"This is the bartender from Mickey's. He talked to the young lady last night in the bar."

"What's your name?" Joe asked the man, a short balding redhead.

"Kenny Cooper. We spoke after the Wilkes kid's killing."

"Right. Did you know this victim?"

He shook his head. "Not really. Just to say hello to when she came in for a drink."

"Did she come in often?" Aggie asked.

"Not really. Maybe two or three times a month."

"So you didn't know anything about her?" Joe asked.

"Just that she worked up at Huntington House."

"What did she say last night?"

"Not much. She seemed to be stewing about something, just sitting there by herself. She had two beers. It wasn't until she was leaving that she said anything to me at all."

"What did she say?"

"I asked her if they'd ever found out who'd killed Wilkes. And she said maybe they would soon."

"That a direct quote?"

"As near as I can remember."

Joe looked over at Aggie.

"Guess we're going to have take a ride back over to Huntington House today," he said.

She nodded: "Guess we are."

48

Liz stood at the window of her bedroom, looking down onto the grounds. She hadn't been downstairs yet. For some reason, she just couldn't make herself do it. She felt as if she'd gone back in time, and she was back in those terrible first few days after she'd come to this house, missing David terribly, feeling so all alone, hiding out in her room.

"Mrs. Huntington?"

She turned. It was Mrs. Hoffman at the door.

"I'm sorry to intrude, but you haven't answered the phone."

"No, I haven't. That's because I don't wish to be disturbed, Mrs. Hoffman."

The housekeeper regarded her indifferently. "Normally I would respect that. But Detective Foley is downstairs, and he insists he has to see you."

Liz felt cold terror race down her arms and into her fingertips.

"He first asked for Mr. Huntington, and I told him he'd left for Europe just a few hours ago. Then he said he had to speak with you."

Liz opened her mouth to speak, to blurt out the thoughts that had suddenly raced through her head, but when she realized she wasn't even sure what those thoughts were, that they were just vague, unformed fears and suspicions, she closed her mouth and said nothing.

She followed Mrs. Hoffman downstairs.

What was the real reason David had left here in such a hurry? Had he found something during his search of the house? Had he found out whatever it was that Rita had said was going on under their roof?

Lis steeled herself as she entered the parlor. Detectives Foley and McFarland were sitting on the couch waiting for her. They both stood as Liz entered. Mrs. Hoffman remained behind her. As much as Liz didn't like her, she was glad the housekeeper was with her. For some reason, she didn't want to face the detectives alone.

"Good morning, Mrs. Huntington," Detective Foley said.

"Good morning," Liz replied. "I'm sorry my husband isn't here. I'm sure, had he known you were coming, he would have waited."

Why did she feel the need to say that? Liz wasn't sure.

"I'm sure he would have, too," Foley said. "For now, maybe you can answer a few questions for us."

"I've already told you everything I know about Jamison."

Detective McFarland looked coldly at her. "We're not here about Jamison Wilkes."

"Well, if it's about Audra or those other missing girls, I don't know anything—"

"Rita Cansino was murdered last night," McFarland said.

Liz couldn't reply right away. It was as if the words didn't make sense to her, as if the detective had just spoken in another language she didn't understand.

But then the words penetrated, and Liz felt as if she might vomit.

"Mrs. Huntington," Foley said. "Are you all right?"

"Rita was here last night," Liz said, her voice seeming to come from someplace far away. "She worked a party we had . . ."

"What time did she leave here?" McFarland was asking. Her voice sounded to Liz as if it came from underwater.

She felt Mrs. Hoffman take a step forward, coming up to stand shoulder to shoulder with her. "I'd say it was about eleven o'clock that she left," the housekeeper said, speaking for Liz, who could clearly not form words. "What terrible news this is, detectives."

"Did you notice anything unusual about her?" Foley asked.

Liz remembered the strange look in Rita's eyes as she'd taken her upstairs and showed her that room.

"I thought you would want to know, ma'am. After all, you're mistress of the house. You should know what goes on under your own roof."

"What are you saying, Rita?" Liz had asked.

"Just that I think you should find out who that woman is."

Liz stared helplessly at the two detectives, not knowing what she should tell them. Once again, Mrs. Hoffman, cool as ever, stepped in.

"To be frank," she said, "I was planning on firing her this morning."

Liz felt for a chair beside her and sat down. Otherwise, she thought she might have fainted.

"Why were you going to fire her?"

"She's been rather insubordinate at times. Not following orders." Mrs. Hoffman took a deep breath. "Last night, during the dinner party, she went upstairs when she should have been serving. I think she was tired, and was taking rests in one of the servants' rooms."

"Did Mr. Huntington know about this?"

"We had a conversation in the kitchen after the party was over. I mentioned Rita to him, and told him that she had been insubordinate."

"Did he know you were going to fire her?"

"He may have presumed," Mrs. Hoffman said.

Liz noted Detective McFarland write something down in her book at that point.

"Did Rita know that you intended to fire her?" Foley asked.

"I don't believe so. But she knew we weren't happy with her."

"Mrs. Huntington," Foley said, turning his eyes to her. "Do you have anything to add to this?"

"No," she said in a small voice.

Liz didn't know if Mrs. Hoffman was aware that she'd gone upstairs to the servants' quarters with Rita last night. She might have been seen them; Liz had done nothing to hide her movements, walking straight through the kitchen when she'd come back down. But if Mrs. Hoffman did know, she was saying nothing about it to the detectives. Why?

Because of the questions they might ask.

Liz remembered the words she'd exchanged with Rita.

"If you send Mr. Huntington up there," Rita had said, *"I guarantee you that he'll report back that there was no girl there."*

"How can you guarantee that, Rita?"

"Trust me, Mrs. Huntington."

Liz feared that if she told the detectives about her visit to that room, she'd cast suspicion on David somehow. David—who had acted so strangely in the middle of the night and taken off at dawn.

"Is there anything else you can tell us?" Foley was asking.

"I don't know anything else," Liz managed to say.

"Why did your husband leave so early this morning?"

"He . . . he had some urgent business in Amsterdam."

"What kind of business?"

"I don't know . . . I don't understand his business. Something about an investor. . . . A hostile takeover attempt . . . I never understand what David is talking about when he talks about business."

"I see," Foley said, writing in his notepad.

"Was this a scheduled trip?" Detective McFarland asked. "Had he planned on leaving this morning?"

"No," Liz admitted.

"So the decision to leave was made sometime last night?"

"Yes," Liz said. "He heard from Paul Delacorte, who's on his board of directors, and whatever Delacorte told him upset David. That's when he decided to go. You should speak with Dr. Delacorte. He'll explain it better than I can. He'll explain that David left for very good reasons that have nothing to do with—"

She stopped speaking. She caught the cold glare from Mrs. Hoffman's eyes.

"Nothing to do with what, Mrs. Huntington?" Detective Foley asked.

"I don't know what I was going to say," she replied. "Like I said, I don't understand business. Talk with Paul Delacorte. I'm sure he can answer your questions."

"We'll do that," Detective Foley said. "But in the meantime, we've also asked your husband to return home as soon as possible for questioning."

Liz's eyes lit up. "You've spoken with David? What did he say?"

"We left a message for him," Foley told him. "On his cell phone."

"Oh, but he can't access his voice mails when he's in Europe. His international mobile plan is down—he keeps meaning to have it fixed, he says, but hasn't gotten around to it . . ."

"That's rather odd for a man who travels as much as he does, isn't it?" Foley asked.

"Yes," Liz said. "I suppose it is."

"We found a contact for him on Rita's phone," Detective McFarland explained.

"Rita's phone?" Liz asked.

"It was called 'David's International Mobile.' " McFarland read off the number from her notepad. "Do you recognize that one?"

Liz shook her head. "No. That's not a number I recognize." She was having a hard time processing this new information. "Rita had a contact for David on her phone? A private mobile number?" She laughed. "It can't be him. It must be some other David . . ."

"The voice mail announced it was David Huntington of Huntington Enterprises."

Liz stared straight ahead, not saying a word.

"Are you sure there's nothing else you can tell us about Rita Cansino?" Foley asked.

Liz remained silent. Mrs. Hoffman said, "Nothing else comes to mind."

"You'll call us if you think of anything else?"

"Of course," the housekeeper replied. "Won't we, Mrs. Huntington?"

"Yes," Liz said quietly. "Of course."

"Thank you for your time," Detective McFarland said.

Mrs. Hoffman walked them to the door. Liz remained standing in the parlor, staring straight ahead of her.

But she saw nothing.

49

Inside their car, Joe and Aggie looked over at each other.

"Huntington was having an affair with Rita," Joe said.

"Seems possible," Aggie admitted. "You think he killed her to keep her from telling the wife?"

"Seems possible," Joe echoed.

"So what's the connection to Jamison and Audra?"

"Maybe he was having affairs with them, too," Joe quipped, starting the car.

"I suspect there's more to this than just an extramarital affair," Aggie said.

"I suspect you're right," Joe said, backing out of the Huntington driveway. "A whole heck of a lot more."

"The chief's not going to like us involving David Huntington," Aggie told them as they headed down the street.

"We can't worry about the chief right now. We have a murder to solve."

"But we'll have to worry about him eventually."

"So let's wait for eventually," Joe said.

He stepped on the gas.

50

"Nicki," Liz said into the phone.

"Hey, sweetie! You remembered! My first full day back on dry land!"

At the sound of her friend's voice, Liz started to cry.

"Liz?" Nicki asked. "Oh my God, babe, what's wrong?"

"I . . . oh, Nicki . . . I'm so afraid."

"Afraid of what, honey?"

"There's been another murder . . ."

"Oh, my God, no. At your house?"

"Of a girl who worked here." She sobbed. "And I think . . . I think she and David . . ."

Liz couldn't go on.

"You think she and David what, honey?" Nicki asked gently.

"I don't know what I think. But just now, on the news, they're reporting on Rita's murder and it's all so terrible and they're saying that David is wanted for questioning. He's a 'person of interest,' they're saying."

"Oh, no, baby. Where is David?"

"He left for Europe this morning. He was acting so weird before he left."

"Oh, my poor Liz . . ."

"I can't reach him. But Rita . . . the girl who was killed . . . she had a number for him on her phone. A number I never knew."

"Liz, sweetie, don't despair . . . don't panic . . ."

"There are reporters outside in the street. A couple of them got onto the property and were banging at the door. We didn't answer. We're not answering the phone." She caught her breath. "Oh, Nicki. Something terrible is happening here."

"Hang tight, baby," Nicki told her. "I'm going fly down to be with you."

"Oh, no, Nicki, there's no need . . ."

"Yes, there is, Liz. You're upset. And I'm only in New York. I don't have to be in Atlantic City for another two weeks. I've wanted to come to see you anyway. It's a short flight."

"It's really, okay, Nicki, you don't need to do that. I just needed someone to talk to . . ."

"Well, now we can talk in person. I'm going to look at flights and call you back. In the meantime, just chill, okay?" Nicki's voice was warm and reassuring. "I'm coming down to be with you. Everything is going to be all right."

Liz was still crying when she ended the call.

She looked around the room.

She was completely alone.

But the fragrance of gardenias overwhelmed her.

51

"Those men in the street," Mrs. Martinez told Variola, stumbling breathless into the kitchen through the back door, "they are like hyenas. Shouting at me, grabbing at me."

"What did you say to them?" Variola wanted to know.

"Nothing, of course." The older woman's eyes hardened as she looked at the chef. "But what they told me . . . I cannot abide this any longer."

"Be careful what you say now."

Mrs. Martinez was shaking her head. "Rita was a foolish girl. A troublemaker. But she didn't deserve to die."

"No, she did not," Variola agreed. She took a deep breath. "She did not deserve to die."

"This can't go on," Mrs. Martinez said. "I am done with it. From here on out, I am done. Even if I have to quit my job here. I am done. I have my children, my grandchildren to think about."

Variola frowned. "Oh, but I'm afraid it's not that

easy, my dear. Not that easy to walk away from. Once you get involved, Papa Ghede does not forget."

Mrs. Martinez became distraught. "I thought this would help my family! That's why I became a part of this . . . for no other reason. I am not like the others . . . you know that! I thought I could help my family by taking part. We have struggled so much . . . been poor too long!"

"I know your reasons," Variola said quietly.

Mrs. Martinez grabbed hold of her arm. Variola stiffened.

"But now I can't risk anything happening to them," the older woman cried. "I can't risk my babies! My little Marisol and Luis!"

"You risked them the moment you agreed to take part," Variola told her coldly.

"I had no idea . . ." Mrs. Martinez dissolved into tears.

Variola shook herself free of her and moved across the room. "For now, just go about your duties as usual. Say nothing."

Mrs. Martinez looked over at her, terror shining in her bloodshot eyes. "All of my duties?"

"All of them," Variola responded in a low voice.

"I can't . . . not anymore."

"Do it for Marisol and Luis, if you're so worried about them." Variola lifted the tray she had prepared earlier, holding a bowl and a pitcher. She handed it over to Mrs. Martinez. "Now get moving."

The other woman hesitated, then took the tray. "It can't go on . . . it's not working. Not the way we had hoped."

"Go on with you," Variola said, looking away from her.

"We had such great hopes for you, Variola. We had thought you could do what you promised. But now . . . it is all falling apart."

Variola said nothing as she lifted a large knife from a drawer. She slid her fingers along its shiny, sharp blade.

"When does it end?" Mrs. Martinez asked. "Tell me, Variola, when does it end?"

Variola turned savagely on her, brandishing the knife. "Go! Do what you are obligated to do! Ask me no more!" The fury spewed from her lips. "Variola will tell you when it ends! You do not tell Variola!"

Mrs. Martinez gasped a little, then turned and ran up the back stairs with the tray.

Variola dropped the knife onto the countertop. It rattled against the granite. She covered her face with her hands.

52

Liz sat on a concrete bench in the back garden, her hands folded in her lap, surrounded by spiky red alpinias and spidery blood lilies. The buzzing of bees filled the air. The sun was almost directly over Liz's head, baking down on her, causing beads of sweat to pop out on her brow. Her eyes were fixed on that ungodly cow angel, standing several feet away from her, its white marble glowing in the sunlight.

But it was the sculpture's black wings that held Liz's gaze.

What sort of place was Huntington House? Why had Dominique commissioned such horrible things?

And was she really gone? Or did her spirit still wander the earth, as the servants believed, killing those who had angered her in some way—like Audra, Jamison, and Rita?

And if so, would she strike next at Liz, who had, after all, removed her portrait and dared to try to take her place as mistress of Huntington House?

She knew it was absurd. Completely irrational. But

Liz would rather believe that the ghost of Dominique, and not David, had slit Rita's throat.

He killed her because he was having an affair with her, Liz thought to herself as a beautiful yellow butterfly danced above the flowers. That was what Rita had been trying to tell her. She'd had an affair with David, and they'd conducted it in the last room on the left of the servants' quarters. And, if Rita was to be believed, there was another woman there last night as well. Another of David's paramours? Had Rita discovered them? Is that why David had killed her?

No, she said to herself, shutting her eyes. *David didn't kill Rita! Dominique did!*

She had tried reaching David, of course. But all she had was an email address. She didn't have that secret number that Rita had had—that secret number that confirmed for her, like nothing else, that David had been carrying on an affair with the chambermaid. Maybe not recently; Liz left open the possibility that the affair had happened while Dominique was still alive. But still . . . if he'd cheated on one wife, Liz thought, he could cheat on another.

She ran her fingers through her hair. A couple of birds in the tree above her began a high-pitched chatter.

David hadn't loved Dominique, at least not at the end. This Liz knew. He'd been very unhappy; Dominique had been vain and difficult. So maybe David might be excused for having an affair under those circumstances.

But then who was the woman Rita saw go upstairs, if not yet another girlfriend of David's? Was that room in the servants' quarters, the last one on the left, the place where he had gone after he left Liz, ostensibly to search the house? Had his real purpose been to join his ladylove, hidden in that room? Had he then told the woman that they'd been caught, and that she had to leave? Had he then driven over to Mickey's bar and slashed Rita to death?

The police had come by and taken David's car. No doubt they were searching it for blood and other evidence.

Liz wondered what Paul Delacorte had told the police—if he really had emailed David about business problems brewing abroad. Had he really encouraged David to get on the next plane to Amsterdam to manage the situation? Liz wondered if Delacorte might be in on any shenanigans, if he knew of David's affair and was helping him shield it. If so, Liz wouldn't have been surprised. She remembered the old lech's hand on her knee last night.

She felt sad about Rita. She had been so young, so pretty. She'd never really felt she could trust Rita, but the young woman had been kind to her last night. Still, as Liz thought about it, Rita's kindness to her had possibly been a ruse, a way to get her upstairs. There, Rita had hoped, she'd surprise David's latest girlfriend by introducing her to his wife. Did Rita see it as some form of revenge for having been dumped by David?

But if that scenario was true, then where had the woman gone? Was Rita wrong about which room she'd entered? Had the woman slipped out somehow before they got there? But the door was locked from the inside. None of this made any sense at all.

Liz supposed the easiest thing to believe was that

Rita was unstable—hysterical. There was never any woman who snuck upstairs. And Rita's killer was some stranger at the bar, with whom she'd flirted, and who followed her out to her car and killed her for whatever psychotic motivations drove him to do such things. None of this had anything to do with David, or with her. On reflection, that seemed the easiest to believe—the theory that made the most sense.

So why didn't Liz believe it?

Because there were two other dead employees of Huntington House, and a third one just made the likelihood of all of them being coincidences very low indeed.

She had no one she could talk to about any of this here at the house. Mrs. Hoffman had merely said tersely that it was best they said as little as possible to the police and to anyone until David returned; we wouldn't want to make the scandal any worse, she asked, would we? Then the housekeeper had disappeared somewhere in the house. Liz had thought about talking with Variola; the chef had offered a sympathetic ear in the past, and Liz thought Variola might be able to help her feel better again now. But in the end, she'd agreed that Mrs. Hoffman was right: until they heard from David, the best thing was to say nothing to anybody.

She was conflicted over the fact that Nicki was coming to see her. It was a sweet, lovely gesture, of course, and certainly Liz would be glad to have a real friend to lean on, someone unconnected to this house and its secrets, someone who would be there for her and for her only. But Liz also knew Nicki's tendency to stir the pot. Nicki wasn't known for her discretion; Liz was going to have to insist that her friend not go around telling off Mrs. Hoffman—or worse, snapping at detectives Foley and McFarland when they asked questions that seemed too tough on Liz. Nicki was likely to start shouting at the reporters in the street, and no doubt she'd confront David, too, when he came home, badgering him to tell what he knew.

Liz sighed. She was going to have to keep Nicki on a short leash or she just might set a match to this powder keg, making everything much, much worse.

If only there was one person she could trust . . .

At that very moment, a hand gently gripped her shoulder.

"I hope I'm not disturbing you," came a familiar male voice.

Liz looked up. Roger stood above her, looking down at her. The sun reflected the quiet concern in his eyes.

She sprang up and was immediately in his arms. "Roger!" she cried.

"There, there, Liz," he said softly in her ear.

"Oh, Roger, it's all so terrible."

"I know. I heard it all on the news. The police are publicly asking David to return from Europe as soon as possible."

She looked up at him. "They're calling him a 'person of interest.' "

"That doesn't necessarily mean suspect."

"I know, but . . ."

He placed his hand gently against her cheek. "You can't possibly think he had anything to do with Rita's death, do you?"

"I . . . I don't know what to think. He acted so strange before he suddenly left . . ."

"David often acts strange when it comes to business matters."

Liz nodded, breaking free of Roger's embrace and taking a few steps away from him. She had let herself forget for a moment that there were eyes everywhere in this house.

"I just worry . . ." Liz couldn't finish. "Oh, Roger, she had a private number for David on her phone. An international mobile number."

Roger nodded.

"You knew this?" Liz asked.

"I never knew for certain, but . . ." He hesitated, then spoke. "Liz, during the last couple months of Dominique's life, we all noticed how . . . how close David and Rita had become."

"So he *was* having an affair with her!"

"I don't know how close." He hesitated again. "But Dominique suspected as much."

"Did she confront Rita?"

"Not that I know of. There wasn't really all that much time. Rita hadn't been here very long before Dominique died."

Liz's brain was processing this new information. "So then . . . possibly . . . when David and I returned here, Rita was hoping their romance might continue."

"Do you think it did?"

"I don't know." She thought about it some more. "Actually, no, I don't think it did. David was only here such a short time, and we were always together. Unless he was sneaking off to see Rita in the middle of the night after I was asleep . . ."

Even as she spoke the words, she recalled last night, how she had fallen asleep expecting David at any moment, only to wake up and realize he hadn't come back . . .

"Oh, Roger, I don't know what to think," Liz said, and she started to cry.

Once again Roger wrapped his arms around her. How good his arms felt.

"You don't deserve this, Liz. You deserve to be treated like a queen."

He reached down and kissed her on the forehead.

She looked up.

Their eyes held.

He bent down to kiss her on the lips.

But at the last moment, Liz pulled away.

"They're watching us," she whispered.

"Who's watching us?"

"This house! Everyone!"

"Liz, maybe you need to get away for a while."

She stared at him. "That's what they want. They want to drive me out of here."

"Who wants that?"

"Mrs. Hoffman." She paused. "Dominique."

"Dominique is dead."

"I've been smelling gardenias all morning. All through the house. Even out here."

Roger sighed. "Are you being serious, Liz? Are you trying to tell me you think her ghost is responsible for all this? Have the servants' stories finally gotten to you?"

"I just know that something very strange is going on in this house. And while yes, it looks bad for David, I think Rita's death is part of something much larger, much more sinister."

"And why do you think that?"

"Because Jamison was killed after telling me that he believed Dominique's ghost had killed Audra, and because Rita was killed after she tried to tell me something about a woman who had snuck into the house."

"A woman tried to sneak into the house?"

Liz nodded. "Rita said she saw her come in the back door and go upstairs to the servants' quarters."

"And where did this woman go in the servants' quarters?"

"The last room on the left."

Liz noticed what could have been a slight flicker of recognition in Roger's eyes.

"I suspect that's where David and Rita used to meet to carry on their affair," Liz continued. "Rita assumed the woman was there for a similar rendezvous with David. But she wasn't there when we went inside, Roger. There was no woman in the room!"

He smiled kindly. "So Rita was mistaken. Or deliberately lying."

"The door was locked from the inside, Roger. Someone had gone into that room! And then promptly disappeared!"

He took a step toward her, attempting to take her hand. Liz resisted him.

"Liz," Roger said. "Listen to yourself. You're not making sense."

"I didn't claim any of it made sense," she replied.

"So you think the woman was a ghost. Dominique's ghost, most likely."

She looked away. "I don't know what to think."

Roger laughed gently. "But if so, Rita knew Dominique. She would have recognized her."

"Maybe she did. Maybe she thought seeing Dominique back from the dead would scare me to death. I don't know, Roger. All I know is that both Jamison and Rita tried to give me some information, tried to warn me in some way, and immediately thereafter, both of them were murdered. There has to be something in all of that."

"So are you going to give the police this information?"

"I'm waiting until I speak with David. I owe him that much."

Roger was nodding. "Of course." He let out a long breath. "Oh, Liz, I wish I could help you. I just don't know what to say to all of this."

She smiled, and this time took his hand on her own initiative. "Your friendship means the world to me."

His face tightened. "David has no idea how lucky he is."

"You're sweet, Roger."

"If I were him, I would never leave you. I'd always be by your side."

He lifted Liz's hands to his lips and kissed her palm.

"Have your parents heard the news?" she asked.

"If they have, they wouldn't call me," Roger replied. "But I'm sure they know. This won't be very helpful for Huntington Enterprises stock."

"I have to believe that David is innocent," Liz said.

"And therefore, these murders are the work of some avenging ghost."

"David wasn't here when Audra was killed," Liz reminded him. "He was on a cruise ship somewhere in the middle of the Atlantic, with *me*."

"That's a pretty solid alibi."

"So whoever killed these three people—"

"You don't believe the three deaths could be unre-lated?" Roger interrupted.

Liz shook her head emphatically. "No. That's just impossible to believe. The same killer murdered Audra, Jamison, and Rita—and for similar reasons, I believe. And whether human or something else, something we can't explain, there is some connection to this house." She paused and looked over at him. "To Dominique."

"What do you intend to do now, Liz?" Roger asked.

"I'm not sure. I need to speak with David before I do anything. But then . . . I don't know what I'm going to do, but I'm certainly not just going to sit around here and wait for the next knife to swing through the air. Because I'm pretty sure the next target will be me."

"Liz," Roger said, troubled by her words. He squeezed her hands in his. "You know I'm here for you. I will do everything I can."

"Thank you, Roger." She carefully extricated her hands from his. "But the first step is to wait for David to get home, presuming he responds to the police's call that he return."

"It wouldn't be like David to ignore the law. He'll come if he's ordered to do so." Roger sighed. "But the weather might be a problem. Have you heard about the hurricane off Cuba?"

"No," Liz admitted. "I switched off the television after hearing the news about Rita, and I have studiously avoided being online."

"The fear is that it's going to slam right into the Florida coast, a direct hit, on Wednesday. It's a pretty powerful storm, too. Could be a category five. If David doesn't get back in the next twenty-four hours, that could delay him another few days at least."

"Well, whenever he gets here," Liz said, "that's when I start asking questions." She looked at Roger with hard eyes. "And if I don't like the answers, then I'm going to see Detective Foley. I hope David will go with me. But if he doesn't . . ."

Liz didn't finish the sentence. But it was very clear that one way or another, she would eventually tell the police everything she knew and suspected.

"May I at least take you to dinner tonight?" Roger asked.

"Thank you, but I don't want to be seen in public. Too many reporters asking too many questions."

"Then I'll have dinner sent in to the gallery. I'll send my car around. What do you say?"

"All right," Liz agreed.

His face lit up. "Excellent. Expect the car around seven."

"Thank you, Roger."

He kissed her hand again and left.

She was, perhaps, playing with fire. She couldn't deny her attraction to Roger, and he clearly felt the same way about her. But she needed a friend. And right now Liz could think of nothing she would like more than a quiet dinner alone with Roger.

53

The dark narrow hallway was strung with cobwebs. Every few minutes Variola had to stop and peel the sticky strings from her face. Her way was lit only by a series of bare bulbs that hung from the ceiling, casting a dim, pinkish light along the narrow corridor. The odor of musty rooms and damp wood was everywhere.

She steeled herself. What she intended to do was not going to be easy. But she had to do it. There was no longer any other way. Things were spiraling out of control.

At the end of the hallway was a door. It was a small door, unlike any other in the house, barely large enough to fit through. Each time Variola had passed through that door in the past, she'd needed to lower her head and pull in her shoulders. On the other side of the door, the room was equally as small. How it stank inside that room. Variola shuddered to think of it.

She reached the door and paused.

Do it, Variola, she told herself.

In the deep pocket of her jacket, she felt the knife, wrapped in soft fabric.

The taking of a life was repugnant to Variola. But this thing behind the door . . . that was no life. It was a mockery of life.

She placed her hand on the doorknob.

But at that very moment the door opened, and Mrs. Hoffman stood in the doorway, the white mask of her face staring at Variola. In her hands she held the tray that Variola had given to Mrs. Martinez earlier.

"What are you doing here?" Mrs. Hoffman hissed.

Variola took a step back. She quelled the sudden thumping of her heart and projected an outward calm. "What I always do when I come here," she said.

"You never come this time of day."

"Maybe I need to come more often."

Mrs. Hoffman stepped out of the room, bending her head so that she could fit, and closed the door behind her.

"You said it wasn't working."

Variola eyed her cagily. "Maybe I was wrong."

"You don't think you were wrong." Hoffman eyed her just as cagily in return. "You came here to do something else."

"What else would I come here to do?"

"After what you said to me the other day," the housekeeper told her, "about shifting responsibilities and changing allegiances, I don't think you need to come here at all anymore."

Variola's large eyes opened wide. "At all? What would you do then?"

Mrs. Hoffman smiled. "I think we would do just fine."

Variola laughed, the sound echoing in the narrow corridor. "You really *do* think you have become that powerful, that you no longer need me. Well, you are mad, Hoffman. I've always thought so, but now I know for sure."

"Haven't you heard?" Mrs. Hoffman asked. "There's a hurricane headed this way."

Variola was momentarily at a loss for words. "You can't think that you can do such a thing on your own . . ."

"But I can! I would like you to help me, but if you refuse, I will do it on my own."

"Impossible," Variola said.

"It's hard accepting the fact that you're not needed anymore, isn't it, Variola? Did you think we had learned nothing from you? You've been a very good instructor, I'll grant you that much. How very much we've learned from you."

Variola's dark eyes flashed. She pushed past Mrs. Hoffman and took hold of the doorknob again. It was locked. But locked doors couldn't stop Variola.

Yet—it would not yield to her will.

"What have you done?" Variola spun around to face the housekeeper. "You have no idea of what you are playing around with. Papa Ghede will not allow—"

"I don't give a flying fuck about Papa Ghede. He's your god, not mine." Hoffman gave her that strange approximation of a smile. "Besides, it is not what *I* have done, but what *she* has done. The power flows through her. I am merely her handmaiden." Her eyes glowed. "Did you really think you might replace her as head of this coven? That I might serve *you*?"

"Without Variola, you are playing a very dangerous game."

Mrs. Hoffman smiled. "If I were you, Variola, I'd pack my bags and leave this house at once. I can't fire you myself—I'll have to wait until Mr. Huntington returns, of course—but wouldn't it be a pity to end your glorious career convicted of murder?"

Variola glared at her.

"I think the death penalty in this state is lethal injection," Mrs. Hoffman went on. "But they ought to burn you. Isn't that the only way to kill a witch? By fire?"

"The only one who will burn is you, Hoffman. In hell."

What passed for a smile crossed the housekeeper's face. "You see, you don't frighten me anymore, Variola. She and I—we have found ways to protect ourselves."

"You're deceiving yourself," Variola told her.

"You couldn't open that door, could you? You no longer have power here, Variola. Your reign is ended."

"I'm going to stop you," Variola promised.

"I don't matter," Mrs. Hoffman said. "I never have. It's always been *her*. And *she* has passed out of the realm of your control, Variola. There is no way you can stop the dead."

She turned and made her way down the dark corridor, leaving Variola standing alone outside the door.

Yet try as she might, Variola could not get inside the room. She tried the knob, she tried summoning every ounce of her power and strength—but the door was truly closed to her. Her way was barred. How had Hoffman done it?

Variola vowed that she would find out—and that she would win.

Because if she didn't—everyone in this house would be destroyed.

54

The car was waiting outside the gallery to take Liz back to Huntington House, but she didn't want to leave. The wine they had consumed—two whole bottles between them—was making her head spin a little, and she felt warm and safe in Roger's cozy lounge, sitting on the small couch beside him, talking about anything and everything these past three hours.

"Thank you for dinner," Liz said. "It was just what I needed."

"You don't have to leave," Roger replied, taking her hands in his.

"We both know I *do* have to leave," she told him, extricating her hands from his grip and standing up. "I'd like nothing more to stay here and keep talking, but . . . it's late, Roger."

She had shared everything with him. Not just her fears and worries about David and the house and Dominique, but also the stories of her father abandoning her family so long ago, and her mother's struggles with alcohol. She'd shared the recent telephone conversation she'd had with her mother, and all sorts of long-

suppressed guilt had come spilling from her mouth—
how she'd abandoned her family by taking the job on
the cruise ship just as her father had once walked out
on them. She'd only made it worse by running off and
marrying David without telling any of them. Now they
were going to hear on the news that Liz's husband was
wanted for questioning in a murder. What a way to
meet him!

Liz had started to cry at that point, and Roger had
held her tight. Resting her head against his chest, she'd
listened to his steady heartbeat. Roger spoke low, in
comforting tones, telling her he suspected she'd spent a
lifetime blaming herself for other people's problems.
She needed to stop doing that, he said. As he'd spoken
those words, he'd stroked her hair. Liz had felt so warm
and protected.

She was smart enough to know where the night was
headed. Each time things got a little close, she extricated herself, just as she had done now, standing up
from the couch and telling Roger she really needed to
get home.

He stood facing her. "Liz, if David—"

She put a finger to his lips to silence him. "Don't
say any more."

"But Liz—"

"Roger, I have to hear him out. I have to let him
make this right, if he can."

"And if he can't?"

"Then . . ." Her voice hesitated. "Then, I don't
know."

"Then can I tell you that I love you?"

She looked up at him, into those soulful eyes of his.
"Oh, Roger, don't say—"

But he was kissing her. She couldn't have stopped him. Even if she had wanted to.

It was bliss. Liz wanted to cling to him.

But she pulled away.

"No," she said. "This is wrong. I have to give David the chance to make things right."

Roger just nodded, and backed away.

"Thank you for everything," Liz said, grabbing her purse, realizing the wine was making her walk a little unsteadily. "Really, Roger, everything. Please know how grateful I am."

"I'm here if you need me," he said, and walked her to the back door.

There, away from any reporters, was the car he'd hired for her. Liz slipped into the backseat. She watched as the car drove away from the gallery. Roger stood on his back step waving at her until the driver finally turned the corner and headed back to Huntington House.

Back home—*Could this ever truly be home?* Liz wondered—she was plunged right back into a dark chasm in her mind full of doubts and despair. For those few hours with Roger, she'd escaped those thoughts. But now here, back within the polished marble of Huntington House, Liz was once again tormented. The wine was muddying her thinking, so she couldn't reason herself out of it. All that kept running through her mind was: *Rita tried to show me something. She was genuinely surprised when nothing was in that room. If a woman had indeed gone in there, who was she? And where had she gone?*

The house was eerily quiet. Mrs. Hoffman and Variola were presumably sound asleep in their rooms, and the other servants had all gone home. Liz stood motionless in the parlor, breathing in and out, trying to calm her sudden attack of nerves.

Her head was spinning faster now. She'd put away a whole bottle of wine. She tried to force herself to think clearly. To scissor through the thick haze that was clouding her reason. But she could hear only one thought banging around in her brain.

One thought only.

She knew what she had to do.

Slowly, silently, Liz moved from the parlor through the dining room and into the kitchen. The chrome and granite and stainless steel sparkled in the moonlight that poured through the window. Liz took a deep breath and crossed through the kitchen. She opened a drawer of the cupboard and withdrew a pin very much like the one Rita had used. She gripped it tightly in her fist. Then she resumed walking.

She paused at the back stairs and looked up into the dark.

The last room on the left.

Carefully Liz ascended the stairs, not wanting to awaken Variola or Mrs. Hoffman. She had one goal in mind. One goal only.

There *was* a woman that night, she firmly believed. Rita really *had* seen someone go into that room. So, the question was, how had she gotten out?

There had to be a way.

And might the answer to that puzzle shed light on other mysteries of this house?

Liz reached the top of the stairs and paused again. She could hear her heart beating in her ears. She felt dizzy—the wine really had a hold on her—so she moved away from the stairs, suddenly fearful that she'd topple down to the kitchen floor.

In the darkened hallway, she made her way.

She reached the last door on the left.

The door will no doubt be locked from the inside, Rita had told her.

Why do you say, "no doubt"? Liz had asked.

Because that's what the instructions always were, Rita had replied.

Who had given Rita those instructions? David, clearly. This was where they had met, where they had carried on their affair under Dominique's nose. Now who was meeting David here? And was Dominique still aware of it—still angry—still seeking revenge?

The door was locked. Liz opened her fist and removed the pin with her other hand. With trembling fingers she inserted the pin into the hole in the doorknob, fumbling around until she managed to pop the lock.

The door opened with a tiny creak.

Liz stepped inside.

She felt for a light switch and flipped it on.

Once again, no one. Just a twin bed and a small dresser. Liz pulled open the dresser drawers. They were all empty.

She looked around the room. No way out. The window was too small for anyone to fit through, and besides it seemed sealed shut. There were no trapdoors on the floor, no escape hatches in the ceiling.

Liz moved over to the closet. The door was ajar. She stepped inside, nudging the pair of wire hangers on the rod, sending a soft tinkling sound through the room. Liz moved her fingers up and down the back wall of the closet. No, nothing there either—but then, just as she was about to take her hands away, she felt something.

A small groove running the length of the back wall of the closet, all the way down to the floor.

Liz fished out her phone from the pocket of her pants and turned on the light. She saw she had several messages from Nicki—she'd turned off the ringer on her phone so as not to be disturbed while she was having dinner with Roger—but she'd have to read them later. Right now she had more urgent business. She trained the light on the back wall of the closet. Yes, she could see the groove. It was very difficult to discern, but now that she had felt it, she could see it clearly enough. Liz pressed against it. A soft, scraping sound followed.

Her heart was threatening to burst up her throat and out of her mouth. Liz pressed harder against the wall. Suddenly, without any warning or any further sound, the back wall of the closet slid inward. It was a door.

Liz shined the light of her phone into the darkness behind the wall. *I've heard things*—her mind was racing—*footsteps—they seemed to be coming from within the walls . . .*

Despite the bright white light, she couldn't make out much. She took a step closer, moving her head slightly through the opening. She could now see out a small, very narrow passageway leading off to the right. The passage couldn't go very far, Liz speculated, as it would end at the back wall of the house.

Steeling herself again, she took a step into the passageway and shined her light forward. As she'd anticipated, the corridor did indeed end at the back wall of the house. But there was a ladder at the end that led up into a hole in the ceiling and another that led down into a hole in the floor.

Liz realized the truth: these passageways led all through the house, between the walls!

For a moment she felt brave enough to go farther, to take the ladder up into the attic or down into whatever lay below, and see what she might find. But she quickly rejected the notion. Liz had seen enough horror movies in her day to know that wasn't a good idea. No way was she climbing through the walls of the house by herself, at night, a little woozy from too much wine.

So she backed out of the passageway into the closet. There was plenty of time to ask questions—of David, of Mrs. Huntington, of Thad the caretaker—later. At least she knew now how the woman Rita had seen had gotten out of the room.

Liz's heart settled down in her chest.

But as she was sliding the secret panel closed, the overhead light in the room behind her suddenly went out.

Liz spun around, shining the light of her phone into the darkness.

"Who's there?" she asked.

She caught a flash of something in the dark. The light from her phone was like a spotlight, picking out only the occasional shape in the room but failing to illuminate everything. Liz moved it frantically back and forth. Once again she spotted something—the flutter of some fabric—but then it was gone, and despite her attempt to follow it with her light, she couldn't find it again. But she could hear something now. A rustling sound.

And it was coming from behind her.

She hadn't closed the panel all the way. In terror Liz spun around, shining her phone in that direction, just in time to see a face—

A deformed, twisted, purple face—

The woman she had seen outside, in the sculpture garden!

Hideous bulging eyes—

Swollen cheeks—

A mouth contorted to the side of her face—

Long matted gray hair—

And hands like talons reaching out for her—

Long gnarled fingers encircled Liz's forearm, and she screamed. Her phone went flying from her hands, skittering across the floor.

"Get away from me!" Liz cried, yanking her arm away from the woman.

In the darkness Liz backed away. Where had the woman gone? It was too dark in the room for Liz to see clearly. She spun around, afraid the woman was behind her. Then, off to her right, she heard a whooshing sound. A shard of moonlight from the window revealed the source.

The long, shining blade of a knife swinging through the air.

In that instant, Liz was overwhelmed by the fragrance of gardenias.

"No!" she screamed as the deformed woman leapt at her from the darkness, knocking her violently to the floor. Liz kicked, clawed, and punched at the thing on top of her, knowing that at any second, that knife could make contact with her flesh and then it would be over.

But all at once, the woman withdrew, scuttling away in the darkness. Liz sat there panting on the floor, covering her head with her hands, too terrified to move. She could still hear the woman moving around the room, swinging the blade through the air. Was she planning to leap at her again?

Liz knew she had to make a run for the door, which was still open. It was her only hope. But just as she was about to get to her feet and run, hands were suddenly back on her, gripping her by the shoulder. Liz lunged upward and took a swing at the woman's face.

"Liz!"

Her fist stopped short of its goal. The face above her was not that of her attacker.

It was Nicki.

"Liz, what's wrong?" her friend asked. "What's happened here?"

Liz could see by the light of the moonlight that they were alone in the room. The deformed creature must have escaped through the secret panel. She tried to speak, to tell Nicki about the danger they might still be in, but all that came out of her mouth were sobs.

"There, there, kiddo," Nicki said, wrapping her arms around her. "Everything's going to be okay now. You don't have to worry about a thing anymore. Nicki's here."

55

Joe Foley sat looking at three photographs he'd placed in a row on his desk.

Jeanette Kelly. Tonesha Lewis. Lana Paulson.

The first two were friends of Audra McKenzie, and had gone missing around the time of Audra's death. The last girl was just reported missing yesterday by her sister.

Jeanette was a freckle-faced redhead. Tonesha was a striking African American beauty. Lana was a little bit older than the other two, blond, with a certain hardness to her eyes and the tattoo of a star on her neck.

There's no reason to think there's a connection, Joe told himself. As far as he could see, Lana Paulson didn't know the other two. And girls go missing every day.

But what had compelled Joe to place the three photographs together on his desk was one small fact: Lana Paulson had disappeared on the same night that Rita Cansino was killed.

"So what?" he muttered to himself, gathering up the photos and returning them to their respective files. It was just a silly hunch.

But Joe tended to trust his silly hunches. They'd often turned out to be right in the past. Ever since the day he'd found his mother dead.

Maybe this hunch would be the exception to the rule. Maybe this one would be wrong. Still, he'd keep the name Lana Paulson in mind. He'd ask David Huntington, when they finally got to question him, if he'd ever heard of her.

They'd certainly caused a stir by announcing to the press that Huntington was a "person of interest" in the Cansino murder. Given the two other murders of Huntington House employees, the media was running wild with theories: could the esteemed David Huntington be a serial killer, offing his employees one by one? The fact that he'd been a world away when Audra McKenzie was killed didn't stop their speculation. And it was serious enough, apparently, for old Mr. Thomas Huntington to come down to Florida to look into it.

The old man was sequestered with his lawyers in Chief Davis's office at the moment. "Any word from in there yet?" Joe asked, leaning across his desk to Aggie's.

She shook her head. "They've been at it for almost two hours."

"The chief is a personal friend of old man Huntington. I wonder what sort of deal they're cooking up."

Aggie gave him a look as if to tell him to be careful what he said.

Joe sighed. The chief hadn't been pleased when they'd told him that they needed to question David Huntington. Only after much cajoling from Joe and Aggie had he agreed to allow them to publicly announce that Huntington was a person of interest in the Rita Cansino murder investigation. Of course, that had brought David's father spitting and sputtering down from New York, protesting against the insinuations and the slander against his family.

The door to the chief's office opened. Out filed three dark-suited, somber-faced lawyers, followed by a tall, distinguished, silver-haired, square-jawed man of about sixty years of age. His dark eyes darted around the station like a hawk's, landing on Joe before passing on to Aggie and then to the others.

"Don't worry, Tom," Chief Davis was saying, clapping him on the back. "We have it all under control. David needn't worry about a thing when he gets back."

"I should hope not," Mr. Huntington said. "I expect you will do your part to quiet these completely unfounded allegations being bandied about in the press."

"We will do what we can," the chief promised.

Joe watched as Mr. Huntington and his lawyers strode out of the station, chins held high, their postures defiant. But Joe could read through that: they were scared out of their minds. What would this scandal do to Huntington Enterprises, especially if it ended up with their rising young star David Huntington arrested for murder and hauled away in handcuffs?

Once they were gone, the chief let out a long sigh and made his way to Joe and Aggie. The chief was a getting a little soft in the gut—it happened when you were taken off the streets and consigned to a desk all day—but he still had the build of a prizefighter, short and stocky, with big arms and shoulders straining against his crisp white shirt.

"I knew this wasn't going to be easy," the chief said to his detectives. "I still wish we hadn't gone public with David's name."

"We had to exert pressure on him to return, Chief," Joe replied. "He has not responded to any of our repeated calls or to any of our attempts to reach him by email. Even the local police in Amsterdam haven't been able to get in touch with him."

"He may be hiding out," Aggie said. "Never planning on coming back."

"David Huntington is an upstanding member of this community," the chief told her sharply. "He is not some criminal on the run. The Huntington family has done a great deal for this city, for this state—indeed, for this country."

Joe sneered. "And I imagine that's just what Old Man Huntington was telling you in your office."

The chief ignored his comment. "I want you to put out a statement saying that David is not considered a suspect," he said. "Insist that he is merely wanted to provide information. Stress that he is *not* a suspect in this case."

Joe smirked. "Can I imply he's a suspect in *other* cases?"

"Don't get smart, Foley."

Joe stood up. "Come on, Chief. We have a lot of questions about this guy. He gets back from his honeymoon and bingo! Jamison Wilkes is murdered. He's planning to fire Rita Cansino—with whom he was likely having an affair—and bingo! She's found dead, too. And he disappears in the middle of the night, flying off to Europe, and won't return our calls."

"You have no proof he was having an affair with Rita," the chief replied. "And it wasn't David who was going to fire Rita. It was that head housekeeper of theirs.

He doesn't know which maid is getting hired or fired. He's above all that."

"You have to admit it all seems a little fishy, though, Chief," Aggie observed.

"And that's not even taking into account the death of his wife," Joe added.

The chief frowned. "His wife was alive and well last I knew."

"I'm talking about his first wife," Joe said. "Dominique."

"Oh, please, Foley—"

Joe grabbed a stack of papers on his desk and thrust them at the chief. "I've been going over Captain Hogarth's testimony—"

"A lying sack of drunken shit," the chief snarled.

"Why did he change his testimony to say he really had been at the helm of the yacht the night Dominique died? That she hadn't gone out alone? That in fact, he'd taken her out and he had seen her husband on board with her?"

"Because he was trying to extort money from David." The chief folded his arms over his chest. "The inquest discredited Hogarth's second testimony. I called him Captain Hogwash."

"Why would he change his testimony and risk being charged with reckless endangerment or involuntary manslaughter? He stated, for the record, that his conscience was troubling him, that he'd been paid off to hide the truth, to say that Dominique had gone out on her own."

"I interviewed him," Chief Davis said, flexing his muscles under his shirt and coming face-to-face with

Joe. "I decided he was an unreliable witness. Are you questioning my judgment?"

Joe backed down, but just a little. "I just thought it was an odd thing for Hogarth to do, to try to change his testimony after the fact."

"I'm sure his intent was to extort some money from David." The chief shook his head, threw up his hands, and then turned away from them, indicating the conversation was done. "The death of Dominique Huntington has nothing to do with the current investigation," he said over his shoulder. "Zero. Zip. Nada. Now get back to work."

Both Joe and Aggie watched as the chief strode back to his office, slamming the door behind him.

"Well, we're clear where he stands at least," Aggie said.

"I did a little research into Huntington Enterprises," Joe told her, sitting back down and sighing. "Guess who one of the major stockholders in the company is."

"Not the chief," Aggie said.

"Nope," Joe told her. "His son." He paused. "And his brother. *Two* of his brothers, in fact."

"That doesn't mean anything," Aggie told him.

"No," Joe said, but the tone in his voice made clear he didn't believe what he was saying. "It doesn't mean anything at all."

56

Nicki stood at the top of the stairs, looking down into the marble foyer of Huntington House, the morning sun filling the room, reflecting off all the marble and the glittering chandelier. On the wall going down the stairs one of Liz's photographs was hanging, but around it there remained an imprint of a much-larger picture than had once hung in its place. Dominique's portrait, Nicki realized. How it must have tormented poor Liz.

At the moment, Liz was sleeping soundly. Nicki had given her a Xanax after finding her in such a state last night. What a strange welcome Nicki had gotten in this peculiar house. She'd found a flight as soon as she could, wanting to beat this hurricane that the forecasters were saying was getting close to the Florida coast. Liz hadn't responded to her calls or texts, so she'd just come to Huntington House on her own, arriving late, and banging on the door. Had something happened to Liz? Nicki was getting frantic.

Finally the door had been opened by what looked

like an automaton. Right away Nicki had known it was Mrs. Hoffman, the creepy housekeeper with all the plastic surgery that Liz had told her about. Nicki had the sense she'd roused Mrs. Hoffman from bed, though she was fully dressed. She'd introduced herself, and Mrs. Hoffman had asked her into the dark and quiet house. She'd known that Nicki was coming, she said, but hadn't expected her so soon. Nicki explained she'd wanted to get a jump on the hurricane. Mrs. Hoffman had acted as if she hadn't heard the weather reports. She explained that Liz had gone out to dinner with her brother-in-law, and she wasn't sure if she was back home yet. But if Nicki would wait in the parlor, Mrs. Hoffman told her, she'd go upstairs and check.

Waiting in that dark room all by herself—Mrs. Hoffman hadn't even turned on a light for her—Nicki had felt terribly jittery. But she'd practically jumped out of her skin when she'd heard a scream. She recognized the voice. It was Liz. Hurrying off in the direction of the sound—through the kitchen and up some back stairs—she'd found her friend cowering in a heap on the floor of a plain little room. Liz had been nearly impossible to console, babbling about a woman with a knife and a secret passageway. Then Mrs. Hoffman, drawn by the commotion herself, had come in. She had helped Nicki get Liz up to her room and into bed.

At that point, Liz had been too overcome to say much, and after the Xanax, she'd passed right out. Nicki had slept on the daybed in her room, despite Mrs. Hoffman's offer to fix up a guest room for her. No way was she going to leave Liz alone for the rest of the night.

Now, standing at the top of the stairs, Nicki couldn't help but wonder about her friend's state of mind. All of this terrible, nonstop speculation on the news and online—speculation that her new husband might be a murderer—had sent Liz over the edge. She'd always been a bit of a nervous nelly—Nicki remembered how Liz would shake before going onstage the first night of a show—and all this had apparently been too much for her. For weeks she'd been imagining ghosts. Now she was imagining strange women brandishing knives coming out of the walls at her. Nicki needed to get Liz out of here. Her friend needed help. A therapist. A psychiatrist . . . a doctor . . . someone.

As she stood there, looking down, Nicki was surprised when the front door suddenly burst open, almost as if blown by a powerful gust of wind. A tall, gray-haired man barged in, barking orders even before he was fully in the room. "Hoffman! Get out here!" he shouted. "Hoffman! Where are you?"

Nicki pulled back at bit so that she wasn't seen. But she kept an eye on what was going on in the foyer. That creepy Mrs. Hoffman emerged, and greeted the newcomer.

"Mr. Huntington," she said. "I wasn't aware you were coming."

"I took an ungodly early flight and I'm flying back to New York in a couple of hours to avoid the goddamn hurricane that's heading this way." He was looking around the foyer impatiently. "Where's this daughter-in-law of mine?"

So that's David's father, Nicki realized.

She knew she had better get Liz up and dressed. Old Mr. Huntington didn't seem like a man who liked to be kept waiting.

Rushing back into Liz's room, Nicki pulled open the drapes. Blindingly white light filled the room. "Come on, sweetie," she chirped. "Time to rise and shine."

Liz moaned in the bed.

"Liz, you've got to get yourself ready," Nicki told her. "Your father-in-law's downstairs."

Liz opened her eyes. "My—father-in-law?"

"Yeah. And he's impatient to see you. I just heard him talking with Mrs. Hoffman in the foyer."

Liz sat up. "Oh, God, my head hurts."

"It's the Xanax, on top of the whole bottle of wine you drank."

"Oh, God, I really drank all that . . ." Liz's eyes suddenly opened wide. "I had the worst dream . . ."

"And that's all it was, sweetie, a dream," Nicki assured.

Suddenly Liz clutched Nicki's blouse. "No, no, it wasn't a dream. It was real. That woman—her face—she tried to kill me."

"Sweetie, you were drunk. I found you by yourself in a room at the back of the house. You were hallucinating."

"No, no, I wasn't. It was *real*, Nicki. There's a secret passageway in the closet, and she came out of there."

Nicki's heart broke. What had happened to her sweet, innocent, intelligent friend in this house of horrors? She stroked Liz's cheek. "We can talk about it later, honey. You've got to get yourself ready to meet your father-in-law. I'm sure he's here to talk to you about David."

"I should tell him." Liz said. "I should tell him about the secret passage and the woman—and how I smelled gardenias, Nicki!"

"Are you saying the woman you saw was Dominique?"

Liz shook her head. "No, that can't be. Dominique was beautiful. This woman was a monster."

Nicki smiled sympathetically at her. "Oh, sweetie, it was all in your mind. Just like everything else. We have to get you out of here. I want you to come to Atlantic City with me. We'll both get on a flight as soon as this hurricane blows over, and you can spend some time with me setting up my new place. You need to get out of here, honey, away from all this craziness and the cops and the reporters at your front door."

Liz was rubbing her temples. "It seemed so real . . ."

They were interrupted by a hard knock at the door.

"Mrs. Huntington?" came the brisk voice of Mrs. Hoffman.

"She'll be down in fifteen minutes," Nicki called out to her. "I'm getting her up and ready now."

"Very well," Mrs. Hoffman said through the door. "Please tell her Mr. Huntington is here to see her. Mr. *Thomas* Huntington."

"Yeah, she knows." Nicki turned to Liz and motioned for her to stand up. "You want to take a quick shower?"

"Yeah," Liz said, swinging her legs off the bed. "Maybe that will clear my head."

"Sweetie, I wouldn't say anything to the old man," Nicki advised her, following her into the bathroom. "I'm pretty certain this is a guy who has a battery of lawyers always walking two steps behind him."

Liz slipped her nightgown up over her head and turned on the water full blast in the tub. "Why should I worry about lawyers?"

"Who knows? But this guy's son might be arrested for murder . . . he's going to look for anything you say as evidence to get him off."

Liz frowned at her. "I have to believe that David is innocent, Nicki."

"Maybe he is. Let's hope so. I just want to make sure things don't get more difficult for you."

Liz sighed. "So if I start sounding crazy, talking about ghosts and women with knives . . ."

"Exactly. He'll send the cops over here to investigate *you*."

"But what if that crazy woman who attacked me is the same one who killed Rita? And the others?" Liz stepped into the shower, pulling the glass door to enclose her. "Shouldn't the cops know about that?" she shouted over the rush of the water.

Nicki didn't answer. Poor Liz. She really believed there was a woman coming out of the walls and running around the house with a knife. She had gone stir-crazy in this place. And who wouldn't? With that asshole, absent husband of hers—whose innocence Nicki wasn't convinced of—and that creepy housekeeper breathing down her neck?

The sooner Nicki got Liz out of this madhouse the

better. Maybe they could even get out this afternoon. Why wait until after the hurricane? Even if they had to rent a car and drive, they should get out now.

Nicki was afraid if they waited any longer, it would be too late.

57

The buoys clanged as the waves slapped hard against the pier. Gulls were circling in mad sweeps through the dark gray sky. The air was warm and humid. The papers in Joe's hands were curling from the moisture in the air, so he thrust them into his jacket pocket and continued on down the pier.

He scanned the line of boats off to his right. Leather-faced sailors were mooring them tightly to the pier. A few boats had been taken out of the water and were secured to metal contraptions. The pier was abuzz with activity, with a sense of urgency. The weather forecasters were calling the hurricane "Caroline," and she was said to be a doozy.

Joe scanned the names of the boats, looking for the one that had been written on his paper. These captains sure could get creative. *The Codfather. Boobie Bouncer. Marlin Monroe. Aquaholic.* Joe smiled. The name he was looking for was simpler. The *Kathleen Marie.* He spotted it finally, close to the end of the pier. As he hoped, a man was tying her up.

"Ahoy there," Joe called down to the man.

The man, who appeared to be seventy but was probably younger, looked up at him. His eyes were black. His face was like snakeskin, brown and rough and scaly. Large, sandpapery hands gripped a thick stretch of rope. He didn't smile. "Who you looking for?" he asked.

"Captain James Hogarth," Joe said. "Is that you?"

"I don't know anybody else by that name."

"Wonder if I could speak with you for a minute."

"Kind of busy, as you see. Trying to get ahead of Caroline."

"Yeah. They say it's going to be a big one. Some talk of evacuations from low-lying areas."

Hogarth shrugged. "We've been through hurricanes before. We'll get through this one as well."

"I imagine we will." Joe opened his hand to reveal his badge. "I promise I won't take up much of your time."

Hogarth studied him with his black eyes. "I thought I was done talking to cops."

"Well, you never talked to me."

The captain threw down the rope. "I'll be up in a second."

Joe watched him as he climbed around his boat, a surprisingly agile old man. The wind was whipping along the pier, and caught Hogarth's long, thinning white hair, sending it flying upward, making him look for a moment like one of those toy trolls Joe remembered from his childhood. With his big, strong hands, Hogarth gripped the ladder and hauled himself up the pier. He took his time, but Joe didn't note any resentment in the old man's walk toward him. It was almost as if he had expected to be questioned again, and welcomed it.

"So I presume this is about the Huntingtons," Hogarth said when he reached Joe.

"Why do you presume that?"

"Because their names are back in the news. Another murder of one of their people." Black eyes danced under bushy white brows. "This time maybe David's got himself caught."

"You say that as if you think he's guilty," Joe observed.

"Everyone knew he'd been carrying on with that girl."

"Did his wife know? His first wife, I mean."

For the first time Hogarth smiled, revealing a mouthful of broken, missing teeth. "Dominique knew everything."

"Why did your change your testimony?"

Hogarth laughed. "I thought that case was closed."

"You originally said you hadn't taken the boat the day Dominique was killed, then you said you did. Which is true?"

The smile disappeared from the old man's face. "Am I going to be arrested for something?"

"Not if you didn't do anything wrong."

"Isn't giving false testimony a crime?"

"We have ways of overlooking that if you can give us other helpful information."

Hogarth shook his head, as if he was disgusted by the whole conversation. He yanked out from his stained white T-shirt a small gold cross on a thin gold chain. "I believe in Jesus Christ, Detective. I believe that telling lies is a sin, That's why I changed my testimony. Because I couldn't live with the lies I told." He looked back down at his boat. "She was not a good woman. But she didn't deserve to die. No one deserves to have their life ended by someone else."

"So you did take the yacht out that day? And Dominique was on it?"

"It's just as I told your chief. It was a beautiful day, not a cloud in the sky, and Dominique wanted to go out on the water. I took her, sir, yes I did." Hogarth's face clouded. "But Chief Davis wouldn't believe me."

"Why do you think he wouldn't believe you?"

"Because of what else I said."

"And that was?"

Hogarth looked at him. "Surely you know, if you've come to see me now."

"Tell me anyway."

"I told him that once we were out at sea, I saw that David Huntington had come along for the ride as well. I hadn't seen him board. Perhaps he'd already been on board, waiting for us."

"Did you speak with him?"

"No, sir. But I heard him. I was up on the bridge, and I heard loud voices, a man and a woman. That surprised me, because I thought Dominique was the only one on board. I peered down into the cabin as I saw her with him."

"With David."

"Yes, with her husband."

"Are you certain it was him? You were looking from above, and from photographs I've seen, the Huntington yacht was a rather large vessel. Are you sure you got a good look at him?"

"Who else could it have been? It was *him*. It was David Huntington."

"Then how do you account for him being at the house, that same day?"

"I *can't* account for it. Just like I can't account for that storm that suddenly whipped up." Hogarth gripped the cross in his hand tightly. "The sky got as black as night and the waves were so high they were coming up onto the deck. I couldn't keep the boat steady. Within no time it was breaking apart underneath me. I called down to Dominique but she didn't respond. It was like she wasn't on board anymore. Like neither one of them was. They would have answered me in such a storm. The boat's not that big. But I never saw her or him after hearing them argue."

"What happened then?"

"The storm was raging. I figured I was a dead man, that I'd go down with the ship."

"But you didn't."

"I had my life jacket on, and though I went under, I came up again and managed to grab ahold of some of the debris, and finally made it to shore. The storm ended just as quickly as it had come up. Suddenly the seas were calm again. Still, it was late before I made back it to land, and when I got there, I went straight to Huntington House to tell them what had happened."

"Who did you tell?"

"Mrs. Hoffman, the housekeeper."

This surprised Joe. There had been no mention of Mrs. Hoffman in the report.

"You told her that Mrs. Huntington was dead?"

"I told her that I feared the worst."

"What was Mrs. Hoffman's reaction?"

"She was white as a ghost, but then again, she always is." A small smile cracked across Hogarth's face.

"She was upset, but she seemed to know already, even if she acted as if she didn't."

"How could she have known already? There was no Coast Guard report of a storm, and no report of a capsized boat until they found remnants of the yacht the next day."

"You want my opinion? I think David Huntington made it back in the lifeboat and he told her."

"Did you see him at all?"

Hogarth shook his head. "I've never seen him since, except on the news. Mrs. Hoffman insisted I spend the night there, since I was so wet and cold. But in the morning, she handed me an envelope and told me, since the yacht was destroyed, they wouldn't be needing me anymore."

"What was in the envelope?"

"More money than I ever dreamed of seeing in one place."

At that moment the wind kicked up again. Waves were crashing over the boats.

"This is going to be a big one," Hogarth said, looking away. "I'm going to have to bring *Kathleen Marie* up to dry land, I think."

"First you've got to tell me why they gave you all that money."

"They said it was for my years of service. But Mrs. Hoffman, she has a way of telling you things without actually saying them. She spoke of Dominique's death as if somehow it could be construed to be my fault. She wasn't blaming me, she insisted, but she implied others might. So it was best that I say I wasn't at the helm of the ship that day. It was best to say Dominique had gone out on her own." He frowned. "The money guaranteed my silence."

"But it didn't."

"Nope. Look, Detective, I took that money in the first place because my daughter, Kathleen Marie, was sick and I thought it could maybe help her. But no amount of money was going to save her. She was in the end stages of leukemia, and I realized that taking that money was like making a deal with the devil, and you know that never works out. In fact, it might have even hurt Kathleen's chances of getting into heaven." Hogarth took a step closer to Joe. "Blood money. That's what it was. I took that envelope and handed it back to Mrs. Hoffman and went down to the station to speak with Chief Davis. Don't you see, Detective? They gave me that money to keep me from implicating David."

"Well, now, he can't be blamed for a storm."

"But what he did, he did before the storm hit. I called down to the cabin at the first sign of rough waters. And no one was there. At least, Dominique wasn't."

"Where had she gone?"

"I think David threw her overboard while they were arguing."

"You wouldn't have heard this?"

"Not necessarily. And besides, just seconds later, by my reckoning, the storm kicked in, so that's what I was focused on. That's when I think David took the lifeboat and left me to go down with the ship. When I showed up alive, I was a problem that had to be dealt with."

Joe narrowed his eyes at the captain. "It's a compelling story, but you have no evidence to back up your accusation. It's far more believable that the storm knocked Dominique overboard, perhaps as she was trying to secure the lifeboat for herself."

"That storm is hardly a believable alibi."

"Why's that?"

"Because there was no indication of a storm before it hit. No forecasts. Nothing. Not a cloud in the sky. Later, the Coast Guard would record that a brief storm had indeed struck the area, but they were baffled that they hadn't seen it coming. And its duration—let me tell you, Detective, I've been sailing these waters for forty years and I've never seen a storm whip up like that out of nowhere so suddenly and then disappear just as quickly."

"Then how do you account for it?"

"I told you. I don't." Hogarth sighed. "Except . . . maybe there's something to those stories the servants always told. Stories about witchcraft and black magic."

"You don't buy any of that."

"Maybe not fully. But there's something in that house. Dominique . . . she had some curious hobbies. Have you seen those statues of angels with the heads of cows? And when they brought that vodou priestess in to cook for them—"

"Vodou priestess?"

"Variola. The chef. She and Hoffman and Dominique were always whispering together, scuttling around through the house . . ."

Joe took out his notepad and asked Hogarth to spell the chef's name for him.

"I don't know what else to tell you," the old man said after he was finished spelling. "I'll happily come down to the station if you like and give my testimony again—that is, if you can get the chief to listen to me this time."

"I'll let you know if that's necessary, Captain."

Hogarth rubbed his rough hands together. "Well, I've really got to hustle and get *Kathleen Marie* out of the water and tied up safely somewhere. Can I go now? We done here?"

"Yes. That's all the questions I have for now. Thank you."

Hogarth nodded and returned to work, scrambling down the ladder to his boat like a man far younger than his years. Joe watched him for a while, then looked out at the crashing sea. Sails and banners were flapping furiously. The sky had become even darker. The hurricane was approaching quickly, Joe realized.

And it was going to be a doozy.

58

Liz paused outside the parlor, trying to gather her wits before she met her father-in-law for the first time. This wasn't how she'd imagined it would be. She'd imagined David would be with her—not running from the law on a murder charge.

"Go ahead," Nicki whispered to her. "He's in there waiting for you."

Liz took a deep breath and was about to step inside the parlor when she heard Mr. Huntington speak. "Where is that little girl?" he was asking Mrs. Hoffman. "I can only stay a few moments longer. The pilot of my chartered jet is telling me that we only have a very small window to get out of here before the hurricane hits. By the way, have you prepared the house?"

"Thad is shuttering the windows even as we speak," Mrs. Hoffman replied efficiently. "We've been through hurricanes before, here. We know the drill."

"There's quite a bit you'll have to teach this little girl," he said.

Nicki fumed. "Where does he get off calling you a

little girl? I've got a mind to walk in there and tell him off."

"Nicki, please, don't make things worse." Liz sighed. This was precisely why she hadn't been thrilled with the idea of her friend visiting. "Let's just smile and make our way through it."

Not very convincing smiles stretched across both women's faces. Liz lifted her chin and stepped into the parlor, Nicki following behind.

"I'm sorry I kept you waiting, Mr. Huntington," she said, extending her hand.

Her father-in-law shook it briefly, his eyes appraising her. "Unfortunately this will have to be a very brief visit," he said.

"That's too bad. I had hoped our first meeting would be more pleasant. By the way, this is my friend Nicki Stone."

Nicki chirped a "Hullo." Huntington barely gave her a nod.

"But I'm sure you want to get out before the hurricane makes landfall," Liz continued, turning to Mrs. Hoffman. "On my way down here, I saw Thad. I'm pleased to see he's battening down the hatches."

The housekeeper just stood there stonily.

Liz returned her gaze to Thomas Huntington. "Have you heard from David?"

The old man stiffened. "I was about to ask you the same thing."

"Not a word." Liz stood opposite him, meeting his gaze without flinching. "Why do you think that is?"

"I assume he's deep in negotiations with this Dutch miscreant who's trying to take over our company's assets. When he's in the midst of business, David has a laser-like focus."

"You think he hasn't gotten the messages from the police to return, or to at least contact them, regarding the murder of Rita Cansino?"

Huntington's eyes hardened. "David understands priorities."

"I would think his priority should be to clear his name."

"I have just come from a meeting with the police chief, Davis," Huntington told her. "He assures me David is not a suspect, and they will be calling a press conference to make that clear."

"Of course I want to believe that David is innocent," Liz said. "But I'd like to hear that from his own lips. If you speak with him, Mr. Huntington, would you ask him to please get in touch with me?"

"I'm sure he will do so at his first available opportunity. In the meantime, Elizabeth, you do understand the necessity of not speaking further to anyone—no police officers, no detectives, certainly no reporters."

"I have no intention of speaking to anyone until I've spoken with David."

"Very good." The old man took a step toward her. Liz could see the family resemblance to her husband: the same high cheekbones, square jaw, and chocolate-brown eyes. But there was something hard in the old man's eyes, something mean. Cruel. "And among those you should avoid would be my younger son, Roger."

"Roger?"

"I understand you had dinner with him last evening."

Liz glanced over at Mrs. Hoffman, who kept her eyes averted. "Yes, I did. He was very kind in offering me a chance to get out of the house after all this terrible news."

"Roger is not to be trusted."

"I'm aware that he and David have not always seen eye to eye, but Roger has been very kind to me—"

Huntington took another couple of steps closer to Liz, who found herself taking a step back, feeling all at once a little bit threatened. Nicki placed her hand on Liz's arm for support.

"You listen to me, young lady," the old man seethed, wagging a finger at her. "You have no idea what sort of a hornet's nest you've stirred up by befriending Roger. I assume you know about, or have at least figured out, David's little dalliance with the dead girl, Rita Cansino?"

"If it happened, it happened well before he knew me."

"It happened," Huntington told her harshly. "And Dominique found out about it."

"That's all in the past," Liz said defiantly. "It might make detectives suspect David in Rita's death, but it has nothing to do with my marriage or my relationship with David."

"*I'll* say it might make detectives suspect David. Do you know *when* Dominique found out about the little tryst David was having with the chambermaid?"

Liz said nothing, just kept staring at her father-in-law.

"*On the day of her death*," he told her, enunciating each word exactly. "That's why she left in such a state. That's why she ran out of here claiming she needed to get on the water to think. Isn't that right, Mrs. Hoffman?"

The housekeeper nodded emotionlessly. "Yes, sir. She was quite distraught."

"But what right did she have to be distraught, Hoffman?" the old man asked, moving away from Liz to confront the other woman. "Wasn't Dominique being a bit hypocritical in reacting so histrionically to the discovery of David's affair?"

Mrs. Hoffman's face remained unmoved. She said nothing.

Huntington looked back at Liz. "You see, Elizabeth, David was merely retaliating against his wife. My late daughter-in-law had an army of lovers, and she did very little to hide them."

Liz looked away. She remembered the portrait of Dominique, the arrogance in her face, the flaunting of her beauty.

"But the final straw for David," the old man said, lowering his voice and approaching Liz once more, "was the affair she was carrying on right before her death. Do you know who with?"

Liz held his gaze. "No," she said in a small voice. "And I don't want to know."

"*Roger*," Huntington spit, as if he had tasted something bitter and wanted it off his tongue. "David's own brother! It was *Roger* who drove my son to madness. After Dominique's death, David had a complete emotional breakdown. That's why we sent him on that cruise." He paused. "That was why my wife and I were not pleased at David's sudden remarriage. We felt he wasn't quite ready . . . not yet stable enough for another commitment."

Liz was reeling.

Roger—and Dominique! He had never told her . . . Was that why he had pursued Liz? Because he had a vendetta against his hated older brother, and seduced his wives out of spite?

And David—so unstable—so unstable that he might well have killed Rita . . .

Liz thought she might faint. Her knees buckled a bit. Nicki, standing next to her, held her up.

Mr. Huntington was slipping back into his coat. "That is why I want you to stay far away from Roger. A friendship with him could make everything much, much worse. Speak to no one. Say nothing." He turned to Mrs. Hoffman. "You'll see to that, won't you?"

"Of course, sir."

Without a further word, the old man hurried out of the parlor. Mrs. Hoffman escorted him to the front door.

When they were alone, Liz turned to Nicki.

"Cover for me with Hoffman," she whispered. "Say I've gone upstairs to lie down. That I'm very upset and I don't want to be disturbed."

"What are you going to do?"

"I'm going to see Roger."

"Sweetie, not a good idea. You heard what the old man said—"

"I'm not listening to that old blowhard," Liz said, her lips tight with anger. "Roger's been the only one who'd been kind and honest to me since I got here, and I need to hear what he has to say."

"But Liz, it's raining pretty hard out there now—"

"I can handle a little rain. Give me your rental car keys."

"You don't have a license. What if you get pulled over?"

"I'll take that chance."

Reluctantly Nicki gave her the keys.

"I'll be back shortly," Liz said, hurrying out toward the kitchen and the back door.

"Be careful," Nicki whispered after her. "Suddenly I have a very bad feeling."

"You're not alone in that," Liz replied.

59

Thad had secured the shutters over the large plate glass dining room windows. He knew it was the eastern-facing windows that were in the most danger of shattering under high winds. About a decade ago, they'd lost most of the windows on that side of the house as well as a part of the roof to Hurricane Frances. Just as Thad had gotten busy with repairs, Hurricane Jeanne had blown through and undone all his work. That was when Mr. Huntington—the older one, the one who was huffing and puffing in the parlor at the moment—had had these shutters installed, so they could protect the house's east flank when the next big one hit.

And it seemed Caroline was indeed going to be a big one.

That worried him. But other things besides high winds and rains worried Thad this afternoon. Things even more powerful than a hurricane.

He remembered other gatherings that had taken place in this house on stormy nights. The skies would darken and cars would arrive out front, and people would gather in the parlor. Dominique would be dressed all in bright red, and a thick, spicy incense would be lit, and then all the servants would be sent home. The servants knew that a good thunderstorm in the late afternoon would always be enough to send them home early.

Thad was remembering those gatherings now because he'd smelled that same incense burning from somewhere in the house. He couldn't place exactly where the aroma was coming from, or who might be burning it. But he had a pretty good idea.

It was Dominique. She still walked through this house.

He remembered the day she died. He remembered the weeping and wailing after the news was brought to them—from Mrs. Hoffman, not the dead woman's husband. He remembered the chanting that had afterward drifted down from the attic, led by Variola's lyrical, Haitian-accented voice. And he remembered the sudden salty stink that had filled the house—the stink of the sea.

When he heard commotion in the kitchen, Thad had gathered his courage and made his way there. But when he went through the door, the kitchen had been empty. Still, what he saw there had left Thad horrified.

Dirty seawater was everywhere. Slimy green seaweed clung to the counter.

They'd laid her out there, Thad thought to himself.

Somehow their witchcraft had brought Dominique back from the sea. And ever since then, she had walked this house.

Thad had never seen her, but he had felt her. He feared her, too, ever since he had attempted to take down her portrait from its place of honor.

And now, all these deaths. Audra, Jamison, Rita. Thad knew Mr. Huntington wasn't the killer. He felt certain that all the murders were committed by Dominique. Her restless ghost simply refused to give up her claim on this world. How Dominique had hated Rita, whose affair with Mr. Huntington had been common knowledge among the servants. That was why she had run off that day on the yacht. Now, at last, she had taken her revenge. Who was next?

Once again, Thad thought he knew.

Liz. Dominique planned to kill Liz. Today. During the hurricane. When her powers were at their greatest.

He had to warn her. He had to get that poor sweet girl out of this house. He felt in his bones that Dominique was going to strike soon. The approach of the storm, he believed, was really the approach of Dominique.

Even as he entertained such theories, he knew what Carlos would tell him: "Thad, mind your own business. Nobody wants to hear your ghost stories." Thad and Carlos had been together for twenty-four years, and never in all that time had Carlos ever given Thad's belief in the supernatural one iota of consideration. "There's no such thing as ghosts," Carlos would say. "Dominique's body was washed out to sea and surely eaten by sharks. She can't come back, Thad. She's just a few pieces of bone and gristle floating through the Atlantic." Carlos was a practical man; if he didn't see a thing right in front of him, he didn't believe the thing existed.

But Thad had a very different point of view. Dominique had never been eaten by sharks. They'd brought her back. Somehow their little witches' coven had summoned her bloated, waterlogged body back to this house. And now her spirit was getting ready to strike. He had to warn Liz. She and her friend should get in the car immediately and get as far away as they could.

He could finish the shutters later. The hurricane wasn't scheduled to hit for another couple of hours. It was more important that he find Liz.

But she didn't open her door when Thad knocked. He tried calling to her, but there was no answer. He tried the knob; it was locked. Concerned, Thad hurried downstairs. He found her friend, Nicki, seated in the study, reading a magazine.

"I'm looking for Mrs. Huntington," Thad said to her.

"She's sleeping," Nicki replied.

"It's really important I speak with her."

Nicki looked puzzled. "Can't it wait? She said she wouldn't nap long."

"No. I've got to talk to her now. Before the storm hits."

Nicki seemed anxious, as if she was hiding something. "I'm sure Mrs. Hoffman can give you instructions on preparing the house—"

"It's not that." Thad glanced around, to see if anyone was around. Satisfied they were alone, he stepped into the study. "Look, you've got to get her out of here. Immediately."

"Why?"

"Because it's not safe. When Audra died, there was a storm."

"Who's Audra? Oh, wait, the girl who died here . . ."

Thad nodded. "Believe me, it's not safe. I can feel it. Something's going to happen."

Nicki looked unconvinced. "Liz told me that all of

the people who worked in this house were very superstitious."

"I'm not being superstitious. Look, there's something in this house . . . a force. A bad force. You can believe it or not, but if you're her friend, you'll get her out of here."

"Well, I agree with you that there's something bad in this house. And you can rest assured that I am going to do my level best to get Liz out of here just as soon as the hurricane blows over."

"It'll be too late then," Thad said, his voice getting desperate. "Please!"

Nicki stood and approached Thad. She seemed to be studying his face.

"You're being sincere," she said. "I can see that. You really believe these stories that Dominique haunts this house."

From the neck of his shirt, Thad pulled out the jade pendent that he wore around his neck on a chain. "This protects me," he said. "I tried to get Mrs. Huntington to wear one, too, but I don't believe she has."

"No, she has nothing like that around her neck." Her eyes flickered away, as if she was troubled. "Look, I don't know you, but I know that Liz likes you. So I guess I can trust you. Last night she claims she had a very disturbing encounter."

"What happened?" Thad asked.

"She was up in the servants' quarters . . . in a room there. I found her, terrified, screaming, curled up in a ball on the floor. Someone had tried to kill her, she said. A woman . . . with a knife."

"Dominique."

Nicki looked confused. "I don't know what to believe anymore. Liz said the woman came out of a secret passageway in the closet—a passageway that went in between the walls of the house."

"In between the walls . . ."

"You're the caretaker of the house. Is such a thing possible?"

Thad nodded. "There *are* such passageways. They were built in the 1920s so the people who lived there could hide their liquor. It was Prohibition. They built passageways to move the liquor in and out of the house." He shook his head. "But you can't come out of them the way she described, in some closet. You'd have to cut a hole in the wall to access them."

"Well, according to Liz, there's an entrance through a closet in the room where I found her last night."

Thad looked at her. "The last room on the left, I expect."

"I believe that's the one. How did you know?"

"It was where Mr. Huntington used to carry on with Rita. It was hardly a secret. Maybe he used those very same passageways to meet her there."

Nicki shuddered. "I'll level with you. Liz isn't here. She went out on an errand. Don't tell anyone else. She'll be back in a moment. And whether you're right or wrong about ghosts and imminent dangers, I'm going to take your advice. Liz and I are going to ride out this storm at a hotel. We'll leave as soon as she gets back. I'll find a way to convince her."

"Good," Thad said. "And in the meantime, I have a certain closet I need to inspect."

60

The first place Liz went looking for Roger was at his gallery. But when she arrived there, pulling up in Nicki's little rental car, its windshield wipers swishing back and forth against the heavy rain, she'd found the gallery closed. The front windows were boarded over in anticipation of the storm. So she had decided to drive over to Roger's house.

Liz had never been to Roger's house before. He'd made promises to have her—or her and David—over for dinner, but he'd never actually set a date. She had the address—it wasn't terribly far from Huntington House—so she headed back that way.

She decided not to call or text Roger ahead of time. She didn't want to prepare him in any way for what she was about to ask him. She wanted to see the honest look on his face when she asked him if he'd had an affair with Dominique.

Roger's house, at least compared to Huntington House, was rather modest. It was all one floor, with lots of metal and spun glass. Probably not more than ten years old, Liz estimated as she turned off the ignition of the car and sat looking over at the house, waiting for the rain to subside just a bit. But that wasn't happening anytime soon, she realized, so finally she pulled up her hood and made a dash for the front door.

"Liz!" Roger exclaimed when he saw her. "Is anything wrong?"

"I just needed to speak with you. May I come in?"

"Of course, of course." He stepped aside so Liz could enter. "Is it okay to drive? I've just been watching the news. Looks like we are about to receive Caroline full-force."

"Just a lot of rain so far," she told him. "I think we've got a little time before it hits."

She glanced quickly around the room. And the first thing that struck her was how similar Roger's house was to his gallery. Every wall was cluttered with paintings not unlike the ones Liz had seen at the art show—disturbing images of headless statues and floating eyes and obelisks set against bright red backgrounds.

"May I take your coat?" Roger was asking.

But she barely heard him. Liz's eyes had fixed on a sculpture on a table in a prominent spot in Roger's living room. It was the bust of an angel—with black wings and the head of a cow.

"I see you still don't fully approve of my taste in art," Roger said, coming up behind her. "Some of them are pieces by Naomi Collins. I often display the work of my artists here in my home. Helps when I have parties to promote the gallery."

Liz said nothing as he took her coat, shaking the rain off it in the foyer before hanging it on a rack.

"May I pour you some sherry? Or something stiffer?" Roger smiled. "It looks as if you could use it."

"No, thank you," Liz said, pulling her eyes away from that obscene cow angel. "I'm still recovering from all that wine last night."

"Is that why you've come, Liz? You're upset by what I said."

Liz had a flash of memory from the night before. Roger's brown eyes, so full of compassion. *"Then can I tell you that I love you?"* He had kissed her after that.

She had liked it. She had felt so good, so happy, so safe, in Roger's arms.

Liz took a deep breath and looked over at him now. "I'm not upset," she told him. "But I do need to ask you something, and I need you to be honest with me."

"Of course."

"Did you have an affair with Dominique?"

There it was: the expression Liz had hoped not to see. Roger's eyes revealed the answer to that question before he even had a chance to speak.

To his credit, he didn't try to lie. "Yes," he told her. "Yes, I did."

"And David knew about this?"

Roger nodded.

"That was part of the reason for his breakdown?"

He sighed. "I heard my father was in town. I see he's paid you a visit."

"Yes, he did."

"He's always hated me. I wasn't the son he wanted. I could never do what David did, which was to kiss Dad's ass and follow his orders without question."

"Did you love her?"

Roger's eyes focused on her. "Not the way I love you, Liz. You are good. She was evil. You are life. She was death."

She felt as if she might cry, but she held back the tears. "I don't know what to say. Except now I understand why David hated her so much."

"And why he hates me."

"Was David with her on the yacht on the day of the accident?"

"Why do you ask that?"

"Detective Foley asked me. I didn't really think about it at the time. Now . . . well, now I'm wondering."

"Yes." Roger looked at her emotionlessly. "David was with her."

"So . . . he made it back safely, but she drowned?"

"That's right."

Liz felt dizzy, much as she had back at Huntington House while talking with her father-in-law. She steadied herself by leaning against the back of Roger's couch.

"But that's not the official story," she said. "The official story is that Dominique went out alone. Why not tell the police and the Coast Guard that David was on board too?"

"Because he didn't want to be accused of murdering her."

"Surely he can't be blamed for a storm."

"But Dominique went overboard before the storm. At least, that's what the captain later asserted."

"The captain? I didn't know there was a captain on the yacht that day . . ."

"In the official account, there wasn't."

Liz couldn't hold back the tears any longer. They slid down her cheeks and dropped off her chin. "What are you telling me, Roger? That David killed Dominique?"

He remained emotionless, just standing there across from her, staring at her. "Given what he'd discovered," he said, "he would have had reason, wouldn't he?"

"And Rita? He killed her, too, because she was going to tell me."

"Oh, Liz." Roger's gaze softened, and he held open his arms.

Liz rushed forward and allowed him to hold her. She sobbed against his chest.

"There, there, my love," Roger said softly, his lips near her ear. "I'm sorry I never told you about Dominique. It was in the past. I thought it was no longer relevant." He gently lifted her chin with his fist. "If it matters, she hurt me, too. You see, I wasn't the only one she was cheating on David with. There were others . . . bellboys, gardeners, deliverymen. She was an evil woman, Liz. She's destroyed David, but you see, I won't let her destroy me."

"He's going to go to jail," Liz said, the reality of her husband's predicament fully hitting her. "He might even be . . . put to death."

"Sweet girl, don't think about any of that right now . . ."

"I've got to go," she said, pulling out of Roger's arms. "I've got to get back."

"Yes, my love, you should go back. But remember, I am always here for you."

She managed a small smile in his direction. "I appreciate that, Roger. Your friendship means the world to me."

"You forgive me for not telling you about Dominique?"

"Yes," she said. "She used you, just as she used so many others." She choked up. "Just as she used David."

They walked to the door and Roger helped Liz back into her coat. "You'll see, my love. When this storm is over, and the sun shines again, all will be better."

"I'm afraid then it will only be worse," Liz said. "If David doesn't come home on his own, they'll have to extradite him . . . and then there will be a trial . . . the headlines are just going to go on and on . . ."

"Listen to me, Liz." Roger gripped her by the shoulders and looked deeply into her eyes. "By this time tomorrow, everything will be better. Can you not feel the power that approaches? This storm is going to be one of the great ones. Let's not be afraid of its power, my darling, but instead, let's harness that power to fulfill our dreams."

"I've never heard a hurricane described that way," she said.

"Feel the power, Liz. Tap into it." He kissed her on the forehead. "I will see you very soon, my love. Don't despair. Better days are ahead of us."

She tried to smile, but Roger's words were almost unfathomable to her. What was he talking about? As Liz turned to leave, her last glimpse before leaving the house and heading out into the rain was that terrible, awful cow-headed angel with the black wings.

61

There it was, Thad realized. The seam in the back wall of the closet. How had Thad never discovered it before? He'd been caretaker at Huntington House for a long time. But he did very little work in these mostly unused servants' rooms. He supposed that was why whoever had made this entrance had placed it here, because it was less likely to be discovered.

Now he had to figure out how it opened.

Thad pressed his fingers along the seam, much the way one opened a roll of Pillsbury dough. Harder, harder, he pressed, moving his fingers down toward the floor. And then, just as he expected, the panel popped open just a little bit, making a scraping sound as it moved away from the rest of the wall.

Thad shined his flashlight inside.

He saw nothing but cobwebs. But a little farther down, he spotted a ladder. Rather like a library ladder, flat against the wall. It went up into an opening in the attic and down through another opening into the floor below.

He took a step inside the passageway. Thad was a

big man, so it was a tight fit. He could barely turn around; his shoulders touched each side of the corridor. He made his way to the ladder, aiming his flashlight first up and then down. He could see nothing. Which way to go? He decided up, and took the first step, shining his flashlight ahead of him.

The ladder led into the attic, but not the part of the attic he'd been in many times. Thad had always noted the peculiarity of Huntington House's attic. It was a warren of small rooms, which were accessed only by going through one to get to another. There was no central corridor, no open space. Now he understood why. *This was where they met, those witches*, he thought to himself. *This was where they conducted their rituals.*

At the top of the ladder, Thad swung his flashlight around. A maze of very narrow corridors led off in various directions. He realized these passageways were the insides of the walls of the attic rooms.

As soon as he took a step forward, he smelled the gardenias.

"I'm not afraid of you, Dominique," he called out, touching the pendant around his neck.

Thad aimed his flashlight down each of the four passageways that led off in different directions. All he could see were cobwebs. But closer to him he noticed something else: a light switch on the wall. He flicked it up, and a series of bare lightbulbs along the ceiling sputtered into life, casting a dull yellow light down the passageways.

He wasn't sure which way to go. Where did these passages lead? Thad chose the corridor closest to him, where he thought perhaps the smell of gardenias was the strongest. He had taken only a few steps when he caught the scent of something else, something both sweet and sour.

"Hello!" he called, peeling cobwebs from his face.

From outside he could hear the wind starting to beat the house. He had left the windows unfinished. The storm was approaching, and Mrs. Hoffman was going to be angry with him. He should turn around right now, go back down the ladder, and get back to work. But something compelled him to go on. The smell of gardenias was getting stronger, but now it was braided with something else, something foul, something that reminded Thad of the dead mice he'd find in the basement.

At each bend of the corridor Thad noticed more ladders going down through openings into other parts of the house. *The walls are all passageways*, he realized. *Every single wall in the house*.

The stink of dead mice now threatened to overwhelm him. But Thad knew whatever lay putrefying up here was a lot larger than a mouse. The odor had become so thick, so gaseous, that he could nearly taste it on his tongue. He clamped his hand over his mouth and nose. He was just about to beat it the hell out of there and go downstairs and tell Mrs. Hoffman what he'd found when he turned a corner and beheld the source of the stink.

The corridor dead-ended against the wall. And there, propped up in sitting positions, were three corpses. Thad suppressed a scream and forced himself to draw closer to the grisly sight with his flashlight. The corpses were women, he discerned, two of them very decomposed, little more than purple rotting flesh and protruding bones dressed in long gray robes. From the hair on one of them Thad deduced she had been African American, but that was as much as he could tell. The third corpse wasn't nearly as decayed as the other two. Its face was gray and sunken, but its hair was still blond and its facial features still identifiable. Thad noticed the little blue star that was tattooed on the corpse's neck.

He covered his mouth and nose more tightly with his hand, fearful he was going to vomit. The three dead women looked like deflated balloons. Except that, in this case, instead of air, all three appeared to have been drained dry of blood.

"Dear Jesus," Thad finally muttered, the horror washing over him. He turned, ready to head back down the corridor. Who could have done this? Was this work of Dominique? Could a ghost really do such a thing? Or was Mr. Huntington really a serial killer as the press was suggesting? Three dead women—in the walls of Huntington House! Thad was horrified. How could this have happened here? He was supposed to be the caretaker of the place!

He rounded the corner and started down the passageway. He saw a shadow moving along the wall before he saw who approached.

And suddenly the smell of gardenias was everywhere.

"Oh, Jesus, no!" Thad managed to cry out when he saw the face of his killer. Then he heard the swish of the blade through the air and felt it slice through his throat.

62

Liz steered the car as best she could through the streets, which had become more like small rivers now, filling up with rainwater. The windshield wipers of the little rental car struggled to keep up with the torrential downpour. Every once in a while Liz got a clear glimpse through the windshield. Even though it was afternoon, the sky had become almost black. Palm trees bent against the ferocious wind.

But it wasn't the approaching hurricane that frightened her. It was the thought of David being arrested for murder, and the resulting trials she would have to endure.

David was guilty. Liz couldn't deny that anymore. She had married a murderer. Her mother's voice came at her in snatches, rather like the rain that periodically slapped against the car windows: *Impulsive! Foolhardy! You barely know this man you've made your husband!*

Mom was right. Liz felt the tears burn again in her eyes. She had allowed herself to believe David was her Prince Charming, and so she had run off and married him, letting her heart rule her head, carried away by the passion and romance of the moment. Finally, she thought she had found someone who loved her—who wanted to be with her—unlike that cruel, terrible Peter Mather, who had used her for a while and dumped her. Finally all the struggle, all the taking care of other people, was over. Somebody was going to take care of her for a change! David had made Liz believe that she was love-able, and she had allowed that deep, craving need of hers to blind her to the truth about him: that he was a manipulative killer.

What else could she believe, after what Roger had told her?

And then there was Roger. Roger . . . who had professed his love to her.

Did she love him in return? Or did she still love David, despite all this horror?

Liz didn't know. She truthfully did not know how she felt. She pulled the car into the driveway of Huntington House, the gate opening at the click of her little remote. At the end of the driveway the remote also opened the garage door for her. She would put Nicki's car inside the garage for the duration of the storm. But when the door had finished ascending Liz was startled to see the garage was full. David's cars were there, of course, and Mrs. Hoffman's and Variola's. But the garage could hold ten cars. And every single stall was filled with cars that Liz didn't recognize. Expensive cars, too. Porsches and Mercedes Benzes and Bentleys.

She left Nicki's little rental in the driveway and hurried up the walk through the rain.

Coming through the back door into the kitchen, Liz was struck by how quiet and still the house was. She saw no one. "Hello?" she called, her voice echoing as she wandered through the dining room into the parlor.

From out of the shadows Mrs. Hoffman suddenly appeared, startling Liz.

"I thought you were upstairs sleeping," the housekeeper said.

"Whose cars are those in the garage?" Liz asked.

"I allowed some of the servants to park in there given the storm."

"Since when do our servants drive Bentleys?"

"Your husband pays very generously," Mrs. Hoffman said.

Liz didn't have time to spar with the old harridan. "Where's Nicki?" she asked.

"I'm not certain. But we may need her help. We're going to need everyone's help to finish the shuttering of the windows. The shutters are heavy. It will take two of us to pull them in. Thad started the job, but it's not finished, and he's nowhere to be found."

"That's not like Thad. Perhaps he's attending to something else more urgent."

Mrs. Hoffman shook her head. "The way these winds are blowing, nothing is more urgent than these windows."

"What time is the storm expected to hit full-force?"

"In about an hour. They've evacuated the coast. It's a wonder we still have power."

Liz was making her way toward the stairs. "I'll get Nicki and we'll help secure the windows."

She found her friend in her room, packing.

"We're getting out of here," Nicki said as soon as Liz entered.

"Nicki, the roads aren't passable. It's a miracle I got

back here in one piece. There are National Guardsmen in the streets. Everything's closed down, and it's just going to get worse."

"I don't care, we've got to find a way."

"What's gotten you all worked up?"

"Thad." Nicki drew close to Liz's face. "He said we're in danger here."

"I suppose he talked about ghosts."

"Whatever the danger is, Liz, he convinced me it exists."

Liz frowned. "When did you speak with him?"

"Just a little while ago."

"Because Mrs. Hoffman can't find him. He was boarding up the windows of the house but left the job unfinished. That's not like him, especially with the storm so close."

Liz noticed the strange, frightened look that appeared in Nicki's eyes.

"What is it?" she asked her friend.

Nicki shuddered. "He's gone up to that room."

"What room?"

"The room I found you in. The one where you were attacked by that woman."

"So you believe me now that I really *was* attacked?"

"Yes, because Thad believed it. I told him about it, and he went up to investigate."

Liz suddenly shared Nicki's fear. "You're telling me that he went up to that room, and he hasn't come back down?"

All at once, a truck seemed to ram into the side of the house. The whole structure shook under an unbelievably powerful gust of wind. Liz almost lost her footing. Hairbrushes and lipsticks went flying off her dresser. A lamp fell over and crashed.

Seconds later, all the lights in the house went out. The two women were left standing in darkness.

Nicki screamed.

The room filled with the fragrance of gardenias.

63

Variola was coming down the back stairs into the kitchen when she saw Mrs. Hoffman approaching, her stony face even more rigid than usual.

"Where is she?" the housekeeper demanded.

Variola smiled. "Ah, did you go looking for her? Did you find the door wide open and observe that she was gone? Spirited away, so to speak?"

"*Where is she?*" Mrs. Hoffman asked again, more urgently now.

Variola moved across the room and lit several candles. The power appeared to have gone out. The storm was getting stronger.

"She is with me," Variola said.

"How did you get to her?"

Variola scowled. "Did you really think that you had found a way to lock a door against me? That I was not powerful enough to find my way inside?"

Hoffman folded her arms over her chest. "If you aren't going to help us, then we will have to do things on our own. Tell me where she is before the storm has passed!"

"Oh, yes," Variola said, teasing her. "We're having a bit of weather, aren't we?"

"What have you done with her?" Hoffman shouted.

Variola snarled. "Only what you would have been incapable of doing without me."

Variola remembered how clumsy Hoffman had been in the beginning, learning the art of vodou. Dominque had been a quick study, taking to the arcane knowledge with ease. But for Hoffman her abilities had developed slowly, sometimes torturously. She had become quite strong in recent days, Variola acknowledged. It had taken quite a feat of strength to seal Variola off from that room in the attic. Hoffman's accomplishment had both surprised and frightened Variola. If Hoffman were allowed to gain the upper hand, to proceed unobstructed, to do things her way, Variola feared what might happen. There had been so much bloodshed in the past year. And there would be more, much more, if Hoffman were allowed to continue unchecked.

Yet clearly Variola had overestimated her rival's powers, for with a little concentration, she had been able to smash through the barrier Hoffman had erected and enter the room freely. Once again Variola had taken charge. Now, with the hurricane approaching, she knew she could end all this madness right here and now. If she was successful, she could stop the bloodshed.

"I will make a bargain with you, Hoffman," Variola told her now. "I will conduct the ritual when the storm is at its peak, but you must agree to my terms."

"I will never recognize you as head of this coven," Hoffman warned.

"I have no interest in your coven! It was your idea—

yours and hers—Dominique's—to bring all these people in, promising them that their greed would be sated."

"Dominique required followers. That was how her power grew. You know that, Variola. You've been trying to bolster your own standing by recruiting Rita and even little Liz."

"I have no need of followers, not anymore. I have no wish for power. I am not one who has ever been motivated by greed or money—"

Hoffman laughed softly. "Come now, Variola. Let's not rewrite history at this late date, shall we? You came here and agreed to teach Dominique, and to help her form a coven, because she paid you a great deal of money. You became rich beyond any of your dreams."

"Every bit of that money has been sent back to my devastated island! And I came here because I was destitute and alone—I had lost everyone! I came here hoping to find a community of like-minded people, who would listen to what I told them, who would heed Papa Ghede's warnings that the power he gives us was never to be wasted on selfishness or revenge . . ."

"I told you once before," Hoffman snarled. "He's your god, not ours."

A blast of wind struck the house, throwing open the doors of one cabinet and sending its dishes smashing and clattering across the floor.

"The storm nears," Variola said. "We have no time to argue. We only have time for you to accept my deal, or not."

"What is your deal?"

"I will conduct the ceremony. I will do what you ask. But after that—you must leave this house. Go far, far away. Leave us all in peace."

Hoffman's eyes narrowed. "But what about the coven?"

"Find a new one." Her eyes locked onto Hoffman's. "She will be restored. She will be strong enough by then to do so."

"Completely restored?"

"Yes."

"You have been promising to restore her for a year. Why should I believe you will be successful now?"

"Because the storm is the power we have needed. What you ask—to completely restore her—is not easy. The act requires far greater power than we have been able to muster ourselves."

"I was having success my way," Hoffman told her.

Variola spit out a laugh. "Your way? All your way did was create a monster."

Hoffman was silent. Another gust of wind rattled the house.

"All right," she said. "Restore her to what she was, and we will leave here."

"You cannot break this bargain. I will ensure that if you do, anything I accomplish today will be reversed."

"We will leave Huntington House."

"I want to be free of you, and of her, do you understand?" Variola asked, her voice rising in anger. "I should have known when I came here that your vanity was the least of your evil. The both of you! Melting off a double chin . . . removing some fine lines around the eyes . . . that was not to be the end of it. Lies and deceptions . . . ending with that terrible day on the yacht."

"Do not evoke that terrible day," Hoffman said.

"Except that wasn't the end, was it? The true evil came after . . . I have tried to stop you, Hoffman . . ."

The housekeeper tightened her lips. "But you couldn't, could you? And know this, Variola, if you fail today, I will destroy you . . . and I will restore her my way."

"But if I succeed," Variola said, "you will both leave here and never return."

"That is our bargain."

They glared at each other, like cats. There was no shaking of hands between them. Their eyes were enough.

"The others have already gathered," Hoffman said. "They are upstairs. I contacted them and told them I would be conducting the ceremony."

"Oh, yes, I've seen them. I just came from up there." Variola smiled. "How excited and eager they all are to participate in a great ceremony they've heard so much about. But how pleased—and relieved—they were to learn that I would be in the driver's seat. They weren't all that keen on watching you bungle things and lead them inadvertently to hell."

Hoffman didn't take the bait. She refused to respond to the insult. "Just please bring Dominique back," she said in a small, forceful voice.

"We should begin," Variola said. "The storm is nearly on top of us now." She turned toward the stairs, then paused. "Are Liz and her friend secured?"

"I've sent someone on ahead to take care of them."

Variola's face grew tense. "I do not want them harmed. Do you understand? Just make sure they are safe from the storm, and far enough away not to hear nor interfere with the ceremony."

"It will be taken care of."

"I mean it, Hoffman! Harming them could hurt the ceremony." She drew close to the housekeeper's face.

"How many times do I need to tell you that bloodshed is never necessary?"

"The blood is the life," Hoffman said emotionlessly.

"They are not to be harmed," Variola told her again.

"Fine."

They both turned and headed upstairs.

64

The wind was slapping against the house with such force that it seemed as if the whole place was being pushed off its foundation. Outside the window the palm trees were nearly horizontal. Liz pulled the heavy curtains closed.

"Stay away from the windows," she told Nicki. "At any minute they could blow in."

Nicki was lighting some candles so that they could see. "We should be in the basement," she said. "Isn't that where they say you should go in hurricanes?"

"Yes, but do you really want to go hide in some dark basement room in *this* house?"

Nicki shuddered. "Good point."

"Let's go downstairs anyway," Liz said. "Mrs. Hoffman said several of the servants were staying for the duration of the storm. We'll stay wherever they're staying."

"The servants all left," Nicki told her. "At least, most of them did. Mrs. Hoffman told them to go as soon as the storm started to approach. I saw them drive away."

Liz made a face. "She told me just the opposite . . ."

"I think the only one to remain was that older lady, Mrs. Martinez . . ."

Liz was really bewildered. "If all the servants are gone, then whose cars are in the garage? I'm certain Mrs. Martinez doesn't drive a Porsche or a Bentley . . ."

Suddenly a loud crash was heard on the roof above them. Instantly Liz knew it was the sound of tiles being torn up by the wind.

"We should definitely go downstairs," she said. "That roof might not last much longer."

She turned on the flashlight on her phone; Nicki did the same. Together they ventured out into the hallway, two lasers of light cutting through the darkness ahead of them.

They saw no one. The entire place seemed deserted. Outside the wind howled but inside there was a sort of a hush, a silence that seemed to echo. Where was everyone? Mrs. Hoffman was perhaps still trying to shutter the windows at the back of the house, but Liz thought they were beyond worrying about that now. Better to take refuge in a room with all interior walls and let the storm pass over them. Whatever damage the hurricane was going to do the house now was out of their control.

"The study," she suddenly said to Nicki. "That's probably the best place to hide out. There's no windows, and it's secure in the center of the first floor."

"Okay," Nicki agreed, following her toward the stairs.

Just at that moment, a large picture window ahead of them shattered inward in a tremendous, earsplitting explosion. Two seconds later and Liz and Nicki would have been directly in front of the window, assaulted with hundreds of shards of broken glass. They would have been terribly wounded—or possibly even killed. Nicki screamed and clutched on to Liz. Wind and rain shrieked through the open window.

"Come on, we've got to hurry," Liz said as they made their way to the top of the stairs.

Halfway down, they stopped. The light on Liz's phone had illuminated something that terrified her far more than the broken window.

The portrait of Dominique once more hung in its place at the landing.

Tall, imposing, indomitable. The eyes of the dead woman seemed to glow as they looked down at Liz.

"How—?" She found she couldn't speak. "Who—who did this?"

"That horrible Hoffman woman," Nicki said. "I think she had a girl-crush on Dominique."

"She's trying to drive me mad," Liz said, trying to stop herself from trembling.

"As soon as the storm passes," Nicki told her, "we are getting the hell out of here. I don't care if trees are down and the roads are flooded. We'll *walk* if we have to."

Liz just stood there, shining her light upward and staring into Dominique's eyes.

You thought you could remove me.

The dead woman's voice was clear in Liz's mind.

You thought you could replace me.

I am mistress of Huntington House, and always will be.

You are just a worthless little girl.

"I'm strong enough to stand up to you," Liz hissed, whipping her flashlight off Dominique's face. "Come on, Nicki. Let's get to the study."

They ran down the rest of the stairs and across the marble floor of the foyer.

But they found the door to the study locked.

"Is anyone in there?" Liz shouted, banging on the door.

"I hear someone out in the kitchen," Nicki said, looking in that direction. "Hello? Someone out there?"

Liz felt a hand on her shoulder. She spun around. No one was there. But the fragrance of gardenias once again filled her nostrils.

Nicki headed off toward the kitchen, calling to whoever was there. But Liz stayed where she was. She felt defiant. "Show your face," she said, shining her light down the corridor, up toward the ceiling, down at the floor. "I know you're here, Dominique. You've been here ever since I came to this house, taunting me. So show your face! Or are you afraid to? Are you afraid of this worthless little girl?"

There was no reply except the steady battering of the wind outside.

Liz decided she would try to break open the lock on the study. They would be safer in there. She stuck her phone into the front pocket of her jeans and began rattling the doorknob. So intent was she that she did not see the panel slide open in the wall behind her. But she most certainly felt the cold clammy hand that emerged from the darkness within and clamped itself tightly over her mouth.

65

"Liz, I can hear people out toward the kitchen," Nicki was saying. "They're singing or . . . something . . . maybe praying . . ."

She turned around, shining her phone's flashlight back to where she had left Liz. But the corridor was now empty. Liz was gone.

"Liz?" Nicki walked back to the spot outside the door to the study, flicking her light up and down and all around. "Liz, where are you?"

She hurried into the parlor and looked around. No Liz there either.

"Liz!" Nicki shouted, cold fear grabbing hold of her throat.

Another huge gust of wind shook the house. The chandelier swung back and forth like a pendulum, clattering furiously.

"Liz, where are you?" Nicki shrieked.

She tried calling her friend, but got only high-pitched static. The storm had clearly knocked out reception.

Calm down, Nicki told herself. *Liz must have heard*

the voices coming from the kitchen as well and gone out there on her own. That's where she is. No reason to worry. Nicki rushed back down the corridor hoping to find Liz as soon as she turned the corner.

But no one was in the kitchen. Nicki swung her phone's flashlight around the room and picked out nothing but bare countertops and empty stools. The voices, Nicki realized, were coming from upstairs. Up the back stairs . . . where she had found Liz cowering in fear, convinced she had been attacked by a strange woman.

"They *are* praying," Nicki said softly to herself, as she listened again to the voices coming from upstairs. A chant—*Oh, Lord, hear our call*—filtered through the darkness.

It must be the servants who stayed behind, like Mrs. Martinez, Nicki thought. *They must be religious people . . . praying to make it through the hurricane.*

She'd go upstairs and speak with them. She felt strange doing so—like an intruder—but what other choice did she have? She was a stranger in this house. A storm was bearing down and she was all alone. There was no other choice but to go upstairs and try to convince the people that they would all be safer in an interior room on the first floor. Perhaps there was a safe room or storm cellar in the house that Nicki didn't know about. The people upstairs would probably know where it was. Possibly Mrs. Hoffman had already taken refuge there. Nicki would suggest they all take cover, pronto. They could continue praying if they wanted to—heck, Nicki might even join them—but they should really do so from a safer spot.

And Liz would be upstairs. She had to be. She and

Nicki had just gotten separated in the dark, and she'd gone upstairs, just as Nicki was doing now.

She took the steps two at a time, guided by the light on her phone.

Candlelight flickered out into the hall from the last room on the left. As soon as Nicki stepped off the top stair, the sounds of praying ceased.

Nicki opened her mouth to call out, but suddenly stopped. For some reason, she kept silent. She approached the room silently, warily. She flicked off her flashlight.

She stood outside in the darkness, staring into the room. Eight people were seated on wooden chairs that were arranged in a circle around a tall, wide, bloodred candle. Dozens of other candles were lit throughout the room, but this center candle had the brightest flame. Four of the people arranged around the candle Nicki did not recognize, but Mrs. Hoffman was there, seated with her back to the door, and Mrs. Martinez, who was seated beside her. There were also three empty chairs. At the front of the circle, staring out into the darkness of the hallway—and so, presumably, at Nicki—was the Haitian chef whom Liz had introduced Nicki to briefly. Victoria, Nicki thought her name was. Or something like that. Something more exotic. Something with a *V*.

"The power approaches its zenith," the Haitian woman was saying. She stood from her chair. "Praise to our master! Praise to him!"

"Praise to him!" the others all chanted.

The wind outside battered the house. The glass in the windows at the far end of the room rattled in their panes. Nicki thought they might blow out at any moment.

"We beseech thee, oh master," the Haitian woman intoned, raising her hands into the air. "Restore our sister! Restore her to full and vibrant life!"

Nicki could scarcely comprehend what she was seeing and hearing. Dark father . . . oh master . . . restore our sister. What was this ceremony? What were these people doing as a hurricane threatened to take the roof off above them?

She was about to rush into the room—the hell with their crazy ritual!—they had to get to safety! But what she saw in that instant froze her to the spot.

A woman rose from the floor. Nicki had not seen her lying there in the darkness of the center of the circle. She was naked, and she rose and stood trembling in the flickering glow of the enormous red candle. She was looking out into the hall. Nicki shuddered.

The woman's face was bloated and purple, with bulging eyes and a crooked mouth. Her body was distorted; it looked as if both arms had been broken. Her shoulders were uneven; wrinkled breasts sagged nearly to her waist. Sores and bruises discolored the entirety of her body. Slowly one twisted arm moved upward. With a gnarled finger, the woman pointed out into the darkness of the hall. It was Nicki she saw out there, Nicki she was exposing. She opened her mouth. The sound that emerged could only be compared to the angry bellow of a cow.

As one, the entire group spun their heads to glare at the intruder.

Nicki screamed.

66

Detective Joe Foley hadn't lived in Florida long enough to encounter a category 4 or 5 hurricane, but today, that changed. Even though Caroline had been downgraded from a 5 to 4, it was still rolling in toward Palm Beach with winds exceeding 130 miles per hour. All over town trees and power lines were down; the coast had surged and businesses and homes were flooded. Emergency shelters were filled with evacuees. Other people were being advised to take refuge in a basement or in a first-floor room with interior walls. Joe had come into headquarters early that morning, and he'd remain for the duration in case he was needed

He could hear the howling of the wind outside. It sounded like a train barreling toward them. The full impact of the storm wasn't expected for another half hour or so.

"And then what happens?" Joe asked Aggie. "We all get blown to Oz?"

She wasn't in the mood for jokes. Joe knew Aggie was worried about her kids, who, last she'd heard, had been hustled down into their basement by her husband. After that, their phone reception had been cut off. She'd tried calling but nothing went through. The last text she'd gotten from her husband had said their youngest daughter was scared and crying.

"She's only three," Aggie told Joe. "She doesn't understand all the noise coming from outside or why the sun went away . . . it's the middle of the day but it looks like night."

"They're in a safe place," Joe assured her. "Probably in a safer place than we are."

Along with most of the other detectives, Joe and Aggie were crammed into what was usually a storage room on the first floor of the station, a two-story Spanish Revival stucco building with a tile roof and lots of big exposed windows. Most of the windows, though not all, had been boarded over earlier that morning. That was one of the biggest dangers of a hurricane, Joe knew: being in front of a glass window that gets blown out by a gust of wind. He could only imagine the number of emergencies his colleagues on the regular police force would have to deal with before the day was over.

Power was off, but the headquarters had a generator to keep the lights on and the computers working, even if the storm made Internet connection spotty. So even as he listened to the wind whistle through the cracks in the building, Joe decided to get a little work done. He opened the file marked "Cansino" that he had carried with him into this makeshift office. He read again the email communication that had come in from Europe during the night.

**All hotels in Amsterdam and surrounding vicinities
checked for David Huntington, U.S. citizen, and
results were negative.**

That fit with another report Joe had received late last
night from the State Department. There was no record
of David Huntington departing the country on either a
commercial or private aircraft. A follow-up call Joe
had placed to Huntington's usual charter pilot confirmed that he had not flown his client anywhere, nor
had anyone else in his company.

Shortly after getting the report from the State Department, Joe had rung Dr. Paul Delacorte, who sat on
the board of directors of Huntington Enterprises and
who Mrs. Huntington had said suggested her husband
get on a plane to Amsterdam. It was nearly midnight,
but Delacorte had still been awake.

"I did advise David to go," he'd told the detective.
"There's a very aggressive attempt to take over some of
our European holdings, and I felt David would be the
best man to go over there and secure the company's assets. But no, I haven't heard from him."

"Is that unusual? I mean, after all, wouldn't he let
you know how things were going?"

"You seem to want to believe that David is guilty of
this murder, don't you, Detective?" Delacorte had asked.
"Well, maybe he is. You're the expert on that. But I'm
afraid I can't help you anymore. David doesn't report
to me. He reports to his father. You should really ask
him."

Joe had; the elder Mr. Huntington, having arrived
back in New York, had told Joe he still had not heard
from his son. And he had no idea where he was.

At least, that was what he was telling the police.

Joe looked down at the photos of Rita Cansino's body, lying in a pool of her own blood beside her car. Was everyone covering up for Huntington? Did they know where he was? Had the whole Amsterdam story been a ruse? Had he really fled somewhere else?

Joe had to consider the possibility that, after killing Rita, Huntington had realized the need to get out of the country. It would appear that if he had fled, he'd used an assumed name. Maybe he'd kept a false passport for just this sort of an emergency. If he'd killed before— Jamison Wilkes had died the same night Huntington got back from his honeymoon, after all—then he might have wanted an escape plan. A phony passport would have allowed him to get out of the country unnoticed. Maybe, Joe imagined, Huntington was at that very moment sipping a margarita on a sandy beach in Mexico, or Costa Rica, or Venezuela, watching the news reports about the hurricane bearing down on Florida. His wealthy father could funnel him money secretly to allow him to live pretty well for a long time.

Or maybe . . . just maybe . . . he'd never left the country at all.

As a good detective, Joe knew he had to consider every possible scenario.

Maybe David Huntington was still right here, somewhere in this city, holed up in some motel, waiting for the cops to come knocking at his door.

Joe scratched his head. Something about this case just did not fit. Yes, it seemed quite obvious that Huntington had killed Rita. He'd had a motive. He'd left the house shortly after Rita did. He'd left unexpectedly on an unplanned "business trip" in the middle of the night.

But for Joe, it was all starting to seem just *too* obvious. Almost as if things had been arranged somehow for Huntington to appear to be the most logical culprit. Maybe he was . . . in fact, he probably was . . . but something just didn't add up for Joe.

The murders of Audra McKenzie, Jamison Wilkes, and Rita Cansino were all related, Joe was convinced. He believed that in his gut. Nothing was going to shake his conviction on that point. But while Huntington might have offed Jamison, there was no possible way he could have killed Audra, since he was on a cruise ship at the time. That was documented. Witnesses, passports, ship logs. So was it possible that Huntington had an accomplice, or accomplices?

But why? What possible motivation was there to kill all these people?

Somewhere outside an alarm was sounding. The wind was getting heavier now. The whistling Joe had heard earlier had become a long steady wail. Above him, the rafters of the roof were starting to creak.

"What do we do if the roof falls in on us?" he asked Aggie.

"Run to the basement, I guess."

He packed up his files and slipped them into the strongbox he'd brought with him just for that purpose. But even as he put them away, his mind was still racing, still tossing around ideas and theories about the case. He was going to find the killer who'd ended those three young lives—and maybe the lives of Tonesha Lewis, Jeanette Kelly, and Lana Paulson as well, since he'd still not found those three missing women. Everyone was entitled to justice; no one's death should go unrecorded or unsolved. He thought—not for the first time today—of his mother. He thought of her every day, several times a day. He thought of her cold, dead body lying in that tent, killed by some unknown maniac who might still be walking free. No one had ever found any trace of Mom's murderer. Joe had tried himself, but had failed. Someday, he vowed, he would bring the monster who killed his mother to justice.

But for now, the next best thing was to find the killer of Rita Cansino and the others. It might well be David Huntington. A couple of the servants at the house had repeated gossip that David had been having an affair with Audra McKenzie around the same time he'd been involved with Rita, or at least that there had been some intense flirtation. But he couldn't have killed her, unless he'd developed a teleportation device to beam him to Florida from the North Atlantic and then back again. So who did? Who killed Audra? Jamison? Rita? Tonesha? Jeanette? Lana?

Could they all have been killed by different people, but for similar reasons?

Joe was just starting to turn that idea over in his head when a sound like nothing he had ever heard before suddenly cut through the room. Everyone leapt to their feet. It sounded like the scream of a dinosaur from one of the *Jurassic Park* movies, except that it went on and on. Aggie, on edge already, was the first one out the door and into the lobby, where large glass windows allowed them a clear view of the street. But there was no clear view this day. The sky was a deep, metallic gray. Wind and rain obscured everything. But then—they saw—

"Dear God," Aggie groaned.

One by one, the roofs of the buildings across the

street were torn off, as if they were just lids on a row of aluminum cans. In quick succession each roof peeled off, soaring gracefully for a moment through the air, resembling a flying carpet—but then, in an instant, each roof in its turn disintegrated into thousands of shards of orange clay. The pieces went rocketing off in all directions, thudding against the windows of the police headquarters.

"All nonessentials down into the basement!" Chief Davis barked.

"Guess that's us," Joe said. "Can't be solving murders out there right now."

"I hope my babies are okay," Aggie said.

"They're safe and warm, Agg, don't worry about a thing," Joe reassured her as he followed her down into the basement, his strongbox of files tucked securely under his arm.

67

Liz struggled in the grip of her unknown captor. It was a man—that was all she could tell. He had one hand clasped over her mouth while he used the other to hold both her arms behind her back. Since pulling her into the secret passageway and sliding the panel shut, the man had not spoken. Instead, he had hurried down the corridor in the darkness, seeming very familiar with the layout. Several times Liz had tried to break free but she'd had no success. She tried also kicking backward with her foot, but her efforts had no impact on the man.

Finally, some ways removed—so that Nicki couldn't hear their voices through the wall, Liz presumed—the man shoved her roughly to the floor. Liz pulled herself up against the wall, her knees in front of her chest. She strained to see through the dark. The man stood over her, and she could hear him making sounds with his tongue. Terrified, Liz pulled her phone from her pocket and shined the light up at him. She gasped.

It was Paul Delacorte.

"What? Why?" Liz stammered. "What are you doing?"

He smiled. In this strange light, Dr. Delacorte looked like a ghoul standing over her. His eyes were so deep-set that they were lost in shadows. His face looked like a skull.

"I was sent to bring you to safety," he replied. "Such a terrible storm, isn't it?"

"Safety?" Liz got to her feet. "I hardly feel safe being dragged inside the wall like that. My friend Nicki is out there . . ."

"I was only told to bring you," Delacorte said, stroking his short, clipped white beard.

Liz wanted to turn her light away from the sight of him, but she feared being left in the dark with such a creature. "Where is Mrs. Hoffman?" she asked.

"Waiting for you. They're all waiting for you."

"Who . . . are they?"

"Our guests, of course."

From outside they could hear the battering the house was taking from the wind. There were snaps and cracking sounds. Even here, inside the walls, the moisture had permeated. Liz felt sticky and damp.

"What do you mean, guests?" Liz asked. "And where are you supposed to take me?"

Delacorte's smile seemed hideous in the glare of the flashlight. "Oh, we have a little time. They're trying some other things first. But I know what we really need to make our little party a success is you."

"What are you talking about?" Liz screamed at him. "I want out of here!"

"In fact," Delacorte said, ignoring her, "we have so

enough time that maybe we can have a little fun. After-ward, you know, that won't be possible."

"What are you talking about?" Liz asked again, her voice becoming weaker, more frightened.

He took a step toward her. Liz backed up down the narrow passageway, keeping the light from her phone shining directly in Delacorte's face.

"Come on, baby, it's now or never," the man said.

His hands cupped her breasts.

Steady, Liz, she thought to herself.

In one swift motion, she brought her right knee up and smashed it into his balls.

Delacorte let out a shriek of pain and collapsed. Liz turned and bolted down the narrow passageway, shin-ing her light in front of her.

"You goddamn bitch!" Delacorte was shouting. "You goddamn fucking biiiiitch!"

The farther Liz ran the more distant his voice sounded. She had no idea where she was running to, but her brief experience with these passageways had suggested that they ran all through the house. So there had to be other exits. She just had to find one. She flashed her light along the wall, hoping to spot a seam. But she saw nothing. And she didn't want to stop and try to find one, not with Delacorte behind her. She had a sud-den terrifying sense of herself, as if seen from above: a hamster running helplessly through a maze, never find-ing her way out.

"Get back here!" Delacorte's voice echoed through the passageway. It sounded closer now; he was gaining on her. "They are expecting you!"

Who were *they*? And why did the idea of meeting

them frighten Liz even more than being caught by Delacorte?

"You can't get out of here!" he shouted, and now his voice seemed right on top of her. Liz swung her light around. She caught a glimpse of her adversary rounding the corner, panting and winded. She also caught a glimpse of something else: a ladder leading up to the second floor.

"Now listen to me," Delacorte said, removing a syringe from an inner pocket of his jacket. "Don't struggle anymore. There's no point. You don't want to die in here when the hurricane knocks the house to shreds, do you?"

"No," Liz said in a very small voice. "I don't want to die."

"So be a good girlie then," he said, approaching her with his syringe.

I'm an anesthesiologist, she heard Delacorte saying at the dinner table. *I put people to sleep.*

She waited until he drew close to her. Then she attacked again.

Her right hand clenched in a fist, she swung and connected with Delacorte's jaw. His head snapped backward in surprise. Liz heard the syringe go flying from his hand, bounce off the wall, and skitter across the floor.

In a flash she leapt onto the ladder and started up, keeping her phone gripped tightly in her left hand as if it were a magical amulet for protection.

In some ways, it was. Otherwise, she'd be plunged into total darkness.

Making it up the ladder, Liz stepped into a passageway on the second floor. Going up a floor wasn't very smart during a hurricane, Liz knew. But she'd had no choice. It was her only escape route from Delacorte. She hoped she could find an exit up here. She knew there was at least one, in the last room on the left in the servants' quarters. But whether she could find it, she wasn't sure.

Suddenly the house shook. It felt less like wind than an earthquake. There was a terrible, high-pitched screech and the very walls around Liz began to come undone. In an instant the darkness disappeared and there was light—a gray, muted light, but light nonetheless. There was also rain, and falling shards of wood. Liz looked up. A piece of the attic had been ripped off the house. The ceiling above her was buckling and collapsing in a dozen different places. Liz covered her head against the falling debris.

Yet even more horrifying than any of that was what came with the wood and plaster.

Three dead bodies—two of them practically skeletons. They fell to the floor just a couple of feet away from Liz. In the impact, the head of one corpse snapped from its spine and rolled toward her, coming to rest at Liz's feet. Dead, blackened eye sockets stared up at her.

Liz screamed.

68

"Bring her here!" the Haitian woman was shouting. "Bring her to me!"

In a flash Nicki was surrounded by three people, a middle-aged man, a younger man, and a young woman with short black hair and bangs that were cut straight across her forehead. Nicki didn't resist. She was too scared to resist. Nor did she try to say anything. She was trembling too much to speak. She just allowed herself to be pushed into the room toward the Haitian woman, who was wearing a long red dress and bright red lipstick and fingernails.

"Let her witness," the Haitian woman said, her enormous dark eyes locking on to Nicki's. "Let her witness the power we shall bring forth!"

"No, Variola, it is not safe to allow her to see," Mrs. Hoffman said, coming up behind them. "She must be done away with. She cannot be allowed to tell what she has seen here!"

"Be quiet, you miserable woman," Variola snarled. "This is to be done my way. Your way has failed miserably up to now. Look at her!"

She pointed to the naked, cowering woman in the center of the circle, her body bruised and broken, her eyes darting around the room in terror, her voice a series of guttural groans.

"Bring her to me!" Variola commanded again.

Nicki gasped as she felt someone behind her tie her wrists together with what felt like rope. This had to be some surreal dream she was having—someone had drugged her—she must be hallucinating. This couldn't be real! But the rough fibers of the rope being tightened against her wrists were all too real. "What are you going to do to me?" Nicki asked, her voice trembling.

"Keep quiet and we will do nothing to you," Variola commanded.

Nicki was shoved down onto a chair by unseen hands behind her.

"But if she tells what she has seen—" Mrs. Hoffman objected.

"Do you really think Variola does not know how to prevent people from talking? You claim to have learned so much." Variola spit on the floor. "But you know nothing."

Nicki saw the look that was exchanged between the two women. It was clear how very much they hated each other.

In that moment a terrible crash startled them all. Even Variola let out a small sound of surprise. Nicki began to cry, realizing it was a section of the roof being torn off from another part of the house. The wall opposite Nicki buckled outward, with water suddenly seeping in from the seam of the ceiling, suggesting that walls on the other side of this room had collapsed. Nicki cried harder. The hurricane was going to destroy them.

If whatever these crazy people were doing didn't destroy them first.

"It is time!" Variola announced, her face triumphant in the candlelight. "The power has arrived! Can you feel it, sisters and brothers?"

The group of people, who had returned to their chairs in the circle, murmured in agreement. But one woman, middle-aged, stood.

"Shouldn't we wait for the others?" she asked. "Paul hasn't returned . . ."

"There is no time to wait," Variola said. "We must bring her back! We must implore our master to restore her to life!'

"Hail, master," the group chanted. The naked woman standing beside the large red candle in the center of the circle began to moan.

"Sweet Jesus," Nicki cried. "You're calling on Satan!"

Variola shot her a look with those great dark eyes of hers. "Not Satan, you fool! Vodou does not worship the devil! It is not evil we seek, but balance." Nicki saw her eyes shift over to Mrs. Hoffman as she spoke. "Those who use the powers for evil, for selfish reasons, will pay the price." She returned her eyes to Nicki. "We seek to restore our sister to full and vibrant life. A life in which she will hopefully use her powers for good. And to do this, we beseech not a devil, but a great spirit, a spirit who can restore balance to our world."

"Then restore her!" Mrs. Hoffman shouted. "Do what you have promised to do, but have so far failed!"

The naked woman in the center of the circle let out a long, low moo.

Another crash as the wind lashed the house. Several candles flickered out, and the room grew darker. A long crack made its way across the ceiling above them. Rainwater began to ooze through the plaster, dripping on all of them.

"Oh, Papa Ghede, restore her!" Variola cried. "Give our sister the life that was hers before the tragedy! We implore you, our dark and compassionate master! We beseech you!"

Outside the wind reached such a high-pitched frenzy that the candle blew out and everyone covered their ears against the sound. All except Nicki, who feared she would go deaf.

"Restore her!" Variola screamed into the sound. Her face was contorted, her eyes squeezed shut, every vein on her neck standing out in stark relief.

The naked woman collapsed into a heap on the floor.

Variola sat down on the floor herself. "She is restored," she said quietly. "Now we must all move to safety."

Mrs. Hoffman bolted from her chair and went to the fallen woman. "My love," she cooed over her. "My darling . . ."

The woman turned her face up toward the ceiling.

"Speak to us," Mrs. Hoffman said. "Your followers. We are here . . ."

The others had all stood now and were gathered around them.

"Speak to us," Mrs. Hoffman said again.

The dazed, naked woman opened her mouth. The group waited.

And then she let out a long animal bray.

Nicki saw the fury that exploded in Mrs. Hoffman's eyes. She jumped to her feet and lunged at Variola, her hands around the Haitian woman's throat. "You failed again!" she screamed. "Your ways are wrong! Worthless and wrong!"

She was strangling Variola, who tried in vain to pull her hands from her neck.

"Stop, Mrs. Hoffman!" cried Mrs. Martinez, rushing up behind her. "You'll kill her!"

"I want to kill her," Mrs. Hoffman said, shoving Mrs. Martinez aside. "She deserves to die!"

"We need her," one of the men argued.

"We *don't* need her," Mrs. Hoffman replied, but nonetheless she let go of Variola's neck and pushed her away. Variola toppled over onto the floor. "Until we have restored our true leader, I am in charge of this coven. We will do it my way."

"The same way we have been trying for the past year," said the woman with the short black hair. "But that way has not worked."

"The way of death and bloodshed will never work," Variola said, off to the side, looking utterly defeated.

"It has worked better than Variola's way, which was just a lot of hope and prayer and nonsense," Mrs. Hoffman countered. "But the blood . . . it has brought her back, bit by bit. Do you not remember how she was a year ago, unable to walk, unable to comprehend even the simplest words?"

"I refuse," Mrs. Martinez said, and the entire group turned to look at her. "No more. Please, no more! How many lives for hers?"

Mrs. Hoffman turned savagely at her. "As many as is needed! You fool! You are a part of this! You cannot back out! None of you can!" She turned to face them all. "You all came willingly to this coven, pledging your lives and your faith. And you have all benefited from our deal with our dark master." She looked over at Variola. "He has given us a great deal. Call it evil, call it balance, call it whatever you will. But suddenly our coffers have filled with wealth. Suddenly our dreams have been realized." She turned back to Mrs. Martinez. "You gave your soul so that your grandchildren might find the wealth and success that always eluded you. You can't back out now!"

"I had no idea this is what it would entail when Variola told me about it," the older woman replied, breaking into tears.

"It doesn't have to entail this," Variola said weakly. "Don't listen to her."

"But it does!" Mrs. Hoffman shouted. "It is the only way to bring her back! And we are running out of time!"

The walls trembled again against the wind, as if they would collapse inward at any minute like a house of cards.

"What we need," Mrs. Hoffman said, "what we have always needed, is blood."

She turned and looked at Nicki.

"The blood is the life," Mrs. Hoffman intoned.

It was a chant picked up by the others. "The blood is the life. The blood is the life . . ."

Nicki looked at their faces. All but Mrs. Martinez were glassy-eyed, and they had all turned to stare at her.

"No," Nicki moaned.

"No!" Variola shouted, but her voice was weak, and getting weaker.

The others began moving toward Nicki.

"The blood is the life," they chanted. "The blood is the life."

Nicki struggled to free her hands but failed. Attempting to stand, she fell to the floor. The others gathered around her, looking down.

In her pocket, Nicki's phone began to ring, but of course she couldn't answer it. Her ringtone was the theme from the TV show *Bewitched*. A silly little jingle that seemed to go unnoticed by the people who were bearing down on her.

"The blood is the life," they chanted in unison.

Nicki screamed.

69

Gagging, covering her mouth, hoping she wouldn't puke, Liz made her way around the stinking, rotting corpses. Her only thought now was to get out. She'd rather deal with the hurricane than with Paul Delacorte.

She shined her phone ahead of her to give her light. She was disoriented. Was this the way she had come? She had no choice in direction, however, as the hideous debris from the fallen attic had barred off one part of the passage. Liz moved as quickly as she could. She had to find the exit!

It all seemed a terrible nightmare. Could it all really be happening? Where was Nicki? Where were the others? Whose corpses had she seen? What had Paul Delacorte been doing in the house?

Escape seemed futile. Liz saw no exit. She was trapped in here—trapped inside the walls!

"No," she whispered to herself, even as she heard the wind outside and the terrible scrape of wood being blown from the house. "I'll find a way out."

She would need to see more clearly if she was ever to find a seam in the wall indicating an exit. She moved her phone closer to direct the light. As she did so, she noticed that she had a couple bars of reception—she realized in a burst of joy that she could make a call. She hit Nicki's number. It rang and rang until Nicki's voice mail picked up. Liz didn't have time to wait. She hit END and then searched desperately among her recent calls. There was one number she was looking for. Only one number could help her now . . .

She found it. She tapped on it. She heard the first ring as the call went through.

"Please, please," she whispered.

But then the sound became scrambled, and she looked down at her phone. Reception was once again lost.

A loud scrape above her—and Liz looked up to see a whole section of the ceiling peel away and then fly off into the sky. Dark gray skies were revealed and rain poured in on her. Liz felt as if she might be sucked out into the hurricane. She scurried down the passage to a place where some ceiling remained.

As she did so, she spotted a new reason to hope.

A ladder, going down. Whether it was the ladder she'd come up here on, she wasn't sure. Where it led to, she didn't know either. But she knew she had to get off the second floor.

Except—

—someone else was already coming up the ladder.

Hands suddenly emerged from the opening on the floor. In instants there also appeared the head and shoulders of Paul Delacorte.

"There you are, you bitch," he growled. "So you'll go into it wide awake. We tried to spare you some of it by putting you to sleep. But so much for that."

He pulled himself through the opening and stood facing Liz. He grinned.

"But first," he said, "I'm going to finish what I started before."

"No," Liz whimpered.

She could fight, she could push and kick and scratch and bite. But there was no way she could overpower him now. He was right on her, and there was nowhere to run.

"Come on, baby, you might as well enjoy it," Delacorte said. "It's going to be your last time."

His sweaty paws were on her cheeks.

"Nooo," Liz cried.

There was a bang. There were so many noises around her as the wind ripped away parts of the house that at first Liz didn't distinguish the sound as being any different. But when Delacorte suddenly groaned and heaved in front of her, his hands dropping from her cheeks, she realized her attacker had been shot in the back. Blood came pouring from Delacorte's mouth and he collapsed like a melting snowman in front of her, dead at her feet.

Liz looked up. Standing at the ladder was Roger, who held a smoking pistol in his hands.

"Roger!" Liz cried in joy.

"Are you all right?" he asked.

Liz looked down at the crumpled body of Paul Delacorte. "He was insane," she managed to say.

"He deserved to die," Roger told her, approaching her, taking her hand and leading her away.

"We've got to get out of here," Liz said.

"Yes, my darling, we have a greater destiny than this."

She didn't really understand his words, but it didn't matter. Roger was helping her around the debris and toward the ladder that led downstairs. "I thought we could hide out in the study," Liz was saying. "Or perhaps the basement . . . somewhere that the winds can't get to us . . . the storm can't last much longer." She thought of something. "We've got to find Nicki! Hopefully she's found a safe place."

Roger said nothing. But he guided her past the ladder that led through the opening to the first floor.

"We've got to go *down*, Roger!" Liz shouted, the winds picking up again and howling through the holes in the ceiling. "It's not safe up here."

"I'm taking you on another route to safety," he explained. "It's where Nicki is."

Liz didn't understand, but she clutched Roger's hand tightly and allowed him to lead her down the corridor. At last they stopped.

"Here it is," he said.

He dropped Liz's hand and pressed both palms against the wall. Liz heard a scraping sound, and then a panel in the wall slid back. She recognized the closet in the room where she had been attacked. Beyond the closet came the flickering of candlelight.

But Liz wouldn't move. "We have to go downstairs!" she insisted to Roger. "The attic has been ripped off and a whole chunk of the second floor is exposed to the hurricane! It's only a matter of time before this part of the house gets blown away as well!"

"It's safer to go through this way," Roger said, stepping into the passage and offering his hand. "The other way was destroyed."

Liz looked at him, unsure.

Roger smiled. "Trust me, Liz."

She took his hand.

70

Variola, seated on the floor, as far away as possible from the terrible ceremony that was taking place, spied Mrs. Martinez out of the corner of her eye, dithering by the door.

Variola knew it was over. She had lost. The ceremony was draining her of her power, sucking her very life force from her body. Mrs. Hoffman had indeed learned her lessons well. She had mastered the arts that Variola had taught her, so much so that Variola was now powerless against her. Hoffman's power came directly from Variola; she was siphoning it off, bit by bit. The weaker Variola became, the stronger Hoffman grew.

But there was one tiny hope.

Mrs. Martinez.

"Go," Variola whispered, and she prayed to Papa Ghede that her whisper would bounce across the room and resound in Mrs. Martinez's ear.

The look Mrs. Martinez suddenly shot her told her that her prayers were answered.

Variola knew how horrified Mrs. Martinez was by

all of this. How sorry she was that she'd ever gotten involved in such madness. It had started out innocently enough: Mrs. Martinez had been fascinated by Variola's tales of magic in the islands, and gradually she had come to believe that such magic might help her family prosper. She had become an avid pupil, assisting Variola in teaching Dominique and Mrs. Hoffman all the arcane arts. And, lo and behold, her daughter Teresa suddenly was promoted at work. Her two beloved grandchildren started getting all A's in school. Mrs. Martinez credited the vodou gods. She was glad to keep assisting Variola in her ceremonies with Dominique and Hoffman, and eventually their little coven grew. It had been harmless in the beginning. Spells to keep them young. Rituals to enhance prosperity. Love potions for Mrs. Delacorte to prevent her husband from straying.

Mrs. Martinez had never expected bloodshed.

Variola fixed the older woman with her big black eyes from across the room. "Go," she whispered again. She could slip out now. No one was looking. They were all focused on the bleeding ceremony. Variola turned her eyes back to the repulsive sight. That poor girl, Nicki, who had come to this house on an errand of mercy, was hanging from the light fixture on the ceiling, her blood draining into goblets that were held by the two men. At least Nicki hadn't suffered. Hoffman had slit her throat effortlessly, and once the girl was dead, the soulless housekeeper had had her strung up, then sliced her body in various other places, producing a flow of blood like wine from a cask.

"Go," Variola whispered a third time, her eyes returning to Mrs. Martinez.

The older woman hesitated just a second, then slipped out the door. No one noticed her leave. A small smile crossed Variola's face.

"Drink, my love," Mrs. Hoffman was saying to the formerly naked woman, who was now wrapped in a gray robe and seated in a chair. Hoffman held a goblet of Nicki's blood up to the woman's lips. "Keep drinking, my darling."

The woman was responding. Variola couldn't deny that. Her eyes were becoming clearer. She had stopped trembling. She was coming back to life.

Hoffman's magic was potent. She had learned well. Variola had to give her that.

But magic used for evil, for one's own selfish rewards, never came to good. At this rate, however, with her strength draining nearly as fast as Nicki's blood, Variola doubted she would live to see Hoffman's ignominy.

"I believe she has been bled dry," one of the men announced, turning away from Nicki's wasted corpse.

"But she needs more!" Hoffman commanded. "She is coming back to us! She is waking up, but she needs more! And it must be given to her tonight, when the power of nature is still surrounding us, gifting us with life!"

"The blood has stopped flowing," the man told her.

"Cut the body down," Mrs. Hoffman snarled. The man did as he was ordered. Nicki's body fell to the floor, a bony heap.

Suddenly, a sound from the other side of the room. They all turned.

Roger Huntington stepped out of the closet, leading Liz behind him.

71

Maria Martinez rushed down the stairs and through the kitchen. But where could she go? Who could she tell of the horrors being committed upstairs? Outside the hurricane raged. Several of the palm trees were down, crushed against the windows of the first floor. Sheets of rain slammed against the glass like a barrage of stones.

How could she go out there? How could she get help?

Maria picked up the phone in the kitchen. Of course it was out. Her own cell phone had lost reception some time ago.

She could go to the garage and get her car. She would drive through the rain. It was the only way. She hurried out through the sunroom.

But then she remembered the other cars in the garage. She had been there when Mrs. Hoffman had directed the guests where to park. Maria had objected that they were blocking her in, but Mrs. Hoffman had dismissed her concerns. "You'll be the last to leave," she had said. "There will be a lot to clean up after we're done."

Another palm tree came down, smashing through a window in the sunroom. Rain and wind and broken glass whipped inside. Mud was splattered all over the furniture.

A lot to clean up. That was for sure.

No matter what, no matter the dangers outside, Maria knew she had to get out of this house. The danger inside was worse. Mrs. Hoffman would soon realize she was gone. And she would be angry. Very angry. And with her sudden acquisition of power from Variola, what might she be capable of doing to Maria to exact punishment?

She had never expected it all to become so terrible. It had started as a lark—as something fun. Then it had become something Maria had hoped would help her family, whom she wanted so desperately to find the success she'd never had for herself. But it all changed the day of the accident. The day the Coast Guard came to the house and told them Mrs. Huntington had been washed out to sea.

"You don't believe it, do you?" Mrs. Hoffman had asked Maria later that night. "You don't believe that Dominique is dead, do you?"

"What else can I believe?" Maria had asked.

Mrs. Hoffman had taken her to a secret room in the attic and showed her.

There was Dominique's body. Bruised, battered, bloody. But breathing.

How very much Hoffman wanted to believe she could restore Dominique to life. How wild had been her dream! And that creature on the second floor—that shambling, deformed creature drinking a dead girl's blood—was the product of that wild dream.

Maria should have gone to the police after Audra was killed. She had suspected just where the poor girl's blood had gone. But Mrs. Hoffman had threatened her. "What magic has done for your family," she warned, "can also be undone, and worse."

"It was all a lie," Maria said out loud, her hands in her hair, not knowing what to do. "Teresa got that promotion all on her own, because she was a good worker. Marisol and Luis earned those grades through their own hard work. Magic had nothing to do with it."

If that was so, then she had nothing to fear from Mrs. Hoffman.

Except that knife she held in her hands.

Maria had been horrified by how easily Mrs. Hoffman had used it to slice that girl's throat, as if it was something she did every day.

Dear God . . .

Had Mrs. Hoffman killed the others? Had she murdered Audra, and Jamison, and Rita?

Was Mr. Huntington innocent after all?

And what about poor, dear Thad? Something had happened to Thad. His car was still in the garage but he had disappeared somewhere in the house.

More blood on Mrs. Hoffman's hands?

Maria knew she had to get out of the house. Whether it was Mrs. Hoffman's magic or her knife, there was more danger within these walls than outside in the streets. She would push her way through the rain and the wind. She would find someone, a neighbor, anyone. Grabbing a rain slicker in the coatroom off the kitchen, Maria Martinez slipped it on and took a deep breath. Opening the back door, she stepped out into the storm.

72

L iz couldn't quite fathom what she was seeing. Here, in this small room in the servants' quarters, in the middle of a hurricane, were gathered a group of people. Chairs were placed in a circle, and candles were burning. She knew the people: Mrs. Hoffman. Mrs. Delacorte. Mr. and Mrs. Merriwell. Mr. and Mrs. Clayton. Karl, the assistant from Roger's gallery. And the artist, Naomi Collins. They were all looking at her. It was like some sort of strange dream, the kind where random people are thrown together in the most surreal of circumstances.

Except this wasn't a dream. The rainwater dripping down from the ceiling onto Liz's face was proof of that.

There was someone else in the room as well, seated on one of the chairs. A woman, it appeared, from the look of the long dark hair flecked with gray. She was wrapped in a gray robe and her face was down. She was drinking from a goblet.

"You fool," Roger was saying, approaching Mrs. Hoffman. "This was not what we had agreed upon."

"We agreed on nothing," Mrs. Hoffman said, turning her back on him.

"What is going on here?" Liz asked.

The darkness of the room had at first prevented her from seeing what else was in the room. But now she discerned Variola on the floor, cradling what appeared to be a body . . .

"Where is Paul?" Mrs. Delacorte was asking. "Where is he?"

"He's dead," Roger spit at her. "And he deserves to be."

"No!" Mrs. Delacorte screamed, dropping into a chair, covering her face with her hands.

"What is going on in this house?" Liz screamed. "We have got to get out of here! This whole floor is going to get blown away!"

As if to underscore her point, a ferocious gust of wind hit the side of the house. Both of the small windows in the room were shattered, pieces of glass flying through the air. Liz managed to duck, but a large hunk sliced into Mrs. Clayton's neck. Blood spurted out from the wound as if from a faucet.

"Blood," Mrs. Hoffman said, rushing a goblet to collect what she could before Mr. Clayton pushed her away, doing his best to attend to his wife.

Liz was horrified. "What is all this?" Her heart was racing as she looked around. "What sort of ceremony were you conducting here?"

Roger steadied her, taking hold of her forearms. "My darling, it's not what I planned," he said. "This is wrong. Please believe me. I had a much more glorious vision for us. It's all Hoffman's doing. She's mad."

"Mad, am I?" Mrs. Hoffman asked, a quiver of triumph in her voice. "Tell me if this is madness."

She gestured to the seated woman in the robe.

"Rise, my darling," Hoffman commanded.

The woman set aside the goblet she had been drinking from, and did as she was ordered. She lifted her face. Liz gasped.

It was the woman who had attacked her. Her face was still bloated and scarred, but her hair was no longer gray. Now it tumbled lustrously over her shoulders and blew around her face in the wind . . . dark, shiny, locks . . .

Liz knew that hair . . . she had seen it in the portrait . . .

"Dominique," Roger said, his voice low and breathy.

Dominique took several steps toward them. They were steady, graceful steps.

"How is it possible?" Liz asked.

"You would have let our precious Dominique rot away, wouldn't you have, Roger?" Mrs. Hoffman asked. "Your plan instead was to bring your darling little Liz into this coven. You would have made that simpering little fool our new figurehead. You would have denied Dominique her rightful place!"

"Yes," Roger shouted. "And when David was executed for killing Rita, I would have married Liz myself, and taken this house for my own, my father be damned."

"You milked our coven for all it was worth," Hoffman said, shouting over the driving wind. "You have been cashing in quite nicely from your deal with Papa Ghede. But it's over for you now, Roger." She smiled, or, rather, adjusted her lips in a way that passed for a smile on that plastic face. "Dominique is back, and she isn't pleased."

"Dominique isn't back," Roger said, laughing derisively. "You can make her walk. You can restore her hair. But what about her *mind*, Hoffman?" He took a step closer to Dominique. "Go ahead, woman. Speak to me."

Dominique's lips moved to form words, but produced no voice. The only sound in the room was the wind howling in through the broken windows.

"You see," Roger said. "She's still nothing more than a mindless zombie."

"This is all madness," Liz said, backing away from them. "It's obscene!"

From across the room, Mrs. Clayton, on the floor in her husband's arms, made a gurgling sound. "She's dead," Mr. Clayton cried.

Liz gazed over at the dead woman on the floor, surrounded by all this insanity and greed. She couldn't help but think, even in the midst of her terror: *It's a long way from Miss Porter's.*

"We've got to get to safety," Mr. Merriwell was saying. "We'll all be killed up here . . ."

"You'll do as I say!" Mrs. Hoffman declared, her voice straining to be heard above the high-pitched shriek of the wind.

"No," Roger said, and Liz saw him withdraw his pistol from his belt. "You'll do as *I* say."

He pointed the gun at Dominique.

73

Never had Maria Martinez ever encountered anything like the force of this wind. The rain felt like solid walls of water she had to run through as she made her way to the street. A couple of time she was literally lifted off her feet by the wind. She was terrified of being sucked up into the hurricane and then dropped miles from here to her death.

She reassured herself that she didn't have far to go. Just to the next house on the street.

But the gate at that house was closed and locked. There was no use banging or calling to the residents. No one would be able to hear her from the street, and surely the intercom wasn't working. The sound of the wind was so loud it felt to Maria as if she were caught in the engine of an airplane. She thought her hearing would never be the same after this.

Providing she lived through it.

Maria hurried to the next house, running from post to post, clinging for dear life each time. A small prayer of thanks escaped from her lips when she spotted an open gate at the next driveway. Running up to the house as fast as she could, Maria had to jump over fallen palm trees, not an easy task for a woman of fifty-nine. Finally she reached the front door and threw herself at it with a thud. "Please!" Maria called. "Please help me!"

No one answered. Maria despaired. They were probably huddled safely in the basement. Or maybe they had fled farther inland before the hurricane struck.

She was having a difficult time breathing. The wind and rain were so strong it wasn't easy to take a breath. Maria stumbled off the steps back toward the street. She would have to try another house. But she wasn't sure how long she could last out here.

Hurrying down the street, she was utterly drenched. Her hair was plastered to the sides of her face. She could barely see two feet in front of her.

Suddenly, amid the driving rain, she spotted a light ahead of her. A dim, flashing blue light in the middle of the street. Her hopes lifted. "Hello!" she attempted to shout, but the wind devoured her voice. Maria began to run.

But just as she did so, the wind caught her. She felt her feet lift off the ground. Maria felt weightless, powerless. She struggled, but her arms and legs thrashed uselessly through the air. She felt herself losing consciousness just before she was sucked up into the hurricane.

74

"Do you have reception on your phone?" Detective Joe Foley asked Aggie, both of them crowded into the basement of the police station with the other detectives.

"Intermittent," she replied. "Just enough for one text to get through from my husband, telling me they're all okay."

"Good to know," Joe said, staring down at his phone. "Looks like I got a call at some point over the last hour. I never heard it ring, though."

"Gee, I wonder why?" she asked with a smirk. "It's been so *quiet* around here."

"Guess who the call was from."

"The governor, declaring a state of emergency."

"Guess again."

She smirked. "FEMA, asking what they can do for us."

"Nope. Liz Huntington."

"Did she leave a message?"

Joe shook his head. "I suspect she got cut off. There was enough reception for the call to come through, but then it got dropped."

"Maybe she has information about her husband."

"So she called to tell me about it in the middle of a hurricane?"

"Does seem odd. But maybe it was very important."

Joe was staring at Liz's number in the list of missed calls on his phone. "I tried calling back, but I can't get through," he said.

"Maybe it was a pocket dial," Aggie suggested, "as she was hurrying down to the storm cellar."

"Possibly," Joe said.

But he knew it wasn't. He had a hunch. And his hunches invariably were right.

He'd learned that the hardest way possible many years ago.

He kept staring at the phone.

"Soon as this thing is over," he said, more to himself than to Aggie, "I'm going over there."

75

"I mean it, Hoffman," Roger said. "I have no compunction against shooting you through the heart. The cops would call it justified, after they see what you have done here."

On the floor, Variola was barely able to lift her head. *Yes*, she thought. *Shoot her! Kill her! Then the power will flow back to Variola.*

Mrs. Hoffman only smiled. "Such a foolish man," she said. "You always were."

Variola watched. Suddenly Roger let out a scream of pain and dropped the gun, as if it had suddenly become scalding hot in his hand. Of course it was hot: Variola recognized again how well Hoffman had learned her lessons.

"Take the gun," Hoffman ordered Naomi Collins, who obeyed swiftly. She aimed it at Roger, who was rubbing his burned hand. Not so long ago, Naomi had been the toast of Roger's gallery. Now she might be his death.

"It's your choice, Roger," Hoffman said. "You can either rejoin our coven and herald the return of Dominique as our supreme leader, or you can die right here."

Variola watched as Liz grabbed Roger's arm. "They're all mad! Can't you see that?"

Roger shrugged her off. "Very well, Hoffman. You've won. Let the games begin."

"Give her to us," Hoffman said.

No, Variola thought.

Roger shoved Liz forward. "Sorry, darling. Nothing personal. You'd do the same to me if you had the barrel of a gun pointed at you and a coven of angry witches ready to take off your head."

Liz screamed. Mr. Clayton grabbed her by her left arm, Karl by her right. They pulled her toward Mrs. Hoffman, passing Variola on the floor as they did so. Liz looked down and saw the dead body next to Variola was that of her friend.

"Nicki!" she shrieked. "Oh, Nicki, what did they do to you?"

"The same that we shall do to you now, my dear," Mrs. Hoffman said. She held a bloodstained knife in front of Liz's face.

I've got to stop this, Variola thought. *I've got to summon the strength . . .*

"Where is Martinez?" Mrs. Hoffman suddenly barked. "Where has she gone?"

They all looked around. "I didn't see her leave," Naomi said, still holding the gun at Roger.

"The despicable coward," Hoffman grunted. "If she thinks she can survive out there in this storm, she's wrong."

Even as she spoke, the wind stopped. The furious, incessant howling and moaning of the storm ended, and its cessation—the eerie sudden silence—was even more startling than any of the noise it had made. They all looked up. The air was still. Outside the broken windows, the sun was even breaking through the dark gray clouds.

"The storm is over," Mrs. Merriwell said.

"No," Mrs. Hoffman replied, her eyes dancing in the plastic mask of her face. "We are in the eye of the storm! This is the moment of greatest power. We should have known. This, finally, is the opportunity we have been waiting for."

A deathly stillness settled over the room, broken only by Liz's terrified sobs.

"Prepare the ceremony," Mrs. Hoffman announced. "We don't have much time. Who knows how long the eye will last. And if Martinez returns, she may bring company back with her."

"What will we do if she brings the police?" Mrs. Merriwell asked, distraught. "We all have reputations in this town, you know . . ."

"Silence, you old cow. Dominique will take care of everything once she is brought back to her full power." Hoffman clapped her hands. "Bring the goblets!"

Once again she waved the knife in front of Liz, who stood before her restrained between Mr. Clayton and Karl, struggling and crying.

"You will provide the life to bring Dominique back. How fitting that is. You thought you could replace her. But in fact, you will be the means of her restoration."

She placed the tip of the knife against Liz's throat. Liz stopped struggling and stood stiffly in terror.

"Not for you the mercy I showed your friend," Mrs. Hoffman said. "Not for you a single clean cut across the throat. For you, death will come by a thousand cuts, as they say. You will bleed for Dominique, and you will watch as your blood restores her."

I must stop this, Variola thought again, but she was so weak she could no longer even move the fingers on her hand.

Mrs. Hoffman giggled like a teenager. "I've wanted to do this since the first day you arrived," she said.

She swung the knife and sliced into Liz's forearm. Liz let out a yelp.

"The goblets!" she cried.

The blood flowed freely.

And Dominique drank.

76

Everything was blackness, but she could hear voices coming from somewhere far away. "Can you hear us?" a man was asking. "Can you tell us your name?"

Maria opened her eyes. She was in some sort of vehicle, it seemed. An ambulance. Medical equipment. Oxygen tanks.

"What happened?" she mumbled. "How did I get here?"

In her mind, she saw Luis and Marisol . . . playing in the bright sunlight. *They will be okay . . . I did the right thing.*

But what exactly had she done? Maria couldn't remember . . .

"You were thrown pretty bad by the storm." The man whose face hovered above her had kind eyes and a soft voice. "Luckily we were right down the street."

Maria realized the man was wearing camouflage. The National Guard.

The storm. The hurricane.

Oh, sweet Jesus . . .

The ceremony. The blood.

She was running to get help . . .

Maria panicked as the memories came flooding back to her. She tried to sit up. The man in the National Guard uniform gently restrained her.

"You've got to send help," Maria told him. "Huntington House. There are people hurt there."

"Okay, we'll add them to the list," the Guardsman told her. "There are lots of people hurt all over town."

"But you don't understand. They'll kill her. They might already have done so."

"There, there, ma'am, just lie still and try to relax." He motioned over to a colleague. "I think she could use a sedative."

Maria sat up. "No, you must listen! It's a ceremony— a coven of witches!"

The Guardsman just looked at her oddly.

Maria thought of something. "Please! You must get me Detective Foley! I must tell Detective Foley what is going on in that house!"

77

It was something out of a fever-induced nightmare: Liz stood in a hurricane-devastated room being restrained on either side by two men, one of them a business associate of her husband's, the other a young man who had been very polite to her during every previous encounter. All the while Mrs. Hoffman, her nemesis ever since coming to this house, sliced open her forearm and collected her blood in a goblet.

Which she then gave to David's supposedly dead first wife to drink.

The absurdity of it all was not lost on Liz, even in her terror.

"This can't be happening," she shouted, not believing what her eyes were showing her.

Dominique was alive! She had been living in the walls, in a secret room within the house, all this time. She was the deformed, bloated woman who had attacked her. Except now, as she sat there drinking her goblet of blood, Dominique looked different than she had the previous times Liz had seen her: she was looking less monstrous. Her hair was lustrous and dark again, much as it was in the portrait. Her face was less bloated. Her eyes were still protruding and her face still seemed broken, but the blood was reviving her, restoring her, under the black magic that had been practiced in this room.

Nicki's blood had started the process, Liz realized sadly, refusing to look over at the dead body of her friend. No, the process had begun before that, she realized: Audra had been killed for her blood, and likely those two friends of hers who had gone missing, whom Detective Foley had asked her about, had been killed for the reason, too. Those were the bodies she had seen, Liz realized. Unfortunate young women slaughtered to keep Dominique alive.

That was as much as Liz's brain would permit her to reason: just how Dominique had survived the accident on the boat, and whether David knew any of this, and whether Jamison's or Rita's murders fit this pattern, she had no idea. She had no time to think about any of that as the fear suddenly set in, threatening to choke her as it surged up from her gut, once the shock and denial of her terrible situation began to fade.

They're going to kill me.

They are going to bleed me dry!

Mrs. Hoffman will kill me. And the others will let her.

Including Roger.

Liz's eyes darted over to her brother-in-law. He was involved with this coven, as Mrs. Hoffman had called it. He'd been a follower of Dominique's. How much did he know about the deaths of those women? He sat there now on a chair in the circle, his head in his hands. Naomi Collins, the artist whose weird paintings had so unnerved Liz, stood over him pointing a gun—but how easily Roger had accepted Liz's fate, how easily he had allowed her to be taken away.

Sorry, darling. Nothing personal. You'd do the same to me if you had the barrel of a gun pointed at you and a coven of angry witches ready to take off your head.

No, Liz thought to herself. *I wouldn't have done the same. I would have fought back, even if it meant I was killed in the process.*

In that moment, Liz realized something about herself. Even as she was held against her will and was growing weaker as more and more of her blood spilled out onto the floor, she understood she was a fighter, and she'd always been a fighter. So many times she had doubted her own strength; so many times she had felt helpless. Yet she was stronger than she ever gave herself credit for being. She was a fighter.

And she wasn't done fighting yet.

Mrs. Hoffman was back in front of her, brandishing that knife.

"Where shall I make the next cut?" she asked. "That pretty little face?"

Liz's arms were restrained by the two men on either side of her.

But her legs were free.

They think I'm just a scared little girl. That's why they haven't taken more precautions.

They've underestimated me.

With one swift move, Liz smashed her left knee into Mrs. Hoffman, right in the cunt. Mrs. Hoffman howled and dropped the knife.

In that same instant, Liz yanked herself free from the two surprised men.

"Seize her!" Mrs. Hoffman commanded.

The men made a move to pounce at her as Mrs. Merriwell and Mrs. Delacorte rushed forward as well. Liz knew she would quickly be surrounded, and Naomi Collins could easily fire a bullet her way.

But she wasn't captured quite yet.

"You will not touch her!" came a voice. Liz spun around to see Variola, struggling to her feet, seeming to summon every last drop of strength she had in the effort. "All of you, who have defiled the teachings of vodou, *will not touch her*." She turned her eyes—once so magnificent, now so sunken and dim, in Liz's direction. "Go, girl. Go as fast as you can. This is the last Variola can do for you."

Whatever magic Variola had invoked prevented any of Liz's adversaries from moving. As long as Variola stood—trembling, with great will—she was safe. Anger burned in Mrs. Hoffman's eyes as Liz was able to hurry across the room unobstructed toward the door, gripping her forearm tightly with her other hand to stanch the bleeding as best she could. She could feel her head spinning from the loss of blood. She prayed she wouldn't faint.

She wasn't the only one growing weak.

Just as Liz neared the door, Variola collapsed. She had used up the last of her strength, and she crumpled lifelessly to the floor, her body dissolving, as if she had been made of sand.

The second Variola disappeared, Liz saw movement return to the other people in the room. They broke free of their invisible chains. Now the door was out of reach. She would have to get past Naomi with the gun if she went that way. So there was only one route left to Liz for escape.

The secret passageway through the closet.

Liz made a beeline for it.

"Bring her back!" Hoffman shouted. "We need her blood before the eye moves on!"

But Liz was already several steps ahead of them. Through the open panel she ran, taking a few precious seconds to turn around and slide the panel back into place. Then she tore off her blouse and tied it tightly around her forearm to stanch the bleeding. That would hold for a little while. But not for long, she knew.

She turned and ran.

They'll think that I've taken the ladder and gone down to the first floor. They'll go looking for me there.

But Liz had another plan.

With the storm temporarily abated, she would go out onto the roof through the hole the winds had ripped open in the attic. She knew she was taking a risk: she'd have to find a way down from the roof, and she'd need to pray that the hurricane didn't start up again until she was safely on the ground. But the roof, as precarious as it was, was less of a risk, Liz believed, than going downstairs and finding herself cornered by her pursuers on the first floor.

As she ran down the passage she could hear them banging on the panel, struggling to slide it open. Liz could hear Mrs. Hoffman ordering some of them downstairs in case Liz went that route, while instructing the others to follow her into the passage. "Half of you go this way, half of you go that way! Hurry! Hurry!"

Liz ran.

Outside, the winds were gathering again.

78

"The storm will be back soon," Aggie cautioned as Joe pulled on his raincoat and headed out of the station. "I'm not sure you can get there and back in time."

"I've got to go," he said. "I've got to find out why Liz called me."

"And if turns out it was just a pocket dial and you're stuck out there in the worst hurricane Florida has seen in a decade?"

"I'm sure they've got a cozy, well-appointed safe room at Huntington House," he quipped.

Aggie shook her head. "I'm coming with you."

"But the storm—"

"We're partners, aren't we? We're both investigating this case."

Joe smiled. "Then let's get going."

They stepped out into the parking lot. The sky was a bright blue-green: pretty, but ominous, too. Joe didn't think he'd ever seen it that color. The afternoon was unnervingly quiet now after all the noise and furor of the past couple of hours. With the coming of the eye, a hush seemed to have dropped over the city, which sat motionless, holding its breath, waiting for the next assault. The only sounds Joe heard as he and Aggie walked to the car were the faraway drones of house and car alarms that had been set off by the winds. Joe glanced up into one of the few palm trees still standing on the street. Its fronds had begun to move slightly again. He knew Caroline wasn't through with them. She was getting ready for her comeback.

"Get your badge out in case we're stopped by the National Guard," Joe told Aggie as they both hopped into the car. "Murder investigations don't take a break, we'll tell them."

"Not even for hurricanes," Aggie replied.

Joe started the car. But before he'd had a chance to back out, his phone, clipped to his belt, buzzed.

"Joe Foley," he answered.

"Joe, it's Tim Duncan over in dispatch. We have a call in from one of the National Guard mobile hospitals for you."

"Who from?"

"Not sure. A patient. Hold on, I'll patch you through."

Joe looked over at Aggie. "Some patient in one of the Guard hospitals wants to talk with me."

"Detective Foley?" a voice crackled in his ear.

"This is Joe Foley."

"This is Captain Alvarez of the National Guard. I have a patient here, a Mrs. Maria Martinez, who insists she speak to you. She's refusing any treatment until she does. She says it's about a case you're working on."

"Yes, please, let me speak with her." Joe switched the phone to speaker so that Aggie could hear.

"I should tell you," Alvarez added, "that what she's saying doesn't make a lot of sense. She suffered some trauma after getting tossed pretty hard by the hurricane."

"Whatever she has to say," Joe said, "I'm eager to hear."

"Okay, hang on."

A couple of seconds passed. Joe and Aggie exchanged quizzical looks.

"Detective Foley?"

"Yes, this is Detective Foley."

The woman on the other end of the phone burst into tears. "This is Maria Martinez," she said. "I just hope I'm not too late."

79

Liz made her way down the passageway, which reeked of the smell of death. She knew those corpses were in here somewhere. At least now, with all the damage left by the storm, there was some light let in from the outside to guide her: she had no idea where her phone was. Liz just needed to find a place where the damage was so severe that she could step out onto the roof.

She had to hurry. She could hear footsteps behind her now. At least some of them had come into the passageway after her.

A few feet down the corridor she spotted another corpse. Paul Delacorte, his dead eyes still open and staring at her. "Scum," she spit as she stepped over the body.

Up ahead, the light was greater. That was because the entire wall on the right side was gone, along with a huge chunk of the ceiling. Stepping through the debris into the light, Liz realized that she was leaving the secret passageway and returning into the main house. As she glanced around, she saw something else: she was stepping into her own room.

The place was soaked with water and strewn with plaster and broken glass, but her bed, along an interior wall, was just as she had left it not so many hours earlier. Her bureau remained remarkably untouched, with bottles of perfume still standing upright. But only a few feet away the entire exterior wall was gone, exposing a sheer drop down into the gardens. Liz saw with some shock that they were now nothing more than brown, glistening pools of mud.

Only then did Liz spot Nicki's suitcase. Her heart broke. Her friend—who had come down here to support her. Liz thought she might dissolve into a blubbering mass of tears right there on the spot.

I've got to stay strong, she told herself. *They'll be in here after me at any minute. I've got to find a way down to the ground.*

Her plan to escape via the roof hadn't panned out. There'd been no way to get out there that Liz had found. Maybe she would have found some way if she'd gone in the opposite direction. But the only route out of the passage that she'd found had been through the broken wall that led into her own room. For a second Liz imagined Dominique moving through that passage in the weeks previous.

I heard her. I smelled her.

I wasn't mad. I wasn't hysterical.

It was all real.

Liz glanced down through the broken wall at the remains of the gardens. The drop was too high for her to jump. She'd surely kill herself, or break her leg, leaving her helpless against Hoffman and her minions, who would quickly descend upon her. Liz studied the broken beams and plaster. Was there a way she could shinny herself down? If she had time, she might have tied bed-sheets together to form a makeshift rope to lower her-self to the ground. But she didn't have time. She could hear them coming for her now. They were running be-hind the walls. She had been a fool to try to go out this way. She should have risked going downstairs.

She looked again out the window. The only way was to jump . . . she'd rather take the leap and hope for the best than be snatched back by those monsters. Maybe the mud would cushion her fall.

But it was too late. A hand gripped her shoulder.

"Jumping would be a terrible mistake." It was Roger. "Accidents like that could severely mar your pretty face." He turned her around to face him and cupped her chin in his hand. "Look at what happened to Dominique when she fell off that boat and got caught in its rotors."

"Don't touch me," Liz said, pulling away from him and standing precariously on the edge, poised to jump. She noticed Roger was alone; Naomi Collins had let him go; and none of the others had followed him in here. Still, he was as bad as all the rest of them. "I'd rather break my neck than die at the hands of you lu-natics," she said.

"But you see, darling, that's why I'm here," Roger said. "They agreed to let me reason with you. You can become part of us."

"You're lying to me. Not that I'd ever join your loathsome little group, but you're talking bullshit. No way would Hoffman allow me to live. If I live, Do-minique doesn't come back."

Roger leaned in conspiratorially. "After Hoffman ran off, we all decided that we didn't need her. Variola was right. We'll do things our way. We've learned plenty. Hoffman isn't the only one who can call up a spell. We'll overthrow Hoffman. It was my plan all along, and it can still come true."

Behind him, Liz spotted movement. The door to her room was opening slowly, carefully, as if to not make a sound. Liz's first impulse was to cry out, but something made her hold her tongue. She gave no indication of what she saw to Roger.

"I was always very reluctant about this idea of bringing Dominique back," he was saying. "I went along with Hoffman only begrudgingly. But she had certain things on me, and so she made me do things. You know how she can be."

"What did she make you do?"

"I had to kill those poor girls for their blood. I wasn't happy about it, darling. Don't think badly of me."

"Audra . . . Rita . . . you killed them . . ."

"No, darling, just Audra's friends. And then some tramp I picked up at a bar. It was Dominique who killed Audra. She was angry about her affair with David. That was how we learned that the blood is the life. Dominique tasted Audra's blood, and we saw the effect it had on her. Ever since Variola had reclaimed her body from the sea and breathed some measure of life back into it, she'd been a mindless zombie. After she made a meal of Audra's blood . . . well, some understanding returned to her eyes. Some intelligence flickered there. That's why it was decided that we needed to find more blood for her."

Liz glanced over at the door, careful that Roger did not notice. A small hand was coming around from the other side of the door

"And I didn't kill Rita either," Roger went on. "I don't want you thinking I did."

"Who did kill her then?"

Roger smirked. "You still fretting over David? Forget him, Liz. He's a loser. How easily he was manipulated by all of us. Dominique had him under a spell for months, and during the time she's been indisposed, Mrs. Hoffman took care of it."

"You're all mad. You're all sick!"

"They are, darling. Not me. I got into this to be a successful art dealer, not a murderer. I refused to do any more of Hoffman's dirty work after those first two girls, and only under great pressure did I agree to bring her poor Lana." He smiled wistfully. "I didn't even get to fuck her first. Oh, boy, when she found out I was a Huntington, she thought she'd hit the jackpot. I told her to meet me upstairs in that last room on the left. I wanted time for a little quickie with her before I slit her throat and drained her blood, but Hoffman was very insistent that Dominique was getting too difficult to control. Her body had grown stronger. She kept escaping from her room. We saw her that day, didn't we, darling, in the sculpture garden? But her mind remained as weak as ever. She needed another transfusion. So . . ."

The hand grabbed on to the door and pushed it slowly, silently, into the room.

"I know I sound awful, darling," Roger said. "But once we're married, I won't play around anymore. I promise."

"Married." Liz spit the word out like poison on her tongue.

But Roger's eyes were far away and filled with madness. "Once Dominique promised she would marry me, too. She would divorce David and marry me. That was our plan. But no!" His face went dark. "How she taunted me! She knew I loved her! She knew that I wanted her to be with me forever. But still she taunted me with other men. She was always flirting. Always taking lovers . . ."

Liz could see the rage roiling in Roger's eyes.

"David always got everything he wanted," he seethed. "Everything! The best grades, the best positions on athletic teams, the leading parts in the school plays. I was always just in the background. All the teachers liked David and hated me. He even got the most beautiful woman in the world as his wife! But I wanted her! She and I could have been so powerful together."

"Her coven made you rich," Liz said calmly.

"I still have a deal with Papa Ghede," Roger replied, his eyes twinkling.

"Variola always said that deals made with Papa Ghede for selfish reasons will backfire."

Roger snorted. "Variola was a weak-minded fool! She never realized what greatness she could have achieved through her abilities."

Behind them, the hand was followed by an arm, and then a bloated, twisted face. Liz saw it was Dominique.

She suppressed an urge to cry out as the once-beautiful woman slipped into the room. Dominique's eyes were sparkling, but her face remained twisted and broken. She was not looking at Liz, however; her gaze was trained on Roger. Instinctively Liz sensed it was in her best interests not to warn Roger of Dominique's presence. At this particular moment, who was to say who was Liz's greater foe?

"We will destroy them," Roger was telling her. "Come

back with me now. They will all fall behind me when I give the word. Naomi, Karl, the Merriwells, the Claytons, Mrs. Delacorte . . . they are *my* friends, not hers. That's why they let me go. They hate Hoffman, too. They will gather around us and we will destroy Hoffman once and for all."

"And Dominique?" Liz asked, as the woman with the wild eyes slowly and silently made her way across the room. "What will you do about her?"

Roger laughed. "I killed her once before. I'll kill her again."

"You—?"

"That's what Mrs. Hoffman had on me, darling." He smiled almost comically. "You see, it was I who was on the boat with Dominique, not David."

"But . . . the captain said he saw David . . ."

Roger gave her that dazzling grin of his. "We look an awful lot alike, my brother and I. You've said so yourself. Captain Hogarth saw me from up on the bridge, and just for a fleeting second. It was only natural he'd think I was David." He laughed. "And convenient, too. Once this is all over, my love, we'll pin Dominique's death on David, too, when he's tried for the murder of Rita."

Behind him, Dominique suddenly revealed the knife she'd been concealing in the folds of her robe. Liz couldn't muffle her horror any longer and let out a gasp. Roger turned around, but it was too late. Dominique lifted the knife over her head before bringing it down savagely, stabbing Roger in the back.

He let out a cry and staggered off to the side. Liz backed away from him, her hands covering her mouth, watching as one more unspeakable terror unfolded in front of her eyes. Dominique yanked the bloody knife out of Roger's back. It made a horrible suction sound. Roger tried to speak, to say something to Liz, but he couldn't form any words. A little sound burbled from his throat, and then he collapsed to the floor. Dominique, almost gleefully, leapt upon him. Her knife went in and out of him over and over again, blood spraying everywhere.

Liz turned. She knew she'd be the madwoman's next target. The only choice left for her now was to jump.

80

The winds were blowing hard again as Joe and Aggie pulled into the driveway at Huntington House. "Half the roof is gone," Aggie noted as the house came into view.

Palm trees lay uprooted all over the property. The once elegantly manicured gardens were ripped apart and smothered in mud. The place seemed utterly deserted and desolate.

But not for long. Joe had barely turned off his car when he spotted the garage door of the great house being winched up on its cord by a stocky, middle-aged man. He was struggling, breathing heavily. The electric door had to be opened by hand with the power out, and from the looks of it, this was not a man used to manual labor.

Joe and Aggie were quickly out of the car and hurrying up to the garage.

"Where you going?" he called to the man. "Roads are closed. The storm's moving back in."

The man's clothes appeared disheveled. His eyes re-

flected fear when he beheld the police car that was
blocking his way down the driveway.

"Aren't you Lyndon Merriwell?" Aggie asked. "I've
seen your picture in the newspapers."

The man didn't answer.

Joe nodded. "Yes, you're a city councilman, aren't
you? What are you doing at Huntington House?"

That was when Joe noticed the blood on Merriwell's
shirt.

He shined his flashlight into the garage. There were
others inside, standing beside Bentleys and Porsches
and Mercedes Benzes. He recognized one of them as
that weirdo artist who'd been showing her work at Roger
Huntington's gallery, and another one as Roger's assistant.

"She tried to kill us," Merriwell blurted.

"She killed my wife!" another man shouted.

"And my husband!" a stout woman added.

"Who killed them?" Joe asked.

"Mrs. Hoffman."

Joe turned to Aggie. "Call for backup. Keep them
here until then. I'm going inside."

"Joe, if even a third of what Mrs. Martinez told us is
true, it's very dangerous in there."

"That's why I need to go in." He turned back to
Merriwell. "Who's left inside?"

"Mrs. Hoffman, Liz, and Roger Huntington."

Joe leveled his eyes at the man. "What about Dominique?"

The man said nothing. All of the people in the garage
seemed to clamp their mouths shut at the same time.

"We know the truth," Joe said, as he heard Aggie

call in to the station. "We know Dominique Huntington is alive."

He headed around to the side door of the house, his hand on the grip of his gun. All around him the wind blew ferociously, sounding once more like a freight train about to bear down on them all.

81

The car sped down the deserted street, swerving around fallen palm trees and vehicles left abandoned in the middle of the road. The driver gripped the wheel tightly. It was imperative he get to Huntington House as quickly as possible. Something bad was going on there.

He pulled into the driveway, but noticed the police car up ahead, parked in front of the garage, its blue light flashing. He backed out of the driveway and drove around the block.

He couldn't go in through the front door, it seemed.

But there was a way to gain access to the property. A place in the back where the wall surrounding the estate was fairly easy to scale. He'd have to go in that way.

He parked in the street. The wind nearly whipped the door off his car as he got out.

82

"That's enough, Dominique," came the voice of Mrs. Hoffman, stepping into the room.

Liz was poised on the edge, ready to jump down into the mud. The wind threatened to push her over the side even without any effort on her part. Gradually the hurricane was regaining its full steam.

Mrs. Hoffman helped Dominique to her feet from where she knelt beside Roger's body. The knife fell from her hand and clattered to the floor.

"Look at you, my darling," Mrs. Hoffman said. "What a mess you've made."

Dominique's gray robe was drenched in blood. Her hands and her hair dripped with it.

Liz took a deep breath. She knew Hoffman wouldn't let her live. She was going to jump.

"No need to kill yourself," Mrs. Hoffman said, turning those cold eyes behind the plastic mask of her face in Liz's direction. "I'm not going to harm you. The police are on their way. Maybe there's a chance all of us can survive this unpleasantness."

Liz just glared at her, while Dominique growled.

"Oh, my darling," Mrs. Hoffman said, turning to the woman in the bloody robe. "Why don't you go to our secret place and get yourself cleaned up? Put on your pretty white dress. The one you love so much. The one you look so beautiful in."

Liz glanced out into the storm. If Hoffman was right, and the police were on their way, she wasn't going to risk the jump. Hoffman almost certainly still had Roger's gun in the pocket of her robe, and she might still kill Liz at any time. But for the moment, Liz backed away from the sheer drop down into the gardens. The wind was getting awfully ferocious now, and sheets of rain were whipping into the room.

She watched as Dominique walked obediently across the room, turning once to glare at Liz. Then she stepped over the debris into the exposed secret passage and disappeared.

"Now," Mrs. Hoffman said to Liz, "let's you and I talk."

"You're even crazier than I thought you were," Liz replied, "if you think you can somehow bargain with me, now that it looks as if the police are coming and you're about to be caught."

"I'm not bargaining with you," Hoffman said, her voice icy with disdain. "I just wanted to get Dominique safely away. I've spent years protecting her. I'm not going to let them come in and find her."

"Your secret place in the attic is destroyed," Liz snapped. "Or hadn't you noticed?"

Hoffman chuckled. "Silly little girl. You called yourself mistress of this house. And yet you never knew all of its secrets. Dominique and I have many secret places all throughout this house. I will keep her there, safe, and no one will find her."

From outside Liz could hear the sirens of police cars, even despite the wind. They were near. They might have even been coming up the driveway of the house.

"You can't believe this will work out your way," she told Hoffman. "They will come here. They will find you and they will find her. They will see what you have done."

Hoffman glared at her with those ferocious eyes. "Do you really think that I don't know how to protect my precious Dominique? I have protected her ever since she came to this house, when those dark eyes bewitched me, and not with any magic, not with any vodou, but with the purity of her beauty and her magnificence. I won't let anyone get to her. I have killed to protect her, and I will kill again. I killed Jamison when I figured he'd tell what he knew. Foolish boy. I copied his keys so I could have access to his apartment. I copied all the servants' keys. If they were coming into this house, I had to make sure I had ways to control them."

"You killed Rita, too, didn't you?" Liz asked. "It wasn't David at all."

"She was a nuisance right from the start. I should have slit her throat a year earlier and saved all of us a lot of trouble."

"You were going to let David take the rap."

Mrs. Hoffman waved a hand in disgust. "David."

She said the name as if it were something dirty. "His philandering is what sent poor Dominique on her never-ending quest to stay beautiful. If only he had appreciated her . . . because no matter how old she got, she was always going to be the most beautiful woman to have ever lived. He didn't deserve her! After we are through here, and your blood has restored my beautiful Dominque, she and I will be together forever, without any of you sad, pathetic creatures around us. And that includes David."

"The police will search this place from top to bottom after I tell them what's happened here."

"You'll tell them nothing," Mrs. Hoffman replied. "You'll do what I say."

Suddenly there was a voice, calling from below: "Hello!"

Liz recognized it as Detective Foley's voice.

"Go ahead," Mrs. Hoffman said. "Answer him. Tell him where we are."

Liz attempted to shout out to him, but found she could not.

Mrs. Hoffman nodded. "Variola taught me so many useful tricks. Pity that she's not around anymore to see what a brilliant student I was." She shrugged. "Well, I think she figured that out by the end."

Liz gripped her throat, feeling the tightening there. It was getting difficult to breathe.

Mrs. Hoffman withdrew a small wooden doll from her robe. There was a ribbon tied around its throat.

"How very much I should like to just snap this doll's head right off," she said. "But you see, my dear, I've got to keep you alive for a little while more. Just long enough to provide Dominique with one more drink."

Liz tried to move, but found she was rooted to the spot.

"She's almost there," the housekeeper said. "One more good long drink of your blood and she will be restored to what she was."

Liz thought she might pass out for lack of air.

"We're up here, Detective!" Mrs. Hoffman suddenly called out the door. "Oh, please come quickly! Liz is hurt badly!"

As she spoke, Mrs. Hoffman switched the wooden doll into her left hand, while withdrawing Roger's pistol from another pocket with her right hand.

No, Liz thought. *Foley's walking into a trap. And I can't warn him!*

"Up here!" Mrs. Hoffman shouted, positioning herself against the wall so she could surprise the detective. "Please hurry!"

The wind screeched into the room at that moment, dousing them with water as if someone was heaving buckets at them. Liz's hair dripped down the sides of her face. The last of her perfume bottles on her dresser toppled over onto the floor. Her elegant white canopy bed collapsed as if it had been made with toothpicks. A couple of white satin pillows were caught by a whirlwind and drawn out into the storm.

Liz saw Foley appear in the doorway, his gun drawn. Mrs. Hoffman leveled her own gun at the detective.

What happened next took only a matter of seconds, but for Liz, time slowed way down. She saw every step, every tiny action, clearly and deliberately.

As Hoffman gripped the gun with both of her hands, she dropped the wooden doll. It went tumbling through the air to the floor.

Meanwhile, Detective Foley was glancing around the room, his eyes at first seeing nothing. Then he spotted Mrs. Hoffman with the gun and his expression turned to alarm.

Hoffman pulled the trigger. Foley had no time to duck or turn his gun to her.

But Liz had time. With the doll out of Hoffman's hand, Liz was suddenly free to move, and so she lashed out, both fists clenched, slamming them directly into Mrs. Hoffman's face. The monstrous woman screamed as she fired her gun.

Foley was hit. He went down in a spray of blood, his own gun firing uselessly into the ceiling. He collapsed onto the floor and was still.

Mrs. Hoffman was wailing. Dropping the gun, she covered her face with her hands and staggered across the room. "What have you done?" she cried. "What have you done?"

Liz looked over at her. As Hoffman removed her hands, her face broke away in a dozen pieces, as if it really had been a plastic mask all along.

"No!" Hoffman screamed, looking at herself in the mirror. What stared back at her was a ghoul with a pulpy red face and bulging eyes, sinewy muscles and veins exposed. No amount of plastic surgery—or magic—could help Hoffman now. She raised her head to the ceiling and howled like a wounded dog.

"Who would have thought a simpering little fool

like you could destroy me?" She stumbled across the room as the wind raged. "What a world! What a world!"

Raising her arms in anguish and despair, Mrs. Hoffman let out a piercing scream, a sound that cracked the mirror and became one with the wail of the storm. Then, despite her best efforts to repel them, the winds took hold of her and sucked her out into the hurricane.

83

Standing under the overhang of the garage, doing her best to defy the encroaching winds of the storm, Aggie heard gunshots from the house, and then a terrible, unearthly scream.

"Joe!" she shouted into her handheld transceiver. "Joe, are you all right?"

Other police cars were now speeding up the long driveway.

"Hang on, Joe!" Aggie cried. "Backup's here."

Behind her, the people were getting restless. "You've got to let us go," Lyndon Merriwell said. "The storm is doubling back on us."

"You're not going anywhere except with the officers who are arriving now," Aggie snapped, turning to look at them with contempt in her eyes. "I know what you people are. Maria Martinez made a full confession. You're all going to be charged with accessory to murder, on God only knows how many counts."

The people in the garage fell silent after that.

Out in back of the house, a man was scrambling over the wall. He dropped onto the grass and went running through the driving rain toward the house.

84

Liz bent over the fallen police detective. She could hear his radio crackling.

Joe, are you all right? Joe, answer me!

Liz wished she knew how to work the thing so she could respond and let them know what happened. But it didn't matter: it sounded as if Detective McFarland was downstairs, and more help was on its way. Liz just needed to make her way down to the first floor and—

"Where is Mrs. Hoffman?"

Liz spun around. The voice was ragged and hoarse, but strong enough.

Dominique was standing in front of her, wearing a lacy white dress, the same one she wore in the portrait. Her face and hands were still bloody, however, and she was pointing Roger's gun at Liz.

"She fell," Liz managed to say.

"You killed her."

"No," Liz said, her eyes focused on the gun in Dominique's hand.

She couldn't have come this far—survived everything thrown at her—and with salvation waiting for her downstairs—to get killed now.

But that appeared to be Dominique's plan for her.

"You tried to take my place," the madwoman said.

"No," Liz replied.

"This was my room."

"Yes," Liz said. "I should never have called it my own. I always felt you here, Dominque. It was always your room."

"You married David."

"Yes, but no one could ever take your place, Dominique. You are beautiful. You are enchanting and unique. I could never hope to be you, or as beautiful as you."

"Beautiful," Dominique repeated, almost trancelike.

"We're very different women, you and I," Liz told her. "I could never be you. Just as you could never be me."

"You're going to tell," Dominique said.

"I'm not going to tell . . ."

"Yes, you are!" Dominique's voice shrilled in anger, like a child's. "You are going to tell about our coven!"

"No, Dominique, I won't—"

"I have to kill you."

"No, please!" Instinctively Liz lifted her hands in front of her face.

"Dominique, stop!"

It was a man's voice that suddenly barked from behind her. Liz turned to look.

David.

It was David.

He stood in the doorway, drenched and windblown, his eyes wide and desperate.

"Dominique," he said. "Put the gun down."

"David," Dominique said in a hoarse little whisper.

"You don't want to kill anybody," David told her, stepping gingerly over Foley's body as he entered the room.

She just stared at him.

"We loved each other once, many years ago," he said. "Do you remember?"

"Remember," she said. "Love . . ."

"Give me the gun, Dominique," David said.

"No!" She kept the gun pointed at Liz. "You cheated on me! You made me feel . . . old . . . ugly . . ."

"I'm sorry about that, Dominique. Very sorry. But you aren't old and ugly anymore."

"Not anymore . . ."

"You are young and beautiful."

"Young . . ." she repeated. "Beautiful . . ."

David took another step closer to her. Liz held her breath, terrified that Dominique would pull the trigger at any point.

"Look at yourself in the mirror," David was saying. "Turn and look over there. See how beautiful your magic has made you."

Dominique hesitated. But finally her eyes turned irresistibly toward the cracked mirror, though she made sure to keep the gun trained on Liz.

What she saw in the mirror made Dominique scream.

Her face was still twisted and broken. Her eyes were still protruding.

Dominique screamed again.

"Is that how you want to look for the rest of your life?" David asked.

Dominique was sobbing uncontrollably. The gun trembled in her hands.

"All your black magic couldn't help you," David told her cruelly.

Liz braced herself. What was David doing? He was goading Dominique to kill her!

But he knew his wife better than she did.

"That is how you will look for all time," he told her.

Dominique was sobbing. Tilting the weapon in her hands upward, she brought it in close to her chest. Then, in one swift, continuous move, she slipped the barrel into her mouth. Liz closed her eyes against the sickening explosion of gunfire.

That was when blackness overcame Liz as well, and she collapsed to the floor.

85

"Joe, are you all right?"

Foley was sitting shirtless on the floor, leaning against the wall, his left hand gripping his right shoulder, trying to contain the bleeding.

"I blacked out," he told Aggie, who squatted beside him. "I'd be dead if Liz hadn't knocked Hoffman off stride just as she was firing."

He looked out into the room. The storm's second round hadn't lasted as long as the first. The winds were already fading away and the occasional ray of sunlight was piercing the rain and the haze to slip into the room. But what the sun illuminated was grisly. Dominique's brains were splattered all over the floor and the bed. Police photographers were snapping pictures of her body. Two different sets of detectives were interviewing Liz and David Huntington separately.

"Mrs. Delacorte broke down in the garage," Aggie was telling Joe. "She confirmed Mrs. Martinez's account."

"So they really were witches," Joe said in amazement.

"Playacting at being witches, I suspect," Aggie replied. "The Haitian woman taught them vodou, and Mrs. Hoffman became convinced that the blood of the living could restore her precious Dominique."

"Who didn't die on the yacht, apparently."

Aggie shrugged. "Not if those are her brains all over the floor." She smirked. "Either that, or she *did* die, and they raised her from the watery depths with their magic. Vodou can make the dead walk, you know. Or haven't you seen any zombie movies?"

Joe shook his head. "What a deluded bunch of fools." He grimaced as a medic wrapped his shoulder in gauze. "So David didn't kill Rita, or any of them."

"It was his brother and Mrs. Hoffman who wielded the knives, according to the confessions we've gotten. We've found some corpses down the hall that had been drained of blood." Aggie gave him a sad look. "I think they're your missing girls.'

"I wish I hadn't been right about that," Joe said.

"It's all so ghoulish." Aggie shivered. "It'll take some sorting out to determine who killed who, but it appears that David was being set up to take the fall, at least for Rita."

"But Rita wasn't killed for her blood. Neither was Jamison." As the medic pinned the gauze in place, Joe winced again. "I suspect they were both killed because they knew too much, or threatened to expose the cult."

"Coven," Aggie corrected him.

"So many questions still to be answered," Joe said, as the medic helped him to his feet. He waved away a stretcher that was offered to him. "I can walk," he said.

Joe looked over at Liz. She seemed in shock, sitting

on a chair, wrapped in a blanket, her eyes glassy, barely responding to the detectives interviewing her.

"Poor kid," Foley said. "I suspect she'll never be the same."

Aggie helped him down the stairs. Outside an ambulance awaited.

The great shining parlor below had been destroyed. Walls caved in. Parts of the roof destroyed. Trees thrust through windows. The crystal chandelier shattered on the marble floor.

Joe looked up as he passed the portrait of Dominique on the staircase.

It had survived the maelstrom, still hanging evenly in its frame.

But the beautiful face was now a skull.

86

Liz sat staring out of the window into her little back-yard in Trenton, New Jersey. The swing set she used to play on as a kid still stood out there, rusted and bent. Her mother had planted some tomatoes in a small square garden, and from the window could see the red fruit ripening in the sun. It was as if she'd gone back in time, and was a little girl again.

Except she no was no little girl, sitting there in Mom's kitchen, her hands wrapped around a mug of tea.

Mom was standing over her.

"Sweetheart, you know he's sent more roses. They're filling up the living room."

"Give them away if they get to be too much," Liz told her.

"You're going to have to see him eventually."

Liz looked out the window again. "I don't have to do anything, Mom."

"But he's here again."

Liz sighed. "Again?"

"He's in the other room."

"Send him away."

Mom placed her hand on Liz's shoulder. "My sweet baby girl. I wouldn't suggest that you see him if I thought it would be bad for you, honey. Believe me. I only have your best interests at heart. Those trials were horrible. I understand why you needed to get away from all that."

They had all been tried and convicted. Liz's testimony had sent the whole perverse bunch of them to prison.

"But Liz, you need to make peace with all that."

"I'm scared to see him, Mom."

"I know, baby. But you once took good care of me when I was pretty low, and I promise you I won't let anything happen to you now."

"I appreciate that, Mom," Liz said, reaching up and patting her hand.

"It's just that, after talking with him, I think he really loves you." Mom sighed. "He's been here three days in a row now, asking to see you. He's staying at a local hotel. Says he won't leave until you see him."

Liz didn't reply.

"Okay, baby," Mom said. "I'll send him away."

"No," Liz said, turning to her. "All right. I'll see him. Just so he'll stop coming by and bothering us."

Liz's mother gave her a small smile, and headed out into the living room.

Liz returned her eyes to the backyard. How simple life had been when she was very little, before Dad went away, before Mom started drinking, before the whole world seemed to fall down around Liz's shoulders.

How simple life had been then, before she had seen all the horrors of the world.

David stood over her.

"Hello, Liz," he said.

"Hello, David. Why have you come?"

"I've come to ask you to go away with me."

She didn't look up at him. "And why should I do that?"

"Because you're my wife."

Liz moved her eyes up to him. How haggard he looked. How pale.

"I'm not your wife," she said. "Legally, our marriage isn't valid. Your first wife was still alive when we got married. That's the law, David."

"But you're still my wife in my heart."

She gave him a small laugh. "That's not the answer that would convince me to go away with you."

"I love you, Liz."

She looked away. "I don't know what that means."

"You have to believe that they had placed me under some sort of spell. I didn't know Dominique was alive. I didn't know what I was doing when they sent me away. I know it sounds crazy—"

Liz laughed. "After everything I've seen, everything I've been through, that hardly sounds crazy. That sounds utterly reasonable and logical. Of *course* you were under a spell."

He sat down at the table opposite her. "I was compelled to leave . . . you know the police are calling it a posthypnotic suggestion."

"But you're calling it witchcraft," she said. "Or vodou."

"I don't know what to call it," he said. "But I do know that I can't blame it all on Hoffman and Dominique. I have to take part of the blame myself, for the way I walked off and left you in that house of horrors."

Liz fixed him with her eyes.

"I was afraid," he said. "My entire life has been spent trying to please my father. So if they somehow enchanted me into doing what they wanted me to do, it would have been a relatively easy spell to cast. It wasn't really going that far against my will to push me out of that house."

"I saw what they were capable of," Liz said. "Even if the police scoffed at my statements about the witchcraft, I saw the way Hoffman made the gun burn in Roger's hands. I saw how she froze me into place and nearly choked me to death with that vodou doll."

"So you know that I acted against my will in leaving you . . ." He hesitated. "But for whatever part of that came from my own nature, I apologize, Liz. I had no idea when I married you that Dominique was alive . . . or that the witchcraft that she and Variola and Hoffman practiced was still going on. You must believe that."

"I do. But you should have told me so much more than what you did."

"Yes, I should have." He looked as if he might cry. In fact, it looked as if he had been crying for days. "And so I've come to say that I'm sorry."

Liz managed a very small smile. "I appreciate that, David. And I accept your apology."

"So will you go away with me? Can we go somewhere and start over?"

"I don't know," she replied, looking away again.

"But Liz, Huntington Enterprises is no more. The company didn't survive all that scandal. I can go anywhere you want to go, do anything you want . . ."

She just shook her head. "David, I told you that I don't know. That's all I can say for now. That's going to have to be enough for you for now." She looked back out the window. "You see, David, my whole life has been spent trying to find someone who can make me happy, who can fill up the scared, empty space inside me. I was looking for someone else to take care of me, because I was tired of taking care of other people. But you, see that's not what I really wanted."

He just looked at her, not knowing what to say.

Liz took a sip of tea before her eyes flickered back up to look at him. "I had found myself finally, before marrying you. I had set out and discovered I had dreams, ambitions, plans. I gave them up when I married you, David, because I was still thinking I wasn't any good, that I couldn't survive on my own, because I still blamed myself for my father leaving all those years ago." She gave him another small smile. "But see, that wasn't true. That wasn't what I wanted. If I come back to you, David, it has to be because I want to, and because it fits with all the other dreams and goals that I have—not because I'm looking for someone to take care of me. Look what happened when I thought like that."

Still David said nothing. He just sat there looking at her. Did he understand her? Liz wasn't sure.

"Thank you for coming, David," she finally said.

He hesitated a moment, then stood. "Whenever you want to talk, I'm—"

Liz nodded sharply, cutting him off.

He kissed the top of her head, then headed out of the room.

In a few moments, Liz's mother had returned. She sat down beside Liz and took her daughter's hand in hers. Together they looked out into the bright sunny afternoon.